NEGATIVE

Book 1: The Rh Factor War

By D.M. Muga

An Apocalyptic Novel

Copyright © D.M. Muga, 2025

This book is a work of fiction. This book is intended for Mature Audiences Only. It contains graphic violence, vulgar and crude language, sexual content, and scenes of explicit violence and gore. Whereas there are real places that exist within this story, and a great deal of research was put into creating this story into a reality, it is still a fictional story. Unless it is indicated otherwise, all of the characters, names, businesses, places, events, and incidents are fictional. That is to say that they are products of the author's imagination and/or used in a fictitious manner. Whereas the research completed to create this fictional story is designed to entertain and educate on basic survival skills, any resemblance to actual persons, living or dead, or actual events is purely coincidental.

Printed in the United States of America

First Printing: 2025

Acknowledgments

First and foremost, thank you to my readers. Whether this is my first book you're reading or if you've been following me a short while now. Thank you for taking the time to read my works of fiction. I hope that you enjoy the *Negative* world after being affected by *The Rh Factor War*. Enjoy and leave a review if you feel so inclined. A special thanks for all of the help, feedback, and guidance to several special folks. Stephanie, Cate, Lilly Mae & Leila Rae. Thanks for being patient with this novice writer and taking the time to help me continue forth with my writing. Thanks to Jeremy for making sure that I didn't overlook anything. Thank you, Cheree Castellanos (https://www.facebook.com/ForLoveBooks4Editing) for your guidance and support. Also, thank you to my wifey and our kiddos, for putting up with me writing late into the nights and early in the mornings. Your support and understanding are invaluable.

Cheers, and enjoy the first installment to the *Negative Series*. Remember to think for yourself and realize that we have knowledge gaps that we try to fill, for better or worse. Make sure to enjoy the times of peace and cherish every moment. When the chaos eventually comes, handle yourself accordingly and best of luck to you all. Thank you for reading!

Chapter 1: Logan Miller

Day 3: San Diego, California

It was a very warm and sunny day in Southern California. It was quiet and you could hear the trees moving from the light winds of the afternoon, as well as birds chirping in the air. In most other situations, this day would have been a perfect and relaxing day for Logan Miller and his family... but not today.

Logan was standing over Kelsey's newly dug grave at a hastily located cemetery in San Diego, California. Kelsey was his wife of 15 years now... the keyword being *was*. Their anniversary had been several days ago and the reason for their whole adventurous vacation to Southern California. They had gotten married when they were both 21-year-olds. Now his wife had been laid to rest in front of him. Tears began to streak Logan's face as he warmed in the heat of the afternoon California sun.

Holding his hand was his 10-year-old daughter, Harper. With her other hand, she was holding her stuffed penguin tight to her chest. He and Kelsey had just bought it for her three days ago at the San Diego Zoo. With the stuffed penguin being hugged tightly to her chest, Harper had the bottom of her face buried in the penguin's fluff.

Logan looked down at her, seeing that she wasn't crying anymore. This somewhat relieved him since she had been hysterical and in tears, off and on, over the last three days.

They were alone at Kelsey Miller's funeral and no one else would be attending. They were far from home, and they had the cemetery to themselves. In truth, Logan didn't know how many people were even left.

The news was still running, and so was the radio. But none of the news was good. The world had gone to shit in the last few days. None of that really mattered though. The only thing that mattered to him was that he had lost Kelsey, Harper had lost her mother, and little Harper had seen it all... and much more.

It had taken him a couple of days to get his head back on straight, go back for his wife's body, and find a local cemetery. Logan then proceeded to find a backhoe to be able to dig his wife a proper grave so that he and his daughter could say their goodbyes.

Not a lot of other folks were really around, and the few people that were had different problems on their mind other than some guy on vacation borrowing a backhoe to dig a grave for his dead wife. Hell, if the locals had even noticed him, they would have likely asked him to dig more for their lost loved ones. But no one had paid them much mind.

Logan and his little Harper weren't able to get into their Sunday best or anything really fancy, with not having packed formal clothes. He did have some dress clothes back home, and Harper had some pretty little dresses... but that was over 1,100 miles away. All they had packed were summertime clothes. Made sense at the time, considering it was late summer in Southern California.

So, he just stood there in shorts and a t-shirt, with tears rolling down his face in the hot sun, with little Harper holding his hand, squeezing her stuffed penguin.

Before their vacation to San Diego for some fun in the sun, Logan, Kelsey, and Harper lived in Greeley, Colorado. Greeley was in the northern part of Colorado. It was populated but also surrounded by wide-open areas and the views were amazing.

Logan and Kelsey had both grown up in Denver, and had opted to get out of the big city, but didn't want to go too far off the beaten path. So, during the recessions of the 2040s, they were able to buy a nice little home in Greeley. It wasn't anything special, but it was theirs and they had gotten a hell of a deal on it. They had moved in shortly before Harper was born, with Kelsey already at six months pregnant on moving day.

Logan was a mechanic and made decent money, and had overtime available to him on a regular basis. He worked at one of the local auto repair shops, and business was good. Logan sometimes worried that maybe his job would become obsolete, being replaced by some sort of futuristic robotics and AI. But he doubted it would happen in his lifetime. Also, despite the stereotypes about mechanics, Logan was not a tool or an idiot. He could and would learn and adapt, when and if the time came.

Kelsey had been a realtor, working with a few of her friends that she knew in the business. She had done well for herself. In fact, during some years she made a good deal more than Logan. He neither cared nor was offended by his wife pulling in more cash than him from time to time. In fact, he welcomed it. They were getting pretty damn close to paying off their home in the next five years, and then they would focus on saving up for little Harper to be able to go to college.

Neither himself nor Kelsey had a full-fledged college education, with a degree and all. Kelsey had gone to community college classes to get her head around being a realtor and had gotten her license years back. Logan just worked his way up through the trade and found himself settling into a nice local and rather busy auto repair shop.

Kelsey's parents weren't wealthy, by any means. But they were good people and always willing to help out with Harper. Logan didn't know his father, with him out of the picture since he was little. Once Logan had graduated high school, his mom had picked up and left. Apparently, she had plans to move to Reno, with her most recent boyfriend. It didn't bug Logan much... He already had a job during high school, and was able to rent a room from a family friend. He had heard from his mom every now and then, but she was pretty much out of his life.

All that mattered to Logan was that he had found Kelsey and was smart enough to not let her go. Together, they had built a life for themselves, and they both wanted Harper to have more opportunities than they had.

By no means did they think that Harper absolutely had to go to college to be successful. That was obviously not true. The two of them didn't have fancy degrees. They had their high school diplomas and did a lot of hard work and grinding afterward to get what they had... and Logan considered them pretty damn successful. Yes, they may have married young, and they would never be rich. But they were happy, and he knew that was a true success. Hell, they were on a week-long vacation in sunny California!

Harper was ecstatic to fly on an airplane and go to California. If he was being honest, so was he. And he knew Kelsey was too. They didn't have much time for big vacations in the last decade. There was also the lesson of the last batch of recessions teaching them to be frugal and spend wisely... as to not end up like the rest.

The first few days had been amazing! They went to Ocean Beach on the first day to visit the ocean. Kelsey had been the only one to ever have been before. It was truly astonishing, and the look on Harper's face was worth all of the money they had spent to get out here and stay for a week. Logan had guessed that his face looked much like Harper's, staring at the vast and massive ocean.

On day two, they took their little rental car to the USS Midway Museum. Kelsey was into that sort of thing, and whereas Logan thought it was going to be boring, he had enjoyed it too. They even drove over a huge bridge onto a Navy base and through Coronado.

Day three of their long vacation was SeaWorld, and little Harper was beside herself. She was truly an animal lover and had a blast. Which sealed their decision to go to the San Diego Zoo the following day.

That's when everything changed and Logan lost his better half...

The day at the San Diego Zoo had started out great. He and Kelsey were enjoying watching Harper enjoy herself. They had gotten there right as it had opened and were determined to see the whole place. The workers said they could get it done in several hours, and then jump over to the Safari Park. The place was huge and Logan had even had to admit that it was pretty damn incredible.

Just after they had gotten done eating a very overpriced lunch, they went on to the penguin exhibit. Harper said they were her favorite, so he and Kelsey picked her up a plush stuffed penguin on the way out of the exhibit in the gift shop.

Walking back out into the open and hot air, Logan went to get them something cold to drink. It certainly was much hotter than they were used to and they always needed to have something cool in their hands to drink. After paying the vendor with his card, he thought he saw a bright flash but thought nothing of it.

He had turned to walk back to Kelsey and Harper and saw them shading their faces, looking up to the sky. He walked over to them with a curious tilt of his head, and then turned his head to the sky to see what they were looking at.

There had been a cloud in the sky that hadn't been there before, at least that he hadn't noticed before. Before Logan could react, he noticed another flash in the sky and another cloud forming high above them... then another... and then another.

He thought he had seen how one of the clouds formed. It looked like an object was coming down to hit them... like a comet or something, and then he saw a streak of something else hit and the first object exploded into the air, bringing the looming clouds into existence.

It had taken a moment for him to realize what exactly was going on, but the screams from the crowd made it clear that everyone else was catching on too.

"It's an attack! Run!" He had heard in the crowd.

After that there was nothing but panic and chaos. Logan had looked back to his wife and daughter and then rushed them back to the gift shop for cover. They had rushed far back into the exhibit to where the penguins were. He was hoping that if any of those comets, or whatever they were, hit... that the exhibit would protect them. He found that others had the same idea.

They had huddled close to one of the plexiglass viewing walls, with the penguins swimming and walking around like everything was normal.

They were able to calm Harper down somewhat, assuring her that they would be okay while Kelsey held her in her arms.

"What's going on Logan? Is it really an attack?" Kelsey had asked, with rising concern in her voice.

"I don't know, hun. It could be comets, or maybe... I don't know. But it looks like they aren't hitting the ground yet. So hopefully, we'll be okay..." He had said to her.

"Mom, I'm scared..." Harper had said with a fearful look in her eyes.

"It's okay, sweetie. Mommy and Daddy are here and we love you." She had said.

"Yes, sweetie. We love you very much." He had added.

He remembers that she had looked over to him at that point and he wanted to say that he loved her and kiss her. Before he could, he was distracted by a piercing scream across the exhibit and then another shriek followed.

He looked over, across the exhibit, to see a woman holding her son and screaming frantically. It didn't look like the kid was doing very well, with violent convulsions and then foaming at the mouth. After a quick moment, the kid stopped and was perfectly still. Then, other people shaking violently on the ground through the exhibit caught his attention.

Before he could begin to fathom what the hell was going on he heard his daughter scream, "Mom! Mom! MOM!"

He turned to see that Kelsey was no longer embracing Harper. She was now convulsing violently on the concrete floor of the penguin exhibit and Logan's eyes went wide.

With Harper now standing and backing away from her convulsing mother, Logan pulled Kelsey close and her head into his lap, not knowing what to do.

An instant later, foam flowed out of her mouth and her eyes rolled into the back of her head as she went still.

"Kelsey!" He had shouted as he tried to shake her awake.

"MOM!" Harper was now hysterical.

By Logan's memory, there were two other people screaming at their loved ones in the exhibit, trying to wake them up... aside from him and Harper. Though, at the time, he didn't give a damn. He was just focused on trying to wake his wife up.

It had taken him some time to realize and accept that she was dead. It had taken even more time to gather up his strength and try to get Harper out of here and back to the hotel. At the time, his brain didn't want to process the information and he certainly didn't want to leave *his* Kelsey alone on the cement floor of the penguin exhibit at the San Diego Zoo.

After some time of his mind in a tragic haze of disbelief, he started to look around and saw bodies littered on the floor. Harper had been sitting on the floor, holding her knees, clutching her stuffed penguin between her knees and her chest... rocking back and forth and sobbing. For how long she had been like that he didn't know. His mind had been a blur.

He still wasn't sure what snapped him back into reality, but he got the distinct feeling that he had to get Harper out of here... somewhere, but he didn't have a clue of where to go. Somewhere else... anywhere else, where she didn't have to look at her mother's lifeless body.

Finally, he stood up, brushed himself off, and tugged on her, telling her that they had to leave. It had taken a little bit for her to get up and a lot of questions that he didn't have answers to. He had felt so bad about leaving his wife there, but he didn't know what else to do.

He did make a promise to himself and her that he would come back for her.

Once Harper stopped asking questions and got to her feet, she had taken his hand... like she used to do when she was much smaller. She was 10 now and she hadn't held his hand while walking for several years now. And within the other arm, she had clutched her plush stuffed penguin.

Walking out of the San Diego Zoo, he had seen countless bodies on the ground. All of them with their eyes rolled into the back of their heads and foam around the mouth. He did look back up to the sky to see if any of the comets, or whatever they were, were still coming down to hit them and kill them all.

The clouds above were daunting and ominous, seeming unnatural, and he knew in his gut that the foreboding clouds in the sky had done this to his Kelsey and everyone else that had dropped dead to the ground.

Making it to the parking lot and driving back to their hotel he had seen many car crashes, a lot of lifeless bodies in the cars, and not one other person driving or walking around. The hotel was actually very close to the Zoo, so he had originally hoped that there were more people around and that it was just their area affected.

Once getting back to The Dana on Mission Bay (their hotel), he had found out that the surrounding area wasn't the only area to be affected and he had found out more of what actually happened.

With Harper back in their hotel room, he walked back down to shop for some snacks and food, finding no one around. He ended up taking some snacks, water bottles, and some soda cans. He left a note with his room number and name, as a courtesy to be charged later. Not that it really mattered since so many folks were dead... but it was still common courtesy. He wasn't a thief.

After Harper had some food and water, she fell fast asleep and the sun began to set, out over the bay. On any other day, it would have been one of the most beautiful sunsets he had ever seen. His only thought had been about not wanting to come back to a beach or California ever again.

After watching more of the news, after Harper was asleep, he had sadly found out that nowhere was safe anymore in the great United States of America. In fact, for all intents and purposes, all of the North American continent had been affected by the attacks, along with all of South America, Europe, Australia, most of Africa, and the Indian Peninsula... and all with similar attacks as in the U.S.

It was unclear exactly who perpetrated the attacks against the United States, Canada, and even most of Mexico... along with most of the rest of the world. But the news had said it came from satellites in space. And there were only so many global players that were not hit with the chemical weapon agents or CWAs.

Logan had thought, *Satellites in space with fucking chemical weapons! Fucking really!? Whoever did this, must have planned this for some fucking time... The evil sons of bitches!*

Apparently, it couldn't be confirmed where the satellites actually came from, because they had cloaking technology on them. The missiles from the satellites were actually designed to be taken out by the Anti-Ballistic Missile Defense Systems when they had been destroyed high in the sky. Evidently, it created a wider dispersion rate of their weapon payloads, which was not like any bomb or missile Logan had ever heard of before. It had something to do with chemicals and dispersion rates upon detonation.

Despite the news channels saying they didn't know where it came from, the survivors of the attacks in the U.S, Canada, and Mexico retaliated against several other countries.

The U.S still had a good portion of its fleet out and they stayed out, not wanting to be affected by whatever this was.

Not surprisingly, we had weapons in space as well, along with the Canadians, and the Mexicans had sea and air capabilities.

After watching the news for the next couple of days, going back to the hotel store and kitchen for food trips, and taking care of and calming Harper down... he found out a lot more. He felt like he had to know what was going on, especially since he didn't have a damn clue of what was going on and what to do next.

He was hoping that watching the news would give him some sort of idea of what to do and where it was safe.

With the United States using our own cloaking technology from the sea, land, sky, and space... there was a massive retaliation.

Russia, Korea, China, Iran, and Pakistan were all targeted with newly-developed nukes with low residual fallout ratios. Logan didn't understand the specifics of the nukes, but it seemed that new nukes had been developed since the phenomenon that had occurred back in 2023... not too far from where Logan was now.

The results were new cloaking technologies being developed and new nukes where the fallout was minimal, meaning no nuclear apocalypse... which Logan wasn't sure if he believed or not.

The way Logan had always understood it from the old movies and history channels about WWII and Chernobyl, was that nukes could end the world if too many of them were used. But the remaining powers that be, thought otherwise and attacked major cities in each country.

The Korean Peninsula, Iran, and Pakistan were decimated and essentially wiped from the face of the Earth... along with portions of India, Afghanistan, and other surrounding countries as collateral damage. It was truly a scorched earth policy retaliation, with estimates of over 500 million dead from retaliation attacks by the North American Coalition.

In Russia, there had been close to a dozen major hub cities brought down to rubble. Including Moscow and St. Petersburg, along with others, which brought another estimated death toll of at least 240 million. In China, the North American Coalition had targeted the cities of Beijing, Harbin, Tianjin, Dalian, Jinan, Shanghai, Nanjing, Wuhan, Pingyao, along with several others. The estimated death toll in China was thought to be well over 400 million.

The scorched earth retaliation attacks were said to be the largest, fastest, and deadliest coordinated attacks in human history. It had even been nicknamed *Operation Retribution*. The North American Coalition retaliated within 24 hours and took out an estimate of 1.14 billion people. The other affected nations either did not have enough resources or time to join in on the counter strike, and the Americans certainly hadn't waited around for them.

Logan had found himself hoping that those were the actual people responsible for his wife's death along with millions of others, but also found himself wondering if there were other actors and if they had taken out the right people. If those nations were going to retaliate, they hadn't done so yet.

It didn't look like the Korean Peninsula, Iran, and Pakistan were going to be able to launch a counter-attack with their countries being wiped off the face of the Earth. Logan wasn't too sure about China and Russia. But evidently, they were devastated badly enough not to be able to hit the U.S., Canada, and Mexico again... If they indeed did so the first time.

But then again, it had only been a couple of days since the North American Coalition destroyed a good portion of the globe with *Operation Retribution*.

Logan couldn't blame them. They were angry. Hell, he sure as shit was angry. His wife had been taken away from him. Harper would now be forced to grow up without her mother.

The way Logan saw it... if those countries were involved, good riddance. If there were more people involved with his wife's death, they should burn too. And he was sure he wasn't the only survivor that thought the same thing.

It was still unknown as to how many were dead in the U.S., but early reports had the number around 85% of the original population. Early estimates had the death toll of the U.S up to 375 million dead and around 65 million surviving Americans left.

It was hard to tell how many were really gone throughout the world, due to the CWA attacks, but chaos had already begun to take over with the survivors. Technology still worked for now and there were still government officials alive that were unaffected... similar to him and Harper being unaffected. But that was still 65 million people across a country that had just hit 438 million, this year, in 2053.

Logan slowly came to the realization that they were on their own and very far from home.

There were some lucky people on cruise ships away from the exploding chemical clouds of death. There was also the military out in the fleets, away from ports and the submarines deep in the ocean. Additionally, there were the folks that were on planes, above the death clouds. It was inferred that some of the surviving airline passengers showed that the effects of the chemical death clouds were not permanent. The exact exposure time to the death clouds was unknown with some passenger planes succumbing to massive death and some not, depending on when they landed. Some planes wound up crashing, running out of fuel or possibly too scared to land. There was still so much unknown and too much speculation. Whatever had affected everyone else around them, it did not affect him or Harper.

According to the news reports, supposedly, the survivors should have counted themselves lucky, since scientists believed that the attacks were designed to take out all of us. They were still trying to work out what sort of CWAs were actually used. They knew they were of the chemical warfare variety and extremely lethal, and that the death clouds had dissipated and vanished overnight. It was apparent that the news media did not know a lot about what had happened.

Logan knew that those people on those planes must have been scared... and yeah, some had succumbed to the death clouds when they landed, and some even crashed and killed everyone on board. Yet he still wished his family had been on one of those planes instead of down on the ground... Then, maybe Kelsey would still have been alive. Or, even better, they could have gone on a cruise instead of Southern California. That was one of the options when they were talking about this vacation.

Nonetheless, that was all wishful thinking and there was no going back from where he and Harper were now.

Logan had grown tired of the news and the cramped hotel room, with the walls feeling like they were closing in on him and Harper, as well as with seemingly no one else around. It felt like an eerie ghost town. He saw people here and there, but they all looked just as lost, confused, and sad as he did. What he saw most were bodies scattered everywhere... always bringing his thoughts back to Kelsey.

So, on day three of this tragic and chaotic new world, he went out to bury his wife and have a funeral for the loss of his better half and his daughter's mother.

Dammit! Why didn't I tell you that I loved you and give you a kiss! Why did this have to happen! He thinks to himself as he stares down at Kelsey's grave.

He then looks down to Harper and she looks up to him, not saying a word.

He sighs heavily.

She hasn't said much in the last few days... Come to think of it, neither have I... He thinks as he looks into his daughter's blank stare.

"Your mom loved you very much. I know she's gone, Harper... but..." Logan says, without knowing how to finish his sentence.

"I miss her, dad..." Harper replies.

He feels his heart sink and he kneels down next to her and she gives him a big hug.

"I miss her too, sweetie... I miss her too..." He says to his 10-year-old daughter.

At least I still have you, Harper. I'm not sure what I would have done if whatever happened affected you too. Or even worse... if it had affected both me and your mom and left you out here all alone... He finds the thought crossing his mind for the first time and feels ashamed for not realizing it sooner.

They stay there for a while longer, losing track of time, with the sun beating down on them, making it a very warm, late August day. The two of them don't say much, just staring at the fresh grave of his wife, Kelsey... with a make-shift cross that he had fashioned together for her grave, with some flowers they found at the flower store near the entrance of the cemetery.

The day shifts to late afternoon and a much more bearable temperature out in the California sun, much cooler from the early afternoon heat.

After a while, Harper tugs on his arms.

"I have to go to the restroom, dad." She says.

He nods. "Okay, Harper. Let's go find one inside, and then go find some more food at the hotel and figure out what to do next."

She doesn't reply but holds his hand as they walk away from Kelsey's grave. Looking over his shoulder as they walk away he tries to *will* his thoughts to her... Wherever she was now.

Goodbye, Kelsey. I love you. I promise I'll take care of our little Harper and protect her from whatever this is... I love you, babe.

Chapter 2: Emily Collins

Day 3: San Diego, California

Emily and little Laura had a rough last few days. They were finally getting back to the hotel their family of four was originally staying at.

She had acquired a car that the owner was no longer in need of and had driven her daughter back to the hotel to get some decent rest and she was in desperate need of a damn shower. Parking the sedan that she had acquired, she noticed that the parking lot of the hotel was nearly empty.

It would have made sense to her if she had realized that the CWA attacks had happened in the middle of the day a few days ago. But right now, all she could think of was about getting Laura inside, taking a nice hot shower, and falling asleep.

Laura was very heavy. The girl was eight years old and Emily couldn't remember the last time that she had to pick her up. But the poor kid was exhausted from having been at the hospital for the last few days. Her teenager, Bryan, was finally in stable condition and she and Laura had been patched up fairly well and cleared to go "home" and get some rest.

Emily and Laura had been much luckier than her son Bryan, and they had certainly been much luckier than her late husband, Erik... along with at least 85% of the rest of Americans. And the way she understood it from the news, most of the world. Because of what the news networks were beginning to refer to as the Rh Positive Death Chemical from the CWAs.

The Collins family was on vacation in San Diego, staying at The Dana on Mission Bay. It was a late summer trip before the kids went back to school and Erik's way of trying to rekindle their relationship, since recent events...

They had just gotten in the day before the attacks, all the way from Flagstaff, Arizona. It had turned out to be a 10-hour drive but was relatively smooth. Bryan and Laura both had their ear-wigs in, listening to their music and watching their videos. Emily and Erik swapped out every few hours, which was nice for both of them.

It felt nice to be getting along and not arguing. It was funny how getting out of your normal routines often tended to relax you. Back at home, she was a 34-year-old housewife, raising a teenage boy and young daughter, hoping that time could freeze and the little one would never reach that teenage stage. Her husband, Erik, was at work a lot. It took a lot to run a construction business and stay on top of everything, and she knew that. What she hadn't known about were some of his late nights were not work-related. She figured out that part, eventually.

Getting to the hotel, they checked in, walked around the hotel, and watched the sunset. They followed it up with dinner at the hotel restaurant, and then Bryan watched his little sister while Erik and she went out for drinks downstairs.

It had really turned out to be a nice trip starting out, and Emily had her hopes up that things would go back to the way they were before Erik had slept with that secretary that he hired a year back.

Erik's construction company was based in Flagstaff, and it did pretty well. He was at work a lot and said that he needed someone to handle clerical stuff to allow him to get home sooner. Emily specifically remembered when the young woman was hired, not being a fan of the choice, but he had sworn that he would never do that to her and to trust him. So, trust him she did...

In the end, Erik had sworn that it only happened once. Stacy, the damn receptionist that couldn't just leave her husband alone, wanted more than just work sex and that's when Erik cut their relationship off and came clean to her before his mistress could.

Emily knew damn well that it had happened more than once, but that was six months ago and they had been through counseling every month ever since. Counseling is where this whole getaway to the coast vacation came about.

At first, Emily was sort of nervous about the whole paradox conspiracy that supposedly happened not too far north of San Diego back in 2023... But that had been thirty years ago. Hell, that was back when she was a four-year-old kid growing up in Arizona. And nowhere else had been affected in the last three decades. It was all rather hush-hush and honestly, most of the U.S. had been glad to be rid of Hollywood and all of their drama.

So, after much deliberation and six months of counseling, off to San Diego they went. Erik had even opted for one of the suites at the hotel, to give them their own privacy at night.

Yeah, the day leading up to the attacks and the morning of the attacks was actually pretty nice. However, everything after that was Hell on Earth and Emily's nerves were raw and exposed, metaphorically speaking.

They had left the San Diego Zoo midday because Laura was getting hot and tired and Bryan was getting bored and hormonal. Their plan was to grab some food and head back to the hotel and layout by the pool next to Mission Bay. All in all, it sounded nice.

Erik was driving on the 163 North when they were looking for somewhere to get some take-out and head back to the hotel. That is when Erik and herself noticed the strange flashes and clouds quickly forming in the clear skies above them.

Having the radio on, she didn't think much of it, until Erik started shaking uncontrollably. She didn't know what to do, as he shook violently for a few moments. Then his eyes rolled to the back of his head and foam started to come out of his mouth. She had remembered screaming, then the kids began to panic, and then she felt weightless. After that, it was all black.

She woke up, not knowing how long she was out, upside down, in their F-350. She could barely hear Laura crying behind Erik's seat, and she couldn't hear Bryan at all. After a few minutes, her hearing slowly came back, along with throbbing in her head and sharp pains throughout her body.

When she had looked over at Erik, it had become obvious that he was gone already. His head was tilted in a manner that made it clear that his neck had been broken in the crash. She could still see the whites of his eyes and remnants of foam around his mouth.

She didn't have time to process grief and sorrow. Her mind went straight to Laura crying in the backseat behind him. She quickly unbuckled herself, falling to the roof of the truck... with the truck being flipped. The sudden movement and thud against the truck's roof hurt, but she pushed away the pain and crawled across the shattered glass to get to her.

She tried to calm her down as best as she could while she unbuckled her and winced as she carefully pulled her from her seat. Once she was down, she looked to where Bryan should have been... but his seat was empty.

Her stomach dropped at that point and she scrambled out of the flipped truck, frantically looking for her teenage son. She had practically pulled Laura out of the truck and picked her up in one smooth motion once out of the truck.

She scanned the freeway, seeing other cars crashed about... but not her Bryan.

After several minutes of shuffling around the wrecked cars in a panic, she found him. He was slumped up against the concrete divider barrier. She rushed with Laura in her arms over to Bryan.

She found that he was breathing but was not waking up and didn't look good at all. She didn't want to move him. So, she put Laura down next to him and began to look for someone to help them.

Not seeing anyone, she ran back over to their truck, looking for her purse with her iPhone inside. After scrambling around in the wreckage of the truck, she finally found her purse and ran back over to where her kids were. She then scanned the area again, seeing a hospital just on the other side of the freeway. She also noticed she was on an overpass.

She frantically searched her purse for her iPhone and when she finally found it, she dialed 9-1-1.

It took close to a minute for someone to answer, "Hello? Is somebody there?"

"Yes! I'm here! My son is badly injured and my husband is dead. We were in a car accident on the freeway! Please send help!" She had shouted at the 9-1-1 operator.

"They're all dead... All of them... I'm the only one here... All of the other dispatchers are dead. They all just dropped dead." The dispatcher had said.

"Oh, sweet Jesus! Did you hear me? My son is dying! I need your help!" She shouted back at the dispatcher.

"Oh... Okay... Yeah... Sorry. You're the first call I answered since *it* happened. The phones have been ringing, but I was checking everyone here... and they're all dead." The dispatcher replies.

NO! NO! NO! This isn't happening! This can't be happening! And now the 9-1-1 guy can't even help me! She screams inside her head.

"Hey! Get it together man! You are 9-1-1 and I need help, dammit! My son is dying here!" She yells at the dispatcher.

"Oh, right. Sorry. Where did you say you were, ma'am?" Was his response.

Ummm.... Where am I? She thinks frantically.

"Um. I'm on a freeway. We were coming from the San Diego Zoo..." She said as she looked around, seeing the hospital again. "Oh! We're on an overpass and we are right next to a hospital!"

"Yeah. Okay, miss. That sounds like Scripps. Let me see if I can get a hold of anyone for you." The dispatcher replies.

"Get a hold of anyone?! What the hell? You're 9-1-1!?" She blurts out.

"Yes, ma'am. I know. Give me a moment, please. Let me try..." The dispatcher says and then she hears him trying to call out to ambulances around her.

As a few minutes tick away, she begins to go into another panic, looking down at her son slumped over and her daughter just sobbing, looking around in disbelief.

Finally, she hears that an ambulance is on the way and the dispatcher stays on the phone with her until the ambulance reaches them. It had to swerve through wrecked cars on the other side of the freeway.

The young paramedic jumped the barrier and Emily had to help get Bryan on a stretcher. She was very concerned with moving him and asked where his partner was. The poor guy pointed to the passenger seat, where she saw a figure slumped over.

That's when reality began to hit her.

What the hell is going on?!

What did that dispatcher mean, they all died?!

Is Erik really dead?!

Maybe I should have gone back for him... No, his neck was clearly snapped. There's no way...

What the hell happened? Why has everyone crashed and so many people dead?!

These are all thoughts running through her head as the paramedic drives them to Scripps Mercy Hospital, San Diego... With herself and Laura riding in the back and a dead paramedic still strapped into the passenger seat up front.

Once they get to Scripps Mercy, a nurse and doctor meet them outside of the emergency room. Emily helps them get the gurney down and then follows the doctor, nurse, and paramedic into the hospital with Laura holding her hand.

The doctor had told the paramedic to stay and help with the patient until they saw how bad it was. The paramedic didn't protest after they saw all of the bodies throughout the hospital. There were so many bodies everywhere. Doctors, nurses, and patients were everywhere. Some were in beds, but most were just collapsed on the floor with foam around the mouth and their eyes rolled back in their heads.

Once the doctor released the paramedic, Emily thanked him for saving them and helping her son. She remembered that he had forced a smile and told her that he was going back out there to look for more people that may have survived... like her and her kids.

The next 48 hours were a blur of chaos, anxiety, panic attacks, and worrying whether her son was going to live or not. She still hadn't accepted the fact that her husband was gone...

Once Nurse Scott had a chance to check out Laura and herself, it turned out that her and Laura, both, likely suffered mild concussions and had mild abrasions throughout their bodies. Nothing appeared to be damaged internally and there were no broken bones.

Emily knew she was certainly sore as hell, and figured Laura was too. Luckily, Nurse Scott had no problem with giving them pain medications and fluids while they rested and waited for news about Bryan.

Bryan hadn't been as fortunate. He didn't have his seat belt on and had multiple fractures along both arms. His legs were fine. But he did have some serious head trauma and a punctured lung. Finally, after a stressful 48 hours, the doctor had the swelling of his brain down, his lung patched up, and both of his arms casted.

The doctor, Dr Lewis, had said that he needed to be there at least a couple of weeks under observation and to get real casts put on his arms.

Emily had been so relieved when Bryan came out of surgery at the end of day two, still unconscious but alive, that she didn't worry about the *what if's* right away.

But sure as shit... the next 16 hours were spent worrying about what to do and how the hell they were going to stay out here in California until it was safe to move Bryan. After watching a lot of the news and talking to Dr. Lewis, she found out that those were only some of her problems to deal with.

Toward the end of day three, after the CWA attacks with the Rh Positive death chemical clouds, very few patients had wandered into the hospital. Apparently, the news was right about at least 85% of the population dying like Erik and the many others she had seen.

Hell, Erik had almost, accidentally, taken them all out in the process. She had reminded herself with the truth of her husband of 12 years being gone.

They had finally gotten married when Bryan was just over one year old. At the time, she was worried that he was simply settling and would eventually leave her. She then reprimanded herself for reminding herself that he did, in fact, cheat on her.

That is your dead husband you're talking about here. Was he perfect? No! But he was trying and he took care of you and the kids! She found herself thinking over and over again while hooked up to an IV and on pain medications with Laura in the bed next to her, watching cartoons on the television.

She found herself going back to wondering about how many other people may have died in similar situations to their own. Bryan would have surely died if that 9-1-1 dispatcher hadn't picked up, the ambulance showing up, and Dr. Lewis working his magical medical skills.

At some point or another, Dr. Lewis had taken their blood and talked to her about her and her children being Rh Negative. He had gone on to ask what her husband was and she told him that she thought that Erik was A Positive. Emily didn't think much about it at the time. She was A-B Negative. Bryan and Laura were both A Negative. Which apparently was a rarity with blood types and Rh alleles from the parents, with both her kids being Rh Negative. Evidently, and specifically in her case, it was possible for a mother to be Rh Negative and the father to be Rh Positive and their children could be Rh Negative if the child inherits the Rh Negative gene from both parents. It was about a 50/50 shot of a child being Rh Negative in this scenario.

Early on day three of their hospital stay and after the attacks, Dr. Lewis had insisted that she go back to her hotel to rest up, clean up, and come back in the morning with a change of clothes. He promised he would stay there with Bryan and the few other patients that they had at Scripps Mercy.

As it turned out, there were only about 25 staff members left alive after the attacks, and only half of them had any medical expertise. Dr. Lewis was one of only two doctors. He argued that he had no one at home waiting for him, but she wasn't sure if she believed him or not.

So finally, toward the end of day three, she relented and took Laura back to the hotel with a sedan that Nurse Scott had located keys for from one of the deceased hospital workers. She had felt bad, but Nurse Scott reminded her that the other person would not be needing it anymore. She sadly agreed with Nurse Scott.

Emily was exhausted from carrying Laura up the stairs to the third level where their suite was. Once getting to her door, she was worried that her card wouldn't work anymore.

She hadn't seen anybody come in or anyone walking around the hotel area. In fact, she saw no one on the road on the way over here from the hospital.

Luckily, her keycard still worked and thc electricity was still on and running.

Flicking on the lights, she puts Laura down on the closest bed in the suite and goes straight to the minibar and downs a mini vodka. She then proceeds to the bathroom to take a nice hot shower and try to regain some of her composure.

The shower had been nice, but she had to abandon her usually scorching hot shower because of the cuts and scrapes all over her body. Walking out of the bathroom in a hotel robe and drying off her hair with a towel, she sees that Laura was awake.

"Hi, sleepy head. How are you feeling?" She asks her.

She looks at her with a pouty face. "My body still really hurts, mom."

"I know sweetie. It'll feel better in a few days." She says. Hoping that she isn't lying to her daughter.

"Okay..." Laura replies. "Mom... I'm hungry. Do we have any more snacks here?"

Emily looks around and doesn't see any snacks. They had only been there a day before the CWA attacks, but she remembered seeing a hotel store with some food and snacks.

"Why don't you go take a quick shower and then we'll walk downstairs and see if we can't find some food. I saw a store down there and they have a restaurant too. I doubt it's open... but maybe we'll get lucky." Emily says to her tired and pouty daughter.

"Okay... I guess so." She gets up and heads to the bathroom and stops in the doorway. "If we find some good food, can we bring some to Bryan tomorrow?"

Emily feels her heart ache.

"Yes, sweetie. Of course, we can. Now go rinse off and let mommy get dressed really quick." She replies.

This gets a slight glimmer of a smile from Laura and she goes into the bathroom and Emily hears the shower turn on.

Emily goes back to the minibar and pulls out another Vodka, downing it quickly. *One more should do the trick. It's been a long freaking day...* she thinks to herself.

She then drops her robe and proceeds to put on some of the summer clothes that she brought with her.

Afterward, she goes back to the mirrors to look at her bruised and scratched face. She brushes her teeth and avoids eye contact with her reflection, then brushes her hair without looking and throws it up in a hasty ponytail.

Once Laura is rinsed off, she comes out of the bathroom. "Mom, the shower really hurt all of my cuts."

"I know sweetie. It hurt me too. But it's only for a little while and they'll heal faster if they are clean." She replies and proceeds to help her get some clothes.

After little Laura is dressed, she quickly braids her hair and has her get a pair of tennis shoes on. Emily had thought about sandals but didn't want to risk their feet getting cut by any broken glass. Plus, she wanted to be able to run if they needed to. Erik not being around and them being in a new place was really starting to make her paranoid. It also could have been the chemical weapon agent attacks, being referred to as CWAs which brought the Rh Positive death chemical clouds to the U.S. and most of the world, three days prior.

Seeing the sun beginning to set out of their window with the view of the Mission Bay Channel, she walked with Laura out of the hotel room, closing the door behind them, with her purse in hand.

Oh! That's right! Almost forgot! She reminds herself.

She quickly takes Laura back into their room and goes to the hotel room safe, punching in their usual safe code. The small safe unlocks and she pulls out Erik's Glock 19X 9mm. It was an old gun and used to be his father's before he passed away about a decade ago, but Erik trusted it and took it everywhere, so that was good enough for her.

She puts the two extra magazines and holders into her purse, along with the Glock 19X.

Better safe than sorry. She thinks as they had back out from the hotel room.

Reaching the hotel store, Emily notices that no one else is around. She does see several sticky notes left on the clerk's counter. Each had a list of food and a note to charge Logan Miller, in Room 211.

So, there is someone else here... she thinks and instinctively looks around.

Laura comes back with a bag full of snacks in one hand and her stuffed penguin in the other. She was finally smiling again.

"Anything for me in that bag?" She asks.

"Uh-huh. I got sodas and a bunch of snacks." Laura replies.

"Very nice, sweetie. How about we go eat these on the patio out there in the fresh air?" Emily says to her daughter.

"Okay! I'm starving... and we can come back for more to give to Bryan, tomorrow!" Little Laura blurts out.

She nods and smiles at her and then looks back to the sticky notes.

I don't think I want to leave my room number with where we are staying... I'll worry about paying them, if anyone that works here ever shows back up. She thinks and wanders out of the store to go eat snacks and drink some sodas with her daughter on the patio overlooking Mission Bay.

She was still super stressed the hell out, but she knew she had to keep herself together. For Laura...

Damn, I should have brought another shot of vodka. But then again, it's probably not smart getting all buzzed in times like these. Probably for the best that I didn't grab another shot for the road. She thinks to herself, really wanting another pull of vodka but thinking against it in the end.

She checks her purse, reassuring herself that her late husband's handgun is still in there. Seeing the old, faded coyote-colored Glock 19X, she feels much more comfortable eating outside in the open and less anxious about other hotel guests that are alive and still around here.

Chapter 3: Logan Miller

Day 5: San Diego, California

Logan was dreading going into the grocery store a couple of miles south of the hotel. He parks his newly acquired olive drab Toyota Tundra in the parking lot of the Grocery Outlet store and looks back at little Harper in the back cab.

"You ready, kiddo?" He asks her.

She nods. "Do you think they have cereal and milk?"

He sighs. "They will have cereal, but I'm not sure about the milk being any good kiddo. It may be all bad by now."

"But you said that the fridges might still be working because the lights are still on at the hotel." Harper argues.

"Yeah. I did say that, kiddo. But milk is a funny thing, Harper. And stores only stock up for a couple of weeks at a time. I'm not sure if we can trust the milk here."

She gives him a confused look. "The stores back home always had food and milk though..."

He shakes his head. *She's not getting it. And I don't blame her. This is a crap situation, all through and through. But if we get sick from some food, we could be in some serious trouble. Man, I wish Kelsey was here... Let me try this a different way.* He thinks to himself.

"How can I explain this to you, kiddo..." He says and sighs, forcing a smile. "You remember all those big trucks we always see on the roads and freeways?"

She nods. "Uh-huh."

"Well, all of those trucks were bringing supplies and food to all different places, like this store. And with not a lot of people around anymore and not a lot of trucks moving anymore to refill the stores..." He tries to explain.

"Ohhh, I get it. Because of the Cee-Wahs and the *death clouds*, there are no more trucks and nobody left to refill the stores." Harper says, interrupting him.

"Cee-Wahs?" He questions.

"Yeah, the chemical thingies that hurt mom and everyone else." Harper says and then a solemn look overcomes her face as she turns her head and stares out the window of the truck.

Damn, she is one smart little girl. Too damn smart... Cee-Wahs and death clouds and crap. Geez! He thinks as he looks at her, just staring at her for a moment.

"Cee-Wahs they are then, kiddo. And yeah, you nailed it on the head. Good job, kiddo. Are you ready to go shopping now?" He says to her.

She turns back to him and nods.

"Alright then." He says as he opens his door.

Harper does the same and exits the truck from the other side.

He closes the door and hears her door close and he locks up his new truck. He reaches down to his right hip, checking for his newly acquired police-issued Glock G45. He then checks his other hip for the two extra magazines on his belt.

The last two days had been spent clearing out some of the dead bodies around the hotel, aside from laying his wife down in her final resting place. He ended up putting the ones that he found around the hotel into some of the rooms, very far away from his. After figuring out the key-maker at the front desk, he filled up five rooms with bodies that he saw scattered around the hotel.

Luckily, he had found keys on one of the first bodies that provided him with his newly acquired olive drab Toyota Tundra.

Another stroke of luck came when one of the bodies he came across was law enforcement. Logan had taken the poor man's keys, along with his police-issued Glock G45 and extra magazines.

After putting the police officer into one of the hotel rooms that he had designated for the dead, he located his cruiser and took his vest, along with his shotgun and extra ammunition in the trunk. It wasn't much, but Logan was a far ways away from his own firearms in his home... some 1,200 miles away.

He did feel rather guilty putting all those dead bodies into those rooms, but he didn't have the time or manpower to bury all of them. The rooms were the best way to keep them out of the way because they were already beginning to stink. He had found some spray paint in the maintenance rooms and spray painted the doors with red X's to mark them.

He lost track after 40 bodies and was exhausted at the end of every day, coming back to the hotel room with Harper watching cartoons. He made sure that she had plenty of food and water and he had given her one of the radios that he had found on some of the maintenance people for the hotel. In the end, he found eight working radios on the bodies of the dead maintenance workers.

So, Harper would check in on him every so often and he would make it a point to check in on her every hour.

By the end of day four he had made a pretty significant dent with clearing the bodies to reduce the spread of disease to him and Harper, they had cleared out all of the drinks and snacks from the hotel store and anything good in the kitchen of the restaurant. He did notice that each time he went to the store, it looked like there was more missing than what they had taken from their most previous trips.

He began to wonder if anyone else was around and ended up taking the notes that he had left on the counter, crumpling them up and tossing them in a trashcan. It was clear that most everyone was dead around them, but there still might be people around and he didn't want them knowing what room Harper was in when he was out taking care of the dead.

After each long and exhausting day of wearing gloves and a makeshift mask, he was glad to still have electricity and hot water to rinse away the stench of death.

On the morning of day five after the CWA attacks, there was time to go shopping. Fortunately, there was a map in the lobby of nearby stores, including grocery stores. His phone was still working for now, but he didn't rightly trust it anymore.

He hadn't been able to reach anyone back home. No one at all. What worried him more were the alerts for American citizens to keep their phones on them at all times, in case the government needed to reach them and locate them for rescue. That part of the alerts really got the paranoid side of him going. After dwelling on the alerts and the fact that they referred to them as American citizens, Logan smashed his phone into pieces before leaving for the store.

The way he saw it, he didn't need it anymore. He had Harper and no one else was answering or around anymore. He sure as hell didn't want anyone locating him by his phone and the message of rescuing them just seemed off for some reason.

Hell, he thought about it so much on the night of day four that he removed the GPS fuse for the Toyota Tundra and even cut the wires behind the GPS on the dash on the morning of day five... before they were to go shopping for more supplies.

Being a mechanic for most of his life had its perks.

Looking at his reflection in the windows of the Tundra... he knew he probably looked funny as hell with his gun on his hip, wearing shorts and a tank top with tennis shoes.

He grinned at how he must look to others, if anyone else was around and even paid any attention to him.

To hell with it. I'm a beach cowboy and somewhat comfortable in this damned California heat. He thinks as he walks over to the other side of the Tundra where Harper is.

"You ready, kiddo?" He says as he looks at his daughter with her stuffed penguin still in her arm.

And here I thought she finally outgrew stuffed animals. He thinks to himself and grins.

Don't be a dick, Logan. If little Harper wants her stuffed penguin, let her have it. He thinks to himself but hears it through his wife's voice in his head. He finds himself having his breath being taken away with the mental sound of Kelsey's voice.

His thoughts had been the same conversation that they had in the gift shop shortly before she was killed by the CWAs. His mind just replayed it in his mind, like some kind of sick joke.

"Yes... If I can't have the milk, can we get some apple juice and some of those Arizona teas?" Harper replies.

"Sure thing, kiddo. You can have whatever you want in there, Harper." He says with a forced smile, trying to shake the memory.

Stay focused, Logan... Harper is still here. Kelsey isn't. Not anymore. And we need to be careful if you want to make sure that Harper survives this shitshow. He thinks as he looks to the grocery store, uncertain of what's inside.

She smiles at him, one of the few smiles he's seen from her since Kelsey passed.

He feels his heart ache as he thinks of his lost wife... the love of his life. And he forces a smile at his daughter.

He pulls up his makeshift mask over his face and then points to hers, hanging around her neck.

"Mask on, Harper. It's going to stink in there, but the mask should help a little bit."

"Okay." Harper replies as she pulls up her mask.

He nods to her and she reaches out her hand, he takes it in his as they walk toward the grocery store.

Once they get within twenty feet of the entrance, he can see bodies slewed about in the California summer sun had not been kind to them over the last five days, and neither had the birds apparently.

He guides Harper behind him so that she doesn't have to see all of the rotting dead.

"Alright, kiddo. Stay right behind me and do your best not to look around. You won't like what you see." He says to her.

"Okay, dad. I will." She replies and she gets right behind him and uses her free hand to hold onto his shirt.

"Good job... and remember... Do exactly as I say and be super quiet. We don't know if other people are here and if they are good or bad guys." He explains to her.

"Mmhmmm" Harper replies quietly.

Such a smart girl you are, Harper. He thinks as he draws his Glock G45 and holds it in front of him and points down to the ground.

Remember, Logan. Don't point your weapon at anything you don't intend to shoot... and finger off the trigger until you are ready to fire... he reminds himself, thinking back to the weapon safety classes he took back when he was old enough to purchase firearms.

Reaching the storefront of the Grocery Outlet with the sliding glass doors opening, the smell is atrocious, and he knew there had to be a lot of bodies inside the store when the CWA attacks hit with their Rh Positive death chemical clouds.

Maybe this was a bad idea. He thinks and then shakes his head. *No... we need supplies and food. Food, medicine, and whatever else we can find.*

Taking a few more steps forward, he sees that he was right about there being a crapload of bodies everywhere. They're scattered on the floors and the smell is nearly overpowering. The scene was horrifying. And what made it worse was the grocery store music was still playing, as though nothing had happened.

"Dad... it really smells in here..." Harper says quietly.

"Yes, it does sweetie. Let's make this fast, okay?" He replies as he looks back to her.

He sees her nod and he goes to the nearest cart, filled with groceries.

Maybe we'll get lucky and he can get the crap out of here right now. He thinks to himself with a twinge of hope.

Looking into the cart, he can immediately see that half of the food had gone bad and was beginning to rot. He looks up and around the grocery store, tilting his head, seeing if he can hear any movement inside the sour tomb.

After a few moments of standing there, he doesn't hear anything but the cycling of the air and the light grocery store music that was still running after all of this time. The usually light and upbeat music now sounded eerie with dead bodies throughout the Grocery Outlet store.

He looks back to Harper and sighs through his nose.

We can't be in here, too long. This stench makes me want to gag. It's got to be even worse for Harper. She hasn't been disposing of dead bodies for the last couple of days. I'm surprised she's not gagging already... he thinks as he sees Harper's eyes on the floor in front of her and clutching her stuffed penguin tightly.

He looks back around the desolate grocery store, with the shopping music playing lightly over the speakers really beginning to creep him out.

It's now or never I suppose... he thinks with a nod.

"Hello! Is anyone alive in here?!" Logan shouts out.

Immediately he hears Harper yelp and he quickly turns around to see her again.

"Sorry. It's alright sweetie. I'm just double checking that it's safe. We need to get in and out of here as soon as possible. So, if no one is actually here, we don't have to be quiet and can get what we need and go. Sound good, kiddo?" He says to calm her down after just scaring the crap out of her with shouting.

She nods nervously. He then looks around, seeing no change in movement and no new sounds reaching his ears.

"Hello! We are just here for some food and supplies!" He exclaims.

He pauses for another minute and looks back to Harper. "You hear anything, kiddo?"

She finally looks up to him and says, "No... just the music. It sounds a little scarier than normal, dad."

He sighs and nods to her. "Yes it does, kiddo. I was just thinking the same thing. Sounds like we are alone in here. Let's make quick work of this. But still stay close to me."

"Okay..." She says as she takes several glances around her.

What is this going to do to her?... Long-term? He contemplates with concern.

He then looks back to the cart with half rotting food inside of it, looking to see what was good and what wasn't. After surveying and shuffling through it, he figures out that most of it is still pretty good. He tosses out the produce, milk, meat, and juice.

Looking back around at the bodies scattered around the store, he decides to leave the cart where it is and moves over to the next closest cart, surveying it and tossing out anything that even looked remotely unsafe.

"Dad, you're throwing out a lot." Harper notices.

"Yeah, kiddo. We can't risk getting sick anymore. We don't know if anyone is left around in the hospitals. We'll have to figure that out a little later to be honest." He explains.

She looks at him and then to the cart, helping him sort the good from the bad.

After they are done sorting out their two newly gained grocery carts, he finds that they were still pretty full. Between the two, they had a good amount of canned foods, a lot of cereal, two cases of water, some light beer, a bottle of vodka, a bottle of cheap whiskey, paper towels, toilet paper, and several bags of varying chips. He goes to grab another basket for smaller items.

"Alright, Harper. Medicines, vitamins, and first aid stuff first, and then we'll go looking for your favorite foods, some of those Arizona teas, more water, and lots of beef jerky. That crap takes forever to go bad." He says to her.

"Okay. Can we also get some of those frozen burritos and breakfast bowls we get back home?" She questions.

He thinks about this and then replies, "Maybe a few, but not too many kiddo. We don't know how much longer the power and lights will be on."

"Oh... okay..." She answers.

He then looks around. "Which reminds me... if you see a cooler anywhere in here, let me know. We'll fill it up with ice."

"But dad, the hotel has those ice machines and they are still working." She presses.

"They run off of the PowerGrid and we don't know for how much longer it'll be up and running, kiddo." He says, trying to imprint the importance to her.

"Oh, yeah. Okay. I'll keep an eye out." She answers.

He nods to her and they set out through the grocery store, stepping around and over the bodies as they shop for their supplies.

It takes four trips with the small hand basket to fill up their carts with their food and medical supplies. And Harper does spot a medium sized cooler by all of the barbeque supplies. That is when he notices a small propane grill with little Coleman propane tanks. The ones used for camping.

They make a fifth trip carrying the grill and filling the basket with eight small propane tanks, finding an empty cart to unload that and their new cooler into.

Logan and Harper then make one final trip to the meat counter. With most of the meat ranging from gross looking to not so good, he sifts through the refrigerated section with packaged meat and toward the back underneath everything else. It is there that he finds several steaks, roasts, and tri tips that he actually thinks still look good.

We'll have to eat these over the next couple of days, for sure, he thinks, looking at the dates on the packaged meats creeping closer to their expiration dates.

Returning back to the front of the store, he tosses the meat into the cooler. They then go to the ice cooler, grabbing two medium sized bags of ice and he puts the ice in the cooler on top of the meat.

Somewhat satisfied with their haul and very happy to be almost out of the rotting tomb of a grocery store, he looks to Harper.

"Do you think you can push the second big cart of food, Harper?" He asks her.

"What about the BBQ stuff and the cooler, dad?" She questions back.

"We'll have to come back for it, kiddo." He replies.

He can see her scrunch her face, certainly not wanting to come back into this store, once they are out of it and in some coastal air. It would be warm outside with the sun beating down on them, but they were looking forward to that ocean scent and fresh air.

"I know, kiddo. This sucks. But it'll be fast. I promise." he says.

"Okay..." She answers.

They push the two filled and heavy carts out of the Grocery Outlet and are struck with a welcoming breeze and fresh air. It was still the morning and hadn't gotten too warm yet. It was that nice part of the morning still, sunny and cool with the ocean air.

He felt relieved and renewed being out of the grocery store and away from the stench. He lowers his mask and spits the taste of his mouth down on the asphalt. He looks behind him to see Harper copy him, spitting on the ground.

"That was super gross dad. I felt like I wanted to throw up, but I didn't." She says to him, with a sense of accomplishment.

"You did really good, Harper. I'm proud of you. You're a very brave and tough young lady." He says to her with a smile.

He sees her smile again as they push the loaded down carts toward his truck in the middle of the parking lot.

Good, another smile. That's two in one day and it's not even lunchtime yet. That's a good sign... he thinks to himself as they reach his truck, having swerved around several bodies in the parking lot. The California sun had truly not been kind to them over the last few days, rotting out in the sun.

He unlocks it and they begin to unload their supplies into the back cab of the Tundra, not wanting to put them in the bed of the truck where he had all of those dead bodies over the last couple of days. Sure, he had hosed it down each day, but it still seemed gross and disgusting to have food back there. So, in the back cab the supplies went.

"Can I sit up front on the way back, dad?" She asks.

He nods and smiles at her. "You're going to have to Harper, with all of this stuff back here."

She smiles again.

That's three. Nice! We're on a roll today. He thinks, grinning.

When they finish up, they put their two empty carts in the cart return.

Just because the world is a lot emptier now, doesn't mean we get to turn into douchebags that don't put the damn carts in the damn cart return. Dammit, I hate those kinds of people... he thinks as they walk away from the cart return.

They walk back to the entrance of the store and put back on their masks. Harper looks at him as they stand outside the entrance, both of them not wanting to go back in.

"We'll be in and out kiddo." He promises her.

She nods and they walk through the sliding glass doors as they open for them, walking through a wall of stench. The putrefaction of rotting bodies smell worse than the first time around, or maybe the fresh ocean air had just been that good.

He hears Harper gag, but she doesn't vomit.

"I'm right there with you, kiddo. Let's get our cart and get the crap out of here." He says to her.

She nods quickly, obviously trying not to vomit this time and they reach the cart. He quickly turns it around and heads back toward the sliding glass doors and their escape and is looking down at her when they exit.

"Almost out of here and then we'll cook up some of those steaks. Okay?" He says to her as the sliding glass doors open and they exit the Grocery Outlet for a second time.

"Dad?" Harper says, looking forward as they reach the scent of fresh ocean air.

Ah, that smells much better. He thinks as he looks forward and his eyes go wide.

"Did you say steaks, mister?" A young man says to him, about twenty feet away.

Logan takes in the scene quickly, seeing two young men standing side by side. One has an aluminum baseball bat over his right shoulder and the other has a big sword-looking thing over his right shoulder. Both young men were close to his height but obviously younger. And both were staring at him and Harper.

He instantly reaches down for his Glock G45, drawing it, looking through the optical, pointing it at the two young men, and clicking off the safety.

"Get behind me, Harper." He says sharply.

Harper quickly gets behind him and he can feel his body tense up and he thought his hands were slightly shaking. He looks down to his hands and his gun, to confirm they are not, and then refocuses on the two young men.

"Whoa! Whoa! Whoa! We don't want any trouble mister!" One of the young men says and puts both hands in front of him, with his right hand holding the long blade.

"Yeah mister! We just heard steaks and got excited. Didn't mean to startle you and your little girl..." The second young man says and then he looks at the other. "Hey Clint, put down your Nata blade, bro. You're probably scaring the crap out of the little girl."

"Like you're doing much better with that baseball bat over your shoulder, Cole." The young man named Clint replies.

Logan just watches the two young men, not sure of what exactly to do. He wants to just shoot and get the hell out of there, but his gut is telling him to wait it out.

"Yeah... we do probably look like something out of a slasher flick. Especially considering our current sitch." The young man named Cole replies.

Logan then watches as both men look back at him and then slowly put down their weapons on the asphalt of the parking lot.

Once they stand back up, they put their hands in the air.

"My name is Clint, and this is my brother Cole." Clint says.

Logan sighs heavily and lowers his handgun to the ready position. "Hello, Clint and Cole. My daughter and I don't want any trouble. We were just leaving..."

"Okay, yeah. That's cool. We get it..." Clint says and then looks to his brother.

"Thing is mister... we haven't really seen too many people around here since it happened." Cole adds.

"Yeah, and you looked like a nice guy, after we saw you with your daughter putting away your groceries and putting your carts in the cart return." Clint explains.

"And our dad always told us you can tell what kind of person a man is, on whether or not he returns his carts to the cart return or just leaves them out in the middle of the parking lot like a jackass." Cole explains further.

Hmmm... Logan ponders the two young men, looking them over. Looking closer, he begins to notice that the two young men look exactly alike.

They're twins... and it's like they are finishing each other's sentences. He thinks, relaxing somewhat.

"Cole, language brother... the little girl." Clint says to his brother.

"Oh right, sorry little girl." Cole says and then looks at Logan. "Sorry, mister."

This gets a smile from him and he puts away his Glock G45.

"Thanks for that, mister. Never really had a gun pointed at me before. It was kinda scary to be honest." Clint says, with his eyes going wide for a moment to emphasize.

Logan nods. "Yeah, sorry about that. Can never be too sure these days and you two really scared the hell out of us. My name's Logan Miller."

"Yeah, sorry about that. If it's any comfort to you, I'm pretty sure I have a brown streak in my pants now." Cole says with a grin.

"Ewww." Harper says, peeking out from behind him.

Logan sighs and gestures to her to come out from behind him. "And this is Harper. She's 10."

Both young men wave to her at the same time, looking like double vision, with them being identical twins.

"Hi Harper. I'm Clint and this is Cole. We are both 20 years old." Clint says to her.

"Are you two twins?" Harper asks.

Both young men smile and reply at the same time. "Yes."

"So, what are you gents doing out here?" Logan says, trying to find out more about the two young twins.

"Looks like the same thing as you and Harper here. We pulled up and parked and were looking around the area from our car over there." Cole says gesturing to a small sedan not too far from his truck.

Huh, I didn't notice the new car in the lot... I'm going to have to pay more attention. He thinks, reprimanding himself.

"Yeah, and we figured you were cool after a minute and wanted to come and say hi. Like we said, we haven't really seen anyone for days... not since the hospital." Clint says to him.

"Fair enough. But word of advice gents... you don't look like you have the best of intentions carrying around those things." Logan says, gesturing to the bat and the blade on the ground in front of them.

"Yeah... I suppose you're right. But we couldn't get into our dad's safe after everything happened. He never told us the code... and our mom..." Cole says and trails off.

Already knowing where he was going, since so many had been lost. "I'm sorry for your loss."

"Thank you... but yeah, we would be sporting something similar to what you have on you... but we couldn't figure out the code. It's one of those big gun safes, bolted down to the floor." Clint explains.

"Hmmm." Logan replies, thinking of his gun safe back home still locked up and likely no one would be able to get inside of it anytime soon, unless someone somehow found the manual override key.

"Where are your mom and dad?" Harper askes, inquisitively.

Logan winces. "Harper... we don't ask those kinds of questions, kiddo."

"It's alright, Mr. Miller." Cole says.

Mr. Miller... never been called that before. These young men may not look like much at first glance, but they're pretty damn polite. He thinks to himself.

Cole and Clint look to Harper.

"We tried to go find our dad, but he works on North Island... it's a Navy base nearby." Clint says to her.

The Navy, that explains them being so damn polite and proper. Their dad is in the military... Well, he was in the military. He thinks to himself.

"Yeah, Harper. We couldn't get in and what we saw was not good. And when we went to find our mom at the hospital, and talked to Dr. Lewis, we knew they were gone..." Cole explains.

"Oh... I'm sorry." Harper replies.

"Yes. We are very sorry for your loss." Logan adds.

Both young men nod.

"I don't mean to be rude, but... What do you mean, you knew they were gone?" Logan questions.

"Well, Dr. Lewis told us over at Scripps Mercy Hospital, where our mom used to work. He told us after he checked out our blood types." Clint explains.

"What?" Logan says with confusion and then looks down to Harper.

"You see, Mr. Miller. Clint and I were adopted by our parents. And Dr. Lewis said that the news through the media out there was that the survivors of the CWAs had something to do with their blood types." Cole says.

"Yeah, I didn't understand everything, but our mom was A Positive. We weren't sure what dad was, but he never came home after the CWAs and the death clouds, so we assumed the worst after we saw North Island from outside the gates. But Cole and I are both AB Negative, and Dr. Lewis said that all of the survivors he had tested so far are negative blood types, he said something about the Rh Negative factor." Clint explains.

The Rh-Negative factor... interesting, but confusing at the same damn time. That's new information though. So, that's something. I must have missed that information on the news, doing all the clean up around the hotel. He thinks as he looks down at Harper.

She's O Negative, and I'm A Negative... and Kelsey was A Positive. This thought brings heartache to him once again with the thought of Kelsey.

"So anyways, we went there a couple days ago, after we went looking for our dad. And that's what he told us. There were other people there but not a lot. It was all kind of a daze after finding out about our mom... it's been a long last few days..." Cole adds.

"Yes it has." Logan admits.

"Yeah, we were both at the community college, in class when it happened. It was really a mess. We went straight home after that and waited for mom and dad and then you know the rest. We just came out here to restock up on food, water, and supplies. After watching the news for the first couple of days and going around town, we were taking a break from trying to get into mom and dad's safe." Clint explains.

"I lost my mom because of the Cee-Wahs." Harper says abruptly.

Logan looks down at her, not sure how to respond. She looked so normal saying such a tragic thing. He knew she was hurting inside but it didn't look like it from the outside.

"Oh no... I'm so sorry, Harper." Clint says to her.

"Yes, Harper, We are very sorry to hear about your mom." Cole says and then looks up to Logan. "I'm very sorry for your loss, Mr. Miller."

"Yes, sir. Very sorry for your loss." Clint adds.

"Thank you, gents. I appreciate that.... and I was thinking... have you tried your parents' anniversary yet?" Logan replies.,

"Yeah... we tried those numbers too." Cole admits.

"Okay, then... then I advise looking for the manual override key. Your parents most likely put it somewhere close to the safe. In a drawer or on top of a shelf or something.

"Manual override key? Didn't know that was a thing." Clint replies.

Logan nods. "It's a big metal looking key and allows you to get into your safe manually. Most, if not all safes these days have them."

"Oh wow, cool. Thanks Mr. Miller!" Cole adds.

"Not a problem, and Logan is just fine, gents. Also, if you see a cop car on your way back home, take a look for firearms in there. Do you boys live close by?" Logan says and then questions them.

Both twins nod at the same time.

"Yeah, over on Temecula Heights... it's literally down the road," Cole says.

"How about you, Logan, do you live around here too?" Clint questions.

Logans shakes his head. "No, we were on vacation from Colorado out here when everything went down. We're staying in one of the nearby hotels."

"Oh, wow! Colorado. How cool. We've never been. Are you guys heading back there?" Cole questions.

It had been a question rolling around in the back of Logan's mind for some time now. He wasn't sure if the trip was worth it, with everyone dead and gone. The world they had known was gone and they had food, water, and a place to sleep for now.

Logan scratches the back of his head. "I'm not sure, to be honest."

"Well, if you stay around here... can we swap numbers to keep in contact? You two are the only people we've seen for days." Clint asks.

"Sorry, gents. I broke my phone earlier this morning..." Logan says.

"Bummer." Clint replies.

Thinking of one of the extra radios in his truck, he looks at them. "You know what? I have an extra radio. We are just across the bridge, north of us and if you two are within range, you can talk to us."

"Oh! Sweet! That'd be awesome!" Clint exclaims, clearly excited about getting a radio.

"Yes, Mr. Miller. That would be pretty awesome. Are you two staying at The Dana in Mission Bay or the Hyatt?" Cole questions.

Logan eyes him, not sure if he wants to tell him which one.

"We've lived here for the last six years. We know the area pretty well. Dad was going to retire in a couple years..." Cole adds.

These guys seem nice enough... he thinks. Liking the two young twins, Clint and Cole.

"Over at The Dana. And let's go get you that radio and you two go about your shopping." Logan replies.

He pushes the cart to the Tundra with Harper at his side and they follow, leaving their weapons by the front entrance to the Grocery Outlet. Once reaching his truck. He unlocks it and finds the extra radio he is looking for. After showing them how to use it and turn it off to save battery, he hands it over to them.

"Thanks again, Mr. Miller." Cole says.

"Least I could do after pointing a gun at you two, gents. Sorry about that again." Logan admits.

"No worries. We totally get it." Clint replies.

"And when you guys get done shopping later, we can check the radios at noon and maybe just set that as our time to talk to each other once a day. Does noon sound good, say on channel two?" Logan says to the twins.

"Sounds great!" Clint responds.

Logan and Harper then say their goodbyes to the twins and plan to talk again in a few hours, if the radio reaches that far. Logan thinks they likely will, if they do live nearby. These types of radios have a range of up to four to six miles and the hotel was only two miles away.

I guess we'll find out at noon. He thinks to himself.

Once the twins are gone and had started their own shopping, he finishes loading up the truck with the last cart and then returns it to the cart return. Harper gets in the front seat and Logan gets in the driver seat. He turns the ignition and feels the cool rush of the AC hit his face.

"They were nice, dad. I like them." Harper says to him.

"Yeah, kiddo. And yeah, I thought so too. Hey, do you want to be the one that calls them at noon on the radio?" He says to her.

"Yeah!" She says with another smile.

She has been smiles all day, so far... well except with the whole shopping around a bunch of dead bodies part of the day. But hey! I'll take it! He thinks as he drives out of the parking lot and back toward the hotel to unload their collected supplies.

Chapter 4: Emily Collins

Day 6: San Diego, California

"Mom, I'm hungry." Laura says to her as Emily looks at her son, Bryan, still unconscious in the hospital bed.

Please wake up, honey... She thinks as she brushes her hand across his cheek.

Dr. Lewis was staying positive for her and she was appreciative of that. But she heard him and Nurse Scott talking about the lessening likelihood that Bryan was going to wake up. Apparently, anything after 48 hours is not good and their next marker would be after three weeks... which apparently meant that Bryan could possibly never wake up.

Please wake up, Bryan. I'm right here waiting for you. We are both here waiting here for you. Mom and little Laura. Come back to us... she thinks, trying to will her thoughts into the subconscious of his unconscious mind.

"Mom, I'm hungry." Laura says to her again.

Emily sighs, knowing that they need to eat, with their last meal being last night here at the hospital. And now it was nearly noon.

They had run out of food at the hotel yesterday. Luckily, Scripps Mercy Hospital still had plenty of food stored up in their cafeteria and their overstock. What was more fortunate was how kind Dr. Lewis, Nurse Scott, and the remaining hospital staff were. There were only six people left at Scripps Mercy Hospital, as of day six after the CWA attacks brought the Rh Positive death chemical clouds to most of the world.

Out of the twenty-five that survived the CWA attacks, only six had stayed behind and continued to show up to the hospital. In fact, Emily believed that most of them were staying here now... if not all of them.

There was Dr. Lewis, Dr. Calhoun, R.N. Scott, R.N. Nunez, L.V.N. Campbell, and the paramedic that had saved Bryan had come back and stuck it out at the hospital. His name was Joel and he said he had nowhere else to go and no family left.

Emily had to give them all credit where credit was due. They showed up, day in and day out, and helped anyone that came walking through the hospital doors. There weren't many people that came through Scripps Mercy. But there were several over the last six days. Mostly surviving family members bringing in their deceased loved ones, asking if there was anything that could be done... with them carrying their dead family members and unable to process their loss.

Emily had been lucky enough to never have seen this actually happen and only heard it from Joel. But it was still all very sad and incredibly tragic. Which always brought her mind back to her son and whether or not he would wake up.

She did see a set of young twins walk through the halls of Scripps Mercy, looking for their mother. Apparently, Nurse Scott had known her, and once hearing the news of their deceased mothers, she could recall the look of defeat on their faces. They were quiet, didn't talk much after hearing the news, and left the hospital saying goodbye to everyone, very polite-like.

Emily was worried that there were only six staff left at the hospital when there were originally twenty-five. But she didn't blame the ones that left. They had families of their own to search for and not all of them had medical experience and had no reason to stay, with their world falling apart all around them. She was mainly worried that the rest would eventually leave before Bryan woke up.

Those thoughts of fear about her son being abandoned in this desolate hospital, in a dead world, were what really got to her now as she stared at her unconscious and unresponsive son.

"Mom?" Laura says, next to her.

Emily nods, with a few tears falling from her face.

"I know sweetie... come on, let's go find some food in the cafeteria." She says to her.

She feels a stabbing pain of guilt, leaving her son there alone in the hospital room.

She exits the room with little Laura and sees Joel in the hallway on the first floor.

Thanks to the remaining hospital staff, they were all on the first floor now and modified it as best as they could to let people know they were here and able to help with what they could. Dr. Lewis had explained that since there were so few people left in the world, they had to help out as many as they could.

She nods to Joel and he forces a smile.

"I'm taking Laura to go get some food. Did you want me to bring you back anything, Joel?" She says to the young paramedic.

The young man looks at her and shakes his head. "No thank you, Emily. I just came from there. I'll keep an eye on Bryan while you're in the cafeteria though... Dr. Lewis should be back anytime now too."

She smiles at the kind young man. "Thank you, Joel."

"He's going to wake up, you know... you'll see. I've just got this feeling that he's going to wake up soon. You know? I can feel it in my bones." Joel says to her.

She pushes back the tears that she can feel ready to come rushing out of her eyes.

"Thank you, Joel. I hope you're right. I truly do..." She replies as she takes Laura and turns to walk to the cafeteria.

She had to get out of there, just for a little bit. She really hoped and wished the young man was right, but she also remembered the conversation that she had overheard and was beginning to lose hope that he would ever wake up.

Her mind wanders on what it would mean if he didn't wake up as they walk toward the cafeteria.

The fires out here are getting pretty bad. What happens if they reach us and everyone has to evacuate? What do I do then? What if no one stays behind to help me with him or helps me get him out of here? How would I even take care of him on my own if he stayed like this? From what I remember from the news, the Internet, and books... people could be in a coma for years. She thinks to herself as she starts to feel the world closing in on her.

"Mom. I want some cereal and fruit." Laura says to her, pushing her out of her spiraling thoughts.

"Okay, sweetie. We'll see what we can find." She replies.

They reached the cafeteria, and to their luck, they were able to find some fruit still good in the refrigerators. It was getting close but still looked good. The milk hadn't gone sour yet and there was plenty of cereal left in the storage racks.

Emily and Laura sat down to a nice and quiet lunch with their cereal and cold fruit. She had found some juices for Laura and some water for herself. She wanted to drink more coffee but knew that she needed to stay hydrated with the heat of Southern California at the end of August.

She was not used to this sort of heat, coming from Flagstaff. It was close to the same temperature, with San Diego being a coastal city and in the low 80's. But it was still warmer and a different sort of heat, with the sun beating down on you all day. It was nice being in the cooled hospital, but she knew that the electricity wouldn't stay on forever. Which was another major concern of hers, with her Bryan being in a coma.

As if she was catching on to Emily's silence and her train of thought, Laura speaks up. "Mom. When is brother going to wake up, and when can we go home? I don't like it here anymore."

She feels her heart break at her daughter's simple questions. She forces a smile at her and nods her head.

"Real soon, sweetie. Your brother is going to wake up real soon. And then we'll figure out what to do next." She replies, not really believing what she is saying.

Laura seems to accept this answer and goes back to finishing up her lunch.

What are we going to do? If he does wake... no, Emily! When he wakes up... she reprimands herself.

When he wakes up... where are we going to go? Will home be any better than this? It's certainly much less populated than out here... at least it was before all of this. If Dr. Lewis and the news is right, most of the world is less populated with maybe only 15% of us left. Is anywhere even safe anymore? She worries as her and Laura finish up their small lunch quietly.

Before leaving the cafeteria she puts a few more water bottles in the backpack that Bryan had brought on the trip and left in the hotel room. It was much easier to carry than her purse. And the Glock 19X fit nicely inside the front pouch.

She still hadn't really wanted to begin to carry it around on her hip and really hadn't felt the need to. A lot of her time had been spent in this hospital and she would surely feel weird walking around with a gun on her hip in the hospital.

But she sure as hell felt safer knowing that she had the Glock 19X and two spare magazines with her.

Reaching the area where Bryan was on the first floor, not too far away from one of the entrances to Scripps Mercy Hospital, she begins to hear yelling and shouting.

She instinctively looks down to Laura and then looks back in the direction of Bryan and the shouting.

"Oh no! Bryan!?" She blurts out as she yanks on Laura's arms to run down the corridor to see if her son is in peril with Dr. Lewis at his side trying to revive him.

Running down the corridor, she sees Dr. Lewis, Nurse Scott, Nurse Nunez, and Joel with their hands up and she hears someone shouting at them.

"I said I want everything you got! I want Norco's! Percocet! Morphine! Dilaudid! If you got it! I fucking want it! Right here and now, motherfuckers!" A voice bellows.

Realizing that she is in immediate danger and running straight into it, she tries to come to a halt before she can see who is yelling at Dr. Lewis and the others.

To her horror, she comes to a shrieking halt, making a whole bunch of noise and alerting the very loud and angry individual to her and Laura's presence. She looks to Dr. Lewis, and the others, with Joel closest to her and their eyes go wide.

Joel looks ahead of him and then looks at her and begins to move toward her and Laura.

She turns her head to see what Joel was looking at, only to see a middle-aged man, with a potbelly hanging out of his tank top, pointing a gun at her.

Oh no! What's happening right now! She thinks as she turns and crouches over her daughter to shield her from the man pointing a gun at her.

The sound of gunfire fills the hall, the echo blaring in her ears.

She shuts her eyes, thinking the worst as she clutches Laura, shielding her from the bullets that are about to hit her in her back.

An instant goes by and she hears a much younger voice yell out. "What the fuck, Uncle Mark!? It's a fucking mom and her kid for fuck's sake!"

Am I dead??? She thinks as she blinks.

She opens her eyes and sees that she is still clutching Laura, who is terrified in silence.

"I fucking told you assholes not to move! Now look at what you made me do! What the fuck!" The middle-aged man shouts out.

Am I not dead? But how? She thinks as she sees blood start to form around her crouched body as she holds tightly onto Laura.

She forces herself to glance back at what is happening behind her and she feels as though she may just throw up that lunch she just ate.

To her horror, she sees Joel's body inches away from her and Laura, crumpled on the ground, facing them. She can see in his blue eyes that the lights had gone out, with a blank stare. A blank and dead stare, looking directly at her.

Oh no! Joel! A shiver runs down her spine.

"What the fuck, Uncle Mark! Seriously! What the fuck! You said we weren't going to hurt anyone!" The younger voice shouts out.

She looks to the voice and sees a young man, maybe even still a boy, holding a shotgun... yelling at the middle-aged man with the potbelly that had just tried to kill her and Laura. But had actually killed Joel, who had saved their lives... once again.

"Shut the fuck up, Nate! It's this dumb bitch's fault. If her dumb motherfucking ass hadn't come running in, then the other asshole wouldn't have tried to be a fucking hero and got himself shot!" The man named Mark yells back at his nephew, Nate.

The young man named Nate looks over to her with soft eyes and then he looks to Joel's lifeless body. "What the fuck ever! Let's get what we came for and get the hell out of here already! After this! I'm done with your drunk ass! My father was right about you..."

"You better watch your fucking tone, Nate!" Mark says to Nate.

Nate's eyes go wide and he looks back at her and then his uncle.

She can see Mark then look at her, with his gun still halfway pointed in her direction. "This is your fucking fault, bitch! Now get the fuck up and get over there with the rest of them!"

She slowly stands up and shuffles Laura behind her and out of his sight, stepping through Joel's blood to stand next to Dr. Lewis and the others. She cannot help but look down, seeing her and Laura's trail of bloody footprints, as they stand next to Dr. Lewis and the others.

She looks to Dr. Lewis with his eyes still on Joel's body then back to Mark, who is smiling at her with a clear sense of creepiness to him.

"Now! Where the fuck were we?! Oh, that's right! Get me all the fucking painkillers you have! Right fucking now!" Mark says as he tosses a duffle bag over to Nate.

"Here dipshit! Go with that doctor there and fill our bags up and we can get the fuck outta here!" Mark says to Nate, gesturing to Dr. Lewis.

"You're a real prick, Uncle Mark." Nate says, picking up the bag and walking up to Dr. Lewis. "Come on, Doc. Let's get this over with so we can get the hell out of here."

The young man walks away with Dr. Lewis and she is left there staring at Mark with Laura behind her, standing next to Nurses Scott and Nunez, with Joel's dead body still bleeding out on the mostly clean hospital floor.

Mark sniffs the air and grunts, then pulls a small bottle of something out of his left pocket. He uncaps it and swigs the whole thing down and throws it at Joel's body and laughs.

None of them move, and the corridor is silent as the small bottle hits Joel's body and bounces onto the corridor floor, stopping quickly in the pool of blood around his body.

She looks back at Mark as he reaches into his pocket again and pulls out a pack of cigarettes. After a few moments of fumbling around, holding his gun in his right hand and trying to find his lighter and get it lit, he takes a deep inhale of the cigarette and blows it directly at all of them.

"Some fucking hero he turned out to be." Mark says with a laugh.

After a few more awkwardly silent moments of Mark smoking and staring at them, he belches and spits on top of the floor.

"Don't worry, you pussies. We'll be out of here once my fucking nephew gets back here with my spoils." Mark says and grins with that creepy grin.

"Mommy." Laura says with a quiet voice.

Not wanting to draw attention to her, she tries to whisper, "Not now, honey..."

But Mark obviously heard Laura already.

"What is it, little girl? The dead body of that pansy ass nurse is scary to you?" Mark says and begins to laugh uncontrollably. He then begins to cough.

After he is done coughing, he lights another cigarette and then looks back to her, with Laura still hidden behind her.

"Little girl, there are a whole fuck load of dead bodies out there! Hell, the way I hear it! Most of the fucking world is dead! And that poor son of a bitch just saved your bitch of a mother's life... so actually, you should probably say thank you to Mr. Dead Pansy Ass Nurse." Mark says to her daughter.

Emily can feel her blood begin to boil with the disgusting human being in front of her talking to her daughter in such a manner. She was really kicking herself in the ass right now. For one, running in here without knowing what was happening. And for two, not having that damned Glock 19X on her hip.

"Don't talk to her..." Emily says slowly, staring the man in the eyes.

He laughs and then smiles. "Lady... I'll do whatever the fuck I want."

He reaches back into his pocket, pulling out another small bottle of alcohol. He stares at her as he drinks it and tosses the bottle aside, aiming at Joel's body again and laughing about it.

Before he can respond, Emily hears footsteps coming toward them and Mark hears them too, with his attention taken away from her and Laura.

Oh, thank goodness! I thought, with that look on his face... I thought... Emily thinks and then pushes the horrible thoughts from her mind.

"Ah! Nephew! You're back!... That bag better be full!" Mark says as the young man walks past her and Dr. Lewis comes up next to her again.

"It's full alright. Now, can we get the fuck out of here!?" Nate responds to him.

Mark snickers and laughs.

"Sure thing, little nephew of mine. Sure thing... just one more thing we need." He says and then looks directly at her.

"We'll be taking this bitch's little girl along with us... she'll be our little travel companion." He says sourly.

Son of a bitch... I knew this guy was a creep. She thinks as she looks around the hospital corridor, taking in her options.

"What the fuck?! No!" Nate responds with disgust. "What the fuck is wrong with you?! NO! The answer is NO, you drunk piece of shit! Now let's take the drugs and get the hell out of here before you do anything else fucking stupid."

She watches as Mark tilts his head, staring at his nephew. His blank face shifts into a wide grin. That creepy sort of grin. And he begins to laugh.

Crap... what am I going to do? Is he just going to leave it and go or is he going to try and take my little Laura? Because I am sure as hell not leaving her alone with that piece of trash. She thinks, hoping that he forgets about Laura very quickly.

"Sure thing, nephew... Here, let me carry that bag for you." Marks says after he is done laughing.

Nate sighs heavily and walks toward him, handing over the duffle bag, with his shotgun in the other hand. "Seriously, Uncle Mark... what the fuck is wrong with..."

A single gunshot sounds off and the young man is interrupted mid-sentence, stunned in disbelief.

Emily gasps along with the others, as Laura jumps and shrieks.

Mark's nephew Nate just stands there for a moment and then collapses to the floor. The shotgun clattered away from him and away from the rest of them too, further down the hall... toward the closest entrance to the hospital.

"Why?" The young man says in a raspy voice, as he is kneeling on the hospital floor, looking up at his uncle.

Mark grins, pointing his handgun at Nate. "I told you to watch your fucking tone."

Another gunshot echoes throughout the corridor...

Emily watches as the young man's head blows out the back, spraying the wall with his blood.

She then involuntarily vomits on the ground in front of her and she can hear the creepy middle-aged man laughing. She couldn't help it. Her lunch came up and out of her mouth without wanting, along with some bile... leaving a very sour taste in her mouth.

This is not good. Not good at all. She thinks as she finishes vomiting.

She wipes her mouth after a moment, recollecting herself. As she stands up straight, she sees that Mark is lighting another cigarette.

There is no way this piece of shit is taking my little Laura. She thinks to herself as she eyes the man that just murdered two people. One of which was his own nephew.

Mark just stares right back at her and grins, exhaling smoke in their direction.

It's then she sees a flash of movement from behind Mark, near the closest entrance to the hospital. The movement is there and then it's gone.

"So, where were we?" Mark says.

She doesn't answer him and neither do the others. She wants to look for where the movement came from, hoping that it is some sort of saving grace. But she also doesn't want to draw his attention to the only thing that might save their lives and stop this creep from trying to take her daughter.

"Ah, that's right. My new little travel companion." Mark gleams as he tries to peek around her to get a look at Laura. He then reaches back into his pockets finding another small bottle of alcohol and quickly downing it.

She sees movement again. This time she recognized it was definitely a person and that person was edging closer to Mark, now being away from the waiting room areas and at the beginning of their corridor. She sees a head poke out and look around the corner.

With the head being somewhere around 80 to 100 feet away, she cannot make out the face that well, but it looks to be a man.

Whoever he is, he's here to help and can at least give me a distraction to get Laura the hell out of here. She thinks as she sees the man's head.

His whole body then comes into view, down at the beginning of the corridor. The man creeps along the wall into the closest front office opening and then he's gone again.

She focuses her attention back on Mark, who is obviously drunk now and still grinning at her and trying to see Laura behind her.

"You are not taking my daughter." She says to him.

"I'll do whatever the fuck I want, bitch." He says as he laughs and waves his gun around.

She then sees the man down the corridor, commit fully and begin to slowly and quietly walk toward them, coming up behind Mark. She notices that the others are staying still and quiet about the newcomer as well... likely also hoping that he will be their saving grace from this mess.

Need to stall and keep this drunken piece of shit talking.

"What I mean is... why don't you take me instead?" She says to him.

"You? Really?! You'd want to come with me?!" The now drunk and slurring Mark replies.

She watches as the man edges closer and closer to Mark without him noticing. She did notice that the newcomer looked over his shoulder several times, looking back for something or someone.

"Yeah... think about it. She's just a little girl. I'm a grown woman and know what men like." She says with a forced smile and twisted stomach as she sees Mark smile wide.

"Yeah! Okay then... that makes sense... Hell! That makes a lot of sense!" Mark says with excitement.

He waves his gun at her.

"Come on over here then, bitch lady, and let's get going!" He says with a smile.

This guy must have been pregaming before he got here. Holy crap he's trashed out of his mind... She thinks as she watches the man behind her close the gap between himself and Mark.

She watches and cannot help but smile as the newcomer raises his own handgun to the back of Mark's head.

"Drop it douchebag, or you're a dead man." The newcomer says in a calm and stern voice.

"What the fuck!" Mark replies.

"I said drop it, asshole!" The newcomer yells, as his voice echoes down the corridor.

Mark flinches and drops his handgun, with it clanking down to the floor, and then freezing up. The cigarette was still burning in his mouth.

"Good... now get up against the wall, and why don't we sort this whole mess out." The newcomer says calmly.

"Just who the fuck are you!" Mark replies.

"Wall! Now!" The newcomer yells again, sending more echoes down the corridor.

Mark quickly shuffles to the wall opposite of his dead nephew.

The newcomer stands in front of him with his gun still pointed at Mark.

Emily sighs with relief and she can hear the others do so as well.

"You all, alright?" The newcomer says as he looks over at them and then back around at the corridor he just came from. "Well, alright... all things considered?"

Dr. Lewis nods. "Yes, thank you. This man was robbing us and trying to take this woman's little girl. If not for you..."

"Yeah... I heard that part... A real sick piece of shit we have right here." The newcomer says.

"Yeah... he's a real piece of trash alright. He killed his little nephew when he tried to stop him from taking my daughter." Emily replies to the newcomer.

"Fuck you, bitch! You were just ready to run away with me!" Mark yells out at her.

"You really thought that! You're drunk out of your mind! And dumb as rocks!" Emily says as she walks closer to the newcomer and Mark up against the wall.

"You lying fucking whore!" Mark blurts out.

"Yeah, that's enough out of you, buddy." The newcomer says calmly and she watches as he pulls the trigger on his handgun.

Emily flinches, from the report of gunfire, as the man puts two rounds into Mark's chest and then lowers his handgun. The man just stares at Mark's body for a moment.

He looked to her like he was a well-kept man. Despite the fact that he was wearing a t-shirt, shorts, and tennis shoes... he looked like a working man. He wasn't tall, but wasn't short either. His brown hair was short. His skin tanned from the sun, but obviously usually of the whiter complexion. He had a clean-shaven face and dark brown eyes.

Her saving grace, which saved her and her daughter from unthinkable future events, looked like a normal, everyday man.

"Sorry about that... had to be done..." He says, swallowing hard several times.

She nods, looking down at the dead Mark and then back to the newcomer.

"If you weren't going to do it... I was... no way I was going to let that waste of flesh walk around out there after trying to take my little girl. It would have only been a matter of time until..." She says to him before he interrupts her.

"Hold on... give me a second..." The newcomer says as he steps back and walks to the newest open doorway.

He leans over and heaves, vomiting whatever was in his stomach.

"Oh no... I get it... I just heaved up my lunch after watching my friend Joel and his poor nephew get murdered." She says, gesturing to Mark.

But I sure as hell don't feel bad about you dying... She thinks as she looks at Mark, slumped up against the wall, dead.

After a few moments, the newcomer is done vomiting and the others have come closer to them, with Laura once again at her side.

The newcomer looks over all of them and puts his handgun back on his hip.

"Thank you, stranger." Dr. Lewis says to him.

"Yes, thank you..." Emily adds.

He nods at them and wipes his mouth one more time with his forearm. He then looks down to Laura and his eyes go wide and he turns back around.

"Harper! Come on out, kiddo! It's safe now!" The newcomer shouts back down the corridor.

Emily looks down the corridor and sees a little girl around Laura's age peek her head out from the entrance of the hospital. She slowly makes herself seen and walks over to them, eyeing the dead bodies on the ground all around them, clutching a stuffed animal to her chest as she walks.

It seemed tragic to Emily that the children seemed to be getting used to dead bodies everywhere. It wasn't just her Laura, this little girl seemed to be getting used to it as well.

"Come on, kiddo. It's safe now. The bad man is gone and these are nice doctors and nurses." The newcomer says to the little girl.

Once the little girl gets up next to the newcomer, he smiles down at her. "It's alright kiddo. It's just like all of the other ones we've seen."

"But there's a lot more blood with these one's and I heard gunshots. Are you okay, dad?" The little girl asks.

He nods to her. "Yeah, kiddo. I'm fine."

Poor little girl. How quickly they are adapting to all of this... she thinks as she looks down to her little Laura. S*he was so quiet with this whole thing and barely made a noise...*

The little girl nods her head and then takes notice of Laura. "Hi." She says.

Laura hesitates and looks up to her. Emily looks back down to her and then to the newcomer and the little girl.

"Hi there. This is my daughter, Laura. And I'm Emily..." Emily says to her.

"Hello, Emily and Laura. I'm Logan and this is my daughter, Harper. We came here because we heard you all had some news of what happened to us and I wanted to hear more... and it looks like I came at the right time." The man named Logan replies to them.

"Right time... that's definitely an understatement, Logan." Emily says to him, and then takes in the surrounding scene with three dead bodies all around them.

Chapter 5: Logan Miller

Day 6: San Diego, California

"Thank you again for your help with that deranged man. I know the oath is to do no harm, but after everything that has happened, how can people want to hurt other people... We should be coming together and trying to rebuild, not robbing and killing each other." Dr. Lewis says to him as they enter the cafeteria.

"No problem, Doctor. After what I was hearing back there by the entrance, I couldn't very well let it go on." Logan says as he looks over at Harper sitting in the cafeteria with the little girl named Laura and her mother Emily.

"Well, I'm sure glad you did, Mr. Miller. If not, I feared the worst for the rest of us. To think, if he was willing to murder his own nephew, what wouldn't a man like that do?" Dr. Lewis remarks.

Logan scratches the back of his head, not used to praise and he immediately feels guilty for what he had done.

"It had to be done, right? I did the right thing, didn't I? I mean... I just killed a man..." Logan thinks, mulling it over in his mind.

"As I said, Mr. Miller. I'm all for the oath and saving lives, but that man would have likely killed all of us. So, yes... you did the right thing and you'd be smart to not think about it too much." Dr. Lewis says, catching him off guard.

"Oh... sorry, I didn't know I was speaking out loud." Logan says back to the doctor, not realizing he was saying what was on his mind.

"It's alright Mr. Miller. You may just be still shaken up from what happened. Hell, I know I am. How about you go sit with your little girl and I'll go see if I can find you a water and snack real quick." Dr. Lewis offers.

Logan nods and walks over to Harper and the others.

"Hi, kiddo. How are you doing?" He says to his daughter.

"Good! They have apple juice here! We forgot it at the store, dad." Harper replies.

"Hey. We grabbed some juices for you." He admits, defensively.

"Yeah, but not apple juice." She responds.

Logan shakes his head and smiles, ruffling up her hair. "Whatever, kiddo. Enjoy your apple juice."

She smiles and goes back to drinking her juice, looking back at Laura and then him again. After she wipes her mouth, "Hey dad! They are staying at the same hotel that we are!"

"Is that so?" He replies.

Logan looks at the woman named Emily for a short moment. She has medium length, reddish hair, green eyes, a light complexion with freckles, and was close to his size. She looked close to his age and her daughter looked a little younger than Harper. She was petite, but didn't look weak.

She sure looks tired though. He thinks to himself. *But then, I could probably sleep for a week, myself.*

"Yes, Logan. And I would venture to guess that you're the same Logan Miller that was leaving notes down in the store at the hotel with your room number on it." Emily says to him.

He blushes, knowing that was a mistake and he realized it after several days.

"Yeah... the one and the same. That was dumb of me announcing where me and Harper were staying. I know that now..." He replies.

Emily nods and smiles.

"But you were smart enough to carry your gun on your hip in times like these. My mistake was leaving mine in my backpack... but I won't be making that mistake again." She says patting her right hip, where he is guessing there is a holster and gun.

She may be petite, but sure as hell not weak. That's for sure. He thinks to himself.

He looks at her and then to her daughter, Laura. "You have a good point there, Emily. But I was wondering... we haven't seen you two around the hotel at all since everything started."

Emily nods slowly and he notices a change in her demeanor and mood.

"My son is here... Bryan is 13, five years older than Laura. He's in a coma, has two broken arms, and had a collapsed lung... but that's doing better now." She says turning her focus on her daughter.

She puts her hand through her daughter's hair. "And her father... he's... gone."

Logan nods slowly, taking in this new information.

"He..." She starts.

He shakes his head and opens his mouth. "You don't have to explain it to me, Emily... no need for you to relive that... Harper and I lost her mother with the CWA attacks and the death clouds too."

He looks down at Harper sitting next to Laura. Who are both holding the same stuffed animal penguin. Which he is just now noticing.

Huh? What are the odds? He thinks to himself.

"I'm sorry for your loss, Logan. Truly. I understand." Emily responds.

"Thanks, Emily. I'm sorry about your husband and I hope your son wakes up soon." He says to her.

"Me too... me too..." She responds.

He watches the two girls showing off their stuffed penguins to each other and chatting away, drinking their juices.

"Hey, were you all at the San Diego Zoo when it happened too?" He questions.

"Not exactly." She answers. "We had just left and were driving, when Erik..."

You're a dick, Logan! You just told this woman not to relive her husband's death and here you are asking about it! He thinks, reprimanding himself.

"Oh... Okay. Yeah, I'm sorry. Just a strange coincidence with the same stuffed animals the girls have." He replies.

Emily looks at the girls, who both then look at her and smile, oblivious to their conversation and caught up in their own little world.

"Yeah, I thought it was weird too. But they are close in age. With Harper being ten and my little Laura being eight." She explains.

Logan nods. "Yeah, that makes sense I guess. They sure are getting along like two peas in a pod."

"That they are. That they are... it's a nice change of pace." Emily replies.

"Here you go, Mr. Miller." Dr. Lewis says, slightly startling him.

He hands him a water bottle and what looked to be a homemade sandwich.

"Oh thanks, Doctor. You didn't have to go through that much trouble." Logan says to the Doctor.

"No trouble at all. Especially for someone that saved our lives. And someone I then gave some terrible and horrifying news to afterward." Dr. Lewis replies.

"Not a problem, Dr. Lewis. At least now I know. And thanks for the update on that other thing we were talking about." Logan replies.

Dr. Lewis nods. "Best of luck to you, Mr. Miller. If you stick around this area, I'll be around as long as I need to be. Or at least, as long as I can be. The fires are starting to get worrisome."

Yeah, the fires. That's a whole new problem, and after what he already told me... geez. That's not good at all. He thinks to himself.

Dr. Lewis looks to Emily and then back to him. "Now then. I have rounds and patients to attend to."

Logan nods to the good doctor and Dr. Lewis turns and walks out of the cafeteria, leaving just himself, Harper, Laura, and Emily.

He turns to see Emily staring at him with a confused look.

"What news did he update you on?" She asks.

He shakes his head, not wanting to say anything in front of the girls.

"If it's all the same to you..." He says, looking at the little girls with the stuffed penguins.

"If it's about the Rh-Negative factor with the CWAs, we already know about it." She says quickly.

"No, yeah. That's why we came here in the first place... I heard it from a pair of twins that we met yesterday at the grocery store. And I wanted to see if anyone here had any more information that can help me decide what to do next..." Logan explains.

"Identical twins?" Emily questions.

"Yes, twins. Two nice young men. Very polite." Logan answers.

"Dark hair? Brown eyes? Both on the medium-tall size and finish each other's sentences?" She questions further.

"Well, holy crap... yeah! Clint and Cole!" Logan admits, astonished by yet another coincidence.

"Yeah, they came in a few days ago, looking for their mom..." Emily begins and then her mood changes and she pauses.

"Yeah, I know. They told me. They were adopted and both parents died in the attacks. Their mom was a nurse here and their dad worked at one of the Navy bases nearby." He explains.

"Huh, what a small world." She replies.

"And it seems like it's getting smaller, as of recent events." He adds.

She sighs and nods.

There is a moment of silence between them, letting the reality of their situation sink in.

Emily breaks the silence. "Is what Dr. Lewis told you of importance? Because the only reason I'm still around here is because of Bryan."

Shit. She is not going to like what I have to tell her. He thinks, stalling to think of what to say.

He nods. "I would wager it's pretty important to you then. To the both of us really, and everyone else around here. I actually got the radio call from the twins while we were... um... cleaning up."

"Radio call?" She asks.

He nods and pulls out the radio that was clipped on the back of his shorts and shows it to her.

She gives him another puzzled look. "Why not just use your cell phone and call them? The phones are still working... for now at least."

Logan scratches the back of his head and sighs, knowing he was going to come off sounding paranoid.

But then again... we were just attacked with CWAs that took out somewhere around 85% of the world population. Well, that and the nukes from the North American Coalition. He thinks to himself, preparing to tell her about his theory on the phones.

"To be honest, Emily... I don't trust the phones." He starts.

"Don't trust them? Why?" She questions.

"Well, first off. Those things were already used to track our every movement and moment of our lives before the CWAs and the clouds of death that they brought down upon our heads. And now, afterward, we were getting those alerts for American citizens to have their phones on them at all times, in case the government needed to reach them and locate them for rescue." He explains further.

"So... that's a good thing right?" She replies. "Wait... you're not one of those conspiracy nutjobs are you?"

Logan laughs nervously and shakes his head. "No. Not even close. Well, I did remove the GPS from my truck... but hear me out."

She gives him a sideways glance. "You can do that? That seems kind of weird to know how to do that."

"I'm a mechanic, Emily." He explains.

"Hmmm. Isn't that convenient." She replies.

He nods. "It most certainly is, on a regular basis. But hear me out."

"Hold on. Wait a moment, Logan." She says and then looks at the girls.

"Hey Laura." She says and Laura looks up to her. "Why don't you go take Harper and go look for some cookies and treats for all of us to share. I'm sure they still have some treats back there somewhere."

Logan smiles as the two girls brighten up at the sound of cookies and treats.

Harper looks at him with a smile.

She's smiling. More and more. He thinks to himself.

"Go for it, kiddo. Make sure to bring some back for me." He says to her.

An instant later, the two girls are up and running toward the storage areas in hopes of finding cookies and treats.

He finds himself very relieved that Harper is running around, happy-go-lucky. He wasn't sure he was going to see that again anytime soon.

"So... you were saying?" Emily says, bringing him back to the discussion at hand.

He turns back to her and sighs heavily through his nose.

"Yeah... Well, I don't trust the phones and anything else that can track us right now. The alerts say that they are there to help rescue us. I don't buy it, especially after what Dr. Lewis just told me. I'm certainly glad I smashed my phone. I even told the twins to do the same before they come to meet me at the hotel." Logan explains.

"You destroyed your life-line to the world? That's border-line blasphemy. What exactly did Dr. Lewis tell you that I don't know already?" Emily presses.

He nods. "He just found out this morning... but he heard from other friends in the area that a group of people were setting fires to the residential areas along the coastline."

"What?! Who?! What people?!" She blurts out.

He shakes his head at her. "That's as much as I know, but like I was saying. Our cell phones can track us. And someone did this to us." He says, gesturing around him.

She pauses for a moment and looks around the room.

"Someone planned this out and from the sound of it, didn't plan on us being alive. So, now they are cleaning up their mess... what's left of us. Basically, any one that survived the CWAs and their death clouds." Logan says to her.

"Do you hear yourself? I know we just met not even an hour ago. And we both lost people very dear to us. But do you hear yourself?" She begins to question him.

Yup. I knew it. She doesn't believe a damn word I'm saying. He thinks to himself as she shakes her head.

"I mean, come on! I get that someone did this, for sure! But you saw the same news as I did. The North American Coalition... we... nuked the hell out of whoever did this to us. Whoever killed my husband and put my son into that damn coma." She says, with Logan beginning to see some of that fire behind those eyes of hers.

"Listen, lady..." he begins and catches a cold stare from her and she stands up.

He continues, anyway. "I'm really sorry about your husband and your son. And I may not be a super smart guy, but I'm no idiot and I'm not crazy. Yeah, we nuked the crap out of a lot of people for what happened to us. But that's not to say we got them all. And I'm not saying to trash your phone and run away with us. Hell, I don't even know what my plan is yet."

"Run away with you?!" Emily questions.

He shakes his head. "Not like that... I'm just saying there's strength in numbers, and that's what I told the twins. But listen, you do what you want. I'm just telling you what I know and none of it sounds good."

"Well, no shit, sherlock. Nothing is going good right now. You just killed some creep that killed my friend, his own nephew, and wanted to rape my daughter. It's safe to say that we are all pretty screwed right now, Logan. And even if there is some group of people invading the U.S. and burning us out! I can't just leave my son in a coma here to burn! Can I?!" She says, borderline yelling at him now.

Well crap... she's pissed... and yeah, I get it. Her son being in a coma is a real thorn in her side. He thinks to himself, trying to think of what's right to say to her.

"Look... Emily. I get it. I do. I buried my wife a few days ago. This is a real shit deal we are being dealt here... but it is what it is, and this is what we've been stuck with. I'm sorry for stressing you out more than you already are. I know it's a lot to take in." He says to her.

Bringing up the fact that he just buried his wife seemed to calm her down somewhat, or at least catch her off-guard and stop her from yelling at him.

Before either of them can say anything further, Harper and Laura reappear with their arms full of snacks and their stuffed penguins.

He smiles at them and looks down at his watch, seeing it's almost 1:00 p.m.

We need to get going pretty soon to meet the twins. He thinks, recalling telling the twins to meet him at 3:00 p.m. in front of the hotel.

"Looks like you two made out like bandits." Emily says in a newly calm voice.

Just like every other woman I've met. She can turn off the crazy like a light switch... and back on again too. He thinks, remembering the similar characteristic of his late wife Kelsey. Sending a fresh stab of pain to his heart.

"We found all kinds of stuff!" Laura says to her mom.

"Yeah we did!" Harper adds.

"Alright, kiddo. We need to get going. You can take a few, but leave the rest for Laura and Emily, and whoever else comes down here." Logan says to his daughter.

"But dad! Do we have to go right now?!" Harper pleads.

"Yeah, Logan. You don't have to go right away. I'm sorry if I'm kind of being a 'B.' It's just been a rough last week. I didn't mean to bite your head off. " Emily says to him.

He smiles at the woman who must be worried frantically about her son, who had just lost her husband. He wouldn't know what he would do if that was Harper in a coma.

"It's not that. And you're fine. We're good... it's just that I told the twins, Clint and Cole, that we'd meet them at the hotel around 3:00 p.m. and I kind of wanted to change into clothes that didn't have blood stains on them beforehand." He explains.

She looks him up and down and then looks at her own clothes. "Yeah, I could use a shower and change as well. And if you are talking to more survivors, I'd like to be in on it too, but I need to go check in on Bryan."

He nods. "No worries, Emily. Go check in on your son."

He reaches behind him and pulls out his radio.

"Here. Take this and we'll be on channel two. I have another one in my truck and I'll leave it on until you get back to the hotel." He says handing her his radio.

"Are you sure?" She questions.

He nods. "I have more in the truck and a few more back at the hotel. Radio us when you get back and the girls can play some more and we can all talk and pull our resources."

Emily reluctantly takes the radio.

"You hear that, Harper? We are going to get to play later!" Laura says with excitement.

"Yeah! That's what I heard!" Harper replies.

Both he and Emily chuckle lightly.

"Alright then, Logan." She says, holding up the radio he just gave her. "I'll call you on this when we get back to the hotel. We may have to stop along the way to get some food though... what grocery store did you go to?"

He shakes his head. "Don't do it. We grabbed a lot of food on our trip. Plus, you do not want to go through that."

This gets another puzzled look from her.

"There's a lot of dead people, and it smelled really really bad." Harper whispers, even though they all can hear her.

"Ohhhh. Okay." Emily replies.

Laura's face twists in disgust and she shakes her head. "No thank you! I've seen too many of those today."

This takes Logan aback a little bit, with their daughters talking nonchalantly about dead bodies.

What is this doing to them? Are they adapting to death and chaos? Is that really a good thing? He thinks with concern.

"Alright then... we shall see you two a little later." Emily says, breaking the weirdness of their daughters talking about death like it was a television show or something.

Logan nods. "Sounds like a plan. Again, it was nice to meet you, Emily." He then looks at Laura. "And you as well, Laura."

"Bye!" Harper adds.

"Likewise, Logan. And thanks again for saving our butts back there. I don't think that would have turned out well otherwise." Emily replies.

Logan nods to her and smiles.

"But, I learned from my mistakes." She adds as she pats a tan colored handgun on her right hip.

This gives him a mental reminder to take the shotgun he found and offer the creepy dead guy's handgun to Dr. Lewis. Just in case another crazy guy came waltzing through the hospital doors. He hoped that the good doctor would accept it.

"Me too. We'll be upgrading our room arrangements to a suite at the hotel, and I'm going to see if I can't change the locks to a standard lock. Just in case the power goes out for good. Plus, I have to get the twins set up in a room, too." Logan explains.

"Huh. Maybe we'll be neighbors... and maybe you can help me with our locks too. That's not a bad idea." Emily replies.

"Will do." He says and smiles as he turns to walk away.

"Bye Harper! See you later! Okay?" Laura shouts out as they are leaving the cafeteria.

"See you later!" Harper replies and she waves back to Laura and her mom, Emily.

Logan turns his head back to look at the mother and daughter that were just saved from what was sure to be a gruesome fate. He waves to them, hoping that he will see them again.

There were far too few people left in this world of theirs. Seeing another face, and a parent no less, was reassuring that the world hadn't completely ended.

Chapter 6: Michail Lenkov

Day 6: Naval Base Point Loma, California

Micha looks onto the burning homes of Sunset Cliffs, California and wishes that he could remove his FSB PMK-S gas mask from his face to light up one of his cigarettes. His men had found many of them on the dead American scum over the last two days as they worked to clear out the dead surrounding the American Naval Base Point Loma after their submarine docked, three days prior.

The sun was already high in the western sky and Micha could feel the heat of the star beating down on him as the fires raged in the surrounding neighborhoods.

Burn, stupid pindos. Burn and turn your American ways to ash. Micha thinks to himself as he surveys his surroundings.

He was annoyed and hot, and did not like the lack of communication with command. He knew that many of them were dead and gone, but all of them couldn't have been killed. Could they have?

It had been a quiet last few days since they had surfaced, and they had met no resistance, just as expected. But the lack of communication from his higher ups was really starting to get to him. He could tell it was starting to put his men on edge too, and they weren't the types to be on edge.

Major Michail Lenkov had left Zaozyorsk, Murmansk Oblast, Russia several months ago. Which was just next door to Finland. It had been a long and radio silent trip around the globe to the western coast of the Americas aboard the Yasen-class nuclear submarine.

Micha had his men aboard his taxi submarine, along with two other submarines, docking at the American Naval Base Point Loma, three days prior.

Micha was special forces, or Spetsnaz, as were the men and women under his command. He had brought with him 120 Russian soldiers, consisting of two platoons, for the excavation and phase one of the *North American Initiative: New Russia.*

Prior to what would be the mission of a lifetime, invading and colonizing the United States of America, Micha had spent time in many other conflicts in the last twenty years of the Russian Federation. He had the pleasure of conducting operations in Manchuria, Serbia, the Ukraine, Afghanistan, Indonesia, and even in Great Britain. Over that time, he had attained the rank of Major and had been preparing for this particular mission for the better part of two years.

The day that the New World Order Axis set their plans into motion, Micha and many other submarines were off the shores of western America, radio silent and hidden from the lazy American radar and sonar detection equipment.

His men and the crew of the submarines were nervous once they moved out to their predesignated docking ports and excavation sites, with Micha's company being designated with the clearing of Naval Base Point Loma and the surrounding area of what was once America's San Diego.

Once docked, the submarines and their crew members of the Russian Federation were to return back to the Northern Fleet base. However, once they had learned of no contact with the Russian federation Command, he and the COBs (Chief of Boat) decided that the submarines should remain in port and the crews should provide security detail of the base.

He technically held rank over the Captain Lieutenant, but was on an equal playing field with the other two Captain-3rd Ranks. Nonetheless, there was no bickering amongst the fellow officers and they all thought it best to stay and see what the situation was.

In the beginning they were worried that maybe the CWAs were ineffective, but quickly dismissed that theory with them not being blown out of the water once they had docked. So, he moved forward with his excavation mission, preparing for the full force of the Russian Federation and the resupply and reinforcements of the New World Axis Powers in one month's time.

On the first day the base was cleared of the dead, piled up and burned, as to not have their filthy *pindo* bodies spreading any sort of disease that could bring along death to his men.

While his soldiers were clearing the base on day three was when one of his junior officers showed him the news on the American news channels. Captain Vlad Grinkov informed him of the American news networks still running.

Originally, he was baffled by the news, having no resistance at the Naval base. But soon he learned why he had no communication with the Russian Federation Command. The North American Coalition had retaliated and from the news reports, it had been devastating to his homeland and the other countries of the New World Order Axis.

"*Pindo* fucks. Could not just die. Let us have what you have been misusing for centuries." Micha had said to his senior officer, when he found out the news that would set back his mission and the overall goal of the Russian Federation.

"Orders, Major?" Was Captain Grinkov's only reply.

After a quick thought, he decided it best not to tell his men. Not yet, at least. So, he gave the order for his soldiers to refrain from the use of any technology, minus the senior officers. He would tell them, but it would be on his terms and once he knew more.

Captain Grinkov agreed and spread the word to the two platoon commanders, Lieutenant Sergey Petrenko and Lieutenant Roman Mashkov.

It wasn't until later on day three (their first day once again on land) that he had the idea to send out a message over the networks for the American citizens to keep their phones on them at all times, in case the government needed to reach them and locate them for rescue. He originally had laughed at the thought of Americans being over-reliant on their technology and leading him and his men straight to them when the time came.

His next order was to have some of the soldiers round up any technology that can track cell phones. Some of the enlisted men became curious as to why, but did not question their orders.

On the morning of day four, he broke the news to his men and the crewmembers of the submarines that the CWAs had not been fully effective against the lazy American scum. He explained to them that according to the *pindo* news media reports, 85% of their population was dead, leaving somewhere around 65 million Americans left alive throughout the future expansion of their homeland. Unfortunately, most of their homes may be in ruins. On the positive side, most of the world was now dead and the land and spoils were left for the taking. It was just a matter of who took them first.

His soldiers were alarmed at first. However, after he reassured them of his plan to deal with the some half a million survivors in their designated target area of San Diego, the idea of 120 Russian Federation soldiers taking out half a million lazy and inept Americans seemed to excite many of them.

His soldiers were also reassured that any American troops that were on the base must have fled and abandoned their base, since they met no resistance once they had docked. This further excited his soldiers and rallied them to seek out and destroy the cowardly American threat to their mission.

Later on day four, he sent one of his platoons out past the gates of the Naval base to begin clearing the dead bodies and searching for survivors. His men and women used the American technology against them, receiving back locations of survivors who were quickly dealt with.

By the end of day four, Lieutenant Mashkov reported the disposal of close to 500 dead bodies, as well as the locating of 64 survivors in the La Playa sector of their area. Soon after being located, the lucky survivors were executed.

Micha's orders were simple... no survivors. The Russian Federation, along with the rest of the New World Order Axis, planned on all the Americans and most of the world's population to be dead. If there were a few stragglers, Micha had no issue with picking them off.

The following day, Lieutenant Petrenko took his turn and led his platoon further into the La Playa sector. By the end of day five, Lieutenant Petrenko reported close to another 500 hundred bodies disposed of and also reported 47 survivors found and executed. Having heard how weak and cowardly the survivors were when they were lined up for their executions over the last two days, he knew he had to see it for himself.

So, on day six, since their multinational coordinated attacks, he left the security of their captured American naval base and headed more west than the prior two days, into the Sunset Cliffs sector. He allowed Lieutenant Mashkov to take lead and was there simply as an observer of his command, leaving Captain Grinkov in command of the rest of his soldiers, above Lieutenant Petrenko, back at his captured and secured American base.

Once he is done looking at the flames and burning bodies that lay within the homes, Micha gestures for Lieutenant Mashkov to proceed.

As Micha walks alongside Lieutenant Mashkov, in the back of the formation leaving the burning neighborhood for the coastline, he removes his FSB PMK-S gas mask from his face, taking in the fresh coastal air.

Relieved to be free of the mask, he reaches into his breast pocket, retrieving one of his smokes, lighting it up, and exhaling the beautiful taste of another American cigarette. They had plenty of Russian smokes, but for some reason the Americans were able to do something right... make delicious cigarettes.

Taking another drag, he looks over to Lieutenant Mashkov to his right.

"Where is this place that you sent the survivors to, Lieutenant Mashkov?" He asks.

"Major, one of the men relayed the message to phones to meet U.N. troops at the coast. Lieutenant Petrenko scouted yesterday and advised a good disposal site. Less mess for us and the ocean will take care of the American filth for us."

"Good. Very Good. Stupid Americans make it easy for us." Micha replies, taking another drag from his cigarette.

"Yes, Major. It worked good yesterday for Lieutenant Petrenko at a nearby park." Lieutenant Mashkov answers him.

The rest of the walk was in peace, with Micha enjoying the peace and quiet, as they walked to the coast. Micha had to admit, he enjoyed the scent of the American ocean. It was much sweeter than back home. But then again maybe it was the emotions associated with the American coast.

It was now Russia's, and his new home. All that he and his soldiers had to do, along with many other companies along the coast, was clear out the dead and left-over survivors from their CWAs. And from what Micha could tell so far, it was going to be an easy process. It appeared to Micha that the survivors were of the weak and cowardly variety, with the CWAs killing off all of the fighters that had kept any country from ever acting on an invasion of the United States of America.

After striding through the town of Sunset Cliffs, to the cliffs, Micha sees a crowd of survivors along the coast line. He then sees them turn and notice his soldiers. His soldiers do as they have been ordered and stand away from the crowd and wait for Lieutenant Mashkov and himself to reach the front of the formation of 60 soldiers.

When Micha has a better look at the Americans crowded around the edges of the cave and the cliff next to the Pacific Ocean, he notices that many of them are smiling, and even crying, asking his men and women so many questions that they don't understand.

Many of his soldiers did not speak very good English. His English was pretty good, along with Captain Grinkov, Lieutenant Petrenko, and Lieutenant Mashkov. There were a few other men and women amongst his company that were okay at English, but not many.

What gets him most is the smiling.

Why are they smiling like idiots? The fucking idiots. Pindos deserve death for stupidity... not one of them armed. Micha thinks to himself as Lieutenant Petrenko steps forward to address the survivors.

"Silence!" Lieutenant Petrenko yells out in English.

The Americans quiet down quickly.

So docile and meek. Micha thinks to himself.

"We answer all questions! And have food... for you! First, stand in a straight line in front of U.N. soldiers! We help you then!" Lieutenant Petrenko says to the group of survivors.

The Americans look around at each other and Micha can hear a few murmurs of confusion.

Getting impatient, Lieutenant Petrenko shouts out, "Move now! Fast!"

This startles most of them and they begin to shuffle around to become a straight line in front of himself, Lieutenant Petrenko, and all of his platoon, with their weapons in carry position.

Micha can't help but find himself smiling at the idiotic and submissive Americans doing anything they are told as long as they hear *help* and *food*.

By the looks of it, there looked to be close to fifty survivors. There were men, women, and children all lined up. All formed up nice and in a row for his soldiers to mow down with their weapons. If they were lucky, many of them would just fall back into the cave and off the cliffs behind them.

Lieutenant Petrenko looks over to him and Micha nods.

Lieutenant Petrenko nods back and commands his soldier in Russian. "On my command, kill the filthy Americans!"

Micha notices the Americans looking at each other with more confusion and beginning to get scared. Likely once they heard Lieutenant Petrenko's Russian words.

"Wait! I can help you!" An American voice shouts back in Russian from the line of survivors

"Stop!" Micha yells in Russian and then looks to Lieutenant Petrenko who has a look of confusion as well.

Lieutenant Petrenko looks back to the survivors.

"Who said that?!" Lieutenant Petrenko says in Russian.

After a moment, Micha sees a man step forward. He doesn't look Russian or like anything special at all.

The man opens his mouth and replies in Russian. "Me! My name is Nicholas Cross! I can help you! Don't kill me!"

Lieutenant Petrenko looks back to him, looking for an answer of what to do.

"Get him out of there. We can see what he has to say. Then we kill him... maybe." Micha says to his Lieutenant.

Lieutenant Petrenko nods in confirmation and turns to his soldiers, ordering two of them to get the man out of the execution line up. The two men snatch up Nicholas Cross quickly, gaining a lot of confused and scared looks from the others.

Once the man and his soldiers are across the firing line of the other 58 soldiers, Lieutenant Petrenko gives the order in Russian, "Kill all Americans!"

A barrage of gunfire opens up on the American survivors.

They had no idea what hit them and no time to run and there was nowhere to even run to. They had allowed themselves to be boxed in. It was like fishing with dynamite. It was like lemmings off a cliff, quite literally.

Micha watches as the American survivors who survived the CWA attacks for whatever reason, collapsed and fell back from the barrage of bullets riddling their bodies. He watches as some men, women, and children collapse to the sandy ground. He watches as other men, women, and children fall backwards into the cave and off of the cliffs. He even watches some jump from the cliffs, trying to avoid their execution.

He then looks to the American that was just speaking Russian pleading for his life, and smiles at the man, as the man named Nicholas Cross looks at the execution of his fellow Americans in dread and terror.

"Make sure that there are no survivors, comrades!" Lieutenant Petrenko orders.

Many soldiers walk forward up to the edge of the cave and the cliffs, firing down into the dead bodies and those that survived the fall from jumping, only to die in agony and be shot anyway.

Once the gunfire dies down and trickles off, his soldiers shout and holler in excitement from killing more American trash. They are all one step closer to finishing taking and claiming what is now rightfully theirs, after over a century of waiting for this opportunity.

The Russian Federation may be in ruins, and there may not be many survivors from his home, or even any at all. Hell, the whole New World Order Axis could be dismantled. But there was still a massive force of Russians on what was once American soil.

By his estimates, there were 15 other companies of Russian Federation soldiers along the American west coast, with somewhere around 2,400 Russian troops between the companies and the submarine crews now on land.

There may be close to 65 million American survivors, but they were split up and if they all acted like the *pindos* that just died... this land would soon be theirs and they could rebuild Russia, if indeed the homeland was destroyed.

This would be the new Russia, and he would be a key player in claiming their new Russia. This idea was beginning to excite him and he began to entertain the possibilities of leading more than simply a company.

There is more... for the great Michail Lenkov. He thinks to himself, thinking of all of his possibilities.

After a moment, Lieutenant Petrenko catches his attention. "What of Nicholas Cross, Major?"

Micha is pulled from his daze of pondering his great future and looks to the frightened man. He looks at his trousers, seeing that he soiled himself while his fellow Americans were being executed.

"Well. He's no Russian. That's for sure." Micha says to Lieutenant Petrenko.

Lieutenant Petrenko laughs at the frightened man named Nicholas Cross.

The man looks frightened for a moment longer and the danger somehow makes something click inside his head that he should be pleading for his life right about now.

"No. Not Russian. But I can help you. I speak Russian..." Nicholas Cross replies.

"Dah, but so do we." Lieutenant Petrenko replies in Russian.

This gets a laugh out of him and Lieutenant Petrenko.

"But I also speak English very well, being American." Nicholas Cross responds.

"Our English not good?" Lieutenant Petrenko questions, getting another set of laughter from the two of them.

Obviously getting scared, Nicholas Cross studders somewhat. "No. No. Yeah. Yes. You do. But I can help... I know more English. And I know the area. You guys were behind the attacks right? And now you're here to clean up the mess and take America for your own... I'm fine with that. I can help you..."

Micha ponders it over for a moment. *It would be helpful to have a guide. We have maps but have never been here...*

"He is traitor, Major. We should kill this Nicholas Cross." Lieutenant Petrenko says to him.

He looks to Lieutenant Petrenko and then back to this Nicholas Cross, with his eyes wide open like a scared little child.

If the Russian Federation is truly gone, we must start thinking about the bigger picture. No one may be coming in 24 days. Micha thinks to himself, deciding whether to kill the cowardly American or not.

"Maybe yes... but... maybe not..." Micha replies.

Chapter 7: Emily Collins

Day 8: San Diego, California

Emily is looking on to Laura and Harper swimming around in the pool at the hotel. The power had been out for about 12 hours now and it was another warm day in early September in Southern California. The ocean breeze was wonderful and really helped with the smell of decay and the dead. There was also the fact that Logan had been cleaning up all of those poor people that died eight days ago. Nonetheless, it was still warm, with the sun beating down on you all throughout the day, and now without any electricity or A/C from the hotel.

The power had gone out several times over the last couple days, but this was the longest it had been out and she was beginning to wonder if it was going to turn back on. She had checked in with Dr. Lewis over one of the radios that Logan had given her and then given her another to hand off to Dr. Lewis.

That did put her mind a little at ease that she had contact with Dr. Lewis and they still had the backup generators running, and also had solar panels atop the hospital that they could pull from. But she was still very worried.

If the power stays off, the generators will eventually run out. Sure, the solar panels should work for a while, and Dr. Lewis says that they'll be enough to monitor Bryan and perform certain procedures and other medical things in the hospital. But then what? What happens when those stop working? She thinks to herself, beginning to stress herself out again.

"This was a good idea to get them swimming in the pool for a little while. The pool is still pretty clean, having only been a week... and it makes it easier than having them jump into a cold shower if the power stays off." Logan says beside her.

She looks over at him, bringing herself out of her daze. "Yeah, thanks... I thought it would also help them relax a little bit."

Logan chuckles and smiles, looking at their daughters. "Well, they sure seem pretty relaxed... almost as if we aren't living in a mostly dead world now."

She gives him a look, and he must have thought about what he just said.

"Sorry... that was pretty morbid. I just meant..." He tries to explain.

She nods at him, knowing exactly what he meant. They were in a hellish situation and it was seeming to get more hopeless at the end of each day. The last local news channel was still reporting whatever they knew, but it wasn't much and it seemed like it was only one reporter and someone turning on the cameras and whatnot. But then again, they hadn't heard from them since the power went off again, obviously.

"I know what you meant, Logan. And I get it... just try to keep those kinds of comments down to a minimum around the girls." She says to him.

She watches as the man scratches the back of his head and blushes.

"Yeah... will do, Emily. My fault." Logan replies.

Changing the subject back to what was on her mind, "Do you think the power is off for good this time, Logan?"

Obviously glad that she changed the subject away from him and his crass comment, he looks at her and scrunches his face.

"To be honest, Emily... I don't know... maybe." He answers after a short pause.

She gives him a look that must have given away her concern.

"I'm sure the power over at the hospital will be fine, even if the rest of the power stays off for good. And you did tell me that Dr. Lewis said that they have backup generators and solar." He adds.

Emily slowly nods her head. "Yeah, I just hope... I just hope that he wakes up in time..."

She watches as he raises his hand. Maybe to put on her shoulder. But then he stops and lets it drop back down to his side.

"He will, Emily. You'll see... and we'll figure it out from there... the whole group of us. Because there is strength in numbers and we have a nice little group started here..." Logan says to her and then he looks back to their daughters swimming in the pool still laughing and playing.

"They sure seem to like our little group banding together. And to be honest, I think it's really good for them to have some sort of fun in all of this chaos." Logan adds.

Emily nods in agreement, she had noticed a change in Laura, just in the last few days. Laura and Harper were very close in age, and it helped take her mind off of her older brother who was still in a coma. Not to mention, her father who had died in the CWA attacks.

"Yeah. You have a point, Logan. It has been nice knowing that you and Harper are just down the way from us now. Laura sure is in a better mood... and then there's Clint and Cole. I don't know what it is about those twins, but they bring a smile to my face whenever they talk." Emily says to him.

Logan chuckles lightly. "I know the feeling. I think it's the way that they finish each other's sentences and are always on the same page... Plus, they just have that way about them and I have to admit, I like them. They are nice young men and more than willing to help out. They've been a great deal of help over the last couple days since we got them set up in one of the suites just down the way from you and Laura, and not too far from Harper and I."

"This is true... didn't you say they went out fishing not too long ago?" Emily questions.

"Yeah. They are over by the bridge to the south of the hotel. And if they catch anything, we can have a nice little fish fry, right over there along the shore. It'll make one hell of a dinner. And it'll hopefully make us all feel a little bit normal again... at least for a moment." Logan says to her.

"Yeah, that would be nice. And normal would be nice too..." Emily starts. "But I just feel guilty enjoying myself with Bryan in the hospital. Like I should be by his side, trying to wake him up and not leaving him alone."

Logan sighs heavily. "Yeah, no, I get it. And I can see how you might feel that way. But you have to remember... your little Laura needs you right now too. And Bryan... he'll wake up. You'll see. Plus Dr. Lewis is over there."

"Yeah, I guess." She admits, not really feeling better about not being with her teenage son in a coma. Instead, she's poolside, at the beach, possibly planning to have a fish fry later on.

"Hey, if it makes you feel any better... We can all go down to the hospital tomorrow and see how he's doing. The whole group of us. You, Laura, me, Harper, and the twins." Logan says to her.

"You guys don't have to all come down there with us." She replies.

"We can make a trip out of it. Plus, I was thinking, we need supplies and stuff. Like the medical sort of supplies. Just in case, Ya know?" Logan responds.

Yeah... that would be smart, just in case something happens away from the hospital. She thinks to herself.

"But what if Dr. Lewis doesn't have enough to give us some?" Emily questions.

Logan shrugs. "If he does, great! If not, there are plenty of other stores and pharmacies we can go through. But I'd rather ask the good doctor first."

Logan then looks at Harper and Laura and shakes his head.

"I don't want to put Harper through that again... going through a store, walking over all of those corpses. Just rotting away..." Logan adds.

"Laura had mentioned it. So that means that Harper talked to her about it. She didn't say much. Just that it was gross and smelled really bad." She explains to him.

"Yeah. I'm not sure if that is a good thing or bad thing... I get kind of worried how this is going to impact them as they get older... that is if we get through this whole shitshow and get back to some sort of normalcy." Logan says, as he looks around him.

"You certainly have a way with words don't you, Logan? No sugar coating or anything..." She says to him, with a wrinkle of her nose.

Logan blushes again and scratches the back of his head. "Yeah. Sorry... again. I've been told that I can be pretty blunt about things. Maybe it's the whole mechanic part of my brain. I don't know. Kelsey used to have to apologize for me to a lot of our friends."

Emily then notices his mood change, as he mentions his dead wife. His look changes to one of defeat and her heart goes out to him. That was the exact same way that she felt about her Bryan. She also felt horrible about losing Erik, but with Bryan... she felt hopeless and lost. Just like that look on Logan's face right then.

Emily puts her hand on his left shoulder and he glances over at her.

"Hey. You're right, Logan. Bryan is going to wake up. We're going to stick together with our little growing group that we have going on. We'll all go to the hospital tomorrow and find some supplies... and life will reach some sort of normalcy again for our kids. I'm not really sure what kind of normal it will be, but we'll all be there and that's all that really matters, right?" She says to him.

She watches as his eyes squint for a moment and she thinks that he is holding back a few tears.

He exhales slowly. "Yeah, Emily. That sounds pretty alright to me. And sometimes I forget just how lucky we are. A 15% survival rate is less than two out of ten people. That's crazy insane to think about what would have happened if..."

Logan must have seen movement past her, because his eyes darted over her shoulder and he put his hand to his hip. A moment of panic engulfs her and she spins around, putting her own hand to her hip.

After a tense moment peering through the bars and foliage around the pool, she sighs in relief, and hears Logan do the same.

"Whew! It's only the twins." Logan says, with relief in his voice.

She had to admit, she was really relieved too. They hadn't seen much of anyone else lately, but they had all heard the gunfire in the area and then there were the fires. The fires were really beginning to make her nervous, especially since it was a group of people intentionally setting San Diego ablaze, little by little.

"Geez! You think they would have radioed us on their way back." She says to him as she hears the girls still splashing in the pool.

"Right!" Logan adds.

"Hey guys! Going for a swim are we?!" She hears Clint's voice say to them.

Logan laughs and wanders over to the gate to open it for them. The lock had been disabled by Logan the first time the power went out, but it looked like the twins had their hands full.

"Swimming sounds awesome right about now!" Cole says, as they walk through the gate into the pool area.

Sure enough, their hands were full. They both had a pole and a rifle in their right hand, and handheld coolers in their left hand. It was like looking at a side-by-side mirror.

She found herself smiling at the identical twins, looking like a postcard for California hunting and fishing.

"You gents catch anything?" Logan asks.

"Sure did, Mr. Miller!" Clint answers.

"Yeah, we did!" Cole says, plopping his pole and cooler into a chair and beginning to take off his shirt.

She looks back to Clint, who has a wide grin on his face.

He looks at her and says proudly, "We caught eight fish out there on the bridge! They aren't super big catches or anything, but they are enough for all of us to eat, that's for sure!"

"Very nice, boys!" Emily replies.

She then sees Cole running past her as he finishes taking off his socks and shoes, heading straight for the pool.

"Cannon ball!" Cole shouts, as he jumps into the air.

She can't help but laugh as she hears the girls shout in excitement and Cole goes splashing into the pool.

"Any trouble out there, Clint?" Logan says, bringing her attention back to the other twin.

She turns to see Clint nod slowly and sigh. "Not exactly... but the fires are getting worse and I think they are getting closer. We did hear some more of that gunfire, but it was a ways off."

Logan shakes his head, looking at her and then back to Clint.

"Did either of you see where it was coming from?" Logan asks.

Clint shakes his head. "Nope. By the time we sighted in with our scopes, we couldn't tell where it came from. And that's how it went each time we heard the gunfire... it sounded pretty distant though."

Emily looks at Clint as he sets down his fishing pole and his cooler, along with his rifle. He did so in a much calmer fashion than his brother. She looked at the rifle, remembering that Logan had told her that their parents had gotten them both the same rifle.

It was an MVP Patrol, and they even had an extra one that was their dad's. Which they were kind enough to give to Logan, with Logan being very surprised by the offer and also very excited. He had admitted that he has one just like it back home in Colorado. The twins had said something about not being able to get into the safe without Logan's help and advice, so it was the least they could do.

She then sees Clint unhook his holster from his hip with his M&P Shield, which used to be his mother's gun. His twin had a sidearm too, but Cole's was a Springfield XD.

Apparently, once they were able to get into their parents' gun safe, they were able to get their hands on several guns. The total came out to three rifles, four handguns, and a shotgun. With Logan already having a shotgun and all of them now having handguns, the other two handguns and the other shotgun were in the twins' suite.

"Well, that's a good thing that it sounded pretty far off. And good job with the fish, Clint... Logan and I were just talking about how great it would be to have a fish fry." She says to him.

"Yeah, that would be pretty awesome... but right now, I'm following my brother." Clint says as he takes off his shirt, kicking off his shoes and socks.

"It's hot and I haven't showered all day... the pool counts as a shower right?" Clint says to them.

Logan laughs. "Makes sense to me, as long as the chlorine is still good and strong. And considering it's a hotel, chances are it's still pretty damn strong."

"Oh yeah... that water looks nice." Clint says smiling at them and then running full speed into the pool.

She watches as he reaches the pool and goes into the air, making it look like he's still running, but then splashing down into the water an instant later. She finds herself laughing at him, along with the girls and his brother Cole.

"Well, he does have a point... that water does look pretty nice." Logan says.

She looks over to him as he takes off his own shirt, kicking off his shoes and socks, and placing his gun on a nearby chair. She sees that he is very much in shape for a mid-thirties married man. Well, formally married and recently widowed, with her being a widow herself. She could tell that he wasn't lazy from how he looked with his clothes on, but Logan standing there in shorts confirmed that he took care of himself.

"Do you have a suit on under those clothes, Emily?" Logan questions.

She laughs. "Actually yeah, I do. It's what I've been using as underwear for the last couple of days."

He laughs back at her. "Smart thinking. We are in California, after all. So, what do you say? Go swimming with our kids and those two goofball twins, and then have ourselves a fish fry?"

She thinks about it for a moment, trying not to feel guilty about her son being in the hospital, and finally nods. "Yeah. You know what? That does sound pretty nice... almost normal."

"Sounds like a plan then." Logan nods and smiles, walking over to the pool and jumping in nonchalantly.

She finds herself smiling at the group of people she had just met, as they all swam in the pool. The group of people that had, for some reason or another, banded together in what was left of this world. She just wished that her son, Bryan, could be in that pool too... laughing and enjoying life, once again.

Chapter 8: Logan Miller

Day 9: San Diego, California

The fish fry the evening prior had been nice. It was, indeed, a relaxing and an enjoyable time. Logan was reflecting on the afternoon of swimming, grilling up some fish on the outside grills, and all of them enjoying some well needed laughter and conversation. He was thinking about these things as he followed Emily's car back to the hotel, with the twins following him.

He was more than happy that Harper and Laura were getting along famously. It was making his decision to stick around a while longer a whole lot easier. And then there were the twins, Clint and Cole. They were very capable young men, but also had a way of being goofy and raising your spirits. Even in times like these. There were even a few times when he almost forgot about losing Kelsey, just for a moment... *almost* being the key word.

Logan could tell that Emily was enjoying herself too. He knew that she was really stressed out and overwhelmed with the condition of her oldest, which Logan didn't envy whatsoever. He knew he would be losing his freaking mind if Harper was in that hospital in a coma.

But he could tell that Emily had relaxed a little bit yesterday and it was mostly contributed to the afternoon of swimming and fish fry afterward. They had all swam with the kids and watched Clint and Cole wrestle around in the pool like... well, like brothers. All the while, the little girls were laughing and playing in the pool too, having a grand ol' time.

If he was being honest with himself, he wasn't sure exactly what his plans were. Heading all the way back to Greely, Colorado seemed insane, and what was really there for him and Harper? Sure, their home was there. But it wasn't anything huge or fancy. It was nice, but still one of those cookie-cutter homes and it would be a long and dangerous journey just to go back for something that could already be gone by now... considering how bad things had deteriorated in just over a week around here.

There was also the thought of Kelsey that kept him from wanting to go back to their home. It's not like he wanted to forget about his wife. They had been together for over 15 years... If he made it back home, he would be going back to the house that he and Kelsey had made into a home. And that was all based on the *if* part of making it back home.

Did he want to go back for the pictures? Yeah, he felt bad about all of the photo albums that she had made over the years and the baby pictures of Harper. But to risk Harper's life on such a long journey, on the gamble that all of his things were left intact and not burned down to the ground like so much out there... it just didn't seem worth it. He did still have one picture of his family, and maybe that would be enough to be able to hold on to her. Hold on to what their lives were like before all of this madness.

He looks out his window, out onto what is left of San Diego as he drives down the 8 West, going past Old Town San Diego.

Before all of this, they had planned on visiting that little area of Old Town... him, Kelsey, and Harper... just to wander around and enjoy the sunshine of Southern California.

I miss you Kelsey... more than you know... he thinks to himself.

Sighing heavily then looking at Harper in the rearview mirror in the back cab of his truck. She was looking out her own window, holding onto her stuffed penguin that they had gotten at the San Diego Zoo, back on the day that all of this insanity and doom with the CWA attacks that had brought the death clouds.

The stuffed penguin brings his mind back to nine days ago when they had bought the stuffed animal for her. And as fate would have it, Emily's daughter, Laura, had the exact same one.

Well, at least we got to take and pay for that very overpriced picture of all of us at the Penguin exhibit at the San Diego Zoo. Best damn 30 bucks I have ever spent. That's for damn sure. Logan thinks to himself and smiles, remembering the picture they took and then Kelsey had convinced him to buy the very expensive souvenir picture of the three of them.

Thank you for pushing me to get that, babe... he thinks as he looks at the center console of the truck, where the very last picture that they all took together as a family was safely tucked away.

He had made sure to have it close to him at all times. Just in case they had to get the hell out of dodge, and just pick up and leave. He knew that it could very well happen if the fires reached them in the near future, and whoever was lighting the damn things ablaze. He would not be able to live with himself if he lost the last and only picture he had of his wife and family... back when it was whole... back when *he* was whole.

He still felt that empty hole in his chest that he had felt the minute he realized she was gone and not coming back. And he knew it was likely that he would feel that hole for the rest of his life. But what mattered to him right now was keeping his little girl, their little girl, in the back cab of his newly acquired truck, safe and giving her a life that resembles some sort of normalcy.

And one of the major reasons he was sticking around was because of her... she was doing so much better over the last few days with Laura and Emily around. And Clint and Cole really seemed to crack those little girls up.

They had really become a small little unit over the last few days, which really amazed Logan. He wasn't always the best at making friends and was even worse at staying in contact and keeping up with them on a regular basis. That was always more in Kelsey's wheelhouse, being the social butterfly.

But here they were... in a small, modified family unit with four other people, making it six of them now. Six versus this shitshow of a world. It would be seven versus this shitshow of a world, once Bryan woke up. Actually, they had spent most of their day at the hospital, just to provide moral support for Emily and Laura.

Their day was spent helping out what was left of the hospital staff, which was just down to Dr. Lewis, Dr. Calhoun, and the Nurses... Scott, Nunez, and Campbell. So, they really appreciated the help of the twins and himself. He hadn't met Dr. Calhoun or Nurse Candice Campbell on his first trip to the hospital because they were out and about in the surrounding area, getting things from their homes to stay at the hospital for the foreseeable future. As it turned out, the remaining hospital staff had all done the same. They surely seemed nice enough, and it also seemed like the other nurse, Anthony Nunez, took a liking to Candice Campbell. Regardless, the entire remaining staff at Scripps Mercy were incredibly helpful and truly selfless.

Since Logan's last visit, with the drunken asshole that killed his own nephew, there were several more patients in the hospital. Most of the injuries were broken limbs, but one was on life support and it was not looking good for the older man. But there was nothing any of them could do but wait and see. Somewhat similar to Bryan's situation.

The doctors and nurses were kind enough to provide Logan and the others with medical supplies, and said they had more than enough to give them what they needed. They were able to get away with several first aid kits, and they were very well stocked. They also came up on some vitamins, antibiotics, and even some decent pain killers. Dr. Lewis and Dr. Calhoun did have to remind them to only use them if they truly needed them, and Logan had assured them that they would use the medications wisely. It was a huge score for their small little group and they all knew it.

One of the first aid bags was in his truck on his passenger seat. Another in Emily's car in front of him, and the rest of the supplies with the twins. The twins had joked around about having a party somewhere, but it had been obvious that the goofy twins were screwing around, once again. They were still following him in their little sedan, several car-lengths back.

After looking back at Harper in the rearview for a moment, he puts his eyes back on the road of the 8 West Freeway, having to swerve around crashed and stalled cars. Over the first few days, he was able to clear enough of a path around cars to be able to come and go from their very small peninsula with SeaWorld on it. This was where their hotel was located and currently acting as their home away from home.

Nearing their exit on Mission Bay Drive, Logan sees that Emily was able to maneuver much faster than him in her smaller car compared to his truck.

"Damn. She's already at the turn onto the bridge." Logan says aloud.

"What, dad?" Harper says, turning her attention to him.

"Nothing, kiddo. You're good." He replies, looking back at her for a moment.

When he turns his attention back to the road in front of him, he sees that Emily has already made the turn and started going across the Mission Bay Bridge, toward the hotel. He can see her small sedan driving smoothly across the mostly open bridge, swerving around cars.

Then a glimmer catches his eye on the other side of the road.

Slowing down and squinting as he maneuvers around another downed vehicle, it looks like another car is driving on the other side of the bridge, going the opposite direction and heading toward their little group.

Is that another car coming our way? Haven't seen anyone else on the peninsula since the start of this shitshow. He thinks to himself.

Reaching the turn, foliage blocks his view and he begins the turn onto the bridge.

Gunfire erupts somewhere close... Too damn close.

He stomps on the breaks as he hears multiple gunshots ring out, which puts his head on a swivel, him looking all around their surroundings.

Another barrage of gunfire erupts as he tries to discern where it's coming from.

"Shit!" He blurts out, realizing it's coming from the bridge.

"What's that, dad!?" Harper questions with immediate concern.

He looks back at her, as he questions whether to push forward to see if Emily and Laura need help, or keep Harper back where it's safer for her.

"Keep your head down, kiddo... actually, unbuckle and lay down back there so no one sees you... okay?" He says to her.

She doesn't answer back, but does exactly what he says.

He goes to pick up his radio and click the mic to speak. "Emily. It's Logan. What's going on?"

He waits for a response and then clicks the mic again. "Emily. Are you there? What's going on? We can't see you from where we are? Is that gunfire close to you?"

Logan releases the mic, looking in his rearview mirror to see the twins pulling up right behind him. They come to a complete stop but stay in the car as well. Likely listening over the same radio channel that he is trying to get a hold of Emily on.

"Logan! Logan! Are you there?!" He hears her shout through the radio.

The sound of more gunfire fills the air, echoing.

His eyes going toward the direction of the bridge, he clicks the mic again. "Yeah, Emily. We're here. Just before the turn. If you haven't already. Stop your car and wait for whoever is shooting at whoever else to stop and go away... just pretend to be a stalled car."

After he releases the mic, he can hear her shouting again.

"Shooting at us Logan! Two men in a Jeep just started shooting at us! I crashed into a parked car! We're okay! But they just keep on shooting! We're trapped Logan!" He hears Emily's panicked voice shouting out into the radio.

"Son of bitch!" Logan blurts out and he can see in the rearview mirror that the twins heard the whole thing too, with both of them getting out of the car, rifles in hand.

"Dad... I'm scared..." Harper says in the back seat, still laying down.

He looks back at her and nods, collecting himself. "I know, kiddo. It's going to be okay."

His attention is brought back to Emily on the bridge, with the echo for more bullets trying to find her and her daughter.

Shit! They're fucked out there in the open. How many did she say? Two of them? He thinks quickly.

He steps out of the truck and reaches over for the rifle that the twins gave him. It was a Mossberg MVP Patrol with a nice Vortex scope on it. He pulls the magazine, finding it to be fully loaded with .308 rounds. He reaches over to the center console and grabs his spare magazine for it.

As he turns around he sees Clint and Cole step in front of him.

"Logan... Did you hear me? Are you still there?" He hears Emily's voice, now whispering over the radio.

Logan looks at Harper and sighs heavily. He then keys the mic on the radio. "Keep your head down Emily. Is Laura okay?"

He sees Clint and Cole looking at him.

"What the hell are we going to do, Mr. Miller? We can't just leave them out there." Clint says.

"Yeah, Emily said there were only two of them." Cole adds.

"Yeah, No! We're both not hurt, if that's what you're asking! But we crashed into a parked car and we're trapped! They'll kill us if we make a run for it, for sure! What do we do?!" Emily says over the radio.

Logan sighs and tries to peer through the brush to see how bad the situation is. After a quick moment, he finally nods and looks at the twins.

"Alright. Hold tight and keep your head down. We're coming for you." He says back over the radio.

The gunfire eases up for a moment, likely because their assailants were reloading.

Hopefully, they're reloading... And we aren't too late!

"Alright then! Let's go already!" Cole says quickly.

Logan shakes his head and looks to the two of them and back to Harper in the truck.

Clint looks to the back cab where Harper is then back to Logan.

He nods and sighs, "You go, Mr. Miller... go with Cole. I'll stay back with Harper."

Not sure if he should leave his little girl, "You sure, Clint?"

Clint nods slowly. "Mr. Miller. You're the only one that has actually killed anyone yet. Plus, Cole is a better shot than I am... I hate to admit it, but it's true."

He looks to Clint, then Cole, and then to Harper.

If I leave her here and anything happens to her, I don't think I could live with myself... but if I don't go, Emily and her daughter may pay the price. What the hell am I supposed to do?! He thinks to himself, not knowing which path to take.

Clint puts his hand on Logan's shoulder. "Logan... I'll take care of her. I promise."

Shit on a fucking stick...

"Alright... but first sign of trouble, get her the hell out of here and we'll find you later. Keep your radio on you." Logan says to Clint.

"Will do." Clint replies, holding up his radio in his left hand.

Logan looks over to Harper. "Alright, kiddo. I'll be back in a few. You listen to Clint here and do whatever he says. I'm going with Cole to make sure that Emily and Laura get out of there safely."

Harper pokes her head up and peeks over at him. "Okay, dad. Be careful... please."

"Will do, kiddo." He says to her.

He then gives another look to Clint.

"I got this, sir. You can count on me." Clint says to him.

The sound of gunfire was intensifying, once again.

Shit. They don't have much time left. We've gotta get going. He thinks, looking toward the opposite lines of the bridge across the divider.

Logan nods and looks at Cole. "Ready to go, Cole?"

Once excited to move, the moment must have caught up with the young man, because he gulps before answering, "Yeah... but what's the plan, Mr. Miller?"

"Here, follow me... we're going to get the drop on them with them focused on the girls. But stay close and don't shoot until we get closer." Logan tells him.

Cole nods quickly, obviously now getting nervous, having realized he was heading into gunfire. "Lead the way, Mr. Miller." Cole tries to say with a confident voice.

Logan looks to Clint and then to Harper and gives her a wink. She winks back and he takes off running toward the divider of the bridge. Not needing to hesitate any further. Every second would count if Emily and Laura were going to make it out of this alive.

Reaching the divider, Cole almost crashes into him, but comes up right next to him instead, with an abrupt stop.

"Alright, stay low and move fast. We have to get eyes on them and hopefully a clear line of sight so we can get decent shots off. We may only have one chance at this." He says to Cole.

Cole nods, but before he can answer, Logan climbs over the center divider for the oncoming traffic of the Mission Bay Bridge. With there, of course, not being any oncoming traffic these days… only a massive amount of gunfire aimed at Emily and Laura.

Hang in there girls. We're coming for you! He thinks as he keeps low and moves quickly through the crashed and stalled cars.

Running by a few cars, he can smell the stench of death. He dares a glance at one of the cars and sees what looks like a whole family in a minivan, still in the seatbelts, but with the hood of the minivan smashed into a small sedan.

He shakes his head, clearing his thoughts of the dead family and likely the many other people dead inside their cars, being baked inside their cars that are now acting like ovens under the hot Southern California sun, adding more to the massive amount of decaying carcasses of entire families and millions of innocent people throughout California and the rest of the U.S.

Stay focused, dammit! They're counting on you. He thinks, snapping at himself.

This time the gunfire sounded much closer to them and he stopped in his tracks next to a semi-truck.

He then hears gunfire that sounded different from the barrage of bullets flying a moment ago.

Shit! Is that Emily firing back at them?! Damn that woman is crazy. A pistol against what sounds like automatic rifles. He thinks to himself.

Looking back to Cole, he finds that he's stopped just behind him.

"They're close." he whispers to him.

Cole nods and Logan turns his attention back ahead of him where the girls are, thinking that the shooters are likely just past this semi-truck. He knows there is enough room at the other end of the semi-truck for a car to get through, because their vehicles fit through the same gap the several times they crossed this bridge.

But if we go up that way, they might see us before we see them… he thinks to himself.

Cole taps him on the shoulder and he looks back to him.

Cole points underneath the semi-truck and makes a downward waving motion with his free hand.

Go under the trailer of the semi! Why the hell didn't I think of that?! He scolds himself.

He quickly nods and ducks down into a high crawl, going underneath the trailer attached to the semi-truck. After a few seconds on his hands and knees, he's out on the other side and is at the cement guardrail of the bridge. A moment later Cole is right there with him. Logan helps him up and pats him on the back.

Logan looks in the direction of the volley of gunfire and can see the back part of black Jeep about 200 feet up, with a red truck blocking the front part of the Jeep from view.

He then hears the sound of what must be Emily firing back.

At least if she's shooting back, that means she's still alive... but we are running out of time, he thinks with concern for Emily and Laura.

He looks to Cole and points in the direction of the Jeep.

"They must be pretty damn close. We need to get a better look. " Logan whispers.

Cole nods and Logan begins to creep forward. After about fifty feet, he ducks his head down when he sees two figures and hears rifles spraying rounds toward Emily and Laura.

Yup. Definitely full auto weapons... shit... we only have one shot at this. He thinks to himself.

He waves for Cole to come up next to him and they both get into the kneeling position, cradling their rifles.

Looking over to Cole, "We may only have one shot at this Cole. Sight in and let me know if you have a shot. And I'll do the same. They look to be about 150 feet out, so adjust your zoom for about 50 yards."

Cole nods and Logan adjusts his scope and looks down through it on his MVP.

Looking just past the red truck, Logan can see one man and then sees the other, shifting his sight to his right. Both men look to be pretty damn young, probably even around Cole and Clint's age. Both young men had short, cropped hair, with a young man's stubble starting to form on their faces.

Who the hell are these guys? Logan thinks to himself.

He hears what must be Laura screaming, as bullets ping off of the vehicle.

Shit! No time to care. He reprimands himself.

"Hey, Cole. Do you see the guy on the left?" Logan asks him.

"Yeah... and the other guy is the blonde short-haired dude, yeah?" Cole says back.

"Yeah, Cole. You take the guy on the left and I'll take blondie over there. But wait and let me know once you are sighted in. Again, we may only have one shot at this." He says to Cole.

"Okay, yeah. Tell me when to shoot, Mr. Miller. I'm already ready for my guy." Cole replies.

What the hell? Already ready? Holy crap. Who the hell are these kids? Damn video games... he thinks as he sights back at the young blonde man.

Just like the range. You see the silhouette. You inhale, exhale, pause, and gently squeeze back the trigger... but this time it's a real damn person. He thinks to himself.

"Alright. On the count of three." Logan says.

"Mr. Miller?" Cole questions.

"Yeah, Cole?" He replies.

"Do we go on three or right after?" Cole asks.

Logan sighs, thinking about it for a moment. "On three, Cole. Ready?"

"Yeah." Cole replies.

"Okay... one... two... three" Logan says, raising his voice on three.

Logan feels the recoil of the shot, as the gunfire thrashes his eardrums. Quickly, he clears his head and he sights back in, not seeing either man.

"Did we get them?" Cole asks, asking the same question he was thinking.

He pulls his bolt back to the rear, expelling the spent round from the rifle. The brass hits the concrete of the bridge and he loads another .308 round into the chamber. At the same time, he hears Cole do the same.

Logan lowers his aim, looking to the ground, around the red truck. He quickly finds his target on the ground, facedown.

"One down that I see. Do you see the brown-haired guy?" Logan says to Cole.

"Nope, not seeing him... but I swear I got the guy. It wasn't even that far of a shot." Cole says, sure of himself.

"Alright, then. Stay sighted in and I'll move forward." Logan says to him.

He stands and begins to creep forward with his rifle aimed in the direction of the now dead young blonde man. He pauses and looks back to Cole.

"Hey, Cole... try not to accidentally shoot me. Okay?" He says.

Cole chuckles and then replies, "Sure thing, Mr. Miller."

Logan sighs and presses forward, slowly closing the gap between him and where the man he shot was lying dead on the ground about 150 feet up from him. Stepping wide to his right to get a better view, he creeps closer.

With each step, it feels like the world and time are both slowing down around him. He can hear birds off in the distance. He can hear the water below him, underneath the bridge. And he can most certainly hear his own damn heartbeat.

Inching closer to the divider, he exhales with relief, seeing the brown-haired man on the ground too. He quickly brings up his rifle to get a closer look.

Sure enough, he's dead... he thinks and looks back to Cole waving.

Cole jumps and jogs over to him with a proud smile on his face.

Reaching him, he says, "The dude's dead right! I told you that I got him!"

Immediately, the sound of two gunshots filled the air.

"Holy shit!" Cole exclaims and drops to the ground.

Logan quickly drops to the ground right beside him, flat on his stomach.

"Shit! Where did that come from? I only saw two of them." Logan says to him.

He then hears his radio crackle to life with Emily's voice on it. "Logan! Is that you out there? Oh my gosh! I'm so sorry! Are you guys alright?!"

"Seriously, Emily?! That was you that just shot at us?! Yeah, the two guys are down and it's safe to come out." Logan replies back into the radio.

"Sorry, Logan! I thought you were them... we're coming out now... I'm so sorry!" Emily replies back over the radio.

"Son of a bitch... we came out here to save them and she almost damn near killed the two of us..." Logan says to Cole, still flat on his stomach.

Cole laughs. "Yeah, but did you die?"

What the hell? Who the hell is this kid? Logan thinks to himself as he begins to stand back up on his feet, brushing himself off and then grabbing his rifle.

"Did I die? What the crap ever, Cole. I sure as shit crapped my pants! Now, let's get the girls out of here and get the hell off this bridge." Logan says to him.

"Whatever you say, Mr. Miller." Cole says with another light chuckle.

The two of them climb over the center divider, meeting up with Emily and Laura who look scared out of their minds but alive and not hurt... aside from a few scrapes and likely soon to be bruises.

"Sorry again, Logan and Cole. Thanks for coming for us. I didn't know what to do. We were trapped." Emily says to him, with her little Laura holding on tightly to her mother.

"Alright, let's get you back to my truck and get the hell off this bridge." Logan says and pulls the radio up to call back to Clint.

"Hey! Hold up a minute... I'll be right back!" Cole says and jogs over to the two men that they had just killed.

He watches as Cole goes into the Jeep, pulling out a large duffle bag, then back to the bodies, picking up their weapons and stuffing them into the bag.

Seriously? Who the hell is this kid?! He thinks to himself with amazement.

He strides back up after a few moments, smiling. "Better than anything then we'll find in any damn cop car."

"Well, son of a bitch Cole. You really are something else." Logan says to him.

"Thanks, Mr. Miller!" He replies.

Logan can't help but shake his head and smile at the resourceful young man.

He keys the mic on the radio. "Clint. We're good here and heading back to you. We have the girls and they're okay."

"Copy that. That's awesome news! Harper is safe and fine back here. See you in a bit, Mr. Miller." Clint responds through the radio.

"Mom! My Penguin!" Laura exclaims.

Emily looks down to her and then over at Cole and him. "And that first aid kit..."

Logan nods. "I'll get it. You two stay here."

Without waiting for them to respond he strides back over to Emily's crashed car and begins to look for the first aid kit and Laura's stuffed animal.

"Well, this car's trashed." He says to himself.

A few moments later, he had both the first aid kit and the penguin and was back with Cole, Emily, and little Laura.

"Chilly Billy!" Laura exclaims as Logan hands her the stuffed animal.

"Alright... now let's get the hell off this bridge." Logan says to all of them.

"That sounds like a damn fine idea, Logan. Thanks again for coming for us." Emily replies, with a mixture of exasperation and relief in her voice.

"Of course." Logan answers.

I'm just glad that it all worked out, because it could have gone sideways real easily... and Harper would have been an orphan this time. Who the hell were those guys? He thinks to himself, looking back at the dead guys that were just trying to murder Emily and Laura.

"Lead the way, Mr. Miller." Cole says with newfound confidence.

Logan nods, and they all head back to their two remaining vehicles, and back to the hotel and the hell away from this damn bridge. Because if there were two men with military-grade weapons, then there were surely more of the same variety. And that part really worried the hell out of Logan.

Chapter 9: Emily Collins

Day 9: San Diego, California

Looking out the window on Logan's side of the truck, driving past the bridge that she was just nearly killed on was really beginning to stress her out.

We could have freaking died right there! And for what?! Who were those assholes that wanted to hurt my baby and me? She thinks to herself as she looks back at her little Laura.

Laura was in the middle-backseat, squeezing her stuffed penguin, sitting right next to Harper. Harper was holding her free hand, and they were both looking out Harper's window... lost in their own thoughts.

They had to divert their two remaining vehicles back the way they came and get on the Pacific Coast Highway to get across the San Diego River and back onto SeaWorld Drive to be able to safely get back to their hotel. Emily's previous vehicle had been blocking too much of the road on the Mission Bay Bridge, and she certainly didn't want to go back on that bridge, and Logan must have figured that out real quickly, taking the long detour.

"Dad?" Harper says to Logan.

"Yeah, kiddo." Logan replies to his daughter.

"Do you think all the fish and animals are dead over at SeaWorld?" Harper asks.

She sees Logan sigh heavily, not wanting to answer the question.

"Harper... I'm sure one of the worker's let all of the animals out." Emily answers her for him.

Logan looks over at her and smiles. "Thanks. Didn't know how to answer that one."

"Yeah, but what if all the people died, like Daddy did." Laura questions back.

Her eyes go wide and she sees Logan's eyes go wide.

Shit... I don't know how to answer that one. She thinks to herself.

"Well... Laura... we're still alive, right kiddo? So, I'm sure there are others out there and I bet they thought the very same thoughts you two girls just did and let animals out of their cages and pools." Logan answers.

She nods to him. "And thanks for that..."

He smiles at her.

"And at the Zoo too, right?" Harper questions further.

Holy hell with the 20 questions. We just almost died. What's with these kids? Worrying about animals instead of us... she thinks as she sees that Logan is thinking something similar with his eyebrows both going up and eyes going wide.

Emily turns around in her seat to look at the girls. "Yes, girls. In fact... I wouldn't be surprised if we saw lions, tigers, and bears walking around in San Diego."

"Really!?" Both girls say with excitement.

"Holy crap. I sure as hell hope not..." Logan says from the driver's seat.

She chuckles. "Really, Logan?"

"What?... I'm not kidding. We are in Southern California and I'm willing to bet someone let all the animals they could go free. Hell, the crazy bastard is probably lunch by now, from one of the very animals that they set free." Logan explains.

"Logan... not in front of the girls..." She says, shushing him.

"Oh no... I tend to have a healthy fear of apex predators. And the more that I think about it... the more I think that some crazy guy or a bunch of crazies thought it would be a great idea to set all of those animals free in the middle of a big ass city." Logan explains further.

"Hmmm" Emily simply replies, pondering about the possibility of real lions, tigers, bears, and whatever else roaming around San Diego with them.

"Come to think of it, it wouldn't be a bad idea to go take a look at SeaWorld and see what supplies we could find. I mean, they have clothes, water, food, and all kinds of stuff..." Logan says, likely thinking out loud.

"You want to go there? The way you made the San Diego Zoo sound... I'm not so sure that's a great idea, Logan." She says to him.

"Can we go!?" Harper says.

"Yeah! Can we?!" Laura adds.

"Sorry kiddos. With what just happened, we have a few things to talk about once we all get to our rooms and all settled." Logan replies.

Yeah, like who the hell were those guys that tried to murder us with fully automatic guns. Maybe the bag that the twins have can tell us more. She thinks to herself.

"Like what, dad?" Harper questions.

"Well, kiddo... If it's alright with you, I'm going to leave you with Emily to play with Laura in their room, while I go with Cole and Clint." Logan says.

"Okay!" Harper answers with excitement.

"Yeah! And maybe we can go swimming too!" Laura adds.

Holy cow! These kids really recover quickly! Talking about swimming and playing after we just nearly died... again! At least they are handling it well enough. She thinks to herself, looking back at the girls.

She then looks over to Logan. "What were you thinking? I'm guessing you have some sort of plan."

He nods. "Yeah... first, I want to see what's in that bag that Clint and Cole picked up... Man, those guys are bright and on point. I'm super glad we ran into them."

"Me too. And I was thinking the same thing actually." She replies.

"If you want, Emily. You can go relax for a little while up in the room with the girls. I know you must be dealing with a lot right now." Logan says to her.

She sighs and nods. "Yeah, but I have just as many questions as you, Logan. And I need to know. What else did you have in mind? Because that doesn't sound like the end of your plan."

"Alright, and fair enough." Logan responds.

He then turns onto the roundabout on Mission Bay Drive, nearing their hotel.

"And I'm not the only one dealing with stuff here, Logan... You did just kill two men." She adds.

Logan slowly nods. "Yeah, that's what I've been thinking about. And I only killed one. Cole killed the other guy. But there was that crazy drunk at the hospital when we met... so yeah... two men have died by my hands."

She instantly feels guilty, realizing that he was still dealing with taking a life. Actually lives, to be more specific. And he was just looking out for her and Laura. Hell, he just saved them... again.

"I'm sorry, Logan. I didn't mean to be rude about it." She says to him.

He shakes his head. "It's alright. It's something I'm going to have to work through eventually. But right now, we have bigger problems."

"Yeah, like who the hell were those guys?" Emily responds.

"Exactly... and exactly why I want to clear our little peninsula again. Then I want to start blocking it off." Logan says to her.

"Block it off? But how will we get to Bryan and Dr. Lewis?" Emily questions with concern.

Logan nods. "I was thinking about that too... I saw an old road that ran alongside SeaWorld Drive and I think it connects again closer to the Pacific Coast Highway."

"Okay?..." She says with confusion.

"So far, my plan is to block off all of the bridges around us. I think there are only four of them. Clint, Cole, and I can block them off in both directions." Logan explains.

"How are you going to block them?" Emily asks.

"With all of the cars." Logan answers.

Emily shakes her head and smiles. "Well, yeah that makes sense. Dumb question on my part. So, you're going to block off all the bridges and then leave the peninsula open?"

"Not exactly. And I was thinking we should use as many cars as we can find to block off each bridge. Not just one row of cars on both sides. Hell, if we can make it ten rows of cars, I think we should. And we'll mostly block the peninsula, with us having to move a couple cars, every time we need to get off the peninsula to go see your son and do whatever else... because those guys didn't look like your average Joes, and I really doubt they were alone." Logan explains further.

"Yeah... that actually sounds like a pretty good plan, Logan. And you were planning on going to SeaWorld too?" She asks.

He shakes his head. "No, first thing's first. We need to make sure that we have some sort of boundary between us and any more bad guys that are out there. Which may take us well into the night but it needs to be done. Especially after what just happened."

Emily nods in understanding. "Okay. But when you go to SeaWorld, I don't want to be left behind. I can do more than just watching the girls."

Pulling into a parking lot of the hotel, he parks and then looks at her. "Okay, maybe we can get the twins to watch the girls when we go looking for supplies, because I don't want to take them in there and I certainly don't want to leave them alone with the possibility of more of those guys with fully automatic weapons out there."

"Agreed. They have no business being in that place right now. Not after what you told me about the San Diego Zoo." She responds, as the engine to the truck shuts down.

"Yeah, there's that and I wasn't joking about the animals... they could be loose and roaming around." Logan says to her.

"Yeah, most of them live in the water, right?' Emily questions.

Logan shakes his head. "Not all of them, and I hear they have polar bears in there too."

"Shit, maybe I don't want to go with you if there's freaking bears." She answers with a snorted laugh.

Logan laughs lightly back. "Right!"

A moment later, the twins pull up a few parking spaces over from them and they all get out of their vehicles.

"Are there more bad guys, mommy?" Laura asks her, as she gets her out of the back of the truck.

She sighs heavily and looks back at her. "I hope not sweetie. But we have a plan to keep us safe... if there are."

"Okay." Laura simply replies.

"Yeah, Laura. And if there are, my dad will just shoot them. Like he did the other bad guys." Harper adds.

Oh crap! This kid! Emily thinks to herself, as her eyes go wide at the little girl's nonchalant comment about death and mayhem.

"Yes, girls. Your dad, the twins, and I will all keep you safe." Emily replies to them.

Harper smiles and Laura replies, "Okay, mom."

Mom? It's been Mommy forever... When did Mom start? Has that been going on for a few days now and I just noticed? She thinks to herself.

Logan walks over to their side of the truck. "Emily. You should probably hear this..."

She looks at him and then at the girls. "Girls, go stand over there, in front of the truck while me and Logan go talk to Cole and Clint real quick. Okay?"

The girls both nod and go stand in front of the truck while Emily walks with Logan over to Clint and Cole a few empty parking spaces over, next to their small sedan.

"What's up guys?" Emily questions.

"Clint. Tell her what you just told me." Logan says to him.

Clint nods. "Well, Cole was going through the duffle bag that he took off those guys on the drive back..."

"Yeah, those dead Russian guys." Cole adds.

"Russians? What?" Emily responds.

Clint and Cole both nod in unison.

"Cole, here, found a map and other things that all look to be written in Russian. At least we think it's written in Russian." Clint explains.

"Well, they sure as hell sound Russian." Cole adds.

"What do you mean sound?" Emily presses further.

"Show her." Logan responds.

Cole nods, reaching back into their car, returning with what looks to be a radio, but much different looking than their own radios. It's bigger and bulkier.

After a slight pause, Cole turns a knob and the radio crackles to life.

They all listen intently to people speaking on the radio. There are different voices responding to each other. A lot of different voices responding to each other. All the voices are speaking in a different language that is certainly not English and sounds a lot more along the lines of what she would imagine Russian to sound like.

Well shit, there's definitely more of them. That makes things a lot more complicated. Emily thinks with her mind shifting to her son in a coma. *Right now would really be a good time for you to wake up, Bryan... Please wake up, son.*

Chapter 10: Logan Miller

Day 10: San Diego, California

Logan wakes up with aches and pains in his back and extremities as he pulls himself out of bed. He groans and stretches as he gets up, cracking his neck and stretching out his back, hearing multiple pops at every turn.

I'm pretty sure that this is just how my body is going to feel from here on out. Especially after nights like last night with the twins, moving all those damned cars around, Logan thinks to himself as he walks around his hotel suite.

He looks over to Harper, who is still sound asleep, and smiles at her as she squirms under the covers in her own bed in their upgraded suite.

It's worth it for the peace of mind of you being safe... Or at least me feeling like you're safer, kiddo. I'm not sure if we'll ever be safe. He thinks to himself, as he puts on a pair of sandals

He grabs his Glock G45, his radio, and a towel. He walks over to her bed and places another radio on the nightstand.

"Hey kiddo, I'm going to go rinse off. The radio is right here if you need me. I'll be just downstairs... okay?" He says to her.

She squirms around a little bit and responds back to him in a groggy voice, "Okay, dad."

She then rolls back over and engulfs herself in covers once again. He can't help but smile at her.

Even after all of this, she's still not a morning person and likes sleeping in. I'm glad some things never change... he thinks to himself as he walks out of the room and heads downstairs, toward the hotel pool.

The sun had begun to rise to the East and the morning air had a brisk ocean crisp to it. But he knew it and was going to warm up real quick throughout the day. Although he had rinsed off last night in the cold shower of the hotel room, the pool seemed easier for this morning.

The power had come back on for a little while the other day, but it was out again and he was really beginning to think that the power was going to go out for good, if it hadn't already. But what was really worrying him right now, and all of last night, were the Russians over the radio.

Reaching the pool gate, he sees that Emily had the same idea. He sees Laura in the spa that wasn't able to be turned on, and sees Emily swimming back and forth in the pool.

Walking through the gate, he looks to Laura. "Good morning, Laura."

"Good morning... is Harper awake yet?" Laura questions back.

He chuckles at her. "Not yet, kiddo, she's being a lazy bum. But you can most certainly go wake her up, once you're done in the spa. Is that water warm?"

She shrugs. "Kind of. It's warmer than the pool that mom's swimming in."

He smiles at her. "Well, aren't you just a smart little girl."

She beams a smile at him and he walks over to the pool.

He places his shirt, towel, radio, and Glock on one of the chairs and slides off his sandals. He then walks over to the deep end of the pool, seeing Emily come up for air.

"Good morning, Emily. How's the water?" He says to her.

"Holy hell, Logan! You scared the crap out of me!" She blurts out.

He laughs at her. "That explains the color of the water."

She shakes her head and smiles. "Ha Ha. Very funny, mister. The color of the water is because the pump hasn't been on much in the last few days, not because I crapped myself. It's not even brown here, just not super clear blue like it was."

He laughs at her. "Ahhhh, so you admit you crapped yourself. That's pretty gross Emily."

He looks at Laura. "You hear that, Laura!? Your mom said she pooped in the pool?!"

Laura starts giggling and replies, "Ewwww, mom! Gross!"

Emily laughs and splashes water at him. "Shut up, Logan. You know what I meant."

Getting hit with the water, he jumps back. "Man, that's chilly!"

"Shut it, you big baby!" Emily says with a laugh.

He shakes his head and dives into the pool, swimming underwater across to the other side, and then doubling back. Once he comes up for air, he takes in a deep breath, exhales slowly, and wades around in the pool.

"Not so bad once you get used to it, right?" Emily asks.

He nods. "Pretty much, and sure as hell beats a cold shower in the rooms."

"That it does, that it does..." She responds.

"And about the pool water... It'll probably be good for another day or so. I'll see if we can't find more chlorine to dump in here, to make it somewhat cleaner. Especially if we are using it to keep us clean. " He says to her.

"I'm sure we can find some of that around here. Not sure why we wouldn't be able to. Maybe the twins can look for it while we are gone today." Emily answers.

"Ah. So, you still want to make that run to SeaWorld with me, then?" He questions.

"Yeah, I need to get out of here, aside from the hospital. I've been there every day since he's been there and I already radioed Dr. Lewis. He says that there's no change in his condition and that Bryan is stable." Emily explains.

"I would completely understand if you didn't want to go, Emily. It is not going to be pretty. That's the main reason I didn't want to bring the littles. After what we saw at the San Diego Zoo and at the supermarket." Logan responds.

She shakes her head. "I need to get my mind off of Bryan, if only for a little while. I'm going crazy in my head, especially after what happened yesterday on the bridge. But are you sure we should leave the girls here? Is it safe to leave them here?"

Logan nods his head as he wades around the pool. "Yeah. I really think they'll be alright for a few hours. We'll be just down the road and we did a damn hell of a good job blocking up those bridges last night."

"What'd you guys end up doing?" She questions.

"Well..." Logan begins thinking back at the events of last night with the twins.

"We started with the Mission Bay Bridge where those guys were... we got a good twenty cars blocking the bridge in both directions. Locking up the cars, and tossing the keys over the bridge. They won't be coming through that way again any time soon." Logan explains

"What if we need to get out?" She questions.

He nods. *She is pretty damn smart, isn't she?* He thinks, looking at her more closely in her bikini bathing suit. Then instantly feeling guilty... thinking about his wife.

"Yeah, well... we have that route that we talked about, on Old SeaWorld Drive. We only blocked that way by six cars and left the keys in an area where we could quickly find them over there. We put them in a small cooler next to some palm trees, over by the nearest stop light. Worst case scenario, we go 4x4ing over the embankment. But we should be able to get out of here when we need to." He explains.

She seems to be thinking it over as she wades around the pool. He looks back to Laura who is swimming around in small circles in the warmer spa water.

"What about the other bridges? You said there were more?" She presses further.

"Yes, ma'am. There were... and we did the same thing with those bridges, along with the main road of SeaWorld Drive by the entrance to the peninsula, and the same process with any other backroad in the area we could find. We could swing by there and check it out to make sure we didn't miss anything in the dark of the night, but we spent enough time over in that area... we should be good. The bridges weren't that difficult, being bottlenecks and all. But that Sea Word Drive area was a real bitch and real pain in the ass to block off. And it took a while to find cars that we could use too. " He explains to her, trying to ease her mind of their safety.

If he was being honest, he was trying to ease his own mind as well.

"So, all the bridges are blocked off, for sure?" She asks again.

He smiles at her. "Yeppum. About 20 cars blocking each bridge. Both ends of the Mission Bay Bridge, the Ingraham Bridge, and the SeaWorld Drive Bridge. With all of the cars locked up the best we could and keys into the water below. If there are more of those Russian assholes, they are going to make enough noise for us to know they are coming our way. Especially with how quiet it is around here now."

It had been very quiet over the last ten days. You could hear for quite a ways and he was confident that they would hear at least some of the alarms going off if people tried to move the cars to close in on their little peninsula. As far as he knew, they were the only ones left alive on the small SeaWorld peninsula.

"Not going to lie, Logan. I'm rather impressed. That was very smart of you." She says to him.

He can feel himself blush, not being a real big fan of compliments.

"It wasn't just me, Emily. Clint and Cole were a huge help. Those twins are more than resourceful. Hell, I'm not sure if they were lucky enough to find us or if it's more the other way around. Plus, sometimes shotgun maintenance does work." He replies.

She gives him a confused look.

"Nevermind. It's just a turn of phrase." He answers.

She nods and smiles, looking back to Laura. "Yeah, Clint and Cole are very nice young men. Cole is a little goofy sometimes, but I think the girls really like that about him. Clint is the more serious one. Have you noticed that?"

"Yes, I have. Clint is definitely more serious than Cole. But don't let that fool you. That Cole is something else. You should have seen him on that bridge. He was a little shaky on the get-go. But once it came down to brass tacks, he was in like sin. And I think he's handling what we did a little easier than I am..." He says, truthfully.

She wades closer to him, within 10 feet. "Yeah, thanks again for saving us yesterday. And again. Sorry for almost shooting you guys..."

Logan laughs. "Yeah, that would have sucked."

She chuckles back and then her tone turns serious. "Are you doing okay though? With everything going on?"

Logan thinks about it for a moment and then shrugs. "I doubt it. But then again... are you?"

Emily sighs heavily. "Yeah, you've got a point there."

They both wade around in the water for a little bit in silence. After a few moments, he watches as she swims over to the side and pulls herself out. He quickly turns around, feeling somewhat ashamed for looking at her in a bikini as she exits the pool. It just didn't feel right to be looking at another woman.

He had been married for 15 years. Yeah, he knew that Kelsey was gone forever, but it still didn't feel like that in his heart. Plus, Emily had just lost her husband in all of this too. He had to admit to himself that she was attractive and a very nice person. But he wasn't sure if he could ever let himself feel for someone ever again.

He and Kelsey had joked around on date nights when they were out having some drinks about what they would do if they ever lost one another. Kelsey had jokingly said that she would have to find herself another sugar-daddy. But he knew she had always been joking.

On the other hand, the thought of her gone, way back then, seemed to even break his heart. Back then he didn't think he would ever be able to move forward if he ever lost her. Here and now, that feeling felt even more true. Regardless of who it was and what the circumstances were.

He is drawn back from his thoughts of his lost wife, the love of his life... when Emily starts talking again.

"Well, should we all start getting ready for the day? The sooner we get into that dead aquarium, the sooner we can get out and back here with whatever supplies we find." She says to him.

He turns back to see her wrapped in a towel and nods. "Yeah. Makes sense to me. Best to get in there before the heat of the day sets in. And if we have time afterward, we can go check in on Bryan."

"Come on, Laura. Let's go get ready for the day. Mommy is going to go run some errands, and you're going to stay here with Clint, Cole, and Harper." Emily says to Laura.

"Okay, mom." Laura says, and starts climbing out of the spa.

Emily turns to him. "You did mention to the twins about watching the girls? Right? It completely slipped my mind."

He nods to her as he swims off to the side of the pool.

"Yes, ma'am. I did. And they actually sounded rather excited about babysitting." He says to her.

"Of course they did..." She says with a chuckle. "And yes, that'd be nice if we had time to go check in on Bryan. Thanks for keeping him in your thoughts..."

"Of course, Emily. We're in this together it would seem." He says to her and catches an awkward look from her.

"You, me, the girls, and those resourceful twins. Our whole little mismatched apocalypse family slash group-thing we have going on." He adds, trying to cover up the awkwardness.

She laughs. "It is a rather strange dynamic that we all have going on, isn't it? Bryan will really like meeting everyone once he wakes up. He'll love the twins, seeing them as the older brothers he never had. And I'm pretty sure he'll take a liking to you too, Logan."

"I can't wait to meet him, Emily. I'm sure he'll wake up soon." Logan says, not sure if he believed his own words coming out of his mouth.

She nods and doesn't respond, but rather looks at Laura. "Ready to go, sweetie?"

"Yes, mom. I'm ready."' Laura replies, and then looks at him. "Bye, Logan."

"Later , kiddo. I'll go wake up Harper for you." He replies, which gets a smile from the little girl.

She turns back to him. "See you in a bit, Logan. I'm going to get her ready."

He nods, grabbing his own towel. "Right behind you. I need to make sure my lazy bum daughter is up and about, along with the twins."

She smiles and walks off with Laura, heading back to their room.

Logan finishes drying off, watching the sun rise higher in the eastern sky over the horizon of the hills and mountains. Enjoying the peace and quiet of the early morning.

Please let this day go smoother than yesterday... because that was a real shitshow. He thinks to himself.

Chapter 11: Emily Collins

Day 10: San Diego, California

Geez! Logan was not lying! This is absolutely horrible! Emily thinks to herself as she maneuvers around another body of what looks to be what was once a young man, now bloated and leaking some kind of grossness, with the smell forcing her to hold back her vomit.

Once entering SeaWorld, the first stop that they had made was to the left, just past the entrance to the huge clothing store. The gates to SeaWorld had still been open, since the CWA attacks had happened during the prime time of their summer season.

Logan had the great idea to tear up some shirts to use as face masks, to help avoid the stench of rotting death everywhere. Emily hadn't realized how grotesque dead bodies were and smelled after ten days. But then again, who the hell really thought about that kind crap besides serial killers, psychopaths, and apocalypse fanatics?

They were able to quickly locate abandoned rental strollers and used them as grocery carts for supplies and food. Luckily there had been no occupants of the strollers, with the kids and parents likely somewhere in the huge clothing and souvenir store. The thoughts still made her stomach turn and she pushed back down the bile that rose up in her throat.

In the souvenir stores, they were able to stock up on clothing for all of them, along with some souvenir blankets and towels. This would help them out, since they couldn't really do laundry anymore. They both found souvenir bags and filled each with water and whatever food they could find... since it was mostly snacks and junk food in the souvenir shop.

She was, at first, relieved to be putting something around her face to block the smell of bloated and decomposing bodies out in the morning California sun. But she soon realized the tied-up pieces of cloth around their faces didn't do much of anything. The smell was still reaching her nose and felt like it was overwhelming her entire body.

"These pieces of cloth are pretty damn worthless, I feel like I'm going to throw up at every step." She says to Logan.

"Do your best to breathe through your mouth. It helps a little, but not much. And if you see any breath mints, grab them." Logan says to her, through his own mask.

After several minutes of loading up their rental strollers, they were able to find some breath mints and both popped a handful into their mouths to try and stifle the smell and sour taste in the air filled with the stench of death from the many decomposing bodies. Far too many to count, even if she wanted to.

"Alright, let's go load this stuff up and come back for more. Maybe other stores have better stuff." Logan says with a mouth full of mints.

"Okay." She mumbles back, through her own mints.

Heading back to the entrance of the souvenir store, she is looking at a hoodie on the wall.

I wonder if I should grab some for the girls... she thinks to herself and then shakes her head. *It's too damn hot for hoodies. We'll find some when we actually need them... like in a few months. I don't think clothes will be an issue anytime soon.*

With her mind distracted, she accidentally bumps into something. Looking down, she sees a dead and bloated little girl, whose body had turned a reddish disgusting color, with oozing fluids coming from her nose, mouth, and eyes.

The reaction is involuntary, as she turns to her left and vomit comes spewing from her mouth, along with all of the breath mints. Turning to her left and leaning over didn't do a damn thing, since she had a piece of cloth wrapped around her face... with some of her vomit getting out, but most of it still in the mask with her and on her face.

Oh, good lord! She thinks as she begins to throw up again, now realizing that her own vomit is going back into her mouth instead of out and away from her.

She begins to gag and panic, hunched over, not sure how to stop throwing up. The smell of her own vomit, mixed with the decay of bodies is overwhelming and she feels the world start to blur.

She then feels someone next to her side and hands touching the back of her head. She hears muffled words, but can't make them out with her being in a daze. Her mind is cloudy and fuzzy, eyes watery, and she can feel the bile taste of vomit in her mouth and all around her face. She tries to breathe, but ends up inhaling some of her own throw up in her mouth and up her nose... making her gag and throw up all over again.

After what feels like a lifetime, she feels the mask wrapped sound her face loosen and then fall away from her face. She thinks she can see it fall to the floor, but her vision is too blurry.

She hears a muffled voice again, and it sounds close to her, but her head is still fuzzy.

"What?" She says after she clears the vomit from her mouth.

"I said, keep your head leaned over. Here comes some water for you." Logan says. She can make out the words, but doesn't understand what he means.

An instant later, she feels water on the back of her head and she inhales deeply from the shock of having water dumped on her neck. Once it stops, she feels more water gushing over her head and flowing around her face. After a moment she catches on and turns her head to the side with her eyes closed. After a pause, she feels water hit her face.

Once the water stops, Logan says, "Alright, now turn the other way, Emily. You're doing good. Just stay calm and let's get you cleaned up."

She does and then she feels more water on her face, washing away the vomit coating her. She then feels a towel being brushed against her face.

"Here, use this to wipe your face, Emily... and here is a fresh bottle of water to rinse out your mouth." Logan then says to her.

She takes the towel and scrubs her face until it feels dry and somewhat clean. She opens her eyes, standing up again, taking the bottle of water from Logan. She pours it into her mouth, swishes it around and spits it out onto the floor. Following the process several times until she feels all of the chunks and bile is out of her mouth.

She feels hands on her shoulders from behind her, pulling her back.

"Alright now take easy steps backwards and don't look down." He says to her.

She steps back slowly and he guides her to turn around to face him, his hands falling away.

Her vision is no longer blurry and she can see him with his cloth mask still on. His eyes had the sadness on them that she had felt looking down at that poor girl. It was a look that was a mixture of sorrow and concern.

She must have been staring for a moment, because he tilts his head in confusion and then puts his hands back on her shoulder to brace her. Likely thinking she still could pass out.

"Are you okay, Emily?" He questions.

She nods quickly, not saying a word.

He gives a weak smile that she can make out from under his mask, with his eyes squinting.

"Good, I'm glad that you're feeling better... I've got to be honest though. That was pretty damn gross and hard to watch."

She turns her head to the side and spits once more, wiping her mouth afterwards. "Yeah... I don't do well with throwing up, and apparently seeing dead kids..."

She sees him look down to her right, past the rental stroller toward the dead little girl on the floor that had sent her into an involuntary vomiting state.

He takes his hands off of her shoulders and takes a step back. "Yeah... that's pretty shitty. Poor little kid... poor all of them, really." Logan says looking down at the dead girl and then around the souvenir store.

After a moment he looks back to her, looking her up and down. She feels a little awkward for a moment.

What is he looking at? She thinks to herself, not sure what to make of him.

"Emily, you may want to go around one of the aisles and go change your shirt. Your shorts look fine, but your shirt is pretty gross." He says to her.

"Oh." She looks down. "Holy hell... yeah, you've got a point."

"Ugh" She says aloud, as she steps over and around bodies toward where the adult shirts are.

She tries to carefully take off her shirt, but can feel the wet vomit against her skin and face as she pulls it overhead. She holds back the bile in her throat.

Can't just keep on vomiting, Emily. Dammit, girl! Get a hold of yourself! She thinks as she grabs an ugly bright green shirt off the wall.

She wads up the shirt and uses it to try and dry off her skin. Looking down at her bikini top, she sees that it's not all off her and she knows she must smell horrible now.

She turns toward Logan. "Hey, can you toss me another water bottle?"

He looks at her and just pauses for a moment.

"Logan?"

He blinks and nods, "Yeah, sure. Sorry... "

He begins to walk over another bottle of water, and it seems as though he is staring at her pretty hard.

"What Logan? Do I have something on my face?... I know you've seen me in a damn bikini before" She says to him.

His eyes focus on her eyes and she realizes that he wasn't looking directly at her. It was just in her head. He was looking past her.

"What? Yeah, no... is that?" Logan begins, as he hands her the water bottle.

"Is that what?" She says as she turns to look behind her at whatever he was transfixed on.

"I think that's a kid... I think I saw a kid... a kid that's alive..." Logan says with confusion.

"What?! Where?" She begins to scan the area where he was looking, toward the far side entrance of the souvenir shop.

She sees something move around the blue umbrella tables, just outside of the side entrance to the souvenir shop. She tilts her head and tries to focus a little more, trying to make sense of what she's seeing. She drops the soiled green shirt down to the ground.

What's a kid doing out here all by themselves? Are they by themselves, or are there others? She thinks to herself.

"Hey, kid! Are you alright!? Where's your family, kid!?" Logan yells out.

She is startled by the sound of Logan's booming voice, but her focus is still where they think the kid is, behind the blue umbrella tables. She sees a small figure take off behind a tree and start running away from them.

"It is a kid!" She blurts out.

"Shit!" Logan adds and takes off in a sprint.

"Where are you going?!" She shouts out after him.

Logan turns back to look at her as he is running out of the souvenir store. "He's been watching us! Poor kid is probably all alone! Come on!"

"Ah hell..." She says to herself, with the water bottle still in her left hand.

She takes off running, following Logan out of the souvenir store and past the umbrella tables and the tree. She sees him turn a corner and tries to push herself to catch up.

Come on girl! Move those legs! We didn't do all those damn Pilates for nothing! She yells inside her head, getting a burst of speed.

She comes around the turn and sees Logan running down a walkway.

"Damn! He's actually pretty fast! Does he do Pilates too? Geez!" She says aloud.

As she reaches the downward-spiraling walkway, she sees Logan halfway down it and what looks to be a young boy in a bright blue shirt, running into an aquarium looking area. She pauses and looks up to see a gigantic pool.

That's a pretty big pool? What do they have in there? Sharks? She thinks to herself as she begins to jog down the pathway to the underwater pool viewing area.

Once she reaches the bottom, she sees that the viewing area is half open and half covered. With dead bloated bodies scattered all around. She comes to a stop right next to Logan, leaning over, putting her hands on her knees. She looks over to him, with him bent over and his hands on his knees.

"Where's this kid at?" She says, out of breath.

"My thoughts exactly... where the hell did he go?" Logan replies.

He straightens back up and sighs heavily. "He couldn't have gotten far."

She points to the other entrance to the viewing area. "Unless he ran back out of here..."

Logan shakes his head. "Nope... I'm pretty sure he didn't." He says, pointing at a bunch of SeaWorld blankets over a large lump over by the glass viewing wall."

He looks back to her and puts his finger up to his lips and she nods, getting the hint to be quiet.

They both walk slowly and quietly over to the blanket spread over something by the glass viewing wall. Reaching the blanket, Logan crouches down and grabs a corner of one of the blankets.

"Leave them alone!" A young voice shouts out at them.

They both freeze and look off to their right where they see a little boy hiding behind a pillar. He looks frightened as hell, but around the same age as the girls.

"Whoa, little guy! We aren't here to hurt you..." Logan says to the kid.

The kid looks behind him, toward the other entrance, likely thinking about bolting. An instant later, he looks back to where the blankets are covering a large lump... that they had just thought where the boy was hiding.

She looks at the large lump, realizing it was more the size of an adult. She then notices a much smaller lump next to the larger one. More the size of a toddler or even an infant.

"Oh crap..." She mumbles to herself.

"What?" Logan replies.

She nods back over to the blankets. "Back away, Logan... I think he knows whoever is under those blankets."

"Ah shit. Think you're right, Emily." Logan says as he releases his grip on the blanket and backs away.

She turns back to the boy. "Hey... we're sorry. We didn't know. We thought it was you. We just thought that you were all alone out here."

"Just leave us alone!" The little boy shouts.

"Hey, little guy... we're not going to hurt you." Logan explains.

"I said, leave us alone!" The little boy shrieks.

Logan pauses and looks at her, and shrugs his shoulders. As if asking her, *what now?*

She sighs heavily and turns back to the boy who yells at them again. "Go away! Leave us alone!"

"Hey!" She shouts back at the boy.

The boy freezes.

"You do not talk to adults that way, young man!" She yells at him.

She watches the kid go rigid and then step out slowly, in defeat.

Yep, he's a boy alright. She thinks to herself.

"Now! You come over right now! And sit your butt down and stop yelling at us! We are just trying to help you!" She yells at the little boy.

She looks at Logan who is giving her a wide-eyed look. She puts her hand up to tell him to wait a moment.

After a silent moment, the boy walks closer to them and sits down on one of the benches in the viewing area under that shade of the overhead covering. He looks to the now two distinct lumps under the blankets, back to them, and then back to his feet.

"I'm sorry, miss... I just..." The boy starts.

"Good! You should be... "She says, lowering her tone with the second part. "We are just here to see if you need any help and you go off yelling at us. Now that wasn't very nice, now was it?"

The little boy shakes his head *no.*

"Now... if we are done running around SeaWorld and if we're done yelling... my name is Emily, and this is my friend Logan." She says to him, catching her breath.

The boy looks up at her and then Logan, and then back to her. "I'm Diego..."

Emily nods to the boy. "Hello, Diego..."

"Hi, Diego." Logan adds.

"Yes, it's nice to meet you, Diego. Now, what I think my friend here wanted to know is if you were alone out here, all by yourself?" She says to the boy.

Diego looks around nervously.

"It's alright, kid. Emily and I are both parents too. We have two girls around your age, Harper and Laura. How old are you, eight?" Logan questions.

The boy looks at them again and then back to the blankets and the lumps.

After another silent moment, he nods, gesturing over to the lumps. "That's my mom and my little brother Derek... he's only two... he was only two."

Oh dear, Lord. She thinks to herself. *And here I am, shouting at this poor boy.*

Several minutes of silence pass by, with no one really knowing what to say.

"Okay... where's your dad, kiddo? Is he here with you?" Logan asks Diego, breaking the silence.

The boy shakes his head slowly and looks back down to his feet. "No, our dad died... last year. He was a Police Officer and a bad guy shot him."

You have got to be kidding me... she thinks to herself.

She hears Logan sigh and there is an awkward silence for several more minutes. It was her, this time, that broke the tension.

"Well, Diego... I am very sorry to hear about your dad, your mom, and your little brother." She says with a gulp. "Logan and I are parents, we have two girls back at our hotel, not too far from here. And I have a son too, Bryan. He's a few years older than you are."

"Yeah, little guy... Diego. You can come with us if you want. We have food, water, and a place to sleep." Logan says, looking around. "Where have you been sleeping?"

The boy points toward the far edge of the viewing wall where a bunch of blankets are coupled up.

Oh-my-gosh... poor little guy. Here all alone, sleeping on the floor, next to his dead mother and little brother. That's horrible... she thinks to herself.

She looks at Logan and can see he is thinking something similar.

The boy stands up and walks over near his dead mother and brother. She and Logan both watch Diego as he stands next to his dead family beneath those souvenir blankets.

"Wow, Emily. Your little tough love trick seemed to get the kid to listen well enough." Logan says to her quietly.

She nods. "Yeah, I learned with Bryan that sometimes you have to be a tad bit louder with boys."

Before Logan can answer, something catches their attention in the massive pool, behind the viewing wall made of some sort of thick glass. It was a black blur and then it was gone.

"What the hell is in that big ass pool?" Logan says, drawn to the viewing wall to get a closer look.

"I dunno. I've never been here." Emily replies.

She walks up next to him and they both peer into the bright blue water, still looking very crisp. Looking around the edges, she can see what caught their attention... A killer whale swimming around in the tank.

"Wow... I cannot believe that this orca is still alive and swimming. It's day 10 since most anyone would have been around to feed him." Logan says with astonishment.

"Orca? I thought it was a killer whale." Emily questions.

"Yeah, it is. But they're called orcas. Killer whales is just a catchy name they've been called over the years. Makes sense... damn things are like lions in the water. They even hunt great white sharks, taking them down with their whole pod of orcas." Logan explains.

Emily just gives him a look.

He shrugs. "I watch a lot of Discovery Channel and nature shows with Harper. She has a thing for the ocean."

She nods in understanding. "Makes sense. Laura is more into the science and space shows." She replies.

"Hey, Diego. Is there anyone else left here with you at SeaWorld? Have you seen anyone else around?" Logan asks the boy.

Diego walks up next to them and stands next to her.

He shakes his head. "Not since the death clouds happened. There were people I saw afterwards, but they left... It's just me now. I haven't seen anybody else for close to a week now."

Since the death clouds... poor little guy has no idea what's happened, does he? But he sure got the name right. I guess that's pretty much what everyone's been calling them. She thinks to herself.

"Huh... interesting. I wonder how he survived this long then. I know they have to eat a lot of fish a day." Logan says aloud, but clearly just lost in thought about the killer whale.

"Oh, Kotia's been eating..." Diego responds.

"Kotia?" She questions.

Diego nods and then points to the killer whale. "Her name is Kotia. I remember it from the orca show before the death clouds... and she ate the other killer whale, Kana." He says and points down below them.

She strained to look below her, and so did Logan.

"Holy crap!" Logan exclaims.

She looks in a mixture of astonishment and horror, as she sees half of the remains of another killer whale at the bottom of the pool.

"Geez! They really are brutal." Emily says aloud.

"Told ya! Freaking apex predator in action, right there." Logan replies.

They all stand there for a few more minutes, just watching the massive killer whale swim around her pool. It was a peaceful moment filled with dread, death, grief, and astonishment. It felt as though this moment surmised her life now. Actually... all of their lives now. Death was their world now and who knows when they would have time to actually deal with their grief.

She feels a small finger tap her on her arm, and she looks over at Diego standing next to her.

"Yes, Diego?" She says to him.

"Ummm... I think it'd be okay with my mom... if I went with you two. Since you and the man have kids... if that's okay?" Little Diego says to her.

She can feel her heart breaking and she is doing her best to hold back her tears, all she can do is nod. If she tried to speak, she knew she would get all choked up.

"That is perfectly okay, little man. I'm sure you will like Harper and Laura... and Bryan when he wakes up? And again, my name is Logan, Diego." Logan says to him.

"Okay... Logan." Diego replies. "Can I go say bye first?"

Say goodbye? She thinks to herself, trying her best to hold back her emotions.

"Of course, Diego... take your time." Logan replies.

Diego turns back around and walks over to the lumps on the ground covered by the souvenir blankets. He kneels down beside them. "Goodbye mom... goodbye Derek... I'm sorry, but I can't stay here with you guys forever. I love you so much, and I'm sorry this happened to you and I couldn't find help in time..."

Oh my gosh!... I just can't even with this... she thinks to herself trying to hold back her tears.

After a moment of silence, she hears a slight sniffle from Logan next to her.

She looks over at him, seeing him standing there with tears running down his face.

"Are you crying, Logan? You were supposed to keep me from tearing up..." She says with a sniffle and her eyes watering up.

He steps in closer to her and puts his arm around her shoulders. She leans her head on his shoulder, feeling a few tears escape from her eyes.

"Wow... how could I not cry? Poor little guy. I'm not heartless, Emily. I have a damn soul." He says to her.

She lightly chuckles as tears run from her eyes, dripping onto Logan's shoulder.

They just stand there in quiet tears for what feels like a long moment of silence, but neither of them dare move before Diego does.

"Goodbye. I'll miss you both. And I'll see you again someday. In the ever after, with dad too." He says to them one final time.

Oh, my dear Lord. This is too much. Poor little kid has no one left. What if that had been Laura? She thinks with sorrow and a pang of guilt for having survived and Diego's mom not being so lucky.

She watches as Diego stands and straightens back up, and they both follow him with their eyes as he turns around. He then walks to the viewing glass and looks upon the killer whale that had eaten her fellow orca. "Goodbye, Kotia. I'll miss you too..."

Yeah. I don't think I'd be missing that killer whale. But then again, the poor kid has been stuck with the damned cannibal orca since the beginning of this whole mess. She thinks to herself.

Diego then walks up to them and they part, with a little bit of awkwardness between them.

"Okay. I think I'm ready to go now." Diego says to the two of them.

She nods to him.

"Sounds like a plan, kiddo. We just need to get our carts of supplies and we'll get out of here. In fact, we can pick up some extra supplies for you and you can pick out some fresh clothes, if you'd like." Logan says to Diego.

Diego nods and starts walking back from the way they came chasing after him.

Logan looks at her. "And we can finally get you cleaned up, Emily. I didn't want to say anything when your head was on my shoulder, but you still smell like throw up... and we never did find you a shirt. You're still walking around in shorts and a bikini top."

She feels her face turn red, and looks down at herself, seeing she had dried vomit film still on her chest.

"Oh my gosh. I almost forgot. So gross..." She blurts out.

Diego turns around and stares at them. "It was pretty gross... I saw the whole thing." He says with a matter-of-fact tone and turns back around, walking back up the walkway.

Logan starts laughing. "He ain't lying. I started gagging once I realized your throw up was going back into your own mouth. Freaking gross."

She narrows her gaze at him and punches him in the shoulder. "Shut it, Logan. That's enough out of you."

"Ow!" He says and chuckles again.

She walks away, following Diego, trying to hide the fact that she was still blushing.

What the hell was that? Did we just have some kind of awkward ass moment? And why am I beet red all of sudden? She thinks to herself, walking back the way they came, blushing and not knowing why, with Logan following behind them.

Chapter 12: Michail Lenkov

Day 11: Ocean Beach, California

Micha flicks his cigarette into the water, hearing the hiss as the cherry hits and the butt starts to float into the ocean. He leans on the rail and gazes out across the ocean waters.

He looks to his left at the gaggle fuck of stupid *pindos* at the end of the pier. He can't see for sure through his own men, but he knows that Lieutenant Petrenko is following his orders.

He had ordered Lieutenant Petrenko to have them lined up, as they had done plenty of times in the last week. Only since they came up with the cowardly yet intriguing, Nicholas Cross, had he slightly shifted his orders. Now with one of their own Americans, Micha had Cross ask them all sorts of questions prior to the mass executions.

Apparently the *pindo*, Nicholas Cross, used to work for Sony in San Diego and went to Russia several times, and that's how he knew their language. The cowardly Cross had a way about him, cowardly, but still sly. It made sense to Micha, since his job was in marketing. He would serve them very nicely... in their New Russia... until he was no longer needed.

Stupid pindos with all their pretty things and distractions. It made them weak... what happened to the fierce warriors we heard of in history books of the treacherous World War II? Our grandfathers and great grandfathers were afraid of these weaklings during the Cold War? We should have taken them then. The stupid shit pindos. Look at them... waiting patiently for their slaughter. He thinks to himself, anticipating the sound of gunfire to be heard shortly.

He looks back off toward the shoreline to see the other half of Lieutenant Petrenko's platoon. He then looks back toward the Naval Base Point Loma, their Forward Base of Operations (FOB), and the submarine crew members and the three COBs that he had left in charge of protecting their position. Lieutenant Mashkov and his platoon had traveled across the channel of the San Diego Bay to the North Island Base, expanding their hold in their New Russia, and searching for supplies and more weapons for their ongoing mission.

Micha was still not entirely certain if any of his comrades would be coming over in 19 days. But even if they didn't, he and his fellow countrymen would still take this land for their own and build a New Russia, just as the original mission dictated. Only now, he would be one of the Commanders when the dust settled. That part was looking more and more certain with every day that passed by without word from the motherland.

The wonderful sound of a barrage of gunfire opens up on the American cowards who were led very easily to their executions.

Micha smiles and lights another cigarette, awaiting Lieutenant Petrenko to return with his report and any valuable information on the surrounding areas. He looks North, back on the ocean, and after a few more cigarettes are tossed into the water below, he hears footsteps approaching him.

"Major Lenkov." Lieutenant Petrenko greets him in English.

He had been getting used to speaking more English along with his junior officers since the arrival of Nicholas Cross.

"Report, Lieutenant Petrenko." Micha says back.

"Major, 37 American survivors have been easily dispatched, and with no issue." Lieutenant Petrenko answers.

"Very good. Any intelligence, Lieutenant?" Micha questions.

He hears another set of footsteps approaching.

"Yes, Major... one American worked at a nearby hospital and there were others there." Lieutenant Petrenko informs him.

"Others in a hospital? Good. How far?" Micha questions further.

Lieutenant Petrenko nods. "Twenty-five kilometers to the east, Major."

Micha looks to the sky, with the sun high above him and then checks his watch. It's 1400.

"Too late to go that far today. Did the *pindo* say how many more *pindos*?" Micha presses.

"Yes, Major. Four medical personnel and five patients." Lieutenant Petrenko answers.

"Good. Very good." Micha replies.

"There's more, Major Lenkov, Sir." Nicholas Cross interjects, with him having been standing next to Lieutenant Petrenko for about a minute and Micha purposely ignoring him.

"Shut fucking mouth, Cross. You do not speak to Major Lenkov unless spoken to." Lieutenant Petrenko says harshly.

Micha straightens up and turns, taking another drag of his smoke, looking Nicholas Cross square in the eyes and sees him look to the floor of the pier and his feet.

Cowardly, yet sly... he thinks to himself.

"What, cowardly Cross? What did the cowardly Cross learn from his fellow *pindos* before they were executed?" Micha says to Cross.

Cross looks up to him and then to Lieutenant Petrenko.

"Speak now, idiot!" Lieutenant Petrenko says to Cross.

Micha smiles as Cross focuses back on him.

"Um. Major Lenkov, Sir... the nurse... something Scott... Well, he said that there are more people and they gave a radio to one of the doctors to keep in contact. I guess one of the patients is the kid of one of the survivors." Cross explains.

A radio? More survivors and they sound coordinated. Very interesting. Micha thinks to himself.

"What the fuck does that matter, American?" Lieutenant Petrenko questions.

Cross quickly nods. "Didn't you have two men run off two days ago? I've been hearing your men talk about it..."

Micha narrows his gaze.

Fucking Bortnik and Federov. If they aren't dead yet, they will be when I find them. He thinks with anger.

Yes, he had two of his men not report back two days ago after sending them off on a scouting mission. He was furious with the concept of two of his men abandoning their mission and running off to go live in the luxurious lifestyle of the Americans. What was worse, it set a horrible example for the rest of his men. If they were to ever return and did not have a damn good reason, he was surely going to make an example of them.

"Make fucking point quickly, American." Lieutenant Petrenko says sharply.

"My point is... didn't they stop reporting in somewhere by SeaWorld?" Cross asks.

"What is this SeaWorld? Bortnik and Federov stopped reporting in North of here, on a small peninsula." Lieutenant Petrenko responds.

Micha watches Cross shake his head in annoyance.

Cowardly, but sly. Yes. Micha thinks to himself.

"SeaWorld isn't important. It's like a gigantic ass overpriced aquarium, what is important is that the dead nurse said that the parent of that kid, along with several other survivors, were staying near SeaWorld, right about where your two men, Bortnik and Federov, stopped reporting in to you from." Cross explains.

"Hmmm." Micha replies.

"What is fucking point, Cross?" Lieutenant Petrenko says with annoyance, now.

Cross opens his mouth, but Micha raises his hand and Cross quickly closes his mouth.

"What our cowardly and somewhat smart *pindo* is saying here... maybe Bortnik and Federov did not defect and run away. Maybe Bortnik and Federov are dead.... maybe these people from the hospital killed them." Micha says to Lieutenant Petrenko.

Lieutenant Petrenko pauses for a moment and then replies, "But Major, we have had no resistance or signs of Americans fighting back."

"Major Lenkov... I'm telling you. Just because you haven't had anyone fight back yet, doesn't mean they won't. There'll be more like me, willing to help usher in this new age. And there will be those that fight back." Cross explains.

"Shut your mouth, cowardly Cross!" Lieutenant Petrenko blurts out and backhands Cross.

Cross takes the hit and puts a hand to his face, staring back at Lieutenant Petrenko. Micha watches as Lieutenant Petrenko gets ready to hit Cross again.

Micha raises his hand again and Lieutenant Petrenko halts.

"Change of plans, Lieutenant Petrenko." Micha says.

"Major?" Lieutenant Petrenko questions.

Micha looks to Lieutenant Petrenko and then to Cross.

"Nicholas Cross. Did the dead nurse tell you the channel the Americans were on with the radio?" Micha says to the American.

He watches as Cross smiles, while still holding his face where Lieutenant Petrenko had just hit him.

"Channel two, Major Lenkov." Cross answers.

Micha looks to Lieutenant Petrenko. "Give Mr. Cross your radio, Lieutenant Petrenko."

"But Major?..." Lieutenant Petrenko questions.

Micha nods and the Lieutenant doesn't question him again.

Cross takes the radio and shifts it to channel two. "What do you want me to say?"

Micha smiles, "We go fishing for *pindos*. Play dead nurse, and we see if any *pindos* bite."

Cross nods and keys the mic on the radio. "Hello. Hello. Is anyone there? This is Scott from the hospital. Please! If anyone is there, pick up!"

Cross releases the mic and he waits in silence for a few moments.

After a couple minutes, Micha nods to him. "Again, Mr. Cross. Again."

Cross keys the mic on the radio, again. "Hello. Hello. Is anyone there? This is Scott from the hospital. Please! If anyone is there, pick up!"

Once he releases the mic on the radio, Micha instantly hears a voice come to life on the radio.

"Scott?! Is that you?! Is everything okay?! Is Bryan alright?!" A frantic female voice says over the radio.

"Dah, the Americans answered. And sound like the *pindos* we are looking for." Micha says with a smile. "Tell her that her Bryan is in trouble and to come to the hospital."

Cross nods and keys the mic. "No! Everything is not alright! I'm here all alone at the hospital and Bryan is getting worse! He's throwing up everywhere!"

Once Cross releases the mic, there is a long silence over the radio without the female American answering back.

After a solid minute a man's voice comes over the radio. "If this is Nurse Scott, then tell me what is wrong with my brother, Bryan."

Micha smiles. *Dah, a clever pindo. He is onto the ruse. Maybe all the brave Americans didn't die in the attacks.* He thinks to himself.

Cross looks at him with confusion. "What should I say?"

Micha gestures for him to give him the radio, and Cross hands it over to him. Micha takes a breath, thinking of what he wants to say to the pindo.

"This is Major Lenkov with the United Nations. Here to help. Who is this?" He says into the radio.

After another minute of silence, the male's voice comes back over the radio. "Hello Major... last I checked, the UN was gone. Now how is my brother?"

Micha shakes his head. *Very clever, pindo.*

He keys the mic on the radio. "Bryan is in trouble and we just arrived. No doctors are here, just my troops and Nurse Scott, here. Come see at the hospital."

Once he releases the mic, another male's voice comes on the radio. "Logan, this is Dr. Lewis. Bryan is fine, same condition on the fifth floor. No one else is here, yet. No Major

Lenkov with the UN and no troops. And I haven't seen Nurse Scott today, and the other man on the radio does not sound like him at all."

"Fuck." Micha says aloud.

"Copy that Dr. Lewis. It may be time for an exodus, with Russians knowing where you are. We had two try to kill us the other day. But they were too slow and too damn stupid." The other male's voice responds.

"Stupid fucking American cowboy!" Micha blurts out with a laugh. "He killed Bortnik and Federov! Fuck me!"

Cross looks at Lieutenant Petrenko and he just smiles back at the cowardly Cross.

Micha keys the mic on the radio. "You will die for that, American cowboy, Logan."

There is no response back, and the radio goes silent. After a short pause, Micha tosses the radio back to Lieutenant Petrenko.

"We now know what happened to Bortnik and Federov... this cowboy killed them." Micha says to them.

"Orders, Major Lenkov?" Lieutenant Petrenko questions.

Micha pulls another cigarette from his breast pocket and lights it, taking a deep inhale of the luscious smoke.

He then smiles at Cross and Lieutenant Petrenko. "I always wanted to kill an American cowboy... we are moving now to this hospital."

"Yes, Major Lenkov! Right away!" Lieutenant Petrenko answers and turns around to gather up the rest of his men to head off toward this hospital.

Micha then narrows his gaze upon Cross and can feel him mentally cowering, making his smile widen.

"Where is this hospital, Mr. Cross? You are going to take me there now." Micha says to Cross.

Cross nods quickly. "Yes... yes, I know where it is. It's called Scripps Mercy Hospital and is about 15 to 20 minutes away."

Micha takes another long drag of his smoke, looks back over the ocean, and exhales.

Not all the brave pindos died... good! This would be boring if they did... he thinks to himself.

Chapter 13: Emily Collins

Day 11: San Diego, California

Emily looks over at the three kids swimming around in the pool. Well actually, Laura and Harper were swimming around. The little boy, Diego, was sitting on the steps in the water, looking off into the distance.

The boy hadn't talked much since they brought him back to the hotel. He wound up sleeping in her suite, which made the most sense to her and Logan... with having just his mother and her being a mother.

One of the few things that the little boy said and asked was why her and Logan were sleeping in different rooms. It had made them both chuckle and they explained to them that they were just friends. Apparently the little guy had it in his head that they were married and the girls were both of theirs, along with her son, Bryan. She couldn't really blame the kid. They were all traveling together and staying together in this strange little group of theirs... but it worked for them.

Most of the rest of the day, the boy was quiet and it had been much of the same today. He wasn't being rude or anything. Logan and she agreed, along with the twins, that the little guy probably just needed some time to adjust. The girls were being nice to Diego, but didn't know what to do when he didn't want to play and swim around. Emily found herself hoping that the boy would open up in time.

I'm not sure if we thought this whole thing through bringing him back with us. But what could we do? Just leave him there? She thinks to herself.

She looks over to Logan sitting on one of the pool chairs next to her cleaning his gun... just as she currently was, and just as Clint and Cole were on the chairs next to Logan. Clint had produced a well-stocked cleaning kit from the bag of weapons that came off the dead Russians. And with events of the last few days draining them all, they decided to take it easy for the day, clean their weapons, and plan their next moves. Their location was good and secluded for the most part, but she was starting to wonder how much longer they could all stay there.

"Hey Logan, do you think we should be worried about Diego, being so quiet and all?" She asks him.

Logan looks up from cleaning his gun and looks over toward Diego. He shrugs slightly. "Naw, I think he'll be alright in time... Harper was pretty quiet the first few days after Kelsey died..."

Logan pauses for a moment before he picks back up his train of thought and continues on, "But yeah, think about it. I'm sure Laura was pretty quiet for a few days too. And the poor little guy had been sleeping right next to his dead mom and little brother since this whole shitshow started. And now he's here, away from them..."

"Yeah, I bet it feels like he lost them all over again, Mrs. Collins... I know we were kind of out of it for a good minute when we lost mom and dad. Hell, it still doesn't feel real sometimes." Clint says, next to Logan.

"Yeah, I guess you guys have a point..." She replies.

"He'll come around. You'll see. He's already talking to us, and he ate dinner, breakfast, and lunch with our little group we have here. So, there is that..." Logan says to her.

"Clint and I can take him out to fish with us in a little while. It's what, like two o'clock or something?" Cole adds.

She watches as Logan looks down at his watch. She reaches to her shorts pocket where her phone used to be, just on instinct. It was still weird not having her phone anymore, with all of them following suit with Logan and ditching them. The Russians on the radio had concluded that they were not alone and that they were all likely being tracked.

The Russians being here, with who knows who else, was really starting to worry her. Especially with Bryan still in his coma. And to top it all off, the power hadn't come back since it last went out. They were going on days now without power. She was worried that it was finally gone this time. Dr. Lewis assured her that Bryan was still able to breathe on his own and only needed to be replenished with fluids through an IV on a regular basis. The monitors were just here to do just that, monitor. But if his situation worsened and they didn't ever get the power back up anytime soon, then he would really be in trouble. He had already been in a coma for 11 days now... which was not good, and she knew it.

The problems just continued to add up and it was really starting to stress her out.

"Yup, spot on Cole. It's two o'clock, exactly." Logan answers, bringing her back to the present moment.

Cole chuckles. "What can I say, I got mad skills, bro... I mean, Mr. Miller."

She finds herself smiling and hears Logan and Clint both lightly chuckle too.

"That you do, Cole. That you do... and Logan is just fine. I know you two are super respectful and all, but it makes me feel like I'm an old, stuffy professor or something." Logan says with a smile.

Clint smiles back at him. "I could see you as a teacher... Mr. Miller."

They all laugh lightly. "I don't know about all of that, Clint. But seriously, if we are going to be around each other for a while and it looks like that will be... Logan is just fine, gents."

"And, I'll add Emily is fine with me boys. Mrs. Collins makes me feel old too." Emily adds.

The twins stop laughing and give each other a quick look and nod to each other.

"Okay... Logan..." Clint says with a nod.

"Copy that, Emily." Cole adds and gives her a quick salute.

"And if it's alright with you guys... my brother and I were talking about it, and we'd like to go with you and the kids... when it's time to leave." Clint says to them.

So, it's not just me thinking about leaving? It's on all of our minds about when we are getting out of here. But what about Bryan? She thinks to herself.

Logan nods. "I'm totally okay with that, gents. You two are more than resourceful and definitely lighten up the mood of doom and gloom." Logan turns to look at her. "I think we should all stick together... and once Bryan wakes up, I've been thinking of where to go." He says as he puts back together his handgun and function-checks it before putting a magazine back into the gun.

She sighs in relief. *Good... he was thinking of Bryan too... I know I can handle this on my own, if they all pick up and leave... but that doesn't mean I want to, and the only thing keeping me here is Bryan. I guess we can talk to Dr. Lewis and see if we can move him. But then again, would Dr. Lewis even come with us? Because I need a doctor to take care of my Bryan. Plus, it's been really good for Laura too, having Harper, the twins, and everyone else around.* She thinks as she looks over at the girls swimming in the pool, also glancing at Diego.

He was now past the stairs and slowly wading around in the shallow end of the pool.

Good, at least he's warming up to the girls a little bit. She thinks to herself with a smile.

"Okay, cool! It'd be kinda boring without you guys. That's for sure." Cole replies.

Logan laughs. "Only you, Cole, would think that a devastated U.S. with foreign invaders could ever be boring."

Cole chuckles back. "Hey! I get bored easily." He says as he puts his handgun back together. "All clean, the both of them..."

"You're getting slow brother... I've been done for a good minute." Clint replies.

"Yeah, but are they actually clean?" Cole replies.

Clint laughs. "Whatever... mine's cleaner than your ass. You got some rank coming off you, brother."

Cole laughs back. "Cleaner than my ass ain't saying much, bro. You should probably clean it again."

Logan starts laughing at this point, and so does she as she puts her old coyote tan handgun back together, function-checking it, and reloading the magazine.

"Well, mine is clean and I sure as hell know how to wipe my ass correctly. And you boys are gross. No swimming in the pool until you get rid of those poop stains. You both obviously have those in those shorts of yours. What? Did you boys not take your diarrhea medicine today?" She says to them.

"Oh! She's got jokes now!" Cole replies back.

"And dad jokes, at that!" Logan adds.

They all burst out in laughter.

Their laughter is interrupted by their radios crackling to life with a man's voice coming through.

"Hello. Hello. Is anyone there? This is Scott from the hospital. Please! If anyone is there, pick up!" The voice claiming to be Nurse Scott says.

They all freeze, look at each other and then back to the radios.

"What did that guy just say?" Clint questions.

"I think he said he was Nurse Scott and sounded like there was trouble." Logan replies.

"Oh no..." She gasps. "Bryan!"

"Hold on... that guy didn't sound like that Nurse Scott dude. He sounded older and different." Logan interjects.

"But what if there's something wrong with Bryan?!" Emily explains.

Logan looks her directly in the eyes and puts his hand on her bare leg. "Everything is going to be fine, Emily."

He stands up. "Alright kiddos. Out of the pool, please. We need to go back upstairs to the rooms."

"Aww, why?" Harper questions.

"Sorry kiddos. But we have to go check in on Bryan, Dr. Lewis, and the others." Logan says to her, and the rest of the children.

"Oh! Can we come?!" Laura questions.

"Ummmm." Logan says and looks back to her.

Before she can reply, the radio goes off again and she already has hers in her hand, not realizing she'd grabbed it.

"Hello. Hello. Is anyone there? This is Scott from the hospital. Please! If anyone is there, pick up!" The voice, claiming to be Nurse Scott, says over the radio again

She quickly keys the mic and responds, "Scott?! Is that you?! Is everything okay?! Is Bryan alright?!"

A moment passes and the voice comes back on over the radio. "No! Everything is not alright! I'm here all alone at the hospital and Bryan is getting worse! He's throwing up everywhere!"

"Oh my gosh! Bryan! He's awake!" She blurts out to everyone else, as she shoots to her feet. "We have to go down there!"

Logan gives her a sideways glance. "Emily..." He says as he puts his hands on her shoulders.

"He's awake, Logan! And he's hurt! We've gotta get over there!" She shouts at him, not meaning to.

"Emily..." He says again calmly. "Take a deep breath..."

She nods quickly, inhales deeply, and exhales, then repeats it one more time, trying to calm herself down. "Okay... now can we go?"

"Of course, Emily. But hold up a minute. That guy does not sound like Nurse Scott... and something sounds off. Dr. Lewis would have notified us if Bryan had woken up. Not Scott..." Logan says to her.

Now she tilts her head and gives him a sideways glance. "What are you saying?"

"Mrs. Collins... I mean, Emily. I spoke with Scott for a while the other day and that voice definitely does not sound like the guy I was talking to." Clint says to her, stepping up next to Logan and her.

Cole follows in right next to him, and she can see the girls and Diego getting out of the pool. They all looked concerned with her shouting and the radio going off.

"I'm with Clint. That dude does not sound the same as the other dude..." Cole adds.

She looks back to Logan, with his hands on her shoulders. "Let me see the radio real quick, Emily... please."

She pauses. "But Bryan..."

"We're still going down there... just let me check something first." he says to her.

She sighs and reluctantly hands him her radio.

He takes the radio and gently nods to her, stepping away and keying the mic. "If this is Nurse Scott, then tell me what is wrong with my brother, Bryan."

She looks at him with a confused look.

"Good play, Logan. If he isn't Scott, there's no way he's getting both of those questions right." Clint says to him.

Ah... I get it. She thinks to herself.

Logan looks over to the twins. "Looks like we may need to go on another trip, real soon... either way this turns out, we need to get Bryan out of there."

The twins nod in unison.

"What do you need us to do, Logan?" Clint asks.

"Yeah... whatever you guys need." Cole adds.

Before Logan can answer, she hears a male's voice come over the radio. Much different than the one claiming to be Nurse Scott. "This is Major Lenkov with the United Nations. Here to help. Who is this?"

"Th U.N.?" Emily questions.

"I thought they were all pretty much dead with the rest of the world?" Clint questions further.

"They are... and this voice sounds pretty damn Russian and like one of the voices we've heard off and on for the last few days." Logan says to them.

"Sure as shit does! These must be more of those guys that tried to kill Emily and little Laura." Cole chimes in.

Emily looks to Cole and then back to Logan with the radio in his hand. "Logan, this isn't good."

"I know... don't worry. We'll get your son out of there. But first we have to know what we're running into." He says to her.

She nods to him. "Okay."

He nods back and keys the mic on the radio again. "Hello Major... last I checked, the UN was gone. Now how is my brother?"

After a short pause the very Russian sounding Major comes back on the radio. "Bryan is in trouble and we just arrived. No doctors are here, just my troops and Nurse Scott, here. Come see at the hospital."

Once the Major stops talking, she hears the familiar voice of Dr. Lewis on the radio. "Logan, this is Dr. Lewis. Bryan is fine, same condition on the fifth floor. No one else is here yet. No Major Lenkov with the UN and no troops. And I haven't seen Nurse Scott today, and the other man on the radio does not sound like him at all."

"Oh, thank goodness!" Emily blurts out.

"I knew it! Fuckling liar..." Logan says to them.

Logan keys the mic on the radio, "Copy that Dr. Lewis. It may be time for an exodus, with Russians knowing where you are. We had two try to kill us the other day. But they were too slow and too damn stupid."

"What are you doing? Are you trying to piss them off?" She questions.

Once he releases the mic on the radio he looks into her eyes. "Emily, they have already proven they want us dead. It's no longer a matter of pissing anyone off. Plus, I need Dr. Lewis to really think about leaving that hospital."

She stares at him for a moment, narrowing her gaze. "You better know what you're doing, Logan."

The radio comes back to life with the Russian Major's voice, "You will die for that, American cowboy, Logan."

"Oh shit, Logan! You sure pissed off that dude!" Cole blurts out.

"Damn! Yeah you did..." Clint adds.

"Shit." She mutters under her breath.

"Don't worry, Emily. It'll be fine... hopefully. But it looks like we have new plans now." He says to her.

New plans? How the hell does my son fit into those new plans? She thinks to herself with serious concerns, staring down Logan in front of her.

She watches as he twists a knob on the radio and after a few clicks, she hears Dr. Lewis's voice back on the radio. "Logan? Emily? Are you guys there? Can you hear me?"

She gives Logan a curious look.

He nods to her. "Dr. Lewis said that they were on the fifth floor and they are actually on the bottom floor. I figured he meant to switch channels."

"Ohhhhh." She replies.

"Nice catch, Logan." Clint adds.

Logan then quickly keys the mic. "Dr. Lewis. Yeah, but we don't have much time. They may scan the other channels once we stop answering the Russian Major guy. Get whatever staff you have and patients left and get ready to get the hell out of there. I'm coming to bring you back here and then I think we should have a serious talk about getting out of California."

"We're leaving? But what about Bryan and the kids? Where are we going, Logan?" She questions and quickly looks at the girls and Diego, who are now quickly putting their clothes back on over their bathing suits.

"Hold on, Emily. Please..." He says to her.

She goes to open her mouth, but Dr. Lewis comes back on the radio. "Unfortunately, Logan... I think you may be right. We'll start getting ready for transport to follow you. We have five patients and there are four of us left. Again, we haven't seen Scott all day. But all the patients are moveable... even Bryan."

She sighs in relief after hearing about her son being able to be moved safely.

Logan keys the mic again. "Copy that, Dr. Lewis. Probably best to stay off the radio for now. We'll be there in 15 minutes. Leaving now."

Logan then hands her back the radio and looks to the twins. "Clint, Cole... can you guys get everything ready for us to get the crap out of here by the time we get back? Also, watch the littles. I do not want to take them on this trip if it turns sideways on us. Be ready to hit the road in like thirty minutes, once Emily and I get back with the others."

"Yeah, we can do that. But Logan... where are we going?" Clint says to him.

"I have a few ideas of where to go. I've been thinking about it. But we can talk about that later. Thank you for watching the kiddos while we're out." Logan says to the twins.

"No problem, Logan." Clint replies.

"Yeah, we got things covered here and we'll be ready for a crazy road trip once you guys get back." Cole adds.

"It's just you and me going, Logan?" She questions.

He looks at her. "Well, I was pretty sure you were going no matter what I said, and we need the kids to be ready to get the crap out of here. Plus, I don't want them anywhere close to those crazy Russians... so, yeah... I figured Clint and Cole could hold down the fort and get us ready to move."

"You can count on us, Logan." Clint says.

Cole follows up with a quick salute to Logan that turns into a serious face. "Yes, Sir. Do or die, Sir!"

Logan chuckles. "Well, the plan is not to die, Cole. But I appreciate the enthusiasm."

"Ummm, right. Sorry, Sir... I mean Logan." Cole responds.

Clint shakes his head and smacks Cole upside his head. "You're a dipshit."

"Hey! What was that for?!" Cole blurts out, rubbing the back of his head.

"Mom? Where are we going?" Laura says, interrupting their conversation on skipping town, with her, Harper, and Diego walking up next to them all.

She kneels down in front of her, looking at her, Harper, and then Diego. "We're going on a road trip. But first me and Logan need to go get your brother and we'll be right back, okay?"

Laura nods quickly. "Okay."

"Okay." Harper says with a nod too.

Diego just gives her a blank stare.

She sees Logan kneel down next to her and look at Harper, and then Laura and Diego.

"Alright kiddos. Here's the deal. We're leaving the beach and I'll let you know where we're going once we get back with Laura's brother. I need you kids to listen to Clint and Cole and pack up and get ready to go...." He says to the kids.

They all look up and over at Clint and Cole.

"Think of it as a race, little ones." Clint says to them.

"Yeah, a race I'm going to win...." Cole says with a chuckle.

This gets smiles from the kids, a chuckle from Logan, and even a smile from her.

She and Logan both stand. She turns to the twins. "Please..."

Clint and Cole both nod to her.

"We got this Mrs. Collins... um, Emily." Clint says.

"Yeah, you can trust us, Emily!" Cole says with another quick salute to her.

She smiles and shakes her head. "Thank you, boys."

Logan looks at her. "Come on, let's get going."

"Right..." She says and then looks back to the kids. "You kids behave and we'll be back soon."

"Okay!" Laura and Harper both say and she sees Diego nod slowly.

"We'll be back as soon as we can, but be ready to go in a half hour." Logan says and both twins assure him they'll be ready to go with the kids.

Logan grabs his rifle and she does the same and they both head out from the pool area, striding quickly toward Logan's truck. Once inside the truck with the engine roaring to life, Logan backs them out of the parking spot and heads to the main road, most certainly heading for the smallest roadblock, past SeaWorld, along Old SeaWorld Drive.

She looks over to Logan while holding her rifle between her legs, ready to see her son and get him the hell out of the hospital. Him still being in a coma was certainly an issue, but right now they had to get him and the rest of them out of there.

But where are we going to go, once we get back to the twins and the kids? She thinks to herself.

"Logan?" She questions.

"Everything's going to be fine, Emily. We're going to get there in time and get the hell out of there. We got this." He says to her.

Logan then drives onto the dirt around the roadblock, not caring to move the cars. "Hold on!"

She grabs a hold of the *oh shit handle* and he drives around the roadblock with no issue, just a lot of bumps.

"Okay... yeah... but then where are we going?" She questions further.

"Yeah, I've been thinking about that a lot... my home is too damn far... Your home is a good idea, but there may not be a lot of room for everyone... so I was thinking about this trip that Kelsey and I went on with Harper when she was much younger." He explains.

"Where'd you guys go, Logan?" She presses.

"The Grand Canyon." He answers.

"The Grand Canyon? Why there?" She asks.

He nods. "Think about it, Emily. It's isolated and off the beaten path. We may have to do some cleanup. But there's a lot of room for all of us and we can figure out the rest about food and water. There's bound to be food and there is the fresh water supply from the river. And I think it's less likely to be attacked by invaders. I mean why would they go to a national park instead of the major cities."

"Hmmm.... I guess it's not a horrible idea." She responds.

"Yeah, and if it doesn't work out... we move on and find something else. Away from those Russians and whoever else is with them." He says back to her.

"Now that part I really like but first things first. Getting Bryan, Dr. Lewis, and the rest of those people out of there." She replies.

"Couldn't agree with you more." Logan responds as he drives toward the hospital, swerving around stalled and crashed cars to go get her son and the others to safety.

Chapter 14: Logan Miller

Day 11: San Diego, California

"Slow down, Logan!" Emily shouts at him as he cuts the turn pretty hard coming off the 163 Freeway.

"No time to slow down, Emily. Just hold on to something." He says back, focusing on turning into the parking lot at a high speed.

"Logan!" She yells at him.

He comes to a skidding stop, spinning the truck around and nearly flipping the damn thing trying to avoid hitting parked cars in the back parking lot of the hospital.

"Holy crap! That was close. Maybe I do need to slow down a bit..." He admits.

"Yeah! You think?! We're no good to anyone if we are dead or get into a crash. Geez! Just get us there in one piece." She says to him.

He nods, "Good point..."

He presses on the gas lightly in the parking lot, heading north and then turning west to come around to the front of the hospital... hoping that Dr. Lewis and the others are ready to go.

"There they are!" Emily says, pointing once they see the Scripps Mercy Plaza front entrance.

"Good! They are moving like their lives depend on it..." Logan says.

He stops, puts the truck in reverse and pulls up onto the sidewalk.

"What the hell are you doing now?" She says to him.

"Flipping a bitch, so we can get the crap out of here. Once they are ready to go, we need to ghost this place before those freaking Russians show up." He says to her.

"Oh... right... sorry, you just scared the hell out of me back there." She replies.

"Scared the hell out of myself too. But I wasn't sure how far those crazy bastards are and I don't want to be here when they come looking for us." He answers her.

He comes back up off the curb and maneuvers the truck to stop right in front of the first ambulance parked in front of the entrance to the hospital.

He opens the door, reaching back in for his MVP Patrol, leaving the truck running. Emily does the same, and they both head to the first ambulance.

"How long do you think we have?" She says to him.

He shakes his head. "It took us damn near twenty minutes to get here and around all of the obstacles in our way... I dunno... minutes maybe."

"Minutes?! You're joking right?!" She exclaims.

He shakes his head. "Nope, and I don't think that Russian Major guy is joking either."

"Shit!" She blurts out.

"My thoughts exactly." He says as they reach the back of the first ambulance.

"Bryan!" She exclaims, seeing her son strapped to a gurney in the back of the ambulance with Dr. Lewis trying to stand over him, making sure he was secure. Logan quickly sees a figure in the front passenger seat, just past the doctor.

"He's doing fine, Emily. And we are just about ready to move." Dr. Lewis says to her.

Logan looks behind him, seeing two other ambulances lined up.

"How are we looking, Doc? Who do we have in those ambulances?" Logan questions.

"I'm in this one with Bryan here and another patient up front with a broken arm... say hello Paul." Dr. Lewis says.

Logan looks to see the head turn, with a man looking back at them close to his own age. "Hello."

Logan waves. "Hey, Paul." He says to the man that he's seen in the hospital before but never actually took the time to talk to.

"Are you sure he's alright to move, Dr. Lewis?" Emily presses.

Dr. Lewis nods. "Whereas, it's not ideal... he's safe to move. I've packed all the fluids that I could and we already had a stash of medical supplies in case we needed to leave in a hurry. We thought about it back when the fires started happening all around the area."

"Good thinking, Doc. What else are we waiting on? Any word from Scott yet?" Logan questions.

Dr. Lewis shakes his head. "I fear Scott is not coming back..." He pauses for a moment and then continues, "Nunez and Campbell are in the next ambulance with two patients in the back. One I didn't want to move, but we have no choice, given the circumstances. We had to do surgery on the older man, Tim. He's recovering nicely, but it's a risk moving him. The other one, a teenager with a broken arm, is recovering from a head injury, and has nowhere to go, just like Paul here... her name is Allison."

"Yup, was out here on business and my driver crashed the car when all of this happened... and I found my way here." The guy Paul says from the front seat.

Shit... we do not have time for life stories. He thinks to himself, checking his watch.

"Hey, Doc. I don't mean to rush you, but I got off the radio with that Major guy close to 25 minutes ago now. I think we should kick rocks real soon, here." Logan says to him.

"Agreed... go check on Nunez and Campbell, and then on Dr. Calhoun and the last patient in the back." Dr. Lewis says to him.

"Alright, will do!" He says and looks at Emily. "Stay here and check on your boy. I'll be back in a flash and we can get the hell out of here."

"Okay." She replies back.

Logan is off, jogging to the back of the next ambulance, carrying his rifle in his left hand. Reaching the back of the second ambulance, he sees the two nurses, Nunez and Campbell, along with the two patients strapped to the gurneys.

"How are we doing back here? Dr. Lewis wants us moving in a couple minutes and I'd have to agree with him." Logan says to him.

Nunez sighs. "We're moving as fast as we can..." He says to him, giving him a stare.

Campbell looks at him. "Logan, right?" She says to him.

"Yeah... Do you two need any help?" He says, then looks to the unconscious patient named Tim, and then to the teenager, Allison... who was awake, alert, and looked scared as hell.

"No, we'll be ready in a minute. Anthony here is just overstressed is all." She says and looks at Nunez.

"Aren't we all..." Logan adds, with a sarcastic look aimed toward Nunez.

Campbell nods. "That's for sure... but yeah, we're about done here. But Dr. Calhoun may need some help." She points to the ambulance behind him, the last one of their makeshift little convoy. "She's strapping in the last patient that we have."

He looks behind him, seeing the back door within view, still open. He quickly looks down at his watch. *Shit... we are running out time...* he thinks to himself.

He looks back up to Campbell and Nunez. "Got it... we're out of here in a couple minutes."

"Where are we going? By the way." Campbell questions.

"We'll figure that out once we are out of here." Logan replies.

Before she can answer, he takes off to the back of the third and last ambulance. Coming around the back open door, he sees Dr. Calhoun strapping down another man, close to his own age but with two broken legs, who was sitting up in the adjusted gurney.

"Hey, Dr. Calhoun... how are we looking back here?" Logan asks the doctor.

She turns to him and nods. "Doing just fine and about ready to go. Dr. Lewis updated me on the situation while we were getting the patients ready." She says as she begins to walk back out of the ambulance.

"Yeah... I think the sooner we are out of here the better. We don't want to be here when those Russians show up." Logan replies, as looks around the area, getting more nervous.

She steps down out of the ambulance and goes to the back driver side door, getting ready to close it. "We're all ready to go back here. We'll follow you and the others out of here..."

Before he can respond, he hears tires screeching further down the road to their South. He looks and sees a blue van that had come to a screeching halt. He watches as the front two doors open up, with very similar looking guys to what they saw at the bridge the other day.

"Ah shit..." He mumbles as he sees the two men raise what he can only assume to be more automatic weapons.

"Oh no..." Dr. Calhoun says with a gasp and she goes to spread her body in front of her patient.

Logan looks at her in awe, as he takes a knee. "Doc! Get down!"

But it was too late... a volley of gunfire erupts, hitting all around the doctor, the ambulance and around him. Now looking back in front of him, he sights in with his MVP Patrol, seeing the assailant that got out of the passenger side door. He can feel his breathing being sporadic and he tries to calm his breaths as he aims at the first shooter. He holds his breath and squeezes the trigger.

The report of the rifle fills the air.

Exhaling, he pulls back the bolt on his rifle, releasing the empty cartridge, and then pushes it back forward. He blinks and then sees the first man was down.

"Shit! We need to get the hell out of here, Doc!" He exclaims looking to his right to find Dr. Calhoun was riddled with bullet holes and blood splatter.

"Dammit! You fucking dickbags!" He yells out as he sights back in on the driver of the van. The Russian assailant steps forward, firing a barrage of bullets toward him, but apparently still aiming at Dr. Calhoun and the ambulance.

He sets the crosshairs over the Russian's chest, holds his breath, and quickly squeezes the trigger.

"Shit! I missed the bastard!" He blurts out, still hearing bullets being sprayed all around him.

He pulls the bolt to the rear, expending the cartridge, and slamming the bolt home, reloading the next round. He sights back in, blinks, and then holds his breath. This time trying to gently squeeze the trigger.

After the echo of his own rifle dulls in his ears, the gunfire stops, and he sighs in relief with the second assailant now down and not getting back up.

"We need to go now!" He says to no one around him as he sees the doctor is certainly gone and dead.

He peeks at the man with two broken legs, who was also very unfortunate to be sitting up in the gurney... now covered in blood and bullet holes.

Before he can think, he hears another sound come from behind him, like a side door to a van opening up. He quickly turns and sees several more vehicles pulling in behind the blue van, with a man stepping out and raising what looks to be some kind of big ass rocket launcher. Something Logan had only seen in movies and video games.

"You've got to be fucking shitting me..." He says to himself, as he looks in disbelief.

He stands and turns to run back toward his truck and the others. As he's running, he hears more gunfire erupt behind him, but he is out of their sights with the last ambulance with the dead Dr. Calhoun and patient blocking him. He sees Nunez and Campbell standing there in shock.

"Get in the damn ambulance and let's go! Now!" Logan says to the two of them.

They are in shock and awe, but end up slamming the back doors to the ambulance shut and are moving toward the front cab as Logan is reaching Dr. Lewis's ambulance. He hears more gunfire from behind them as he sees the back of the ambulance closed up and reaches the passenger side window.

Seeing the window rolled down he stops, quickly looking in, seeing first Paul and then Dr. Lewis in the driver's seat. "We gotta go now!" He exclaims, avoiding telling him the news of Dr. Calhoun and the last patient.

"We're ready to go!" Dr. Lewis says with alarm.

"Alright! Stay close and keep up!" He says back and moves toward his truck at the front of their little makeshift convoy.

At that instance, he feels a blast of heat, along with a deafening roar, and the ground shakes beneath his feet.

"What the shit..." He stammers out, as he turns around to see the back ambulance was in the air and coming back down, crashing to the ground.

"Ah, shit. Fuck me sideways with a pinecone, that's not good." He says as he turns his attention back to his truck.

He looks up and doesn't see Emily anywhere but notices the driver side door to his truck is shut with the passenger door still ajar.

"Dammit, Logan! Run!" He hears Emily's voice shout.

Shit... move dammit! He thinks, focusing himself and bolting for the passenger side door.

Once reaching the door, he jumps in, yelling "Go! Go! Go!" as he slams the door shut.

He can hear more volleys of gunfire erupting behind them and sounding as though it was getting closer.

"Which way?!" She shouts as she presses the gas, accelerating the truck abruptly.

"Back the same way we came!" He shouts back.

She nods and focuses on the road, turning right at the end of the parking lot and heading back the way they came, aiming toward the 163 Freeway. She makes the next sharp turn and Logan looks behind them to see Dr. Lewis's ambulance behind them and then a moment later, Nunez and Campbell right behind him.

Pulling out of the parking lot she yells in a panic, "Where's the on ramp?!"

"Screw it! Go up the offramp, where we came in! Maybe we'll confuse and lose those crazy Russian assholes!" He yells back with adrenaline mixed with anger and fear running through his veins.

She nods, guiding them onto the offramp of the 163 Freeway, retracing the path from which they came. Logan is frantically looking behind them trying to discern if they are being followed. After several tense minutes, they reach the 8 Freeway and all he sees behind them are the two ambulances.

"Do you see them anywhere?!" Emily questions.

"No, but that doesn't mean they aren't too far behind us." He says, beginning to catch his breath.

"Shit, Logan... what the hell happened back there?" She questions, as she turns on the 8 West.

"The Russians showed up as Dr. Calhoun was closing the doors on the last ambulance... and she freaking stood in front of her patient, trying to block him... they didn't stand a chance." He says to her.

"Oh no! Really?! How many of them?!" She questions.

"Only two at first... and I got lucky with taking them out before they took me out. Then some crazy asshole with some kind of rocket launcher jumped out of the van as more cars started to show up." Logan explains in half-shock of what happened as their three-car makeshift convoy drives down the 8 Freeway.

"Holy hell, Logan?! Is that what that was? It felt like a bomb went off." She replies.

"Well, I guess a bomb did go off. It was crazy and it was so damn hot. If I had been back there, I'd be dead for sure... and Harper would..." He says, trailing off with that last part.

Oh shit... I just almost died and Harper would have been all alone in this shitshow of a dead world... what the fuck, man! You gotta be more careful. He thinks to himself.

"Logan... you are not dead, thank goodness... and Harper is safe. But we need to figure out our next move. Should we get going right after this?" She says to him, obviously catching onto his panic.

"After this?" He mumbles.

"Yeah, Logan. After this. You said something about the Grand Canyon. Remember???" She says to him.

The Grand Canyon... that's right! He thinks to himself.

He turns back around to look behind them to decide if anyone is following them.

I don't see anyone out there. But after that... they'll sure as hell be looking for us. Shit, what do we do? He thinks to himself.

"Logan?" She presses.

He nods quickly. "Yeah, the Grand Canyon still seems like a good idea. But traveling right now, right after that... that doesn't seem smart."

Swerving around cars down the 8 Freeway, she glances at him. "What about at night? What about tonight, Logan?"

"Yeah, that's smart, real smart. We can leave with the cover of the darkness to help hide us from those murderous bastards. Let's get back to the hotel and make sure that we are all ready to go and then leave after the sun sets. We can drive slowly and without lights until we are far enough away from here, because the 8 Freeway is the fastest way out of here. Hell, to my knowledge, it's the only way out of here that we know of." He says to her with a plan forming in his head, coming back to his senses.

"Right, we get back and keep quiet and hidden until nighttime. And we can ask the twins. They must know the area pretty damn well." She says to him.

Logan nods and reaches for the *oh shit handle* with a shaky hand as she exits the freeway heading towards the Old Sea Word Drive road with the smallest roadblock and their only way in and out of their small little peninsula.

He looks in the side rearview mirror as the two ambulances follow their lead, going up over the embankment and driving around the blockade.

"We need to get off the road and out of sight..." He says to her.

"I know, Logan. But what if they are following us? How do we get out then?" She questions.

"The only back up plan is a damn boat, but I sure as shit don't know how to work one... I mean, we can probably figure it out." He says to her.

"But isn't that how those Russians got here?" She asks.

He shrugs. "Either by sea or they landed at the airport. But yeah, if it was by sea, we would be double screwed with plan B. Let's just hope that they didn't see which way we went with all of the commotion back there."

"I don't know, Logan. I don't like it." Emily replies.

He shakes his head. "Me either. Not one damn bit. But all we can do is wait it out. Your idea about leaving at nighttime sounds like our smartest option at this point. But first we need to get back to the kids and keep quiet until the sun goes down."

"I'm working on it, Logan." She responds to him, with her focus on the road and getting them to safety.

"Yeah, nice driving by the way, Emily." He says as he turns again in his seat, scanning the area, trying to figure out if they were being followed.

Her knuckles are white, gripping the steering wheel, and she was stressed the hell out, but she still turns to look at him and gives him a half-smile. "Let's just hope we lost those crazy Russians. That's really sad about Dr. Calhoun and that other guy. But I'm glad you are alright. I thought for a second there... never mind." She says and turns back to the road.

"That I was dead?" He questions.

She shakes her head and looks straight ahead at the road. "Let's not worry about that right now, Logan. You're fine... we're fine... for now. Let's just try to keep it that way and get the hell out of here."

"Alright, and yeah. We sure as hell cannot stay around here anymore. That Russian Major already sounded super pissed off. And after I just killed two more of his guys, I'm sure he's not going to be very happy about that either." Logan says with a sigh.

Emily doesn't say a word as she turns on Mission Bay Drive. Logan double checks that the two ambulances are still following them and no one else... hopefully.

Chapter 15: Michail Lenkov

Day 11: San Diego, California

The air smells of barbeque and structural fire. He had become accustomed to the smell over the last week of clearing out the area around the Naval Base of Point Loma. The burnt remains of human beings now just smelled like an overcooked barbeque.

It was 1440 at the Scripps Mercy Hospital front entrance, and he had just missed the cowboy and the other American survivors that had killed two of his men... now four of his men.

Despite the air being rife with burnt and crispy smells, he could still smell the salt of the ocean and the sun was still high in the sky. Even afire, this place was still much more pleasant than back home.

He hears footsteps approaching him as he gazes upon the scene left for him, only having missed the *pindos* by minutes. Some of his men got here in time, but not enough of them to stop the *pindos* from escaping.

"Major Lenkov... most of the Americans on the radio got away sir." Lieutenant Petrenko says to him.

Micha is staring at the charred woman, several feet off to the left of the ambulance that is still on fire from the firing of an RPG-7 by one of his men. She was obviously blown away from the ambulance by the explosion. She wasn't killed by it though. He could tell by the holes throughout her body that his men had killed her prior to Lebedev using his RPG-7.

The charred woman is not completely burnt, with the left side of her flash burned from the explosion and the heat of the rocket, still smoldering, her clothing melted to her body and sizzling against her dead skin. Leaning in closer he can read her name etched into what appears to be a doctor's coat. At least what was left of her coat.

You were Dr. Calhoun. Not likely the woman on the radio. She was not at the hospital. And certainly not the Dr. Lewis from the radio giving away my ploy to lure in the pindos. He thinks as he gazes upon the half-burnt remains of Dr. Calhoun.

He looks into her eyes, with her left eye blackened from the blast. But her bright green right eye was still wide open. He tilts his head looking at her half-charred face and then over the rest of her body.

You were a beautiful pindo woman, Dr. Calhoun. And having more medical personnel around would be beneficial to the survival of my troops in the coming days. Certainly, if the excavation platoons are all that is left of the Russian Federation. Yes, we may need to rethink our policy of killing all pindos on sight. He thinks as he stands back up again.

He stretches and arches his back slowly as he straightens out, cracking his back as he leans back. He feels the sweet release of the pressure in his facet joints and the entirety of his back. He then stretches out both arms to extend the release of pressure, feeling that rush of swift release from built up tension.

He nods slowly. *Yes, we will rethink this strategy. Certainly, if the pindos are as beautiful and skilled as you, Dr. Calhoun. Overtime, we can train and breed the stupid fucking pindo ways out of these Americans.* He thinks with a grin. *Dah, at least the beautiful ones. No need to keep the men, dogs, and pigs of the pindos... except for maybe Cross. Cowardly Cross is clever, but also entertaining and amuses me.*

He turns to the ambulance with the back ajar, with one of the doors now on the ground several feet away. He steps closer, looking into the burning ambulance, seeing pieces of what used to be a person in the back of the ambulance thrown all about.

Very interesting. He thinks, looking over the remains once more. *Neither of you pindos are the American cowboy on the radio... Logan.*

He looks back to Dr. Calhoun's charred remains. *You are a woman...*

He then looks to what was left of the pindo in the back of the ambulance with half of his body still trapped in the gurney. *And you are in pieces, with some of you still strapped to the gurney. The Logan on the radio did not sound injured.*

He looks back at his two dead men, next to the blue van and his mood sours and his thoughts shift away from the possibility of acquiring beautiful and gorgeous *pindo* women, retraining and repurposing them.

Dah. The fucking cowboy, Logan, is still out there. He thinks with a scowl.

"Major?" Lieutenant Petrenko questions, trying to gain his attention.

"Yes, Lieutenant Petrenko. I heard. The fucking *pindo* cowboy and other *pindos* got away."

"Major, Ryadovoy Lebedev reported that the man that shot Petrov and Volkov evaded our scouts." Lieutenant Petrenko explains.

"Dah... the clever American cowboy, Logan. With his brother, Bryan, the woman on the radio, and the Dr. Lewis. And more *pindos*, yes." Micha replies as he reaches into his breast pocket, extracting a smoke and lighting it.

"Yes, Major... the men reported that there were two other ambulances and another vehicle. The scouts searched, but... no sign of their current location, Sir. " Lieutenant Petrenko explains.

Micha takes a long drag of his smoke and exhales. "This cowboy intrigues me..."

"Major Lenkov... What are your orders, Sir? Are we to expand the search for the cowboy and other Americans or finish our primary mission with clearing the region?" Lieutenant Petrenko asks him.

Micha exhales another cloud of smoke and eyes Lieutenant Petrenko. "Are you questioning my commitment to our mission, Lieutenant Petrenko?"

Lieutenant Petrenko doesn't even flinch at the question, staring back at Micha. "No, Major. Your devotion to our mission and the Russian Federation is why I follow you, Sir... the mission is to take the region prior to our reinforcements that are to arrive in 19 days."

Micha grins. "Yes. Reinforcements that are to arrive in 19 days. What if reinforcements do not arrive, Lieutenant Petrenko? What do we do then?"

This thought had been on his mind for some time now. They were nearing two weeks without communication with the Russian Federation Command. He was becoming more and more certain that The North American Coalition's retaliation had wiped out most of his homeland, along with the rest of the New World Order Axis and the reinforcements that were to be arriving in 19 days.

His men were still handling it well enough. But there were some rumblings of what the new mission would be if the Russian Federation reinforcements did not show up when they were supposed to. The zero communication with Command was increasing the likelihood that no reinforcements would be arriving to aid them with taking what was left of America as their New Russia.

Under his command, his troops were already able to dispose of close to 2,000 bodies and execute several hundred American survivors. It was a long way off from the estimated 65 million American survivors left alive in the ruins of the U.S. But it was certainly a good start.

He was annoyed... annoyed putting it lightly, with the loss of four of his men. In all actuality he was enraged, but did not want to overly display this to his men. In truth, he wanted this cowboy's head on a pike for taking out four of his men.

He was down to 116 of his Russian soldiers, with most of his men and women being of special forces, or Spetsnaz... consisting of two platoons for their excavation mission of the region. There were still the COBs and the crew members of the three Yasen-class nuclear submarines that brought them here, totaling 63 more Russian troops... if need be and if he was able to convince or coerce the COBs that he did not outrank.

Still, this Logan and his group of pindo survivors posed a threat... however small of a threat. It was likely pure luck being able to take out four Spetsnaz soldiers and this Logan was just that lucky. Yet, if he continued to lose men by the cowboy's hand, it would most definitely affect his image amongst his troops. His men would begin to build rumors of this Logan and any other *pindo* survivors with him. That is, if the rumors hadn't already begun to spread throughout his ranks.

Lieutenant Petrenko Looks at him squarely. "Major Lenkov... Again, I will follow you, Sir. This is to be our New Russian home. You will lead us to glory and victory, Sir."

Micha exhales another cloud of smoke off to his side.

"Dah. Good. Very good. And yes, we will be victorious, Lieutenant Petrenko." Micha replies.

"Yes, Major. One question, Sir... why do we need the *pindo* Cross around, Sir?" Lieutenant Petrenko questions.

"Dah, yes... the cowardly but clever Cross." He responds.

"Yes, Sir. Why not just execute the cowardly Cross, like the rest of the American *pindos*?" Lieutenant Petrenko presses.

Micha shrugs. "The *pindo* entertains and amuses me. When he stops entertaining and amusing, then he dies... but not before. Understood?"

Lieutenant Petrenko nods. "Yes, Major. Understood. As you command. What are your orders for the cowboy and the others?"

"Dah, yes, the cowboy... do you have a map of the area, Lieutenant Petrenko?" He questions back, as he flicks his cigarette away from them and into the ambulance that is still on fire, the flames starting to dissipate.

"Yes, Major." Lieutenant Petrenko responds.

Lieutenant Petrenko pulls out a folded map from his cargo pants and hands it over to him. Micha nods and they walk about to the blue van closest to them, walking past his two fallen soldiers, cursing Logan in his mind as he walks past them.

Once reaching the hood of the van, he opens up the map and begins to study it. After a moment, Lieutenant Petrenko points to a spot on the map.

"We are here, Major." Lieutenant Petrenko says to him.

Already knowing where they were and not wanting to reprimand him for assuming he didn't know where they were, he simply nods. "Yes, we are, Lieutenant."

Lieutenant Petrenko must have gotten the hint, because he steps away and doesn't say another word as he studies the maps and looks to the surrounding areas.

If it was me... I would either be on one of those small islands or the surrounding peninsulas just north of us. And that area is the last known area where Bortnik and Federov were before the cowboy Logan killed them. Just like Cross pointed out... Something about Sea World. He thinks and grins at his quick thinking.

He turns back to Lieutenant Petrenko and gestures for him to come closer. Lieutenant Petrenko steps closer, standing next to him, looking at the map over the hood of the van. Lieutenant Petrenko doesn't say a word. He simply looks at the map, waiting for him to speak first.

After a moment Micha opens his mouth. "Lieutenant Petrenko, dispatch a patrol to scout this area." He says pointing at the peninsula and the two small islands just north of their position.

"Yes, Major. What are the orders for the patrol?" Lieutenant Petrenko replies.

"Have them observe and report back on any movement. If there is, they are not to engage. They are to report back and we will surround the *pindos*." He replies.

"Major... a patrol of six will be able to suppress the American threat." Lieutenant Petrenko replies, questioning his decision to have them only observe and report back.

Micha nods to him. "Dah yes. But that is not the point. Is it, Lieutenant Petrenko? If they find this cowboy, Logan... he did kill four of my men. He must be made an example of. Any rumors of him must be stamped out and his head on a pike will do just fucking fine." He says with a smile.

"Yes, Major Lenkov... I have heard rumors beginning to spread amongst the soldiers. There were only murmurs before the last two men died. Now there are sure to be louder rumors about the American cowboy, Logan." Lieutenant Petrenko replies, gesturing to the two soldiers, Petrov and Volkov, dead on the ground.

"Dah, yes. All the more fucking reason to crush him. He does intrigue me, but enough is enough. His head will be removed from his body once we locate him and the other *pindos* he's with. He got lucky here and the other day. He will not have the same luck when he meets our entire force. How do they say... three strikes and you are out..." He says to Lieutenant Petrenko with a chuckle.

"Yes... it will be done, Sir. The patrol will stay out overnight to observe and report back to me and I will keep you up to date, Major Lenkov." Lieutenant Petrenko responds.

"Good. And have some of the men take what they find in the hospital here. It is sure to have more medical supplies that we may need in the days and months to come... in our new homeland." Micha adds.

"Yes, Sir. Right away." Lieutenant Petrenko replies and begins to stride away.

"Lieutenant Petrenko?" He questions.

Lieutenant Petrenko halts and turns about to face him. "Yes, Major?"

"Send me the cowardly, yet clever Cross. He will show me what is in this area where the *pindos* may be hiding, and tell me more about this SeaWorld place." Micha says to him.

Lieutenant Petrenko's face scrunches up. Likely not wanting to talk to the cowardly Cross, Micha notices this and smiles.

"When he stops being entertaining and amusing, you can be his executioner." He adds

Lieutenant Petrenko provides a look of satisfaction. "Yes, Major. Thank you, Sir."

"Dah, and Lieutenant Petrenko... remind me later to change our policy of which *pindos* we execute and which ones we repurpose." Micha says to his subordinate, recalling his earlier train of thought while gazing upon the charred, but still beautiful remains of Dr. Calhoun.

"Major, I don't understand..." Lieutenant Petrenko replies.

"Not now, Lieutenant Petrenko. Explanations and orders later. Deal with the patrol for now." He answers.

"Yes, Major Lenkov. Right away." Lieutenant Petrenko responds swiftly.

Lieutenant Petrenko turns back around and heads away to go order some of his platoon to search and pillage the hospital for anything they might need or want, and to summon the cowardly Cross.

Micha chuckles again, and reaches for another smoke. He lights it and takes a deep drag of the flavorful American cigarette.

He looks back to the map, looking at the amusement park called SeaWorld just north of their current location, just over a bridge-crossing. He exhales a cloud of smoke onto the map and grins.

"As they say... you can run, but not hide, American cowboy. This is not the wild wild west anymore, *pindo* Logan."

By the time he is just about done with his smoke, he flicks it away and lights up another as the cowardly, yet clever, Cross walks up to him.

"You wanted to see me, Major Lenkov?" Cross asks him.

Micha smiles and exhales his smoke into Cross's face. Cross squints his eyes, but does not dare move away or look to become agitated.

Micha chuckles at this. "Hello cowardly and clever Cross. I have questions for you."

Chapter 16: Emily Collins

__Day 12: San Diego, California__

Emily looks to the sky as she is putting Laura into the back cab of Logan's truck. *The moon isn't quite full, but it's a clear night and the moon light will help guide our way out of San Diego.*

She sees Logan loading Harper into the seat across from Laura. Both of the girls were still sound asleep, slightly fidgeting as they were buckled in. Little Diego was awake and alert, but as quiet as a mouse in the middle seat between the girls. She told him he could go back to sleep once inside the truck, but there he was... awake and looking around but not making a noise.

I wonder how he got along for so long on his own, over at Sea World. I'm sure it definitely changed him, watching his mom and little brother die and then sleeping next to them for 10 days. We've only had him a couple days and we are already moving him very far away from here. Poor little guy. She thinks to herself, staring at the young boy.

As if the kid could read her mind, he looks over at her and forces a smile. It was one of those smiles that kids do for pictures, when they really didn't want to have their picture taken at that exact moment.

She smiles back at Diego, nods to him, and sees Logan looking at him and then her. Logan goes to speak, but she quickly shushes him, in fear of waking up the kids. He nods in understanding and then both step back and quietly close the back cab truck doors.

She walks back to the bed of the truck and Logan follows. He looks over the filled bed of the truck and then to her.

"You ready to go? Are we forgetting anything?" Logan asks her.

"Yeah... and I'm really not sure. You packed most of the stuff. Why are you asking me?" She replies with a look of confusion.

He's the one to force a smile now, and scratches the back of his head. "Yeah, sorry. Kelsey was the one that usually made sure we didn't forget anything..." He then looks off to his right and behind the truck to see the ambulance. There is an awkward pause.

Well, this is awkward for sure. I'm not your wife, Logan... I know we are traveling together and all. And yeah, you're cute and all... but your wife just passed and so did my Erik. She thinks with a wince of pain about her dead husband. He had his faults, but had still been her husband.

She stares at Logan more intently and then looks back to the kids in the back cab of the truck. *We are kind of like a family now... I guess. But what does that make you and me? How the hell did we even turn into a warped little family unit? We even picked up another kid together... What's that all about?*

He interrupts her strange train of thought. "Looks like Dr. Lewis and Paul are ready with your boy Bryan, asleep in the back. Which means that Nunez and Campbell are ready behind them, with that guy Tim and the girl... Allison, I think her name was."

She follows his gaze and sees Dr. Lewis in the driver's seat and Paul in the passenger's seat, buckled up and ready to go.

"Looks that way. I sure hope that Bryan is alright back there." She says with concern.

"I'm sure he will be fine, Emily... as long as we all get out of here soon." He replies.

Cole and Clint then walk up to them, with Cole walking up on Logan's side of the truck and Clint walking up on her side.

"We ready to get this show on the road?" Clint asks with a smile.

Logan nods. "Yeah, I think so gents. You all loaded down with that new truck you found up front?"

Cole smiles. "Isn't she a beauty? Hardly any dents and practically a brand new F250, and 4x4... Now we have a truck too, Logan." He says, as he pats Logan on the back.

Emily can't help but smile at the young man's cheery demeanor and she sees Logan smiling too.

"But yes. To answer your question. We are ready to go, Logan. Am I still riding with Emily, here? And you're up front with my brother?" Clint says next to her.

She nods to him. "That's still the plan, Clint. You don't mind if I drive though right?"

"Not at all, Emily." Clint responds with a smile.

She smiles back. "I figure you're a better shot anyways, if we run into any trouble."

"I'm not as good of a shot as my brother, but I'm good enough to get the job done." Clint replies.

"Yeah, Clint will cover your six, for sure!" Cole blurts out.

Emily's eyes go wide, looking to the back cab to see if there is any movement with the kids waking up. She obviously can't see anything through the tinted windows and in the dark of the night

"Geez... keep it down brother..." Clint scolds his brother in a hushed voice.

Cole's eyes go wide and he covers his mouth. After a moment he removes his hand. "Sorry... my bad." He says in a hushed voice, but still not very quiet.

She sees Logan shake his head and gesture for all of them to head past the tailgate of the truck and to Dr. Lewis' ambulance.

She follows his lead along with the twins.

Once they are gathered around the driver's side of the ambulance, Dr. Lewis rolls down his window. Emily can see the moonlight mixed in with the lights from the dashboard reflecting off the doctor's glasses.

"Everything alright?" Dr. Lewis questions.

Logan nods. "Yeah, Doc. Just wanted to check and make sure that we are all ready to roll out of here."

"Yes, I believe so. The plan is still the Grand Canyon, right? How far is it again? And are you sure this Southside place is a smart place to go?" Dr. Lewis asks.

"That's the plan, Doc. And yeah, that place was legit last time we were there. Like I was telling you all earlier... the Southside Haven Lodge. It used to be called something else, like Moose Ridge or Maswik, or something like that. Anyways, after some new owners took over about a decade ago, they really decked that place out. They have it running off of solar and one of the workers told me the water supply comes from down in the Grand Canyon itself. We were there during a blizzard a few years back. We were snowed in and couldn't really go anywhere for a few days. And we still had power and everything. It was really nice and right next to the South Rim of the Grand Canyon. Hell, the more I think about it, the more I think it's a perfect place to hide out and ride this thing out." Logan explains what he had already told them about several times throughout the afternoon and evening.

The place did sound nice and almost too good to be true. She hoped it was true and they would have a nice place with running water and even electricity. The twins had assured them they would figure out the food situation and there would be plenty of animals to hunt out there. She knew that to be true, with her living an hour away in Flagstaff. They had been to the Grand Canyon a few times too. But had never stayed at that particular lodge. It was usually just a day trip, since they lived so close.

Logan then looks at her. "How far did you think it would be Emily? You know that area better than me."

"It took us close to 10 hours to get here from Flagstaff, and the Grand Canyon is only about an hour from us. So, anywhere from 10 to 12 hours I'm guessing... " She says to Dr. Lewis and the others.

"That sure is a long way... you do know where we are going, right?" Dr. Lewis questions.

Logan nods and so does she.

"I'm from Flagstaff, Dr. Lewis, and Logan took that same route out here from Colorado." Emily states.

"Sure did." Logan adds.

"Plus!" Cole chimes in. "We have our handy dandy map here, and it's even the old-fashioned paper kind." He says while pulling out his map from his back pocket.

She smiles and shakes her head. *This guy...*

She sees Logan grin and pat Cole on the back again.

"Yup. We'll be fine... as long as we make it out of San Diego without being seen." Logan says.

"Yeah, about that. Is it really necessary to drive without headlights? It seems kind of risky..." Dr. Lewis questions.

"The way I figure it, Doc. It's safer than those Russians and whoever else they've got out there with them seeing us." Logan replies.

"Yeah, Dr. Lewis. As you saw earlier. Those guys mean business. They nearly killed my daughter and me the other day. And earlier they..." Emily adds, not wanting to finish her sentence.

Dr. Lewis nods. "Yes. That was truly tragic about Dr. Calhoun. She was a good person and an excellent doctor... you guys are right. It just seems dangerous, is all."

"I'm not going to lie, Doc. It is dangerous. But then again, I have a strong feeling that things are going to be pretty damn dangerous from this point forward in our lives." Logan responds.

Emily thought about this for a minute. *From this point forward in our lives... he's not wrong. That's the sad part. We have to travel over 500 miles right now, possibly getting caught by foreign invaders. Most of the world... what 85%?... is dead now. Including Erik.*

She looks toward the inside of the ambulance to where she knows Bryan to be. *And then there is Bryan still in his coma... Logan's right. Danger and death have become a part of our lives pretty much overnight.*

"Okay then. So how far should I trail Emily and when should we start using the radios again?" Dr. Lewis asks for clarification.

That's actually a good question about the radio. I didn't think of that... she thinks to herself, being brought back to the conversation.

Logan nods. "These kinds of radio can go up to around 25 miles and who knows what kind of radios those crazy Russians have."

"Right!" Cole exclaims.

Clint quickly smacks his brother upside the head. "Damn bro. The kids are still sleeping."

Cole covers his mouth again quickly with his hand.

Clint shakes his head and chuckles. "Hell of a shot but not much of a thinker, my brother."

Cole pulls his hand away from his mouth. "Hey... that hurts." He says, trying to sound hurt and defensive, but his grin gives away his sarcastic inclination.

She smiles and sees Logan chuckle silently.

Logan opens his mouth again to speak. "I would say we keep our distance from one another. At least the rest of you from me and Cole. Let us scout up ahead and stay back about... I dunno... 10 or so car lengths. At least until we get out of San Diego. So, maybe an hour to be safe and make sure we are out of their range. Does that sound good?"

"Sounds good to me." Dr. Lewis replies.

"Me too. And remember. We're taking the 8 until we get to El Centro. Then we are heading North through Glamis and through the desert into Arizona." Emily explains to all of them, knowing the route and being from Arizona, and having been to the sand dunes and camping areas of Glamis on several occasions.

"Right... we may need you up front around that point, Emily. Since you say you've been through that way a lot more than the rest of us." Logan says to her.

She nods, knowing the area pretty well. "Yeah. Erik and I used to take the kids out to Glamis to ride quads and camp out for long weekends during the fall and winter seasons... I know the area well enough."

A new thought formed in her head. One she hadn't thought about yet. *What about our trailer back home? Could we use that?*

She looks over at Logan and tilts her head.

"What's wrong, Emily?" He questions.

She shakes her head. "Nothing. I was just thinking... We have a good size trailer at home. It's a 30-foot Attitude trailer. And if Erik's truck was able to tow it, I'm sure the twin's truck or your truck can too. Should we stop by my house and get it?"

"Hmmm." Logan says and scratches the back of his head. "Sure. It sounds like a good idea. But are you sure it's still even there?"

She shrugs. "Couldn't hurt to check and see. I know you say this place is all hooked up with solar and whatnot. But what if it's not. Or what if it's burnt down to the ground like what happened around here."

Logan slowly nods. "You've got a good point. I'm hoping the Southside Haven Lodge is still up and running after all of this, but that's a pretty solid back up plan."

"Yeah it is." Clint adds.

She sees Cole nod quickly, trying to keep quiet and not shout again.

"Sounds good to me too." Dr. Lewis adds.

"Alright then. That solves it. We're stopping by the Collins' home to pick up what I am guessing is a very nice trailer. Even if we don't need it. It will be nice to have it for a backup plan down the road." Logan says to the group.

He then looks at her. "Plus, Emily... you can grab whatever you want from your home and we can bring it with us to the Grand Canyon. I'm sure there are keepsakes that you'd like to hold onto.

She nods and smiles at Logan, already having the thought in the back of her mind when thinking about going back to her Flagstaff home.

He really is a nice and thoughtful guy. Plus, he did save mine and Laura's life. Yeah, there are certainly worse people to be stuck with during the collapse of Western civilization and pretty much the whole freaking world. She thinks, staring at him.

"Should we start heading out then? It's just past one o'clock in the morning." Dr. Lewis says to them all.

"You're right, Doc. We should get going. It's late enough and if any of those crazy Russians are out there... Hopefully, they are all sleeping by now."

Hopefully! She thinks to herself.

"Remember. No headlights and radios for the first hour, and trail behind my truck at least 10 car lengths. If there's any trouble, hide and get out of here." Logan says to them.

"But what about..." Emily starts.

"Get them out of here, Emily. Get my Harper out of here." Logan says with emphasis.

She exhales slowly and nods, understanding his love and fear for his daughter.

"Let's get this show on the road then." Cole says with excitement in his voice.

Logan smiles and pats him on the back.

The four of them walk away from the ambulance with Dr. Lewis, Paul, and Bryan.

Once reaching Logan's truck, she opens the door and climbs in, seeing Logan nod to her without a word.

She watches as the two twins embrace in a hug and say something, but she can't make it out, with them being in front of her truck, and her inside with the doors closed. She watches as they both chuckle and Clint heads to the passenger side of her truck and Cole heads to jump in the truck with Logan.

Clint opens up the passenger door and jumps into the truck, quietly closing the door. He looks back to the children and so does she. She sees that Diego is still wide awake, staring back at them. The two girls are still knocked out and fast asleep.

"You alright, Diego?" She asks the young boy.

Diego nods, but doesn't say a word.

She gives the boy a concerned look and then looks back to the front and sees the bright red taillights of the black F250 with Logan and Cole inside.

She hears Clint rolling down his window and looks over to him. "Are you hot, Clint? I can turn on the A/C."

He shakes his head. "No, Mrs. Collins... I mean, Emily. I just thought it'd be smart to listen out for things for a while. At least until we get out of here."

Smart kid... Well, he's not a kid... just super young. But pretty damn smart. She thinks to herself.

"Very smart thinking, Clint." She replies, as she rolls down her own window.

She then looks forward again and watches as the taillights of the F250 get smaller as Logan drives up ahead of them.

She hears the clicking of a radio and she looks over at Clint again.

"Remember not to use that thing until we are out of town. Okay?" She reminds him.

He nods. "For sure. I'm just going through the channels every few seconds or so, to see if I pick up on any of those crazy ass Russians. I thought it'd be a smart move to listen and hear if any of them are around us."

Geez! This kid is freaking brilliant! His twin is kind of a goofball, but these two boys are super resourceful. I mean, wow! She thinks to herself and then releases the parking brake and starts lurching her vehicle forward to slowly follow Logan and Clint out of San Diego.

"I'm really glad you and your brother are with us, Clint. And I'm happy you both decided to come along." Emily says to him.

Clint nods, flipping to another channel on the radio, listening. "Of course, Mrs. C... I mean, Emily. It's not like we were doing anything else special, and there's nothing really left for us here. Except for a bunch of crazy Russian invaders that are out to kill us and take our land. It actually sounds like something from one of the movies our dad used to watch with us as kids."

Emily slowly swerves the truck around some downed cars with the help of the moonlight. She was making sure to drive very slowly, considering they weren't using headlights for a while. She could still make out just about everything, but there was no reason to go over 10mph. At least until they were far enough away to turn on their headlights.

She looks over to Clint after moving past the downed vehicles and smiles at him. "Well, I'm still glad you and Cole decided to come along with us. And I know the girls like having you two around too."

Clint turns his head to look behind them at the kids in the back seat. "Plus, this little cool dude, Diego. Couldn't just let him go on this adventure without us." Clint says to the young boy and winks at him.

Emily looks back and sees him smile. Her heart warms up, having seen Diego smile back. She then focuses her attention back on the road ahead of her, still able to see the very small taillights of Logan and Cole's truck up ahead.

"Looks like we are staying about ten car lengths back. What do you think, Clint?" She questions.

Clint looks up from checking the channel on the radio. "Yeah, looks that way. Nice driving in the dark, Emily.

She looks in the rearview mirror and can make out the silhouette of the ambulance following a few car lengths behind them. "And looks like Dr. Lewis is using our taillights to guide them."

Clint looks in the sideview mirrors and nods. "Looks like it."

She looks to her left and sees that they are passing SeaWorld and getting closer to the freeway onramp. The idea was to get onto the 5 and then jump on the 8, heading east. And far away from all of the Russians in the area.

She sees Logan make a slight right turn, getting onto Old SeaWorld Drive to move past their smallest blockade on the peninsula they called home for the last 12 days.

A few moments later, she makes the same slight right turn and then sees the F250's taillights bounce around a little bit.

"They must be going around the blockade and up over the curbs." Clint says to her.

She guides her way down Old SeaWorld Drive, getting ready to do the same thing.

"Sounds about right. And then to the freeway and we are on our way out of here..." She replies.

An instant later, she is squinting at a pair of bright headlights that suddenly flashed on just in front of Logan and Cole's truck.

Emily hits the brakes instantly.

Oh no! She thinks to herself.

"Shit." Clint blurts out.

"Do you think it's the...?" She begins to question.

The radio crackles to life and they hear a voice come in over the radio in Clint's hands. The voice was obviously Russian, speaking a language they didn't understand.

"Sure as shit. It's those crazy ass Russians... shit." Clint says calmly.

A moment later a new voice answers the first one and then the first Russian responds back.

"What do we do? I know he said to leave them, but..." Emily says to him.

Clint sighs heavily. "I'm sure as hell not leaving my brother."

Clint then drops the radio in one of the cup holders in the center console of the truck and reaches back behind him.

Emily watches as he brings back a small backpack and then opens it up, displaying some sort of small rifle. One that doesn't look familiar to her. She's seen her fair share, but this one looked a little out of her league. She looks back at the children, nervously... wanting to get them the hell out of there.

"Alright, here." He says, handing her the hi-tech looking rifle. "You take this and stay here with the kids. I'm getting out and going up there to see what is going on."

She takes the weapon and watches as Clint takes another identical small rifle out of the backpack. She watches as he unfolds the stock and the rifle doesn't look so small any more. But it certainly looks more expensive than anything that she had ever shot and what they had back home.

Clint then grabs several magazines from the backpack, handing her two.

"Here's one for now and an extra mag. Just in case you need it. If it starts going bad up there, get the hell out of here, Emily. It only looks like one pair of headlights up there. But who knows and it sounded like they called for reinforcements over the radio. So we don't have much time." Clint says to her.

She then hears shouting and looks forward to see the dome light come on from the F250 and can make out the figures stepping out of the truck... Logan and Cole.

Clint goes to open the truck door.

"Clint! Wait!" She blurts out.

He pauses, not opening the door yet. "Emily, he's my brother."

She shakes her head. "No. The dome light." She says, reaching up and turning the witch on the dome light to the off position.

"Oh yeah... good call." Clint replies.

She nods and watches as Clint opens the door and steps out into the cool night air. She opens her door and steps out as well.

"Where are you going? You should stay here." Clint says in a hushed voice.

"Hell yeah I'm staying here. But I'll watch you as you go up. I won't shoot unless I have to. I'll just watch you as you go up there and watch your back." She says to him.

"Alright, yeah. That's smart. I'll be back... hopefully." He says, closing the door quietly.

Before she can say anything, Clint moves forward in a low, crouched sprint toward the blockade about 150 feet up ahead of her and the kids.

She breathes a strong whiff of cool ocean air through her nose and exhales it slowly.

Alright, Emily. They saved your butt. Now it's time to return the favor. She thinks as she closes her door quietly.

She then looks to Diego in the back seat, who is just sitting there quietly and not freaking out for whatever reason. She nods to him and smiles. He forces a smile back at her.

She looks at her machine gun looking rifle and folds out the stock like she saw Clint do.

Now... let's try to figure you out real quick. She thinks to herself.

She looks to the scope... the very expensive looking scope. It wasn't like the rifles that her and Erik had. But it did have some of the same knobs on it. She sees what looks to be colored dots on it. It was hard to tell with just the moonlight to guide her, but she turns the knob anyways, and looks through the scope.

First there was a red dot and then it changed to cross hairs. She then sees a button on the scope and presses it down.

What does this do?... Oh wow! She thinks to herself, looking through the scope. *I can see everything out there, just in white and grayscale. But the white looks like it's almost glowing.*

She shoulders the rifle and looks through the scope again toward where Logan and Cole are and where Clint is nearby. She quickly sees the partial silhouettes of what are likely Logan and Cole, in a glowing hot white appearance through the scope. She then scans and sees another figure kneeling down on her side of the blockade. She quickly realizes that it was Clint. Shifting her sights up and toward the headlights, she squints and can make out at least one more figure near the headlights and what looks like one more stepping out from the driver's seat.

It looks like this thing can see people in the dark, but it's not green like in the movies. Some kind of fancy glowing white vision... she thinks to herself and lowers the rifle.

She checks that her magazine is securely inserted into the rifle and then pulls the bolt to the rear, releasing and letting it move forward, going home and putting a round in the chamber. She then looks to Diego, and sees that all three kids are awake and staring right at her.

Geez! How long have they been awake and just staring at me silently? Creepy kids... but it's good they're awake! She thinks quickly.

"Alright, children. I'm just going to step off over there to the light pole... just right there. If you hear gunshots get down... in fact. Just get down right now and stay down until I get back." She says to her daughter, Harper, and Diego.

None of them say a word, but all nod slowly and then duck down in the back cab.

Alright then... that was easy enough. Not even one "why." What the hell is this world doing to our kids? She thinks and then quickly shakes her head. *Never mind. No time for that now.*

As if to indicate the severity of the situation, she hears what she thinks to be two men yelling in Russian. Yelling at Logan and Cole.

Holy Hell, please just let it be a few Russians... like on the bridge... I don't think we're making it out of this if it's that Major and his whole damn army. She thinks to herself as she swiftly moves to the blacked out light pole and sights in toward Logan, Cole, Clint, and what she hopes to only be two Russians.

Looking through her scope, she thinks to herself. *Yeah, there's definitely only two... for now... but Clint's right, they did call over the radio and that's not good!*

Chapter 17: Logan Miller

Day 12: San Diego, California

"Shit!" Cole blurts out, as they are quickly blinded by the bright headlights of a vehicle several car-lengths in front of the blockade just in front of them.

Logan was blinded and couldn't see the Russian special forces soldier holding an AK-15K with the barrel pointed at Cole and himself. But once the headlights flashed on, that was the first thought that crossed his mind. Some Russian had caught them and now they were screwed.

Shit is right! They were waiting for us to move around at night! He thinks to himself in alarm.

Logan hadn't seen the vehicle in the darkness, only lit up by the moonlight, until the bright lights from the headlights seared into his corneas, and he realized how screwed they were.

"Fuck me." He mutters as he squints.

"What do we do, Logan?!" Cole says, obviously shocked too.

What the hell do we do?! He thinks squinting to look in the rearview mirror, not seeing Emily, Clint, and the children in his truck behind them. But knowing that they were back there somewhere, and likely pretty damn close.

He looks back to the blinding headlights, disorientating his eyes that had become adjusted to the darkness of the night.

Shit. What do we do? If I take off, at this range they probably have us pretty much in their sights. And if they do miss, they could hit the kids, Emily, and Clint. They could hit Harper... he thinks, trying to let his eyes focus back on who exactly was in front of him and how many.

"Vykhodit!" He hears a very distinctive Russian voice yell at them.

"Fuck me." He mutters again.

"Logan?" Cole says, more calmly. "What are we going to do?"

"Vykhodit!" A Russian yells at them, again.

Logan sighs. "They've got us, Cole. And if we try to run, they could hit your brother, Emily, and the girls..."

"And little dude, Diego, too." Cole adds, catching on to how screwed they were.

He nods. "Yeah." He simply replies.

"Vykhodit!" A Russian yells at them, again.

"What the shit do you think they want?" Cole questions.

Yeah, what do they want? Why are they not shooting at us already? The other Russians didn't bother talking at all, and just started trying to kill us. He thinks to himself.

"Not sure. But I'm guessing they want us to turn off the engine and get out of the car." He replies.

"Shit." Cole responds.

"Yeah... shit." He answers as he turns off the ignition to the truck.

"Get out now!" The Russian now says in English.

Cole looks over to him and Logan looks back and nods. "Get out slowly, Cole. Hands up, nice and slow. They haven't shot us on sight yet, so maybe we can buy some time and distract them."

"But what if it's a whole army of them out there?" Cole questions with concern rising in his voice.

He was brave as hell and certainly able to handle his own. But this was a crap situation and if he was being honest with himself, he was scared shitless too.

He pulls the handle on his door and slowly pushes it open.

"If there is, then we really are screwed. All we can do is hopefully buy some time for the others to get the hell out of here." Logan replies.

"Well, shit, Logan, that sucks." Cole responds, as he opens his own door.

"Get out now!" The Russian says in English again.

"You said it, Cole." He quips back.

He steps out into the cool coastal night air, letting the smell of the salty breeze fill his nose. He tries to squint and focus, but the searing pain in his eyes tells him that he is still momentarily mostly blinded by the bright lights.

"Pushki seychas!" The man yells at them in Russian.

He looks over to Cole and Cole looks back with a shrug, with both his hands high in the air. They come together in front of the F250, hands raised. Right about now he was wishing he had dawned that vest he picked up off that cop over a week ago. It hadn't crossed his mind until now, and he sure was kicking himself in the ass for not being more prepared and protected.

Both him and Cole were wearing shorts, t-shirts, running sneakers, with guns on their hips. Probably looking like something these Russians expected all Americans to look like, thanks to Hollywood.

Well, back when Hollywood was around and wasn't stuck in whatever the hell happened some thirty years ago back in 2023. Hollywood and everything else within that circle with a radius of 71 miles was now cut off from the rest of the world and now the talk of paradox conspiracies around the globe. Now "Hollywood" was everywhere over the U.S. It just wasn't called Hollywood anymore and not a consolidated epitome of power and fame in Southern California.

But yeah... Logan was pretty damn sure that him and Cole looked like something out of an American movie to these Russian guys. Shorts, t-shirts, sneakers, and carrying guns at the beach. Like it was a normal every-day Tuesday in the great U.S. of A. Well, at least what was left of the great U.S. of A.

"Pushki seychas!" The Russian yells at them.

Logan's thoughts are rocked back from their appearances and stereotypes of Americans and back to the two Russian soldiers with what he guessed were fully-automatic rifles pointed at them. Possibly, the last few moments of his life. Maybe that was why his mind was wandering, feeling that the end was near and not wanting to focus on impending doom.

"Sorry comrade! We don't speak Russian!" Logan says back to the Russian in front of the headlights with a rifle pointed at him. He tries to say it in a loud, firm voice but without sarcasm.

No shit we don't speak Russian. You crazy shits... why haven't they killed us yet? On the bridge there was no conversation. Just shooting and trying to kill Emily and Laura. Why is this different? He thinks to himself, happy to still be alive but unsure as to why.

He feels the need to look over his shoulder but stops. Not wanting to draw attention to the others.

Another voice yells out from behind the headlights. "Guns down now!"

"Ah! Why didn't you just say so, bro? You guys didn't really think that we knew Russian, did you?" Cole replies, obviously not trying to conceal or hide his sarcasm.

He and Cole both slowly reach to their hips where their sidearms were.

"Medlennyy!" The first Russian voice in front of the headlights shouts at them.

"English douchebags! We don't speak Russian!" Cole replies.

"Careful, Cole." Logan responds in a hushed voice. "We're trying not to get shot here, bud."

"Slow! Guns down slow!" The second voice, behind the headlights says to them.

Well, one of them knows some English. Let's try to use that. And it only sounds like two of them... so far. He thinks to himself.

"Okay! We're putting our guns down slowly now." Logan replies.

He grabs his Glock G45 with his index finger and his thumb to show he wasn't going for it and trying anything stupid. He wouldn't stand a chance against whatever type of rifle that those Russians had pointed at them.

He looks to Cole, seeing him do the same thing. He tries to give a look that says, *shut your damn mouth, Cole. They haven't shot us yet.* But Cole doesn't catch on and just tilts his head in confusion.

Logan sighs heavily through his nose and stands back up after putting his gun down on the road.

"Hey guys, we don't want any trouble. We were just passing through, trying to get home. We have water in the truck if you want it. It's yours. Hell, you can have the truck if you want." Logan says to them, just trying to figure out what they want and if they can maybe bribe their way out of this.

Maybe these were different Russians. Maybe not the same group that they shot on the bridge. Hell, maybe not even Russians at all. Could be a lot of folks that came over here from that area, and I'm betting all of their languages sound about the same... he thinks to himself, just happy that he wasn't filled with bullet holes yet. Keyword being yet.

"Ty Logan?!" The closest Russian in front of the headlights yells at him.

Shit! Definitely Russians. And definitely the same damn Russians on the radio, from the hospital, and on that damn fucking bridge. Shit! Logan thinks to himself, trying to think of what to respond.

Cole didn't skip a beat though. "What?" Cole says, playing dumb. "We don't speak Russian. Remember?"

"Ty Logan?!" The closest Russian shouts again.

Logan looks at Cole who is shaking his head and shrugging. "I don't understand what you mean, bro. Really... it's like you're speaking Japanese to me right now but instead it's Russian." Cole responds.

Fuck me... this fucking guy is going to get us shot. He thinks to himself and looks back to the Russian in front of him with a wince... half expecting to hear the loud report of gunfire.

"Are one of you Logan?!" The second voice yells at them.

The other Russian speaks English, but I don't think he's very good at it. Or he'd be talking more than this other guy... And I'm starting to really think there are only two for now. But these two look like they could take out a whole damn army... fucking shit. We are definitely screwed. Not dead yet but still screwed. He thinks to himself as he opens his mouth

"Who?! No! My name is Frank! And this is my nephew, Cole! We are just trying to get home! But if you want our stuff you can just take it!" Logan shouts back

He then watches as the two soldiers speak in Russian, He had no idea what they were saying, but it sounded slightly like confusion. Then the one behind the lights, next to the driver's side door, raises what looks to be a radio.

He then hears a radio crackle to life and the Russian speaking into it.

Yup. That's a radio. Which means my eyes are finally adjusting. He thinks as he squints, trying to look around.

He doesn't see much else besides the two Russians. After a short silence with the Russian awaiting a response on the radio, he could have sworn he heard some movement from behind the Russians, but they didn't notice it.

Logan looks to Cole and he notices that Cole may have heard the same thing behind the Russians.

An instant later he hears the sound of something jumping on the roof of a car.

What the hell is that?! He thinks to himself.

It was the vehicle directly in front of them. Something big, on all fours, and not human. Logan wasn't entirely sure but it looked like the outline of a huge ass cat staring down at the Russian behind the opened driver's side door.

"Cho za khuynya!" He hears the Russian shout out, and then the radio crackles back to life, distracting the Russian for an instant.

Logan hears a low growl and then the huge cat-like creature leaps onto the Russian soldier behind the driver's side door. He hears the man scream out in shock and agony as he's pushed down to the ground.

"Suka-a-a!!" The Russian soldier in front of the headlights yells out, moving quickly to his fallen comrade, now pointing his rifle in the direction of the huge cat-like creature on top of his fellow Russian.

Then Logan hears a familiar voice in English yell out from behind them. "Cole! Logan! Get down!"

Logan quickly drops down to his stomach, atop the asphalt, feeling the cool touch of the road and the small rocks of the asphalt jab into the palms of his hands and knees, not sure of what's coming next.

He looks over to see Cole doing the same thing. He reaches for his Glock G45 and he watches as Cole grabs his Springfield XD off the pavement and grips it tightly, aiming up toward the Russian now distracted by his fallen comrade being devoured in the brightness of the headlights.

Exactly what I was thinking, Cole! Logan thinks to himself as he sights in.

Logan pulls the trigger and hears the loud report of his Glock, along with Cole's Springfield and more gunshots from behind him.

The Russian soldier jolts around as though he's dancing as bullets hit what is likely his bullet-proof vest and the rest of his body not protected by the vest.

Before the fatally wounded soldier has time to fall to the ground, Logan glimpses movement from off to his left, and another huge cat-like creature pounces on top of the dying Russian, bringing him down hard to the ground.

Cole, him, and what has to be Clint behind them, all stop firing and stare in shock and awe.

Is that a?... He thinks to himself.

"Is that a fucking lion, bro?!" Cole blurts out.

"What the hell is that?!" Clint shouts out from behind the blockade of cars.

"It's a fucking lion, bro! What the hell does it look like!?" Clint shouts back.

"Yeah... and lions hunt in packs... or prides." Logan says, thinking out loud. As he recalls seeing lions at the San Diego Zoo, some 12 days ago. Thinking back on reading the information panel on the lions and how they hunt.

"What?" Clint says to him, eyes going wide... catching on to his train of thought.

"Meaning, there are going to be more of them." Logan says quickly looking around and gets to his feet.

He holds his Glock in front of him, aiming into the dark all in front of him. An instant later, Cole springs to his feet and is scanning the area as well. Logan looks to the headlights and the lioness tearing a chunk from the already dead Russian soldier's neck.

"What?! Are there more Russians already?! It did sound like they called for backup!" Clint shouts from behind the barricade of cars.

"No! Not yet! But there could be more lions out here with us!" Logan replies.

"What?! Where?!" Clint responds, alarm rising in his voice.

"They fucking hunt in packs, bro! Aren't you listening?! I thought I was the dense one... geez!" Cole answers.

"Not now, you two! Cole! Slowly get up and move back to my truck. Don't run... walk slow-like. Real slow-like. They'll chase you if you move too damn quickly." Logan explains, remembering the information gathered from the San Diego Zoo and watching nature shows on the Discovery Channel with Harper.

He takes a step backward and then another. Trying to get back to the open door of their truck. He looks over to Cole, doing the same.

"Are you sure there are more out there, Logan?!" Clint says to him, obviously not having started to walk back yet.

"Clint! I am pretty damn sure. Even if they're not out there. We have two big ass lions right in front of us. Get the crap back to Emily and the kids. Fuck lights out, and fuck going slow. Get in that truck and tell Emily to follow me." Logan says to him in a half-shouting voice. Not wanting to really startle or grab any attention from the two lionesses, clawing away at the two, now very dead, Russian soldiers.

"Right! My bad, Logan! Will do!" Clint says to him, and Logan doesn't hear him again.

Reaching the driver's side door, Logan maneuvers behind it and looks over at Cole on the passenger's side. At that moment the lioness in front of the headlights turns her gaze to him and she snarls.

An instance later, three more lionesses emerge from behind the Russian's vehicle.

"Aw shit" Logan stammers out.

"Clint! Don't walk! Run, bro! There's more of them!" Cole shouts out and jumps into his seat slamming his door shut.

Logan jumps into the truck too, slamming his door. He fumbles for the ignition switch, revs the engine to life, and kicks on his brights.

The pack of lionesses pause and all of them stare at him and Cole, baring their teeth.

He slams on the horn of the truck and the pack of lionesses jump back slightly but don't give up any ground. still only about 20 feet in front of them.

An instant later, he sees headlights come on behind him from Emily and the others.

"Time to get the crap outta here!" Logan exclaims.

He shifts the truck into gear, leans on the horn once more, and presses the gas pedal. He swerves to the left of the vehicle with the pack of lionesses all around it. The lionesses jump out of the way as they snarl. He drives past the huge cats, on and off the curb, and then back onto the road.

He looks over at Cole. "Cole, get on that radio and tell them to drive fast and hard around those lions!"

"But you said..." Cole replies.

"I know what I said, Cole! We'll worry about the Russians once we are away from these damn lions trying to eat us. Now get on that radio! They need to know that they're driving into a whole damn pack of those things." Logan shouts back at him.

An instant later the radio crackles to life after Cole presumably shifts back to channel five on the radio. "Hey guys! There's freaking lions up here! Windows up and drive fast!"

He releases the radio and looks at him. "Logan, are we still going the same route?!"

At that moment, Logan sees lights come across from them on the other side of the San Diego River, to their south.

"That's a whole lot of nope, right there! I am betting that those headlights mean that there are more Russians coming to actually kill us this time! We're headed north!" He replies.

"North?! But, Logan? That route will take us close to the quarantine zone where that dome thing is, or whatever the hell it actually is. Only the military takes that route." Cole replies.

Turning his wheel hard left, the truck lurches and turns north of Friar Road, heading for SeaWorld Drive and the 5 North.

"Right now. At this very moment, I'll take my chances with whatever the hell is up that way. It's better than a pack of lions and an army of Russians. We'll turn off toward the east, first chance we get. But for now, we just need to get the hell away from here!" Logan yells, checking the review view mirror to see Emily's truck now close behind him and the two ambulances that are following them too.

"Good! Looks like they all made it past the lions. Hopefully they take out a few more of those crazy ass Russians." He says to Cole as he turns on the 5 North, heading toward the very strange and mysterious event that created some sort of circle that he had been warned to stay away from since he was six-years-old, back in 2023. But right now, he didn't give a shit. There was still a lot of room between them and whatever the hell the quarantine zone actually was, and they were a hell of a lot closer to lions and Russians. Both of which wanted to kill them.

Once on the 5 North Freeway, the radio crackles back to life.

"Where are we going guys?" Clint asks over the radio.

"North, toward the circle of death." Cole replies over the radio.

"What?!" Clint responds back over the radio.

"Give me that." Logan says, looking over at Cole and snatching the radio from his hands.

He clicks the radio back to life and speaks into the radio, knowing full-well that the Russians could still hear them. "This is Logan. Trust me and stay off the radio until we get there. Those crazy Russians could still be following us if they got past the lions and whatever else escaped, or more than likely was actually released from the San Diego Zoo."

There's a moment of silence over the radio, then it crackles back to life with Emily's voice. "Copy that, Logan. You better know what you're doing."

"Copy that. Over and out... for now." Logan replies and hands the radio back over to Cole and presses down on the accelerator of the F250.

He scours the rearview mirror for headlights behind them that are not from their four vehicles. Not seeing the headlights remerge behind them or any other vehicles in pursuit... yet.

"Do you really think that someone let those lions go on purpose, Logan?" Cole questions.

Logan nods slowly. "I sure do. People are crazy as hell and it's safe to assume that some of the crazy ones survived the CWA death clouds, and I've always heard that California is filled with those types of crazies that mess with wild animals and crap."

"Whoa, Logan! Not cool, man..." Cole says with nervous laughter. "We're all not crazy out here. Plus, I'm kinda happy some lunatics let loose the lions. We'd probably be dead if they didn't."

Logan chuckles back, thinking about how close they just came to death... once again.

"Yeah, you've got a point, Cole. And to be clear, you and your brother Clint are some bad ass Californians. That's for damn sure." He says to the twin that kept his cool with Russians pointing guns at him and lions that wanted to eat them.

Cole is beaming with a wide smile. "Thanks, man! I'm just glad to be out of that situation. Hopefully, it's smooth sailing from here. And all those conspiracies about that circle of death thing are all wrong."

Logan looks over at him. "I'm not going to lie, Cole. We're going nowhere near that damn place. First turn off we can, and we are heading east. No one's heard a word from the people inside whatever the hell that thing is for 30 years now. So, that's a hard pass for us."

"Well, that's good to hear. I thought you were seriously driving into that thing for a second." Cole replies.

"Nope. Just want to have the Russians think that if they were listening in." He responds back.

"Ah! Very smart, Logan. Very smart." Cole answers.

"Thanks. I have my days. Now, do you think you can pull out that map of yours and find us a way east, toward the Grand Canyon?"

"Yeah. Sorry. My mind was still stuck on those Russians, the lions, and now the circle of death. That was really a close one." Cole replies, reaching for the map still in his back pocket and then unfolding it to examine.

"Yeah. A close one for sure, Cole." Logan responds.

Too damn close... I really hope that this Southside Haven Lodge works out and we get to breathe for a little while. He thinks to himself.

"Alright! Cool! I think I found a route to get where we are going from here." Cole says to him.

Logan slows down to swerve around a bottleneck of cars on the 5 North, guiding the F250 around the wrecked and stalled cars to get more distance between them and the Russians... and the lions.

"Good deal, Cole. I'll drive. You navigate." Logan replies with the hope of getting further and further away from everything currently trying to kill them.

Chapter 18: Michail Lenkov

Day 12: San Diego, California

"Lieutenant Petrenko. Explain to me one more time how the American *Pindos* got away. I must have not heard you right." Micha says to his Lieutenant.

"Dah, Major. It does sound unbelievable. But the dead lion proves that Sergeant Sokolov is telling the truth, Sir." Lieutenant Petrenko replies in English to him.

Micha looks down at the dead lioness atop Ryadovoy Lebedev's dead body. He then glances over at Ryadovoy Kiselyov's shredded remains at the front of the vehicle.

Fucking lions... he thinks to himself.

"Sergeant Sokolov split up her forces to cover more bridges. Lebedev and Kiselyov stopped the Americans here, awaiting for Sergeant Sokolov and the rest of the patrol. When they arrived, they saw vehicles driving away and shot this lion. Other lions ran off. The Americans got away too, Sir." Lieutenant Petrenko explains to him.

Lieutenant Petrenko's English was improving day by day. As was his, and a good amount of his troops. They were all still getting used to speaking English in their new lands. It was going well enough, but still slow for most of his troops. He had thought about it last night and even more this morning.

Their tactics and policy of killing all of the *pindos* had been changed earlier this morning, by his order. If they were going to be alone here in their New Russia without any additional support or reinforcements, he had to change the plan. His orders were to kill all adult men. Capture all children and women. If any resisted, kill a few to get them in line and under control. His troops knowing how to talk to the captured would be beneficial over time.

Micha was going to send Lieutenant Petrenko's platoon out in the morning for a sweep of the area to begin with the new tactics, but Sergeant Sokolov's patrol had finally checked in just after he had given the orders in change of tactics against the Americans.

It seems she was sitting on this fucking information of the pindos' escape all night. Thinking of this angered Micha.

"Fucking lions. Fuck's sake. This Logan's luck is fucking stupid. And explain why Sokolov took so fucking long to report in?" Micha replies.

Lieutenant Petrenko nodded. "Sergeant Sokolov reported that they were still patrolling the area afterwards, to see if there were more of them in the area. One of the men that was stopped said his name was Frank. And the other, Cole. Not Logan. But Sergeant Sokolov did report that a Logan, other male voices, and a female voice came on the radio shortly after they found Ryadovoy Lebedev and Kiselyov, here."

Micha shakes his head. "So, it was him! Why did she need to still patrol and not report back to you, Lieutenant?! Was she scared because of her failure?!"

Now Lieutenant Petrenko is the one to shake his head. "If I'm being honest, Sir. Dah, she was afraid. She did not say as much. But she looked afraid."

Good. She's fucking afraid because she knows what I'm going to do to her. Stupid bitch! He thinks to himself.

"Sir. There is something else... good news." Lieutenant Petrenko.

"What fucking good news?" Micha says sharply, thinking of what he'll do to Annika Sokolov before he executes her.

"Sergeant Sokolov and the rest of her patrol did arrive in time to see taillights from one of the vehicles, she thought quickly to use a tracking round in her rifle, and tag the last vehicle." Lieutenant Petrenko replies.

"Did she now?" Micha responds, looking over at Sergeant Sokolov.

She stiffens up once she meets his eyes. He narrows his eyes, and grins.

Maybe you won't die yet, Sergeant Annika Sokolov. But there are fates worse than death. He thinks as he stares at her, reaching for a smoke.

"Yes, Major. We know where they are, currently." Lieutenant Petrenko says, handing him his GPS Coordinates.

Micha lights his cigarette and exhales. "Dah?! Where is this Logan and the rest of those *Pindos*?"

Lieutenant Petrenko points to the screen on the handheld GPS coordinator. "They appear to be driving through the desert, heading east. Instead of North, like the cowboy said over the radio. Or Sergeant Sokolov misheard the direction they were going. Her English is getting better, but still not good yet."

Micha takes another drag from his smoke. "No. This Logan lied on purpose. So we don't follow him to where he is really going."

"Major?" Lieutenant Petrenko questions.

Micha looks away from the GPS coordinator and back at Lieutenant Petrenko and simply nods, exhaling another cloud of smoke. He was really enjoying these American-made smokes.

At least the pindos knew how to do something right. He thinks to himself.

"Let me go after the cowboy, Logan, and the other Americans. Praporshchik Oblonsky can take command of my platoon until my return. And this time, with your permission, we kill these Americans on sight." Lieutenant Petrenko says to him.

Micha takes another drag of his smoke, contemplating his response. He looks over at Sergeant Sokolov, still very angry and annoyed with her patrol letting the Americans get away.

"Stupid fucking lions. That Logan is too fucking lucky." Micha mutters.

"Major Lenkov. Nothing will stand in my way of ridding you of this nuisance cowboy and the other Americans. On my honor." Lieutenant Petrenko adds.

Micha narrows his gaze at his Lieutenant, and then finally nods. "Dah! Fine. Take over Sergeant Sokolov's patrol and take one more with you. And don't let any fucking lions kill you, Lieutenant Petrenko." He says and then looks back to Annika Sokolov. " And don't let her die either. I have plans for Sergeant Sokolov upon your successful return. She will have to earn my respect and her life back after her failure."

"Dah, Major. None of my men will die under my command. I will take Sergeant Sokolov, the rest of her patrol and one other from the platoon. The platoon is in good hands with Praporshchik Oblonsky." Lieutenant Petrenko explains.

"Ah, dah. Reminds me... take the cowardly Cross with you. He will be useful with throwing the Americans off their guard. Use him as a decoy. But do not let him die. He still amuses me. Do you understand, Lieutenant Petrenko?" Micha orders him.

Micha can see Lieutenant Petrenko grit his teeth, not liking the additional orders of taking Nicholas Cross along with him. Micha also knew that his subordinate wanted to be the one that kills the cowardly and clever Cross. But Micha didn't want him to yet, so he would not.

"Dah. As you wish, Major Lenkov." Lieutenant Petrenko finally replies.

Micha nods. "Kill this Logan and the others with swiftness and end the rumors of his defiance. Bring me back his head. If there's nothing left, just bring me back a head and we call it Logan. Check in often, Lieutenant. Do not return until this cowboy is dead and all rumors along with him. Do not let me down, Lieutenant Petrenko... dismissed."

Lieutenant Petrenko comes to attention, salutes him, and Micha returns the salute.

"It will be done, Sir." Lieutenant Petrenko says to him.

Micha smiles and exhales another cloud of smoke. He watches as Lieutenant Petrenko moves away from him and directly toward Sergeant Sokolov and the rest of her patrol. He then focuses his attention back on the lioness in front of him, atop one of his Spetsnaz soldiers.

"Fucking lions." he mutters again.

Another soldier dead and this Logan's rumors will only continue to grow if I don't have his head soon. That makes six of my men dead. These two may have been killed by the lions, but that won't stop the legend of this Logan from growing throughout my ranks. This cowboy needs to die and not turn into a legend that threatens my command and my future in this region. If I cannot handle one fucking cowboy, they will never follow me again. Micha thinks as he stares down at the lioness and the dead body of his enlisted man.

A few moments later, he hears hurried footsteps approaching him.

"Major Lenkov! You can't be serious. I am still useful to you, Major. If you send me with Lieutenant Petrenko, he will surely kill me!" Cross blurts out.

"Dah, Cowardly Cross returns." Micha says with a chuckle.

He turns to face Cross, staring into the depths of his eyes and Cross freezes up.

"Lieutenant Petrenko will not kill you, Cowardly Cross. I ordered him not to. Do as he orders and you will return. I still find you amusing and useful. But do not question my orders again. Or I will kill you myself." Micha says to him in a low and calm voice.

He can see the shock and fear in the man's eyes and it makes Micha grin even wider.

Cross quickly nods and stammers out, "Yes, Major Lenkov."

"Now, go. Out of my sight. Now with you." Micha orders him.

Cross backs up quickly, unsure of which way to turn. After an awkward moment, he shuffles off toward Lieutenant Petrenko and the others.

Micha chuckles again, turning back around to gaze upon the dead lion on his dead soldier. He shakes his head slowly, exhaling another cloud of smoke and smiling.

Fucking lions. For fuck sake. Fucking lions. He thinks to himself, beginning to laugh at the situation and the excitement of Lieutenant Petrenko carrying out his orders and finally ridding him of this cowboy, Logan, and the other American *pindos*.

After a few moments, he flicks his cigarette and turns back around, looking for Praporshchik Oblonsky. He still wanted to do a sweep of the area and begin his new policy with the enemy right away. He knew that it would make his troops happy, most certainly the men. And after thinking of what he wanted to do to Sergeant Annika Sokolov prior to killing her, he knew finding some *pindos* to capture would make him happy as well. They may not be Russian women and children. But with time and practice, they could be... they would be.

It was a new day and new orders. His new orders. Since there was no one else around to give them. Lieutenant Petrenko would most certainly deal with the thorn in his side and his men would be happy by night's end.

All they had to do was capture some more stupid fucking *pindos.*

It still amazes me how long these lazy Americans lasted. At least the women and children can be made of use. He thinks to himself, still scanning for his temporary platoon leader until Lieutenant Petrenko's successful return.

Finally locating Praporshchik Oblonsky, he claps his hands together.

Dah. It's going to be a glorious day for New Russia. For the great beginning of finally building my New Russia. He thinks to himself as he strides over to Praporshchik Oblonsky amongst the rest of his Spetsnaz soldiers.

Chapter 19: Logan Miller

Day 12: Ocotillo Well, California

Logan looks out over the desert region that surrounds him at a U.S. Border Patrol Station where the 78 Highway meets the 86 Highway. The sun was starting to peak over the horizon to the east, the direction they were heading.

Cole had done a good job navigating them out of San Diego and on their way to Arizona, careful to avoid the main freeway and stick to the highways, taking the 52 East to the 67 North, to the 78 East. What was even better was there had been no issues up to this point of needing to refill their gas tanks. This place seemed as good a place as any. No one was here. Not too many dead bodies to worry about. There was the lucky instance of the roadwork being done in the area, with plenty of vehicles with fuel for them to acquire.

Logan was definitely relieved to be out of San Diego, and even more relieved about having a good amount of distance between them and those crazy ass Russians, and not to mention the lions and whatever else was loose out there now.

He looks down at the gas can filling up from the section of garden hose jammed into the Border Patrol vehicle. He takes another swig of water from his water bottle, spitting the remaining taste of fuel in his mouth out onto the desert sand.

It's going to take a while to get this damned taste out of my mouth. For the future, I need to find one of those kits, to make siphoning easier for me. But I'm sure as hell glad that I remembered to bring a garden hose and a couple gas cans during all the craziness... just for this very situation. He thinks to himself, looking behind him, toward the way they just came.

Damn. For a desert, it's pretty damn gorgeous out here. Must be why we saw so many trailers and campers back along the way we just came through. Must be some sort of camping place where folks can ride around... he thinks to himself.

He hears the kids and looks back to the structure where the voices are coming from. He sees the kids, Emily, the twins, and the others walking out of the Border Patrol Station.

Focusing on his little Harper. He knew the Border Patrol Station was clear, having cleared it himself with the twins. But he was still nervous about having her so far away from him.

He takes another swig from the water bottle, swishes it around in his mouth, and then spits it onto the desert floor.

Even being a mechanic, I've never had this bad of a taste from fuel in my mouth. But then again, it didn't happen often, and I did just siphon a crap load of fuel. So, there is that. He thinks to himself, looking back over at the desert scenery.

A few moments later, he hears footsteps approaching.

"It really is beautiful out here, isn't it?" Emily says to him.

He looks at her and smiles. "I was just thinking the same thing."

She nods and gestures back down the highway they just came from. "It's called Ocotillo Wells. It's a place where people come out to camp and ride their dirt bikes, quads, and other toys. We've been here once or twice, but Erik prefers... preferred, Glamis. Which we'll be going through in a little while."

"Yeah, it looks nice." He says to her.

He thinks back to several hours ago, in the twilight hours of the morning, with the Russians and the lions. *Damn, that was way too damn close. If those lions hadn't been there, we would've been screwed for sure. Possibly all of us. Those Russians were no joke. There's no way we could have taken them on our own. They had us dead to rights.*

"You alright, Logan?" Emily questions.

Logan nods slowly. He was still pretty damn shaken up from earlier in the morning with almost being killed and worrying about what would happen to Harper.

"Yeah." He lies to her.

"Hey. Everything turned out alright back there. It's probably best to just not over think it too much." She says to him.

"Yeah. But I can't stop thinking about what would have happened to Harper if I had died back there. Or even worse. What if they would have caught her and the rest of you, after they were finished with me and Cole?" He questions, showing his obvious concern and that he was still bothered and dwelling on the events earlier that day.

"No, yeah. I get it. But if you play the *what if* game, it's not going to turn out well for you and the *what ifs* will eat you alive. Trust me, I know." She says, and he watches her gaze go to the ambulance where her son is still in the back in a coma.

Logan sighs heavily and scratches the back of his head, trying to think of how to change the conversation. Sure, he had almost died. But so had she and Laura, and her son was still in a damn coma.

Way to go, dumbass. You're not the only one in this shitshow. He thinks to himself.

"Yeah. You've got a point. But we need to be more careful in the future. There's not always going to be a pack of lions to save our asses." He says to her with a slight chuckle.

Emily looks back to him and smiles. "Yeah. You've got a point there. That was like an act of God, or something."

"It was something alright. And if I'm being honest. I may need to change my underwear out pretty soon. It's been kinda gross driving for so long, after having pissed my pants thinking about getting eaten by lions." He says with more of a chuckle, this time.

She grins and shakes her head. "Way to make it gross and awkward, Logan."

He laughs. "Hey! I'm just kidding. I'm good, just trying to lighten the mood."

"Uh-huh. Sure you are." She says, with a chuckle of her own.

Harper, Laura, and Diego walk up with Cole and Clint right behind them.

"Hi dad. How's it going?" Harper says to him as she walks over to him and gives him a hug.

"Careful, Harper. Your dad just told me he peed his pants earlier, when the lions came out for the bad guys." Emily says with a grin.

Harper backs away quickly. "Ewww. Gross dad!"

"Yeah, that's pretty gross, Logan. And I've been riding with you this whole time? I was curious about the ammonia smell." Cole says to him with a smile.

He laughs and scratches the back of his head. "Alright, alright, alright. I was just kidding. But I will pee my pants and even crap my pants soon. If I don't go use the restroom."

The group laughs at him, and along with him.

"You're gross, dad." Harper adds.

Emily shakes her head. "Well, the bathrooms were pretty clean inside the Border Patrol Station."

"Yeah, the men's bathrooms were pretty clean too, Logan." Clint says to him.

"Good deal. Cole and Clint, you mind finishing this up for me? The trucks and ambulances are filled up and I'm just refilling this last gas can to put in the back of Emily's truck. Just in case we need it anytime soon. I already put the other gas can in the back of our truck, Cole." Logan says to the twins.

"Sure thing, Logan." Clint replies.

"For sure, Logan!" Cole adds.

"Alright then. I'm off to the potty. I'm hoping they have toilet paper, so I don't have to use my hand." he says with another sarcastic grin.

"Really, Logan?! Now that truly is disgusting." Emily says to him.

"Yeah, dad!" Harper says and starts giggling.

Laura starts giggling too, and he can see Diego laughing lightly as well. It was nice seeing the little boy smile and it was certainly a rare occurrence.

Logan chuckles and walks off toward the Border Patrol Station. "Back in a few, ladies and gents. Don't leave without me."

He hears the group chattering and laughing as he makes his way to the station with the bathrooms inside. Once inside the doorway, he can smell the decay of the body behind the counter that he knew was there from clearing the station when they had arrived. There was one more body in the back room, another in the guard shack at the checkpoint, and one was in his car.

The last guy in the car looked like he was getting ready to go on patrol, with the keys in the ignition, but the Border Patrol vehicle hadn't been started yet. Apparently, none of the Border Patrol Officers had been of the Rh-Negative blood type variety and had all succumbed to the effects of the death clouds from the CWAs.

Seeing the bathroom, his stomach reminded him that he, indeed, had to take a crap. He always found it strange that the closer you got to the toilet the worse it was, like a finish line or something.

He makes his way into the bathroom and the first available stall. He closes the door behind him, pulls down his shorts, hearing the sound of the gun that was in his waistband clank against the bathroom floor, and sits onto the toilet.

His first instinct was to reach into his pocket to grab his iPhone. Just like he always had, to check the news, social media, and whatever else piqued his interest while he was sitting on the toilet.

Oh yeah. No more phones. Looks like going to the crapper isn't going to take twenty to thirty minutes anymore. But at least there is toilet paper. He thinks with a grin, seeing a close to full roll of toilet paper on the wall mount.

Sure enough, after a few minutes he was done and at the sink washing his hands. After scrubbing his hands, he dries them with some paper towels from the dispenser and walks out of the bathroom, feeling much better now.

Walking out of the Border Patrol Station, He feels the morning air begin to get slightly warmer with the desert sun coming up. He then sees that everyone is getting loaded back up and he heads toward Emily's truck, which was actually his truck. But then again, he found it off some dead guy. So maybe it was his, maybe all of theirs, maybe none of theirs really.

I guess right now, it's Emily's truck. Possession is nine-tenths of the law. He thinks to himself with a smile forming.

Reaching the truck, he goes to the driver side window where Emily is. He sees Clint in the passenger seat and nods to him. Clint nods and smiles back at him. He then focuses on Emily right in front of him.

"Are we all set and ready to go?" He asks Emily, putting his hand on the truck and looking at her through the open window.

She looks at his hands with a sarcastically disgusted look on her face.

She's got jokes. He thinks to himself, still smiling.

"You're in luck. They had toilet paper! And I even washed my hands." He says with a smile.

"You're stupid, Logan." She says with a chuckle. "And yeah. I believe we are ready to roll. Clint just put that gas can in the back, with that piece of garden hose you cut up."

"Good deal." He says to her and then looks at Clint. "Thanks, Clint."

"No problem, Logan." Clint responds.

"Do you know where we are going?" Emily questions him.

"Yeah. I think so. Cole is doing a great job of navigating thus far. I think Cole said we're staying on the 78 for a few hours, then the 10 for a bit, then onto the 60 for a while, and then the 89 to the 40 and into Flagstaff." Logan says, thinking back to what Cole had told him about twenty times over the last several hours in the truck.

She nods with approval and responds. "Sounds about right. I'm guessing it's at least another six hours straight through. So, probably closer to eight to ten hours until we come up on my place. We can stay the night there and then head out to the South Haven Lodge in the morning."

"If that's alright with you. I'm okay with it. Are you sure?" He says and then peeks back to the kids in the back cab of the truck, seeing Harper, Laura, and Diego chatting amongst themselves.

It's good to see them all getting along nicely, especially considering we all just almost died by Russians and lions a few hours ago... damn, that was way too close. He thinks, with his mind again shifting back to the early morning events of that same day, and his smile fades away.

"Yeah. I'm sure, Logan. It'll be fine and it'll give us time to get the trailer hooked up and any belongings we need from the house. I'm not sure if we'll ever be coming back. And that's even if the place is still standing." She says to him.

He nods slowly, knowing what she meant. A good amount of San Diego had been afire. And the same could be for her hometown. Hopefully that wasn't the case, because that meant more foreign invaders much further inland. In the end, there was just no telling what they were going to find at the Collins' residence. He had hoped it was a restful night's sleep and some time to unwind. During these times though, nothing was certain. But then again, was anything certain before the world went to war and 85% of the world died off.

"I'm sure your home is still standing, Emily. It's pretty damn far away from the beaches and all of the invading Russians." He says to her, trying to reassure her and himself as well.

"Yeah. But I doubt the Russians are the only bad guys we have to worry about, Logan. Remember that crazy drunk at the hospital? He was probably a normal guy before all of this, and you saw what he did and wanted to do." She replies.

Logan thinks back on the day that he met Emily and Laura, and he had to kill that disgusting disgrace of a human being. He certainly deserved it, but it was also the first time he had killed someone. As it turned out, it certainly wasn't going to be the last time. Sure, he had been training for years, off and on, pretty much his entire adult life... but that was only training. There was no more tapping out, no more rounds and resets. Now, everything was or for keeps and final, with the finality of it all either being alive or being dead. No, it had become blatantly clear that this was a new world and they would have to continue to fight to survive.

Yeah... that creep was the first. Plus a few Russians. Well only one by me. One by Cole, and the other two by those freaking lions. He thinks to himself.

"Yeah. You've got a point. And that's the whole reason that Cole and me are driving up front. Just in case we run into any trouble. It gives the rest of you some time to get the hell out of whatever mess we find ourselves in next." He says to her.

"Plus, what if those crazy ass Russians didn't only have subs or boats or whatever they came here on? What if they have planes too?" She responds to him.

He looks at her with wide eyes. "Shit, I didn't think about that. I was just hoping they were at the coastline." He says to her, lying, and not wanting to bring up that thought in the back of his mind.

It would be easy now to slip into paranoia and think that enemies are all around them. Then again, that could really end up being their reality from here on out.

Aside from everyone here with us, we haven't really seen any old fashioned, good people. We haven't seen a lot of people alive, actually. I just hope that there's still good people out there. He thinks to himself.

She nods. "Yeah, me too. But you never know."

He sighs heavily and then looks back to Harper and the other two. "Yeah. Freaking *what ifs.*"

"Hey, Logan." Emily says to him, he looks back at her right in front of him. "She'll be alright. We're going to be alright."

He smiles at her. "Sure thing, Emily. You're right. But if anything happens to me..."

She shakes her head slowly. "We're going to be fine, Logan. We're going to go hide out at this resort at the Grand Canyon and no one will have much of a reason to come looking for us there. You'll see."

He nods. "Fair enough. But if something does happen. Please..."

She looks over her shoulder at the kids for a moment and then back to him. "Of course, Logan. But you have to promise the same goes for Laura and something happening to me."

He smiles at her. "I promise."

"Oh. And Bryan and Diego too." She presses.

He nods and smiles. "Of course, Emily. But like you said. We're going to be fine. We just have to steer clear of Russians and lions. And they are way back that-a-way." He says gesturing toward the way they came through in the early and dark hours of the morning.

She looks in the direction and then back to him and smiles. "Alright, let's get moving then. So we can get to our place sometime this afternoon."

"Sounds like a plan." He replies and looks back at the kids, at Harper. "Alright, kiddo. I'll see you in a bit. Call me on the radio if you need anything. Behave for Emily and Clint, okay kiddo?"

"Okay, dad. I will. Drive safe and watch out for more lions." She says with a serious tone.

He smiles at her and she forces a smile, obviously still somewhat concerned with what happened earlier. "Will do, kiddo."

He looks back to Clint and then Emily, nodding to them, and pushes away from the truck. He turns and walks up to the black F250, where Cole is likely sitting in the passenger seat waiting for him. He reaches the truck, opening the driver side door to find Cole studying the map.

"How's it going, navigator? Are we all set and ready to go?" He asks Cole.

Cole looks at him with a smile. "As long as you changed your underwear and washed your damn hands." He says with a laugh.

Logan shakes his head and smiles. "I told you guys I was joking. And yeah, I washed my hands."

Cole grins. "Let's get going then. We're still stopping by the Collins' place right?"

"Yep. That's the plan." Logan replies as he takes his seat.

He then closes the door and turns on the ignition, putting the truck into drive, and looks in his rearview mirror to see the Tundra behind him and the two ambulances behind them.

He breathes through his nose and focuses his attention back to the highway.

On the road again. He thinks to himself, pressing the accelerator and bringing the truck back onto the highway.

After a few moments, he looks in the rearview mirror again to see the Border Patrol Station, with the camping area known as Ocotillo Wells getting smaller in the distance behind them.

Driving southeast, he looks to his left and sees what looks to be a huge lake.

"There's a huge lake out here in the middle of the freaking desert?" He questions.

"Yeah. According to the map. It's the Salton Sea actually." Cole replies.

"Huh. Looks pretty damn nice." He replies.

"Yeah, maybe. But it smells like salty death. Geez!" Cole responds.

Logan shakes his head. "I still can't smell a damn thing but fuel, because of that damn taste still stuck in my mouth."

"Well, consider yourself lucky, bro. It's a weird smell out here and I think it's coming from that Salton Sea place." Cole replies.

Logan chuckles. "Yeah. Lucky. Right."

Before Cole can respond with something that was certainly going to be along the smartass variety, the radio crackles to life.

"You guys there? This is Emily. Over." Emily says over the radio.

Hmmm. I wonder what she wants. We just left and we just talked. He thinks to himself.

Cole answers the radio. "Yeah, Emily. This is Cole. What's up? Over."

They had all gotten better with radio etiquette throughout the night, driving along the highways, and it was beginning to show. The twins had advised having call signs in the future. Maybe they'd all talk about it tonight when they were at the Collins' home.

"The kids are hungry and there is a town coming up in about half an hour. Brawley. Should we consider stopping and looking for some food to not use up our own? Brawly is a pretty small town. Over." Emily says over the radio.

Cole looks at him and Logan shrugs. "I could eat."

Cole nods and holds up the radio again close to his face. "Copy that, Emily. We are hungry too. We'll stop in town somewhere. Over."

A moment later Emily comes back on the radio. "Copy that. Keep your eyes open though guys. It is a small town. But you never know. Over."

"She's pretty damn smart, that Emily." Cole says to him.

Yes she is. He thinks to himself and nods to Cole.

"For sure. Tell her we'll be careful but to stay off the radio until we get there, so no one picks up our signal." He says to Cole.

Cole nods and clicks back on the radio transmitter. "Copy that. Will do. Radio silence until breakfast. Over and out."

Emily doesn't respond back and Logan turns his full attention back to the highway, now with the Salton Sea in his rearview mirror and heading more directly east.

The desert area gave way to fields that were meant for farming just a couple weeks ago. Driving through the farm lands, most of the crops looked like they were beginning to die-off with whatever watering system controlled by their farmers no longer operating. Or more likely that the farmers were no longer alive to operate the watering systems.

"How the hell are their farms out here? I mean way the hell out here, in the middle of nowhere?" Logan questions.

"Fun random Californian fact. California can actually produce enough food to feed the whole U.S." Cole says to him.

"You've got to be shitting me." Logan replies.

"Nope. You'd be surprised how much food comes out of Cali. I didn't believe it either when my dad told me. But then I Googled it. And sure enough... Cali could feed everyone, if it needed to. I guess especially now that most everyone is gone these days." Cole says, with the last part sounding sad. Which was not normal for Cole.

"Hey, Cole. If I didn't say it before, I'm sorry about your parents, bud. They sounded like they were really nice people." He says to Cole.

Cole nods. "Yeah thanks, Logan. They were really nice people."

They were both quiet for several minutes, with Logan driving through the farmland, turning southeast once more, following the highway, and then turning back in a more direct east route. He turns on the 86b for a bit, to go straight through the small town of Brawley.

Poor guy. Him and his brother lost their parents in a blink of an eye. And have been nothing but helpful this whole time. Hell, I almost actually shot them when we first met. And they still stuck around to help us and even agreed to leave their home area with us. I mean who does that? These are two badass twins. That's for damn sure. He thinks to himself as he begins to see what looked like a town up ahead of them and their little caravan of trucks and ambulances.

"And I'm glad to have you and your brother with us. To be honest, Cole. I'm not sure if we would have made it out of San Diego without you guys." Logan admits to Cole, trying to break the silence.

He looks to Cole who is just staring forward, strangely quiet and not very Cole-like.

"I'm serious, Cole. You and your brother are pretty badass and we are lucky to have you guys around." Logan says to him.

Cole doesn't answer.

"Cole? Are you alright, bud?" He questions.

Cole finally looks over at him, with an unusually straight face. "I don't think we should be stopping in this small town, Logan."

Logan tilts his head in confusion.

Cole points in front of them and off to the side of the road into the town of Brawley.

Logan tries to focus his vision on what Cole is seeing. "What do you see, Cole? Do we need to turn around?"

"Yeah, I'm pretty sure turning around is a good idea. I'm also pretty damn sure that those are dead bodies tied to those light posts." Cole responds.

Logan squints and can make out the figures on the light poles on the other end of a bridge, just out of town. Sure enough. There was a body on each side of the road, tied up to the light poles.

"Shit." Logan murmurs, and slows down the truck.

As he stops completely he can see Emily's truck and the ambulances stopping behind him. They are about 100 feet away from the bodies, but they are definitely dead and that they have signs around their necks.

He looks at Cole. "Hey bud. Hand me the radio real quick."

"Sure thing, Logan." Cole responds, handing him the radio.

Logan clicks the radio to life. "Alright folks. Hang tight real quick. Cole and I see something. We're going to drive a little close, but be ready to head back the way we came. Over."

Emily's voice comes over the radio quickly. "Copy that. Be careful. Over."

"Copy that, Logan." Candice Campbell responds over the radio too.

"Copy that as well." Dr. Lewis adds afterwards.

Logan hands the radio back to Cole and presses the accelerator again, creeping the truck forward to get a closer look.

"Eyes open, Cole." He says to him.

"Sure thing, bro." Cole replies, reaching for his rifle.

Logan only had to drive a little further up to make out what was written on the signs of the bodies tied to the light poles at the other end of the bridge. They were definitely dead bodies, both men and both had cardboard signs hanging around their necks with big bold letters.

"Rapists." Logan says dryly.

"What?" Cole questions.

"The signs on those dead guys both say RAPIST on them." Logan explains.

Cole looks, squinting. "Oh... well, that's a good thing right? Less bad guys. Right?"

"Yeah, I think so. But I dunno... hanging dead bodies outside of town just doesn't seem normal. You know?" Logan replies.

But what the hell is normal these days, anyhow? He thinks to himself.

"Okay, so what should we do?" Cole questions.

Logan sighs and shifts the truck in reverse, looks behind him, and presses on the accelerator.

"We go talk to the others. But I don't think it's worth the risk." Logan says as he steers the truck in reverse toward Emily and the others.

Chapter 20: Emily Collins

Day 12: Flagstaff, Arizona

Emily looks back to the kids napping in the back cab of the truck.

We're almost there guys. She thinks to herself.

She then looks at Clint. "Hey, Clint. Can you hand me the radio? We are getting pretty close to our exit."

"Sure thing." Clint replies, reaching for the radio in his side door compartment.

It had been a long and grueling last 13 hours on the road. Long road trips are not as fun as the movies make them out to be, especially in the circumstances of most of the world being dead.

After Logan told them what they saw at the edge of town in Brawley, they had all decided to stay away from major cities and drive straight through when they had to. This somewhat changed their course. They wound up taking the 78 to the 10 real quick, then back North on the 95 until they hit the 40.

They had to drive straight through Blythe, even though everything looked dead to the world. Blythe wasn't the most populated city before the attacks, but it looked like the population was close to zero after the attacks, with their band of trucks and ambulances having to swerve around cars and corpses along the streets.

In truth, the freeways and the highways weren't much different. Their train of trucks and ambulances were swerving and maneuvering around stalled and crashed cars, with plenty of corpses for them to see in a state of decay of some sort of liquefaction. The bodies weren't liquid per se, but they were definitely getting there and it was disgusting. Many times, she caught the girls and Diego just staring out the window at a car with bodies inside of it as they swerved around it and drove further along their journey.

A trip that should have only been around eight to ten hours, was going to end up taking them over 13 hours, and she could tell that the kids were not happy. You could call it a mom-sense, or just plain old common sense. Kids being stuck in a car on a road trip for long hours. A road trip through the decay of what was left of America had to be the worst road trip in road trip history, for sure. She knew they certainly were not happy travelers. But then again, were any of them happy at all, about any of this?

Laura, Harper, and Diego were behaving, but you could still see them getting tired and annoyed with being in a car all day. To her surprise though, there wasn't one complaint. Just grunts here and there, trying to get comfortable. Emily was actually shocked that there wasn't even any bickering. She was more and more worried about how much the new world had changed all of their children, if they weren't complaining about being in a car for over 13 hours. Even worse, how would this new world continue to change their little ones.

Once they hit the 40 east she felt better, knowing they were getting closer to her home. They steered clear of Needles, and stayed on the 40. Needles was small, but they didn't want to take any chances if they didn't have to. Pit stops were a dangerous luxury now.

When they hit the California and Arizona border, they had all gotten out and stretched their legs for a little while on the bridge near Topock, over the Colorado River. It was a risk, but a necessary risk, with needing to refuel. It had given them a chance to recharge and look over the water while refueling the two trucks and two ambulances. A little bit of conversation was had, but Emily could feel the stress in the air of being out on the road, out in the open, and not knowing what lay ahead of them. After Logan, Clint, Cole, Campbell, and Nunez siphoned enough fuel from the surrounding vehicles on the bridge to refill their vehicles and the gas cans, they were on their way once again.

Once they got further into Arizona, the scenery changed to more of mountains and greenery compared to the desert, ridges, and dunes. California was nice and beautiful, but she was certainly glad to be out of the Golden State and in the Grand Canyon State. Especially after everything that had happened on what would be referred to as the worst vacation in human history. At least between her and Logan, and when the kids weren't around.

Reaching Kingsman, they continued to opt out of going anywhere near the center of the city, despite how small it was they stayed to the 40, curving around and out of the town, and were getting closer to her home.

The next several hours, they had gone into a quiet groove. Her and Clint rarely spoke, unless there was some sort of road blockage to avoid. The kids were quiet in the back and eventually fell back asleep around three o'clock in the afternoon.

She knew that they were very lucky with little incidents for the 13-hour road trip through dead America... other than the kids having to use the bathroom every few hours and not very happy in a cramped area after the first few hours. And, of course, except for the Russians almost killing Logan and Cole, and then there was the whole lion thing. But she was trying to keep that out of her mind. Everything else had gone mostly smooth since then.

She just felt lucky to be alive and on their way to her home, even if only for a little while. She was also glad that Logan was there, and Harper and Diego, along with the twins, Dr. Lewis, and the others. It was nice to have company and people helping her with her son and it sort of felt like they were all looking out for each other. In reality, they truly were.

Seeing the signs for Flagstaff Ranch Road brought her out of her daze and quiet groove. They were almost there, and there was truly some relief in that. She hoped that things would get better and somehow those crazy Russians would get dealt with and things would eventually go back to normal. She knew it wasn't smart staying in a populated area, and was onboard with Logan's plan for the Grand Canyon. But she was still hopeful that someday she would be able to come back to her home. Someday sooner rather than later.

Clint hands Emily the radio and she clicks it to life. "Hey guys. We need to be getting off here, on Flagstaff Ranch Road. It's the least traveled way to our house. Over." She releases the transmission button on the radio, awaiting their response.

"Copy that. Logan is asking where to go after that?" Cole says back over the radio.

She responds back through the radio to Cole, "It's only about 10 minutes from there, give or take. Take the road to the left and then turn right on Route 66 Highway. Then take another right at Woody Mountain Drive, right next to the campground. Turn left at the roundabout and then just keep making rights until we're on University Ave. It's four rights and then the fifth house on your left, coming from that way. Over"

"Wow... you're going to have to repeat that, Emily. That's a lot to remember. Over." Cole says back over the radio.

She hears Clint chuckle off to her right.

She keys the radio again. "I'll just tell you as we go. Just tell Logan not to drive too fast so he doesn't miss the turns. Over"

"Copy that. He says he'll try." Cole replies back over the radio.

"Hey, why don't we just lead them in?" Clint questions.

She gestures back to the napping kids in the back cab. "Special cargo back there, and also behind us. It was Logan's call to make sure that they'd lead us in. So, if anything happens we have time to react."

"Yeah. Makes sense. Just don't like my brother being in harm's way. Is all." Clint replies.

Emily sighs, knowing how he feels. "Clint, I think we are all in harm's way these days."

"Yeah, I guess you're probably right." Clint replies.

She smiles at him, trying to comfort his concern and then looks forward to see Logan also missing his turn. "Ah shit." She blurts out and keys the radio. "Turn right on Route 66! Geez! I thought you'd guys remember that much!"

She immediately sees the brake lights of the F250 and it turns hard-right on Route 66.

She hears Clint laughing next to her and she can't help but smile. After she sees they didn't crash, that is.

She clicks the mic on the radio again. "Alright, speed racer. Second street up, make a right. Woody Mountain Road. Over."

Clint replies, "Copy that, boss lady."

She grins and guides them the rest of the way to her mountain home in Flagstaff, Arizona. Taking all of fifteen minutes to safely guide Logan and Clint to the front of their driveway. She looks at the dashboard clock, reading 6:05 p.m.

"We're here. Home sweet home." She says aloud, not really to anyone around in particular and more to herself. She was excited to finally be home, even if it wasn't for very long.

"It looks nice, Emily." Clint answers.

"Yeah. It is pretty nice. Well, at least we like it. It's home... It was was home, I mean." She responds back softly.

Logan's voice comes over the radio. "It looks quiet enough, and no one is coming outside to greet us in the neighborhood. I think we're good to go in. Over"

She nods and keys the mic on the radio. "Copy... I was thinking the same thing. The cars on both my neighbor's driveways are there, but it doesn't look like anyone is coming out to greet us. Which probably means..." She pauses and releases the mic on the radio, not having to finish her sentence for them all to know what she meant.

"Copy that. Understood. Where should we park Emily?" Logan questions back over the radio after her short pause.

"Park off to the left, on the small pavement and I'll back up your truck to the trailer on the right. We can hook up the trailer in a bit. Once we get settled and everyone inside. Over." She responds over the radio.

"What about us, Emily? Over." Dr. Lewis says over the radio.

She nods and looks over her street and her neighbors' houses. "Park in the driveways of my neighbors' houses. I would think one of you on each side of my house would be good. If they are home, we'll move once we get settled. Over."

"Copy that." Dr. Lewis replies.

"Copy that as well." Campbell replies from her ambulance's radio.

After she makes a three-point-turn she backs up the truck pretty close to her trailer in the large driveway to the right of her house. Once satisfied, she puts the truck in park, shuts off the engine, and sighs with relief. Part of her wasn't really sure they were going to make it this far. And the fact that it was without any more major problems was amazing.

She steps out of the truck and stretches, seeing Logan and Cole walking over to them. Logan looks in the back cab and sees the kids still napping and smiles at them.

"How'd they do since our last stop?" He asks her.

She shrugs. "They did great. I could tell they were annoyed as all holy hell. But they did great, actually. It was really kind of strange."

Logan nods slowly. "Not the strangest thing to happen, but glad they're doing alright."

"You've got a point." She replies.

"Should we start unloading?" Cole asks.

Logan shakes his head. "No. Only take the weapons you need and whatever food we need for the night."

"Roger dodger, Logan." Cole replies, and goes to turn back to the black F250.

"Wait." Emily says, as she sees Cole freeze in his track and slowly turn his neck around peering at her with a childish grin. She chuckles. "Don't worry about the food part. Save it for the Grand Canyon. We should have plenty of food that isn't spoiled in the house. It's only been 12 days and we have non-perishables usually stocked up pretty good. The winters here get pretty cold and you don't always want to go to the store. So, it became kinda habit."

He sticks out a thumbs-up and smiles wide. "Affirmative, boss lady. No food, only guns." And Cole strides off to the black truck.

She hears Clint laughing lightly. "Sorry, my brother's kind of a dork."

"Kind of?" She replies and laughs back.

Logan laughs too and quips, "Maybe so, but that dork is one hell of a shot."

"Yeah he is!" Clint replies with a wide grin of his own.

Emily is distracted by movement at the end of her driveway and sees Dr. Lewis pushing the gurney with Bryan on it with the aid of Paul and his one good arm. Behind them she sees the nurses Anthony Nunez and Candice Campbell pushing the guy named Tim, who was still unconscious on his gurney and the teenager named Allison walking next to them. Her mind instantly shifts to Bryan to check up on him.

She looks in the back cab at Laura, then at Logan and he nods back to her. "I got her. Go check on Bryan and get them inside. We'll finish up out here." he says to her.

She smiles and nods back and goes to Bryan. Her heart sinks when she sees that he is still in his coma and hasn't woken up yet. She looks to Dr. Lewis as he stops in front of her.

"How's he doing, Dr. Lewis?" She questions.

"He's stable and there's been no change. At this point, no change is a good thing. Now where can we get him and our other patient, Tim, so that they are nice and comfortable?" Dr. Lewis questions.

She nods quickly. "Right. Let me go get the spare keys. I'll be right back." She turns to where their hide-a-way key set was. After a few moments, she has them out of the hide-a-way and is opening her front door. She instinctively goes directly to the alarm system and shuts it off, hearing it beep off and inactive.

Huh... power is still on here. I know we have solar panels like most of our neighbors, but I didn't think it'd still be on, since Erik didn't want to pay the extra cash for the batteries. The sun is still out though. She thinks as she flips a light switch on and sees the light come on. *Well, that's nice at least.*

Focus, Emily. Bryan. If this light works and the alarm still works, so should the garage doors. She thinks and then moves to the garage door.

Unlocking the door and moving into her garage, she hits the garage door opener and the garage door slowly opens. She watches as Dr. Lewis brings in her son with Paul. Nunez and Campbell follow them, bringing in an unconscious guy named Tim with a confused looking teenager following them. She holds the door open for them and steps off to the side.

“Straight through and past the kitchen is a den, next to the living room with the wood stove in it. That should be enough room for them. Move whatever you need to out of the way.” She says to them.

Dr. Lewis and the others comply and go in through the garage door into her house. She hears the squeaky sound of the wheels of the gurney hit her floor and she cringes at the thought of her tile floors being scratched.

Then thinking about how her son is on one of those gurneys, she admonished herself. *Screw the tile, Emily. Hell, screw the whole house. All I want is for both of my children to be alive and safe. Please wake up, Bryan. Come on sweetie...*

The second gurney passes her as she holds the door open. And then the teenager named Allison. This is the first time that Emily had gotten a close look at the girl. She looked to be close to Bryan’s age and was pretty. But her eyes went immediately to the side of her head that had recently been shaved. Even with hair beginning to grow back, she can still see the massive amount of stitches that were on the side of her head.

The teenager looks at her as she passes by her and Emily tries not to look at her injury and tries not to get caught looking at her injury. The girl stops in front of her and she doesn't know what to say.

“Candice and Anthony said this is your home.” She says, not really questioning her.

“Yes it is, and your name is Allison, right? My name is Emily.” Emily responds.

Allison nods. “Yes. And I’ve seen you around the hospital. Your son is the one... the one that is in a coma?”

Emily forces a smile. “Yeah. Bryan. He’s probably around your age.”

She points to the man named Tim on the gurney. “That’s Tim. I met him after my dad died. He stopped some guys from trying to take me and... you know...” She pauses for a moment. “They actually did this to me.” Allison finishes, pointing to the scar on her head.

Emily feels her heart break. “Oh, I’m so sorry, Allison.”

“Tim stopped them both and killed them. But he also got shot... I just wanted to say thank you for letting me and Tim stay here. I hope he’ll be alright. But I don’t think he’s doing very good at all.” Allison says to her.

Emily's heart breaks a little more. "Oh, of course. But you know we are only here for a night and my friend Logan is taking us somewhere away from people and it should be safer."

"Okay. Well, is it okay if we come with you, until Tim gets better?" Allison asks.

Emily's eyes begin to well up looking at the teenager with half her hair shaved off because of some assholes trying to do horrible things to her. "Of course, Allison. That was always the plan, to get everyone out of the hospital and somewhere safe, away from all of the bad guys. Now, why don't you go sit inside for a while. There's a bathroom right through there and a nice couch in the living room. Make yourself at home. We'll make up some food once we get everyone else inside."

"Okay. Thank you, Emily." Allison says in a small and soft voice and wanders into her home.

Emily wipes her eyes clear of tears, and follows them inside to go make sure her son is set up well enough.

Once reaching her den, she sees that Allison found and went into one of the bathrooms, and that the others were putting the gurneys in the den like she proposed. She helps them move some of the furniture out of the way to make room for the gurneys and for Dr. Lewis and the two nurses to be able to get around the two unconscious patients.

"Dr. Lewis. I just heard how Tim and Allison wound up at your hospital." She says to him.

"Yeah. That was one hell of a crazy story. The guy walks in carrying Allison in his arms. She was out cold and bleeding from a head wound. Turns out the guy had two GSWs in his abdomen. He told me quickly what happened to her, that he thought he killed the two guys that did it to him, and then he collapsed once he handed the girl over to us. The damn guy is a hero in my book. That was a few days ago, I think. I'm not really sure anymore. Time seems to kind of bend in on itself now." Dr. Lewis explains.

"Wow. And yeah. I know what you mean. Is he going to be alright, though?" She questions.

"Not sure. Dr. Calhoun did surgery on him and we've been pumping him full of fluids, antibiotics, and pain meds. He's in and out of it, and we were going to lower the dosage on the morphine to bring him back around, but then all of this happened. Thought it best to wait until we got where we were going. He should be coming around in the next few hours, actually." Dr. Lewis tells her.

"Okay, let me know when he's up and we'll find him some food. In fact, we'll get started on that once we get everyone inside and situated." Emily replies.

Dr. Lewis nods. "Sounds good to me. It's nice to be off the road and a good ways away from the Russians. I'll miss San Diego, but the San Diego we left was no longer my home."

"Agreed. And I'm super glad you're with us, doctor. Thank you so much." She responds. "Okay, I'll be back. Use whatever you need and let me know if you need anything."

"Will do. And thanks for getting us out of there in time. Glad to be along for the ride and have a purpose in all of this mess." Dr. Lewis answers.

You're a doctor. A real medical doctor. You're always going to have purpose. She thinks to herself.

"Thanks again, Dr. Lewis. For everything." Emily replies and then heads back out through the garage to her front yard.

Once back outside, she smells the familiar scent of the pine trees on her lot and in the surrounding neighborhood. It smelled like home.

Maybe we'll be able to come back someday. After everything is settled down and the government gets rid of those Russians and whatever else is under control. She thinks to herself as she looks over at Logan carrying a sleeping Harper, Clint with her sleeping Laura, and Cole carrying Diego, who was beginning to stir and wake up.

Walking up to her, Logan asks, "Where can we put the kiddos, Emily?"

Emily nods and points back toward the way she just came. "Straight through there, past the kitchen and living room, just past the wood stove is a hallway. Laura's room is the first one on the left. Down the hall from ours... I mean mine and Erik's" She says pausing. "Laura has a queen size bed in her room and all three should be able to fit. If not, Bryan's room is the third door on the left, if you need more room for them."

"Sounds good. We'll be back in a bit to hook up the trailer and then... I guess we'll take a break." Logan replies.

"Yeah, that sounds good. A break really sounds nice right about now. I'll go get the keys for the trailer and the locks and everything." She replies.

He smiles and then carries his daughter into her house through the garage. Clint follows, carrying her daughter, and she smiles at him and checks that she is still asleep. Cole follows last with Diego, who had fallen back into his slumber and is carried into the house without stirring.

They are out! And I don't blame them. It's been a crazy last couple of days. She thinks, chuckling to herself. *It's been a crazy ass last couple of weeks.*

She heads back inside to their key rack and grabs the trailer keys and heads back outside to their 30-foot Attitude trailer, grabbing an extra hitch and lock from the garage to attach to the truck.

Looking at the trailer, she remembers that they were still paying the damn thing off. They had the money to pay it off for years and only owed about $10,000 on it, but were still paying the minimum payment. Sometimes her and Erik would get into arguments over the interest being racked up and how much extra they were paying. She would argue that they should just pay it off and he didn't want to diminish savings with that kind of hit unless they had too. She and her husband were both smart with money. But she always went with his lead, since he never led them into massive debt and bad decisions before. Well, no real bad decisions aside from his damn receptionist, Stacy.

She walks over to the trailer and unlocks the hitch lock. She then puts the hitch on the truck and the locking bar through the hole, twisting it to the locked position. She heads back to the trailer, unlocks the door, opens it, and peers inside. It had that musky smell of not being used for a few months. It was summer time and they would be going out camping again in the fall and winter. Out to the sand dunes and other desert areas.

No more camping trips to plan, I suppose. Or is this just going to turn out to be one huge and long ass camping trip? She thinks to herself, looking around their trailer. *Well at least we don't have to worry about paying the damn thing off any more. Hell, does money really matter anymore?*

Logan startles her and she hears his voice behind her. "You okay?"

She jolts slightly. "Yeah." She replies as she turns to face him.

"Sorry, Emily. Didn't mean to scare you." He replies, as he scratches the back of his head.

She smiles at him. "It's alright, just lost in thought is all."

"Oh." He replies, obviously not wanting to press on whatever she was thinking about.

"I was just thinking about how I don't have to worry about paying this damn thing off anymore." She says with a smile.

He nods and grins. "Yeah. I guess not. Huh, I wonder if money really matters anymore. At least for a while, until things get to some sort of normal."

She laughs at him and shrugs. "I was thinking the same thing. Huh, weird."

"Great minds think alike." He responds.

She nods at him. "Alright, now let's get his trailer hooked up. You guide me in and we'll get everything ready to go for when we leave in the morning, and then we can make some dinner. I was thinking of spaghetti. I think I have enough of that stuff to feed us all. The bread's probably bad by now though."

"Wait. Are you sure you don't want me to back it in, and you guide me?" He questions.

She gives him a look and he raises his hands.

"Just asking," he answers.

She shakes her head and smiles. "Erik showed me how to do it and I actually do it pretty often."

"Fair enough, Emily. You back up the truck to the hitch and I'll guide you in." he replies.

She nods to him and goes to jump into the truck. After turning the engine over, she looks over her right shoulder and allows him to guide her in. She got it on her first try and smiles with accomplishment.

"First try, like a professional." She says to herself as she kills the truck engine and jumps back out of the truck.

"Damn, Emily. Nice. You weren't kidding. Didn't mean to doubt you. Just don't know many women that can do that." He says to her.

She laughs and says to him, "Well that'll teach you not to doubt me. Now let's finish this up and go make some dinner. Do you know your way around the kitchen and how to cook? I've seen you grill, but can you cook?"

He laughs back. "Now who's doubting who, Emily?"

She shakes her head, chuckles, and shrugs.

She smiles at her friend, Logan. Who now seems to be part of her new makeshift family, along with Harper, and the twins.

She heads over to help finish setting up the trailer for the morning and then she is determined to make some dinner and relax for the rest of the evening in the warmth of her own home. She knew they would all be a little scrunched with the thirteen of them staying under one roof. But she'd figure it out... she always did.

Chapter 21: Henry Torres

Day 13: Flagstaff, Arizona

Torres taps his throat mic. "Copy that, *Bleak*. I see the Russkies too. Let's try to just observe for now. But if you see any signs of aggression, weapons hot. Light those fucktards up. Hopefully we get some intel first though. I want to know why they're following those civilians."

"Affirmative, *Hawk*." Staff Sergeant Blake (aka *Bleak*) replies back over their comms.

"Copy that. Ready to get some Russian kills? Don't have any of those yet. Do you, *Hawk*?" Sergeant Jackson (aka *Thriller*) responds back over their comms.

Torres sighs. "*Thriller*, try to keep a clear fucking head. I'm all for enthusiastically meeting the enemies of the US of A and all, but there are civilians involved and I'd rather not have any of them die. And no. I have Commie kills, but no Russkies yet."

"Copy that, *Hawk*. Head fucking clear. Intel first... if possible, and weapons hot if anything pops off." Jackson replies.

Torres chuckles under his breath, laying low in a prone position on the crest of the roof next to the chimney, across the street from where they saw movement at the house in the far back, between two other residences. Blake was below him on the driveway, prone and underneath an old pick-up truck. Jackson was positioned at the corner house to the West, to his right.

Their focal point was the house tucked away in the back with a travel trailer. The house was dark but they knew there had to be people inside of it. That is where he had seen a figure walking out to the house on the right, their left, with no lights on. A few moments later, a figure walked back into the house tucked away in the back. The figure looked identical to the fist figure, looking to be a young male carrying a rifle. They knew it had to be a different person since they heard their chatter over the radio, for swapping out guard watches for whatever group was in that back house. A few minutes after their changing of their guard duty, had been when the Russians showed up, as they figured they would be. Lucky for the group of civilians in the back house, they were pitch black and quiet.

These civies don't appear to be too fucking dumb. They do have a rotating watch set up. But then again, they do have a team of fucking Russians about to knock down their doors. He thinks to himself.

The house to the left, his right, still had lights on and he wasn't sure if any civilians were inside that residence. This was the main focus of the Russians, with their two vehicles parked down the street and then spread out behind an ambulance and other vehicles in front of the only house with lights on.

He had known they were Russians from their own chatter on the radios. Captain Turner (aka *Hornet*) and 1st Lieutenant Sanchez (aka *Wiz*) had picked up on both groups' radio chatter while their Chinook was en route to survey the transmitter being pinged in this small residential area of Flagstaff, Arizona.

He clicks his throat mic again on their closed network to reach the pilots. "*Hornet*, this is *Hawk*. SITREP. Any sign of more incoming enemy forces? Over."

A moment later he hears Captain Turner come over their comms. "That's a negative, *Hawk*. From the sounds of it, what you have there is what you're going to get. *Wiz* also did a fly over with his MITAD, and didn't see any other hostiles in the immediate area."

Always with all the damned acronyms. Acronyms for this, acronyms for that. Torres thinks as he tries to remember that MITAD stood for Military Issued Tactical Aerial Drone.

"Understood, *Hornet*. Will update shortly. Be ready to provide support. Over and out." Torres replies back.

He looks over the six Russians that look well-equipped and not just like your regular soldiers. And it looked like they already had a civilian with them that they were talking to, and who was getting ready to literally go knock on the door of the house with the lights on.

Only six of them, but they walk the walk. Not your average Joe's, that's for fucking sure. Or your average Ivans in this case. He thinks to himself, surveying the six combatants, fully-geared up, and one even having an RPG on his back. Two were directly in front of him, behind the ambulance. Two off to the right, using the trees as cover, and the other two crouched in the hedges outside of the house where Torres believed there was at least one of the guards.

"Hey *Hawk*. If this is it, should we just drop the fuckers and be done with it? I mean, is that guy really just going to knock on that fucking door?" Jackson says over their comms.

"Hold, *Thriller*. Looks like they have one prisoner already. Let's assess and gather what intel we can. Any hostilities though... weapons hot. Kill them all, except their civilian prisoner. Now mouths shut, ears and eyes open, Rangers." Torres replies back.

Kid has a fucking point, though. Maybe we should just take out these Commie fucks here and now. But Command did say they wanted intel from the fucktards. But then again, I've not always been known for following the fucking rules. Torres smiles, thinking about how he wound up in Military Logistics for the U.S. Army as an Army Ranger, and within the last few years of his active-duty career, so close to retirement.

Henry (the *Hawk*) Torres had been a Ranger since he became an NCO some 20 years ago. He was originally an 11 Bravo, and whereas not every day was sunshine and fucking unicorns, he enjoyed what he did and loved being a Ranger. It was his childhood dream. There really wasn't another option for him growing up. Well, there were other options, of course, but not to him. It was always the U.S. Army and he was going to be a damn Ranger. As it turns out, it never got old for him. It was what he knew and he was good at it.

He didn't have a family, was an only child, and his parents died within a couple years of each other back when he was in his early thirties. It had been a hard hit, but they had him when they were in their forties, so he figured it was coming sooner or later.

He was transferred from the 75th Ranger Regiment in Savannah, Georgia, a couple years back. He had also figured that this was coming for some time, with pissing off all the *right* higher-ups, or *wrong*... depending how you're looking at it.

He did what he thought was right, and that didn't always line up with the progressive U.S. Army's idea of what was right and what was wrong.

They couldn't do too much to him, with him being a First Sergeant and with an outstanding record. But he knew he'd likely get transferred to some fucking desk job eventually, always going against the Brass and the ever-evolving politics of the U.S. Army.

Was he pissed and sour about it? Shit, yes! But what could he do? Orders were orders and he was only a few years out from retirement.

So, he was given orders to take over as the First Sergeant over some logistics POGs. He went to Fort Bliss and was attached to the Mobilization Brigade. It wasn't all bad over the last two years, and he sure as shit was still a Ranger through and through.

The Brass here left him alone for the most part and he only had to last another five years to retire at 30 years and go on to the next chapter of his life. He sure as hell didn't know what that meant. Maybe he would wander the U.S. like a freaking nomad or some shit. Maybe he would start up his own business, somehow. He always saw other Rangers and military elites starting up businesses. He especially liked a group of veterans that made their own brand of coffee. But then again, he knew jack-shit about making coffee. So that wouldn't work. Over the last two years in Colorado, with his life moving much slower than he was used to, he had more time to think, and he started thinking about writing. He didn't get around to putting the pen to paper, but he had some solid ideas.

All he had to do was stop pissing off the Brass for the next five years and he would be fucking golden with retiring at 48. Or at least not piss them off enough to push him out early.

That all changed 13 days ago with most of the world and all of the western world being hit with death clouds from the CWAs that took out close to 85% of the global population.

He had been one of the very few folks left standing and breathing at Fort Bliss when it happened. All around him he watched as men and women throughout the base dropped like flies. There were other survivors, but a lot of good men and women had died from those fucking clouds of death. One of his men, Specialist Conner, had survived along with him. Later they would find out it was because of their blood types being Rh Negative.

The retaliation from the North American Coalition had been swift and cut-throat, and Torres couldn't be happier with the end result. It sure as shit sucked that most of the world was dead now, but at least the sadistic and twisted fucks that did this shit were ground to dust and ashes.

He was close to hitting his breaking point, with cleaning up and taking care of his fellow fallen soldiers over the first week. Not really knowing Specialist Conner up until the attacks, the kid kind of grew on him. There was a dumbass Lieutenant Colonel that had survived on the base along with the other roughly 10,000 of them... out of around damn near close to the 80,000 military men and women and their families that were on the base.

The Lieutenant Colonel wasn't entirely a dumbass, having taken his advice to reach out to the surrounding areas and take in survivors to help establish some sort of normalcy and detour from the region descending into madness. Torres was thankful for that, because he had been to plenty of places where shit situations turned into straight fucked situations when people lost communications and what they knew as their normal ways of life. Lieutenant Colonel Thompson still fucking thought he knew it all and that his ideas were the best way to go. Yeah he was a Lieutenant Colonel, but the Army didn't always end up promoting the best guy or gal to the next rank. Then again, he probably thought the same damn thing about Torres, if he knew about his record of going against the Brass.

So, the second week was coordinated *search and rescues* of the civilian population around Fort Bliss. Torres was put in command of these operations, having plenty of field experience with his 20 years with the 75th. Of course, Torres had offered the idea, but Colonel Thompson played it off as his own.

There was some excitement with taking care of some of the folks that decided it was time they could do whatever they wanted since the U.S. was in complete disarray. But it wasn't anything that he couldn't handle, and he gained a liking to Specialist Conner. He ended up showing himself useful and adept.

That's why he insisted that Specialists Conner tag along with his little ragtag group that was given orders a couple days ago. A Chinook came in two days prior from his old stomping ground, Hunter Army Airfield. Apparently, they had taken a heavy hit as well, with their death toll around 90% of the base. The most intriguing aspect was that they had orders for him to get the hell out of Fort Bliss.

On the Chinook were the pilots, Captain Turner and 1st Lieutenant Sanchez, along with Staff Sergeant Blake and Sergeant Jackson. He knew who Blake was. She was a real piece of work and gained the callsign *Bleak* through her sheer determination to get the job done. She was a solid Ranger, but just needed to be reeled in every now and again before she did too much destruction. Sergeant Jackson was new to him, but was a Ranger and seemed capable enough. He seemed spry and full of piss and vinegar. The younger ones always were.

They were given orders to come over and pick him up, and go investigate the enemy threat to the west. High Command of the North American Coalition had intel that Russian troops were invading the west coast, conducting a scorched earth policy and slowly moving inland. Despite the enemy nations being nuked, their advanced elements had made their way to their destinations and were still carrying out their orders from dead command units.

Lieutenant Colonel Thompson had been irate with having to give him up. Torres found it fucking hilarious and was thankful to get the hell out of the babysitting and coddling operations. Luckily, one of the few higher ups still at Hunter Army Airfield was Rh Negative and he was a full bird Colonel, Colonel Briggs. He outranked Lieutenant Colonel Thompson and there wasn't a damn thing he could do about it.

Torres knew the hearts and minds thing needed to be done to restructure the U.S. But that wasn't his cup of fucking tea. Someone else would have to step up to babysit and coddle all those civilians that had become too complacent and reliant on the government and all the luxuries that America had before this World War III bullshit. He certainly didn't want to have to deal with teaching civilians how to take care of themselves.

Before leaving, he had asked Specialist Conner if he wanted to tag along. The kid practically jumped at the opportunity and Torres found himself happy to have the kid along. It was like training someone new all over again. And he sure as shit didn't want to see Specialist Conner get bogged down in all of the bullshit that was surely inbound for Fort Bliss. The kid showed talent and was made for the field, not some rebuilding and restructuring society bullshit. Again, someone else could figure out those fucking details.

Lieutenant Colonel Thompson sure looked pissed watching them take off in the Chinook heading for MCAS Miramar, in San Diego. Torres found himself smiling and saluting the dumbass as they left.

It took most of the day to get to MCAS Miramar. They refueled at Holloman Air Force Base, and then again at Luke Air Force Base. While in the air, they were scanning frequencies to pick up chatter and picked up a whole lot of it. There were mostly small pockets of survivors, some Russian chatter here and there, and they even picked up a ping of a tracker moving eastward on the ground.

The Russians had probably figured that everyone would be dead in the Great U.S. of A, so they didn't really hide their communications or tracking signals. Honing in on the frequency, they heard radio chatter from a small group of civilians heading to Flagstaff, Arizona. They didn't think much of it, other than the group having a tracker on them, until they heard Russian chatter heading in the same direction some hours later.

Reaching MCAS Miramar, Torres had figured the small element was following the civilians to their destination. After weighing their options and their mission to gather intel, he thought it best to take on a small element of Russians, instead of the massive Command element along the shorelines. Plus, he was simply fucking curious why the Russians would be following a group of civilians. He could also use this opportunity to capture one of the Commie fucks and gather the intel they needed on their enemy invaders.

They were already caught up with the *why*. The resources were here, and the American-Russian relations had been shit for over a damn century. But they needed to figure out the specifics of their plans… the *how*, *when*, and *what* they had at their disposal with their fucking Commie Motherland wiped off the face of the Earth.

So, they refueled at MCAS, and turned back around to Luke Air Force Base. It was his show after all, and Colonel Briggs had chosen him directly to gather intel on the invading enemy force.

Once refueled they headed into Flagstaff, landing in a field outside of town. Once on the ground, Torres left Captain Turner and 1st Lieutenant Sanchez with the Chinook, along with Specialists Conner to provide support for them. If shit went sideways, they'd come pick them up. He liked Specialist Conner, but he wasn't prepared for this kind of engagement just yet. He knew he could trust Blake, and she trusted Jackson, so that was good enough for him.

He trekked the quick five miles with Staff Sergeant Blake and the eager Sergeant Jackson, to where the tracker had finally stopped several hours before.

It was now into the early morning hours of day, still dark as death outside, and he could feel his body becoming stiff and he was reminded of how long he had been out of his old routine since being stationed at Fort Bliss a couple years ago. But his body would get used to it again quickly and he would do what needed to be done, as he always had.

"*Hawk*, permission to engage hostiles? And I did a quick cycle through the frequencies, and I heard the chatter from the group of civilians" Jackson says over their comms.

Looking through the scope of his suppressed rifle, he scans the area to see what Jackson was seeing that he wasn't. He had a different vantage point than himself and Blake. One of the Russians had moved off to the side of the ambulance and out of his view.

Tapping his throat mic. "What do you see and what'd you hear, *Thriller*?"

"One of these Commies is raising their fucking RPG and I think he intends to blow up that fucking house, First Sergeant… I mean *Hawk*. My bad. And I didn't catch the whole conversation, but it sounds like shits about to pop off. " Jackson replied back.

Fuck me. What did these civilians do to piss off these Russians, to travel all the way out here? And they seem quasi-prepared. What the fuck is going on here? He thinks to himself.

"Is their prisoner in the line of fire?" Hawk questions back.

"Affirmative, *Hawk.*" Jackson responds over their comms.

Shit. That's no fucking good. Fuck it. Let's get this party started. He thinks as he keys his throat mic.

"Engage..." Torres begins to say into his comms.

Torres then hears a man shouting in a thick Russian accent. "Goodbye, cowardly Cross! Die like the rest of the lazy American *pindos*!"

The shouting Russian is followed by the sound of an RPG launching followed by an immediate explosion of the projectile reaching its target... the house with the lights on. Then he immediately hears suppressed rifle fire from Blake below him, and assumes Jackson is engaging as well. An instant later, he hears the report of suppressed rifle fire, followed by the shattering of glass windows, and sees the muzzle flashes coming from the other house with the lights off. The house to the left of the house in the far back, where their guard watch was set up.

These civies have some fucking stones on them. I like them already. He thinks to himself.

He taps his throat mic. "Engage hostiles and fucking put them down. Do not engage the civilians in the homes. Stay put and do not move forward. We don't want to accidentally get picked off by possible friendlies."

Neither Jackson nor Blake responds, but he still hears the sound of suppressed rifle fire. He sights in and takes aim on one of the confused Commie fucktards already on the ground.

Ah, my first fucking Russian! He thinks as he sends an expansion round into the Russian's head, with it exploding into pieces.

The Russian soldier stops moving and squirming around on the ground and he puts a few more into the Commie bastard for good measure.

One down for sure. Five more to go. He thinks as he grins and takes aim again. *Fuck me! It's good to be back!*

He quickly rolls over to the cover of the chimney on the roof of the house as he feels roofing being hit and sprayed all around him. The Russians had already pinpointed exactly where he was.

Fuck me sideways. I am fucking rusty… either that, or getting way too old for this shit. He thinks, cursing himself. *Fuck the age and fuck being sore tomorrow. Time to knock off that rust. Let's party, you Commie bitches!*

Chapter 22: Nicholas Cross

Day 13: Flagstaff, Arizona

There's no fucking way that douchebag Petrenko is going to let me live through this. How the fuck am I going to get out this fucked up situation? Nick thinks to himself as he is walking up to the gray house with a dark red door. He was walking up to the house with the ambulance in front of it that the Russians followed all the way from San Diego. The group of people that he was forced to follow all the way from San Diego. Why the fuck did Lenkov make me come all the way the fuck out here? He must have known that Petrenko would try to kill me. Petrenko even joked on the ride over that Lenkov had given him orders to not kill me... yup, that point when that crazy Russian fuck was laughing about it, that's when I knew how fucked I was. Fucking shit. He thinks as he reaches the front door to the house with the lights on.

"Stupid fucking red door. All these pretentious fucks think their red door makes their home so damn welcoming and makes them stand out. Fucking idiots. It's not unique if everyone and their fucking mother has red doors." He says to himself with a half-smile, shortly forgetting how screwed he was as he rings the doorbell. "I sure as fuck hope that you died with the rest of the pretentious and holier-than-thou douchebags. Stupid fucking red door trend."

He waits for an answer at the door, hoping that there isn't one. He looked over his shoulder, seeing the shapes of what must be the Russians setting up for an attack, and he was between them and who they wanted to kill. Plus, he was pretty damn certain that Petrenko was going to kill him regardless.

How the fuck am I going to get out of this one? I survived almost two weeks in this global war bullshit, and half the time I've been with Lenkov and the rest of those crazy fucking Russians. What the fucking shit am I going to do? He thinks to himself, not wanting to ring the doorbell again, knowing that every second mattered at this point.

Nick had been back in San Diego for a few weeks. He had actually just gotten back from Moscow before that. He often went to Russia for his marketing job, and most of the time it was Moscow. He enjoyed getting out of the States and enjoyed Russia immensely. Nick admired the Russian *can-do* attitude and damn they knew how to drink, and the women were absolutely gorgeous.

When he found that they were the ones behind the CWAs, well at least one of the countries behind the start to this whole World War III end of the world bullshit, he was half scared shitless and half fucking excited. Was it scary almost fucking dying and most of the world dead and gone? Yeah, fuck yeah it was. But then again, he could now do whatever the hell he wanted and he enjoyed that.

Hell, he had just had one hell of a night when Lenkov and his Russian Army rounded all of them up. He definitely didn't mean to get caught up with the Russians, when he followed the instructions on the text messages. He just wanted to see what he could get for free out of the supposed support for American survivors. Sure, he had taken the opportunity provided by the death clouds to relieve some jewelry stores of their precious metals and gems, because why the hell not, and they would prove useful down the road. But he hadn't given much thought to long-term survival and his diminishing food situation in his luxurious 2,000 square foot apartment in San Diego. And all that loot was stowed away in his apartment, which was likely burnt down to the fucking ground now, because of those damn determined Russians.

Man, had that been a dumbass idea when he listened to the chick he hooked up with the night before about going and seeing what they were handing out. Her name was Cassie. At least that's what he thought her name was. That night, the night before he was captured, was still pretty damn fuzzy. He should have just let her go off and get killed by Lenkov and his army. But she was hot, and a nice piece of ass. So, he followed along with her, hoping to get some more of that sweet ass.

The look on *hot* Cassie's face was priceless, the second she realized that she and the others were dead as shit. In truth, it really didn't bother Nick much, aside from the fact that she was hot as hell and he wasn't into that whole necrophilia crazy ass shit. The only thing that mattered was that he was still fucking alive. Once he figured out a way to get the fuck away from the Russians, he would find another hot Cassie. He never really had trouble in the women's department, and now he got to use the whole "end of the world" card to pick up chicks. And it sure as shit worked well enough.

Nick knew it was only a matter of time before Lenkov got bored of him, or someone else killed him... like Petrenko. Shit, he was impressed with himself for surviving with those crazy fucks over the last week. But he knew he was walking a dangerous line and his days were numbered. Lenkov and the others always called him *Cowardly Cross.*

Every now and again Lenkov would admit that he was *clever* too. And he sure as shit was. He didn't get to where he was today without being clever and knowing how to play the fucking game to win. The game of life had changed drastically, but it was still a fucking game. Only now, he had the option of doing whatever the fuck he wanted. And if he was going to get back to doing whatever the fuck he wanted, he had to get away from this fucked up situation.

Nick looks back to the red door and a thought forms into his head. *Maybe this is my way out...*

He reaches for the door handle on the red door. *Please let this piece of shit fucking red door be unlocked.*

He clicks on the lever to open the door and finds that it presses down and he hears the clicking of the door being opened.

"Fuck yes." He blurts out.

He quickly looks over his shoulder, and is still holding the door closed.

What do I do now? He thinks to himself.

Thinking quickly, he nods.

If I can just get inside, maybe I can get away. Hell, maybe this Logan and his mini militia will handle my Russian problem for me. Shit, maybe they have hot chicks with them? There was a girl on the radio. He thinks as he pushes the door open, with the door opening inward.

"Okay, yeah. I'm coming in. If you have a gun. Don't shoot. I'm unarmed." He says loud enough for Petrenko and the rest of the Russians to hear.

He crosses the threshold of the lit-up house and doesn't see anyone inside. He takes several strides into the house, entering what must be the home's living room. He sees that there is a kitchen, just past a wall separating the living room from the kitchen, and another living space past the kitchen. Every single light that he saw was on.

"Hello? Anybody home?" Nick says aloud.

He pauses for a moment, listening, and hearing nothing but silence. He takes several more steps, getting closer to the kitchen area, seeing no one and no bodies either.

I don't think anyone is fucking home. But every single light is on. What the fuck? Who the hell does that?... Wait? Is this a fucking decoy? A damn fucking distraction, in case anyone comes along? He thinks and then hears Petrenko's voice from outside.

"Goodbye, cowardly Cross! Die like the rest of the lazy American *pindos*!" Shouts at him from outside.

"Fucking shit!" Nick blurts out and pushes his legs forward to try and run away from the front door, expecting a barrage of bullets to erupt.

He makes it a few steps and then hears a loud explosion and a wave of heat pushes him, picking his body up from where he was trying to run away. It all seems to happen in slow motion in his mind, but there's no sound. He can just feel heat and sees the far wall at the end of the living area, past the kitchen, getting closer. And getting closer real fucking quick.

His eyes go wide as he impacts with the wall with great force, knocking the wind out of him, and he can feel pressure and stinging needles on his back and on the back of his legs. He tries to open his eyes and his vision is blurry, but he thinks he can make out that he is on the ground and staring at a fireplace. Before he can figure out what is going on, his vision gets even more blurry and then it goes dark all together and there's nothing.

It's pitch black, dead silent, and before Nick succumbs to the darkness, he is pretty damn sure that he's dead, or at least about to die here shortly.

Stupid fucking red door. Good luck and welcoming, my fucking asshole. His jumbled mind thinks as he drifts off into the darkness and there are no more thoughts.

Chapter 23: Logan Miller

Day 13: Flagstaff, Arizona

"Logan... what should I do, man?" Cole says over the radio, not bothering to say *Over*, likely being too scared shitless with another group of Russians getting ready to try and kill them all again.

Logan shakes his head. *How in the hell did they find us? They had to have followed us, but how? We ditched our cell phones... How did they track us?*

Clint walks back into the front living room with Emily. Logan had been sitting in the dark in the living room as a last line of defense guard and had only been there for a few minutes. Cole had just swapped out Clint, and he had just swapped out Emily. Clint hung back to talk to Logan for a few minutes, and that's when Cole radioed that they had company... of the killer Russian variety. At least Cole was pretty damn sure it was the Russians. And so was Logan, but he just couldn't figure out how.

"What's going on, Logan??? Clint told me that the Russians followed us?! Are we sure it's them?!" Emily says to him, in a hushed but alarmed voice.

Logan scrunches his face with uncertainty. "Not sure who else would be setting up to mow us down in a hail of gunfire. It could be someone else, I suppose. But my money's on the Russians. I don't know how, but either way... we're in trouble again."

"Plus is though, they took the bait." Clint adds.

Logan nods and then looks at Emily. It had been Emily's stroke of genius to have them all go dark and use her neighbor's house as a distraction and even a decoy. She said she had seen it in some old movie when she was a kid. He couldn't lie, he was impressed. But he would be even more impressed if they made it out of this one unscathed.

"Do you think they'll go away once they find it's empty?" Emily questions.

He shakes his head. "Doubtful. They came all the way out here."

"Yeah... I figured as much. What should we do then?" She questions.

"Only thing we can do. Fight back and try not to die in the process. Our kid's lives depend on it. I doubt there are any damn lions to save our asses this time. So, it's on us." Logan responds.

She nods slowly and so does Clint.

"That's enough motivation for me." She replies.

"Yeah, screw these crazy bastards. Where do you want me, Logan?" Clint adds.

Logan sighs and looks around him, having already gone over the plan in his head if someone tried to attack them. He had just been hoping it was like that old drunk guy at Scripps Mercy, and not an elite and pissed off force of Russians.

"Same thing we talked about after dinner... Clint, meet up with your brother and wait for me and Emily to get set up. Unless you have to, wait until I fire. They aim in my direction and then you guys fire and we will do that back and forth. And... hopefully, we get lucky in this shitshow, and come out on top in the process." Logan says to them.

"Logan? What do you think our chances are of all of us making it out of this one? Or any of us?" Emily questions, in a calm and well-mannered voice for a mother with two children in harm's way, along with a whole group of other people in the back end of her house. The alarm in her voice had given way to some sort of chilly calmness.

He goes to open his mouth, but Cole comes back over the radio. "Hey Logan. They're sending some dude up to the decoy house. He looks like a normal guy. What should I do? Over."

Logan closes his mouth, thankful for having been able to avoid telling Emily the hard truth. He then raises the radio and focuses his attention on Cole and their makeshift plan to protect everyone inside.

"Copy that, Cole. Hang tight. Clint's jumping the fence around back and coming your way. I'm heading to your truck to use as cover, and Emily is posting up at the front of the house. Everyone else is moving toward the back. Give us a few minutes, and don't do anything crazy, Cole. Over and out." Logan says over the radio.

Logan looks at Clint and nods to him. Clint nods back and heads out the back of the house without a word. Logan then looks at Emily.

"Make sure they're all good back there, and if anyone gets past us... give 'em hell, Em." He says to her.

She nods. "You know I will, Logan. I know what's at stake here."

It was the first time he had called her Em instead of Emily, and he didn't know why he shortened up her name, like they had been friends for years or something. But it felt like it suited her and he didn't have time to think of it.

She looked at him with eyes of certainty and she didn't look scared at all anymore. It was dark in the house, but he could still see that look of steeled determination on her face. The air was still and he could smell her standing so close to him.

I hope I look as stoic as she does. Damn! Chances are though, I look like a scared man about to get into a firefight with bad guys that are way out of his league... because they are way out of my league. He thinks to himself.

He was damn impressed, because he sure as hell felt scared. His palms felt sweaty, and he shifted his newly acquired Russian PSA AK-V to his left hand while he wiped his right palm on his shirt and then did the same to his left palm.

Emily and Clint had shown them what they found in that big bag of goodies that they got from the dead Russians. The upgrade in weaponry was amazing and gave them at least somewhat of a chance against the threat outside. Clint had said it looked like there were seven of them, but that they were still outnumbered, with their numbers only being four of them fighting back, and the rest shielding the children and wounded. It really seemed like they were screwed for sure.

Logan sighs. *Can't think that way... but if something were to happen to me, all that matters is Harper.*

"Deal still stands right, Emily? Anything happens to me, you take care of Harper and get the hell out of here." He says to her.

She grins. "Only if you do the same thing for me, Logan. But don't think that way. Think positive. If you automatically think negative shit, then shit turns negative real quick.

His eyebrows raise. "Fair enough, Em. Think positive shit. Got it... wish me luck."

She shakes her head. "I wish us all good luck in this holy mess of a hell storm."

"Right." He replies and turns around, striding to the front door.

He quietly disengages the locks and slowly opens the door. Raising his rifle, he taps the button on the scope to turn on the thermal imaging. Emily may not have known what it was at first, but after all the video games as a kid and teen, he sure as hell did. So did Clint and Cole automatically.

He scans the area directly in front of the house through the pine trees. He can see several silhouettes of vehicles past the black F-250, which is blocking most of his field of vision. He doesn't see any heat signatures through the scope though.

Well, we know you're out there. But if I can't see you. You can't see me. He thinks to himself and dashes over to the cover of the black F-250, hoping that he's right.

Once crouched down, he creeps to the front of the truck and peeks around the vehicle. He thinks he sees movement and then moves back to the cover of the truck.

Careful Logan. This shit isn't like playing fucking Warzone back in the day. There is no respawn, or next round, or a gulag to get a second chance at. Well, these are Russians. There may be gulags eventually... Logan shakes his head. *Dammit! Focus, Logan!*

He then hears a doorbell chime coming from their decoy house. He shifts his AK-V and gets onto his stomach next to the front right tire of the truck. He maneuvers himself slightly underneath the truck and then raises his rifle to scan the area once more, careful not to expose the barrel of his AK-V.

Looking through the thermal option on the optic, he sees the bright lights of the decoy house in grayscale. The man at the front door is a figure of bright white.

Well, I guess it's kind of like playing Warzone as a fucking kid. He thinks with a grin. *Geez! It's almost like they were training us for shit like this.*

He scans to his right, shifting as he does. One of the tires, along with pine trees, is blocking his view of the ambulance in the lit-up house's driveway. Scanning more right, he sees part of someone crouched next to the ambulance in front of the house with Cole and Clint in it.

Shit. There's one of them. He thinks to himself.

He maneuvers his body on the cool cement more beneath the truck to angle himself to the right, where he thought he saw movement moments before. Sighting back in on the AK-V, he quickly sees figures in the bushes along the border between Emily's home and the house with Clint and Cole in it.

Well shit on a stick. There's two more. But I'm betting Cole and Clint have them already in their sights. I mean, shit. They're practically out in the open out there, at least with these scopes and them all focused on the house with the lights on. Lucky for us, they're overconfident and think they have us already. Fucking lucky as shit, but I'll take some luck at this point. He thinks to himself as he maneuvers back to aim at the figure that he can only see part of, who was crouching.

I'll go for this guy, Cole and Clint take out those two. Well, hopefully they're thinking the same damn thing as I am. The guy ringing the damn doorbell doesn't seem to be armed at all. So that leaves three more. He thinks to himself as he hears a loud explosion off to his left where the guy ringing the doorbell just was.

"What the shit was that?" He mutters to himself.

He hears the sound of the suppressed rifles coming from his right, along with the shattering of glass windows from the house they were using as their guard house.

Dammit! That must be Cole and Clint, thinking that was me or some shit. He thinks and then quickly scans over to where the two figures were in the bushes.

He sighs in relief seeing the two figures on the ground. One wasn't moving, but the further one was starting to get back up.

What the hell? He thinks as he sights in and fires off a round at the wounded Russian.

His shot hits home, putting the Russian back down on the ground. Logan waits a moment and watches as the guy starts to get back up again.

No fucking way, what the... he thinks and watches in amazement as the man's head is bright white and then the head is gone. There was a quick spray of head pieces, but the head was bright white through the optic and then it just wasn't there anymore.

Murderous sons of bitches must have body armor on. Shit... of course they do. But it looks like their heads aren't bulletproof. And like someone out there is on our side. He thinks to himself, and then shifts his focus to the front of him, seeing and hearing the battle escalate.

Shit, they have the twins pinned. He thinks as he sights in on the figure that was crouched and only half visible, but now he can see the whole silhouette.

He aims in the lower half of the figure. *I bet you don't have body armor on your asses, douchebags!*

He releases the trigger after a few rounds leave the barrel, and sees the figure fall back. He looks through the optic to see that the figure was a woman, on her back and screaming out in agony. He didn't notice before, and had just assumed that it was a guy.

Holy hell is that a girl? You have gotta be shitting me... he thinks, focusing on the bright white head of a woman screaming through the scope.

An instance later the screaming is gone, along with the screaming woman's head. It was there one second and gone the next, just like the guy that kept getting up.

What the hell is going on? Is that us? I didn't think that our guns could blow off heads like that. Someone is out there, and they're on our side! He thinks as he hears the firefight rage on.

He then feels concrete chipping up at him, and dust flying into his eye. He squints and tries to regain focus and the reality of the situation settles in.

Aw shit! They found me! He thinks as he scoots back quickly and uses the front right tire to block his body as the F-250 takes a barrage of gunfire.

He can feel his heart pounding and it feels like it is going to come right out of his chest, like in the super old movie, *Temple of Doom*. His vision goes slightly blurry with stars forming in his field of vision. He tries to calm down his breathing as he checks over his body to see if he was shot anywhere.

Not feeling any pain, or any holes in his body, he breathes a quick sigh of relief.

Focus, dammit! This ain't over yet! Three are down and there are still three left to go! Focus, Logan! He thinks to himself.

The rapid succession of gunfire coming from the house with the twins in it brings his mind back to attention. He creeps around to the front end of the truck again. He peeks out, seeing that the Russian's attention was now focused on Cole and Clint. He raises his AK-V to sight in on the two Russians in the driveway, now making an advance toward the twins. He looks past them and sees a guy who looks like he's holding a rocket launcher, aiming at the twin's house.

You have got be fucking shitting me! He yells inside of his head.

An instant later he hears glass shatter from the house behind him, Emily's house, the house with Harper, Diego, Laura and everyone else inside of it. The sound of suppressed rifle fire comes from one of the front windows of the house and Logan looks over to see muzzle flashes from the window.

"Oh no." He mutters and looks over to the two Russians in the driveway. One was now down, and the other was shifting to aim at Emily and the others in the house.

An instant later, the Russian is thrown toward them, getting hit from behind, and Logan sees a smoldering hole in the man's back, as he comes to a stop not too far away from him, toward the tailgate of the now shot-up F-250.

Who the hell is out there? Because that sure as shit isn't us. He thinks and then remembers the guy with the rocket launcher. *Oh shit!*

He shifts his aim and sees the guy now shifting his aim toward Emily and the others.

A feeling overcomes him. A feeling that he isn't used to. He felt hot, alert, and something that can only be described as pure fury. It wasn't exactly like seeing red. At least he didn't think it was, with having been training for years and always taught to trust your training instead of being one of those guys that "saw red" and thought they could do unimaginable damage. No, this was different, and pure fury seems about right. He was alert and felt warmed up.

His mind flashes to an image of Kelsey, and then her grave on that hot sunny day in San Diego, California. The next image that crosses his mind has multiple other freshly dug graves next to Kelsey's. Only this time, they all have grave stones on them now. He sees names on several of the gravestones... Kelsey Miller, Emily Collins, Laura Collins, Bryan Collins, Diego Cruz, and Harper Miller.

His eyes go wide, as he watches the man with the rocket launcher move in what seems like slow motion.

"NOOOOOOOOO!" He screams out and unleashes what is left in his magazine at the man with the damn rocket launcher.

After several rounds hit the man all over, the man stumbles and Logan keeps firing. He can feel something that he had never felt before boiling up inside of him. That feeling of alertness and being warmed up was still there, but he felt aside himself and still that feeling that could only be described as pure fury. He steps out from the cover of the truck and launches more bullets from the barrel of his AK-V. He strides forward, firing several more rounds at the man as he fumbles and begins to collapse. He looks down to see one of the Russians bleeding out several feet away from him, not having realized he walked into the middle of them. He aims his barrel down, without thinking, sending some more bullets into the already dying man.

He looks at the man that is face down, off to his left now, with a gaping and smoking hole in his back. He aims at that guy next. But nothing happens as he pulls the trigger. He hits the magazine release button, and lets the mag drop to the cement, reaching for one of two more jammed into the pockets of his shorts. He flips it around with his freehand, jams it into the AK-V, and slams the bolt home.

He knew that he must have looked aloof, walking around in the middle of a firefight in tennis shoes, shorts, and a t-shirt. Only this time, he was wearing the vest he had picked up off that cop car back in the first couple of days. But he could give two shits less what he looked like. Hell, he wasn't even thinking, really. Something else had taken over and he was just along for the ride, looking through his own eyes from what felt like a third-person point of view. He knew his actions were his own, but he was simply doing, not thinking.

He points the rifle at the already dead Russian with the hole in his back and commits to putting several more rounds into him. He then raises the weapon to look through the optic, sighting back in on the dying Russian with the rocket launcher. As he looks at the man leaning up against the ambulance on his ass, he can see that he is trying to raise the rocket launcher again.

"Just fucking die, you sack of shit! And leave us the fuck alone!" He yells, as he sends more bullets flying from his AK-V toward the Russian who is refusing to die.

After a few moments, his AK-V stops firing and he looks over the jammed rifle, trying to figure it out. He tries to clear it but then gives up and tosses it to the ground. He instinctively draws his Glock G45 from his hip, and aims toward the downed Russian by the light from the burning house, aiming at the downed Russian that looked to be dying but was not quite dead yet.

Logan registers that he sees a bright flash in front of the dying Russian, but doesn't have time to process it. The next thing he realizes is that there is a flash of fire, massive amount of heat, and splintering wood flying everywhere. It is then that he notices that his Glock is no longer in his hand and he's flying backwards. No, being thrown backwards by some sort of explosion. He feels the wind leave his body, being knocked out of him as he hits something behind him, and then he feels it give and his body pushing through it.

The next thing he knows, he is looking up at the night sky. He can see pines reaching toward the stars, and the night is clear, with him being able to see stars.

What was I doing just now? He thinks, dazed and confused, from the blast and being hurdled through the fence line.

He tries to push himself to get up, but feels his body is sore and tired. He lets himself just lay there. The world is silent around him, and he looks back up to the overarching pine trees and the stars far above them and him.

Maybe, I'll just lay here for a minute longer? What was I doing anyhow? He thinks, trying to focus his mind.

It seemed important, but I can't remember for the life of me... was I drinking? I don't feel drunk. Oh man, if I am... Kelsey is going to be pissed if I passed out in the backyard. But wait... we don't have pine trees in our backyard. Where the hell am I? Is that a fire I smell? He thinks, straining to look around him.

A face then comes into view. It was the face of a woman. She had red hair, and what looked like green eyes, in the dark of the night. Yeah, they were definitely green. He could tell with the background of the campfire. He felt a sense of calmness and something else overcame him looking at the redheaded woman.

Campfire? Am I camping? Who is this redhead? Something familiar about her. Something happy and sad about her. He thinks as he watches the woman say something to him, but he can't hear a word she's saying.

Then he sees Harper's face come into view.

Harper! He thinks and winces as he smiles. He tries to say her name, but he doesn't hear his voice. Only in his head.

She was crying and he couldn't for the life of him figure out why. Harper then throws herself on top of him and he feels pain shooting through his body, igniting his senses.

"Logan! Can you hear me?!" The redhead yells at him. He could hear her now but it still sounded muffled to him. Like behind a wall or like he was under water and she was talking to him from above the surface.

Her name is Emily. He thinks, his mind coming back to him. *Emily Collins... Em.*

"Daddy! Don't die! Please don't die! I can't lose you too, Daddy!" Harper yells at him, while she is gripping to his chest for dear life.

Lose me too?... Oh no... Kelsey. He thinks, beginning to remember what happened close to two weeks ago.

"Oww, kiddo. You're squeezing too tight." He says to her and she seems to hear him.

"Daddy!" Harper yells again, now with her face in front of him, tears streaming down.

"Logan! Are you alright!?" Emily says to him, now sounding much less muffled.

He strains to sit up as Harper backs up, allowing him to prop his arms behind him like he was on a shore somewhere. But to his amazement, he was looking at several fires past Emily and Harper through a fence line. And his body felt like he was hit by a truck. Or maybe hit with a rocket and thrown through a wall.

His mind races and catches him back up to the present, and he looks around him.

"Holy shit, did we win? And did I just get hit with a fucking rocket and not die?" Logan blurts out.

He focuses on Emily and Harper next to him, with Cole and Clint walking up to him from the back of the house they were in, and there was another man with them. He was in what looked to be a military set up, and he was carrying one hell of a big ass gun.

"Yes, I think so, Logan. With the help of Mr. Torres here and his friends." Emily says to him.

Harper grips him in an embrace again. "Dad! I'm so glad you are okay. I thought you'd died!"

He chuckles. "I'm alright kiddo."

At least, I think I am. He thinks to himself and starts to pat over his body with his left hand. *I'm sore as hell and feel like shit, but I don't feel any holes. Is anything broken though?*

"Let dad try and stand up, okay kiddo." He says to his daughter and she releases him and backs away slightly.

He attempts to stand and his legs tremble as he comes to his feet. He felt pain shooting through his entire body, but nothing felt like it was about to fall off. He was just in a shit load of pain. Like he just went through a damn wall or something. In reality it was really just a fence line.

Emily and Harper both come to his aid as he forces himself to stand. Harper is on his right, holding him around the waist and Emily has his left arm around her and over her shoulder, bearing some of his weight. He could smell the mixture of sweat and her scent. It smelled nice. Along with the smell of burning wood. Almost like they were all just camping out in the woods. His mind began to drift out again until she spoke.

"I don't think standing is the best idea right now, Logan. You were lucky not to get hit with that damn rocket, but it did send you flying through that fence." Emily says to him.

"I'll be fine, Em." he says, forcing a smile, and not sure if he was lying or not.

"All the same, we should have Dr. Lewis take a look at you. And I'm sure Mr. Torres probably wants to talk to us about what's been going on. He's with the Army." Emily replies to him.

"Yeah, dad. Have Dr. Lewis make sure you're not dying." Harper adds.

He chuckles at this, feeling pain in his chest. "Roger that, kiddo. Will do."

Cole, Clint, and the Army guy, Torres, reach them.

"I'm starting to get why those Russian bastards were referring to you as the American Cowboy. You're Logan, I'm guessing. I'm First Sergeant Henry Torres with the U.S. Army, or what's left of it anyways. You can call me Henry or Torres. Whichever is fine by me." First Sergeant Henry Torres says to him with an outstretched hand.

Logan reaches out his own hand, and winces in pain as he does, but still shakes the man's hand. "Nice to meet you Henry. And yes, I'm Logan, and I'm guessing you were the one shooting with that big ass gun of yours."

First Sergeant Henry Torres looks him in the eyes and then he sees the rugged and rigid face of the man turn into a wide smile. "Nice to meet you, Logan. Damn impressed you survived that! Hell of a show to watch!"

Chapter 24: Emily Collins

Day 13: Flagstaff, Arizona

Emily helps Logan walk back into the house where Dr. Lewis is in the back with the rest of their group. Harper was on the other side of Logan, helping him walk as best as she could. He wasn't complaining, but he was wincing with every step. She knew he had to be in pain, having gone through a fence line, launched backwards by some sort of rocket launcher.

A freaking rocket launcher?! Seriously?! When are we going to catch a break? I really hope that it stays quiet for a while now. But how the hell did they find us? She thinks as she goes through her kitchen toward the back of her home. *We certainly can't stay here any longer. That's for sure.*

Reaching her further back living room, next to the fireplace, she sees Candice tending to her Bryan and Anthony checking over the guy named Tim who had saved Allison.

Seeing Dr. Lewis overseeing the two nurses, she looks around for Laura and Diego and doesn't see them, along with the teenager with the scar on her head, Allison.

She looks to Dr. Lewis. "Dr. Lewis? Where are the children?"

Dr. Lewis looks up and sees them halfway carrying Logan as he struggles to walk.

"Logan! Are you injured? What happened? Were you shot? Where does it hurt?" Dr. Lewis replies, ignoring her question.

She hears Logan chuckle lightly and then feels him wince again. "It hurts just about everywhere, doc. I don't think anything is broken and I don't think I have any new holes, but I'm hoping that you have some killer pain meds left on you. My head is hurting like a son-of-a." Logan replies.

He was covered in scrapes, bruises were already beginning to form, could have broken something, probably had a damn concussion at the very least, and here he was making jokes. He did still smell nice though. She caught herself wondering if he always smelled this way or if only after a gun battle with killer Russians. She found herself grinning and shaking her own head.

"Always with the jokes, Logan." She replies.

"He got hit with a rocket and went through a wall." Harper blurts.

"Oh, dear Lord. What? How are you still alive?" Dr. Lewis responds.

"Not exactly hit with a rocket but pretty damn close. A rocket launcher hit one of the pines out front and sent Logan here flying through the fence line. He's still pretty dazed and wobbly... but seriously Dr. Lewis, where are the children? Where's Laura?" Emily chimes in.

"Over here, ma'am! They're in this room and I'm looking over them. They're doing fine, all things considered." The patient named Paul says, as he leans up against a wall with a rifle tucked into his shoulder and the barrel aimed at the ground, using his only good arm, since his left was still broken and in a cast.

She nods to him. "Thank you Paul! Were there any issues with them?"

He shakes his head. "Aside from the invading Russian douchebags, nope. They were quiet as mice. Kinda creeped me out actually. Kids not crying or screaming with a battle raging at your front door. But I just checked on them. They're all sitting on the floor against one of the walls and all kinda stared at me as I peeked in on them."

She nods back. She was really starting to worry about how accustomed all of the children were becoming to the constant chaos. But that would have to be something to deal with another day.

"Thank you, Paul. I truly appreciate it." She says to him.

He smiles at her and Dr. Lewis interrupts their conversation. "Now, if you don't mind, let's get Logan down on this couch over here. I need to take a look at him. We need to make sure that there are no internal injuries."

"Okay." She says as she and Harper help Logan onto the couch and he lies down. She watches as he winces a few times and jolts as pain must be striking through his body.

I hope you're alright, Logan. We already have a good amount of us injured and wounded. She thinks and then looks at her son.

"Dr. Lewis. How's Bryan doing?" She asks him.

Beginning to look over Logan, he speaks to her. "He's stable and hasn't changed. But I can't say the same for Tim. His vitals are beginning to drop, and I'm concerned."

She looks to Bryan and then Tim, thankful the bad news wasn't about her son. But then felt bad for not caring too much about the man that risked his life to save a teenage girl from unspeakable horrors.

She then sees First Sergeant Henry Torres walk into her home with Cole and Clint ahead of him.

"Is he going to be okay, Emily?" Clint asks.

"I'm sure he's going to be fine, Clint. The dude walked away from a rocket attack, like he was a freaking terminator or something. Did you see his crazy ass out there?! He went full throttle kill-mode for sure!" Cole replies to his twin brother.

Emily smiles, and shakes her head. "Dr. Lewis is looking him over, now."

She looks at the rugged looking Army man. He was older than her. Maybe a decade or so she would guess, but he looked like the world had aged him much further than that. It wasn't so much gray hair or looking old and frail. He looked strong and good for what she guessed was pushing 50. It was in his eyes and face. He looked rigid and rugged. He didn't look tired though.

He nods to the twins. "That's for damn sure. But how the hell do you boys know what a terminator is? Those movies were before my time."

"They made more than one, First Sergeant." Clint replies.

Cole chuckles. "Yeah, more like 20 of them, First Sergeant."

Emily sees the Army man give them a confused tilt of the head, like they said something off or wrong.

"Our dad was in the Navy for a long time." Clint adds, catching on to his confusion.

"Ahhhh. It all makes sense now. Got it. Good to go. Good shit." Henry Torres replies, and then looks around. "Is he around here too?"

Cole and Clint both shake their heads and don't answer.

"Oh. Sorry boys. I didn't mean to..." He begins.

"It's okay. A lot of people have lost people these days. Logan and Emily here took us in and we decided to go with them to the Grand Canyon." Clint replies.

"Yeah, we have all been in San Diego since the start of it. We lived there for years, but Logan and Emily's families were just visiting the area when it all went to shit." Cole adds.

"Oh, I see. And these Russians followed you all the way from sunny San Diego?" The Army man replies.

"Yeah, how the hell, man?!" Cole questions and looks over at Clint.

"Not a clue, brother." Clint replies and shrugs.

"Yes, Mr. First Sergeant Henry Torres. We were thinking about that too. We aren't quite sure how they did that." Emily replies.

"Well, we know how. They put a tracker on one of your vehicles. One of my men found it on that shot up ambulance out front, next to the dead Russian with the RPG. He was dead when we came upon him. Good riddance, but their prisoner that we pulled from the wreckage of the house next door let us know that they were tracking you all... and Henry or Torres is fine by me, ma'am." He replies.

"Wow, um, Henry. You guys work fast. They put a tracker on us and they had a prisoner?" Emily responds, astonished at how much he knew that they didn't.

"Huh. Maybe they did it when we ran into those lions, back in S.D. We did see those other headlights turn up as we were racing out of there when those lions were saving our butts and eating those crazy Russians that were about to kill you and Logan." Cole says, turning to look at his twin brother.

"Yeah, they did. That was scary as shit. I wasn't sure if they were going to try and eat us next or what the hell was going to happen. Freaking wild, man." Clint replies, scratching the back of his head.

"You got to be screwing with me. Real shit lions ate the Russians." Henry replies and then looks back to her. "Sorry ma'am."

She smiles. "You can swear, it's not like I don't cuss, Henry. I'm a woman, not a nun. I just try not to do it so much around the children." She says looking over her shoulder at Harper hovering over Logan, with Dr. Lewis still examining him.

"Fair enough." Henry says to her and then looks over at Harper and Logan, and then looks to Dr. Lewis. "Hey Doc, after you finish checking out *Wyatt Earp* over here, can you take a look at their prisoner? He looks okay, for the most part but is pretty banged up. He is complaining about his ribs and right arm though..." Henry then looks at Logan on the couch. "But shit, Logan. You went up against a rocket launcher with a damned side arm and fucking won. Call me impressed. That was some Wyatt Earp shit. Well, if they had rocket launchers back in the Wild Wild West."

I'm still surprised he made it through that too. She admits to herself.

She looks to Logan on the couch, who focuses on them but still seems pretty dazed. "To be honest, it's all kind of a blur right now. I just remember being worried about Harper, Laura, Emily, and everyone else back in the house... and then there was fire and flying. And now here I am."

Geez. Dr. Lewis must have already given him pain meds. He's pretty damn fuzzy right now. She thinks to herself.

Henry chuckles. "There was fire alright. Haven't had that much fun in a damn good minute. And it sure as hell was fun as shit to watch you all in action. And civilians nonetheless. Once again, I am impressed with you all." Henry replies with a long whistle afterwards.

She turns to look back at Henry and gives him a look, which he must have registered.

"Sorry, ma'am. Didn't mean nothing by it. I'm just an old Ranger. And just damn impressed is all." Henry says to her, as he puts his hands on his hips. "Going against those Spetsnaz... Well, let's just say that not everyone can pull it off. Good on you all."

She nods to him and smiles. "Well, thank you Henry. I just wouldn't call what we went through as a *fun* time. I'm sure the only reason we were able to pull it off was because of you and your Rangers. So, thank you. But you said there was someone else injured? A prisoner?"

"Yes, ma'am. The guy says his name is Nicholas Cross. And we pulled him from the rubble of that house next door." Henry says to her and then looks toward Dr. Lewis checking over Logan.

She looks back over at Dr. Lewis as he looks up and looks back at Candice and Anthony. "Campbell, Nunez. Would you two mind going and checking on the gentleman outside before we move him. Not much we can do for Tim but wait, and Bryan is stable... for now."

That last part stung Emily, hard. *"For now," is not a good sign.* She thinks to herself.

She looks at Bryan, and watches as Candice and Anthony both make their way toward her, the twins, and Henry Torres.

"Where's this guy at?" Anthony asks.

"You two doctors too? Wow, imagine that luck." Henry questions.

"Nope, but we are nurses, sir." Candice replies.

"Is that good enough for you?" Anthony chimes in.

Henry laughs. "Yup. More than good enough for me. Meant no harm by it. Just thought it pretty damn stunning that you all have a full medical team in your group. And I'm not a Sir. I work for a living." He says, winking at Anthony.

Anthony tilted his head in confusion for a moment. She didn't understand what he meant by the last comment either. But she did recognize when men were doing their manly intimidation bullshit. She had seen Erik do it all too often. And she was betting that this guy Henry would end up winning this intimidation game. He didn't look like someone you wanted to cross.

"Emily, we're going out there with the First Sergeant. He said he has more of his men coming in on a Chinook, and we want to see that." Clint says to her.

"Shit yes, we do." Cole chimes in with a grin.

"We'll find out what we can from their prisoner dude and whatever else we can." Clint adds.

"Okay. You boys did amazing out there. Thank you very much!" She says as she walks over and hugs each of them and gives them a peck on the check.

Each of the twins blush afterward and smile.

"Of course, Emily. Glad we could help." Clint replies.

"And glad we all didn't die." Cole adds. "And we saw you being a badass out there too. Mowing down those Russians through a window. Pretty badass yourself, Mrs. Collins." Cole replies, smiling and scratching the back of his head again.

She smiles back at the twins, who had followed them all the way from their home. She hadn't known them very long at all, but they felt like instant family. Like her own little brothers or something.

"Alright boys, have fun with your helicopter and find out whatever you can. We need to be leaving sooner rather than later. I'll be out there in a bit. I need to check in on Laura." Emily replies.

"And truly, thank you again, Henry. I don't know what we would have done if you and your Rangers hadn't shown up." Emily says to Henry.

"Of course, ma'am. Fighting enemies, foreign and domestic, is what we do. Looks like there'll be a lot of that from here on out. Glad we could help and you all are alright." He says back to her.

She nods at him. "You're probably right about that, Henry."

He's rigid and rough around the edges, but seems like an all-around good guy. He sure as hell came to our rescue. I don't think all of us would have made it out of this one without him and the rest of his Rangers. She thinks as she looks back over at the dazed and drugged up Logan laying on the couch.

"Alright then, ladies and gents. Let's move out." Henry says and the rest of them follow him out of her home.

She could have sworn she heard Anthony muttering something. He must have because she did for sure hear Candice *hush* him.

Men, with their manly games. She thinks, shaking her head.

She looks back to Logan, Harper, and then Dr. Lewis. "How's he doing Dr. Lewis?"

"Well. He definitely has a concussion, so we shouldn't be moving just yet. Nothing looks broken. But he's going to be sore for a while. I gave him some pain medication that is already kicking in. He shouldn't fall asleep for at least several hours and then if he does doze off, wake him up every couple of hours. I can't do extensive testing, so better safe than sorry. He's very lucky though." Dr. Lewis says and then looks down at Harper hovering over her father. "If I'm being honest, I'd like to give him the day."

So, It looks like we won't be leaving today then. Hopefully, there won't be any more damn Russians. Or at least Henry and his Army guys are sticking around for a little while. She thinks to herself with concern.

"Okay, Dr. Lewis. Thank You. Thank you for everything." She replies.

He nods and smiles. "Of course. It's what we do, Emily. We did take the oath, after all."

She smiles back at him and puts her hand on his shoulder as she walks past him to go check in on Laura, along with Diego and Allison.

"And thank you for standing guard of our little ones." She says, reaching Paul in the hallway.

"Of course, ma'am. Least I can do. Got to make myself useful somehow. You all are the ones fighting off Russians and whatnot. Shit. I wish I could do more." Paul replies.

"Oh, don't worry. I have a feeling there's still a lot to do in the coming days. In the coming weeks and months, actually." Emily replied

He shakes his head up and down in understanding. "Yeah. You've got a point there. Life ain't getting back to normal anytime soon."

She thought about this as she walked past him and reached Laura's room where all of the children were... except for Bryan. She turns the doorknob and feels her heart swell, seeing Laura sitting in the middle of the three, with Diego to her left and Allison to her right.

"Hey guys. How are we doing?" Emily says.

The three kids just looked at each other and then back to her. Laura rises to her feet and runs over to her, giving her a huge hug. "Are you okay, mom?"

"Yeah, sweetie. I'm okay. How are you doing?" She replies.

"Good. Paul told us it was over and we won against the bad guys. Is Logan, Cole, and Clint okay? Harper ran out to check on her dad. I told her not to go." Laura says to her.

"It's okay sweetie. And yeah, they're okay. Logan bumped his head pretty good, but he'll be fine. Some Army guys showed up and helped us get rid of the bad guys." Emily explains to her, simplistically.

"That's good. I'm glad the bad guys are dead." Laura replies.

Glad they are dead? Wow. What is this world doing to my sweet little Laura? She thinks to herself, with worry.

She looks over to Allison and Diego. "How are you two doing?"

Allison gives her that blank and dull stare that she has and replies back, "Okay."

Diego doesn't say a word, but rises to his feet and walks over to her and Laura. He then steps off to her side and gives her a hug as well. She feels her heart melt at the poor kid opening up.

"You kids must have been so very scared. I'm sorry you had to go through that. Looks like we'll be here for one more day and then we'll head out to the Grand Canyon. Okay? I think the Army guys are going to stick around to help us out, for the day at least. And then we can go on our permanent vacation. Sound good?" She says to them.

Allison doesn't say a word but simply nods. As does Diego and Laura, who are still hugging her.

She hears footsteps behind her and turns to look over her shoulder to see Dr. Lewis coming into the room.

"Emily, you should come out here." He says to her.

"What's wrong Dr. Lewis? Is it Logan?" She says feeling her heart drop.

He shakes his head. "No. It's Bryan..."

Her heart sinks even further and she feels her knees go weak.

Oh no. Not my baby boy. She thinks to herself with tears welling up in her eyes.

"He's awake, Emily. He just woke up as you walked out of the room... and he's asking for you." Dr. Lewis tells her.

The dread of death drifts away as she feels ecstatic and pure relief. Now the tears do come flooding out.

"Really???! He's finally awake? Is he okay???" She says in a cracked and crying voice.

He nods with a thin smile. "Yes, Emily. Your son is awake and he seems to be doing okay. But I'll need to run some more tests."

Oh, dear Lord! Thank you! My son is alive and awake! She thinks to herself as tears are streaming down her face.

"Let's go see brother, sissy. Okay?" She says to Laura, looking down at her.

Laura looks up with wide eyes. "Okay!"

Her heart fills up with even more joy as she sees her daughter's face light up from news of her brother.

"Can I come too?" Diego questions.

She chuckles through her tears. "Of course, sweetie."

She looks over at Allison, who is now rising to her feet as well.

She laughs again with tears running down her face. The joy of having her baby boy awake. Even though he's a teenager now, he'll still always be her baby boy.

She looks to the ceiling above her, and pushes her thoughts to the sky. *Thank you! Thank you for bringing my baby boy back to me!*

Chapter 25: Logan Miller

__Day 14: South Rim of the Grand Canyon, Tusayan, Arizona__

Man, I feel like I was hit by a truck? How long am I going to be sore for? This is twenty times worse than those times that I slacked off from the gym and training for a while, and then jumped back like I was the frigging Hulk or something. Then I was sore for what felt like weeks. And even ten times worse than when I fell off that trail and tumbled for freaking 50 feet down a damn mountain! Man! I really hope it doesn't take as long as that time to recover from this. What was that, a couple months of healing time? And plus, I'm older now... getting older sucks. Logan thinks as he grimaces, looking out the window at all of the wilderness around them.

He shifts and adjusts in the passenger seat of their newly acquired Toyota 4Runner.

Screw it. May as well just start getting used to being sore all the damn time. These are shit times and the world is at war. So, I guess I should just be happy that I'm alive and well, and so is Harper. My body will either get used to it or it won't. Logan thinks to himself, trying to shift into a more comfortable position in the front passenger seat.

"Are we there yet, Cole?" He asks the driver of the 4Runner in a sarcastic exasperated tone.

Cole laughs. "Does it look like we're there yet, Logan? And you're the one navigating, now. You tell me?" He says back with a chuckle.

Logan laughs back and then winces. "Right. Valid point, my man, valid point. But to answer my own question, yeah, we are about there. I think we should be coming up on the South Rim Entrance."

Cole looks over at him. "What do you think we'll find? Do you think we'll be able to relax for a bit? Damn, I hope they have a pool."

Logan smiles at the young man. "Not sure. And I hope so, bud. But I don't remember the Southside Haven Lodge having a pool. I really didn't look for one though, so maybe."

"Well, as long as there aren't any Russians or anyone trying to kill us, I'll be happy with that." Clint says from the seat behind Cole.

"Yeah. Me too... me too." He responds back, looking back out the window.

The last 24 hours had been pretty eventful and pretty damn busy. Luckily they didn't have to deal with any more crazy, killer Russians. And they had made a few new friends. The big news was that Bryan, Emily's son, was finally awake.

Logan was a little bit fuzzy for the first part of the day, but refused anymore heavy pain meds after lunchtime at the Collins' home. It was truly a weird scene, once all of his senses came back to him. That and all of the pain.

He was banged up pretty damn good, and he was going to be banged up for a while. Dr. Lewis said nothing was broken, but he had minor scrapes and abrasions all over his body. He did say that he would be a little off for a few days and he wanted to keep an eye on him for his concussion. He sure as hell was lucky and happy for it. It was all kinds of a blur to him. He remembered up to the point of the rocket hitting the tree and sending him flying, and then something about a ball of fire and heat and him smashing into something hard. After that was stars and haze until the morning time.

What he did know, and what truly mattered, is that they had won their little battle. What was more surprising was that they were all safe and sound, aside from him being banged up and the twins having some scrapes and cuts from splintering wood and glass from the battle.

Thinking back, he could certainly recall being enraged and wanting it to be done. He remembered feeling scared as hell of losing Harper, Emily, Laura, and everyone else. And that fuel of fear pushed him into something he had never felt before. It was like pure fury, and he still couldn't really believe himself. He couldn't believe that he stepped out into the middle of gunfire, like some sort of lunatic.

Can't be doing risky shit like that again. Not if I want to see Harper grow up. Not if I want to make sure Harper gets the chance to grow up. This was one of the ongoing thoughts throughout the morning while he slowly came out of the drug-induced fog.

Harper had been by his side all morning. And Emily had been by Bryan's side all morning. She was ecstatic that her son was finally awake, and so was little Laura. He could only imagine how happy they were, and their joy brought back memories of his Kelsey and how much he wanted her to be here with them now.

After a good lunch, he felt a lot more like his normal self... along with all of his new aches and pains. He knew it would be more painful with not taking the pain meds from Dr. Lewis but it was better than being in the foggy haze. He wanted his mind clear, and if that included some pain... so be it.

As it turned out, the twins had been busy while he was out of commission in the morning hours. But that didn't surprise Logan one bit. They really were a useful pair and he was sure glad to have them at their side. Without them, they would likely have all been dead last night.

Well, them and their new friend, First Sergeant Henry Torres. Which he insisted either on Henry or Torres. So, Logan followed suit with Emily and called him Henry. This gained strange looks from his other men, with one of them actually being a woman. And they had one of those big ass helicopters with two rotor systems. When they introduced themselves to the group, the two pilots who went by *Hornet* and *Wiz*, told them that it was a Chinook. The soldiers under Henry went by *Bleak*, *Thriller*, and Conner. Logan knew they were nicknames when the others referred to Henry as *Hawk*. Except for Conner, Logan noticed. That name sounded like a real name. He didn't really care and in the end, it didn't really matter what their real names were. They had helped save their asses. Plus, they brought them up to speed on a lot going around in what was left of the U.S.

While Henry caught them up and gathered his own information from them, the twins went out with *Bleak*, *Thriller*, and Conner. They wound up finding the 4Runner to replace the shot up and mostly destroyed F-250. They were able to pack almost everything from the bed of the truck into the SUV, but whatever didn't fit was put in the Honda Odyssey van they had found to replace the ambulance that was shot up and had turned out to be the reason the Russians had been able to track them so far from San Diego, by the orders of the Major Michail Lenkov. And as luck would have it, the reason Henry and his group of Rangers had been able to track them too.

Which brought up how they found out about the tracker, the Russians, and the insanely obsessive and cruel Major Michail Lenkov... Nicholas Cross. As it turned out, Nick had been captured and forced to help the Russians with locating more civilians, since he knew how to speak Russian.

Logan wasn't too sure on how much he could trust a guy that helped the enemy kill Americans. But the guy had said he was forced to and they tortured him on a regular basis. It was hard to tell if he was telling the truth, since he was in worse shape than himself. As it turned out, a rocket was fired at him too. But with Nick, it had put half of a house down on him. Candice and Anthony had to work him over him pretty well, as did Dr. Lewis. And they did a damn fine job, as they always did. But Nicholas Cross sure as shit didn't look like he was having a good day. The guy ended up having a concussion, multiple large abrasions on his legs, a broken hand, and even a missing ear.

Logan had to admit. That part had to really suck, missing a damn ear. He still wasn't too sure about the guy. He seemed off and a little sleazy, having hit on Candice when the Rangers pulled him from the rubble, and Candice checked him out. Well at least, that's how Anthony told the story.

Time would tell about Nicholas Cross. Henry didn't have room for him on his mission, with being a civilian, but they did. And how could they say no? He was forced to help the Russians and he was injured. And it was clear as day that they intended on killing him with the rest of them. Maybe he was just in the wrong place at the wrong time and had a bad start of it all with this whole shit storm. If Logan was being honest, they all had a rough start of it with this shitstorm, and he was hoping they would find some peace. At least for a little while.

So, Nicholas Cross joined their makeshift group. He was in the back van, with Anthony and Paul. Dr. Lewis was in the Ambulance, ahead of the van, with Allison up front and the still unconscious Tim in the back with Candice looking over him. Emily was ahead of the ambulance, and behind them, with the rest of the kids and towing the trailer. Bryan was able to sit up and start moving around slightly. So he was in the front seat, with the seatbelt securely fashioned. Harper, Laura, and Diego were in the back seat. Logan was riding shotgun, with Cole driving, and Clint in the back seat as they neared the South Rim Entrance to the Grand Canyon.

Before they left the Collins home, likely for forever... Emily had told him how Diego had been opening up a little more and he had noticed it too, with the little guy talking more at lunchtime. He was glad that the little kids were all doing pretty well. Allison was still pretty quiet and standoff-ish, but she was still hanging around with the little ones and even checked in on Bryan every now and again.

Bryan, on the other hand, was super quiet and appeared to be taking in everything slowly. Whereas, they were all at the two-week-mark of this whole shitstorm of a new world, with now 85% of the world population dead along with multiple countries wiped off the map, and well into World War III... it was really only day one for Bryan, and he was just finding out how bad the world was. All things considered, he was taking it well enough for a 13-year-old kid. But he had certainly given Logan some looks when he had been talking with his mother later on in the day. Couldn't really blame the kid. To him, he was just some strange guy that his mom and his sister liked and trusted, and his dad was dead.

It had made him think back to when this all started two weeks ago. Watching the love of his life be alright one second, then the convulsing, and then the life quickly leaving her body. Leaving him here alone, to raise their daughter, Harper. Memories of his lost wife bring fresh stabs of grief to his heart. And his mind drifted to thoughts of her for some time after lunch. Thoughts of how they met, how they started a family, and planning for a much-needed vacation in sunny California. But he eventually had to push those thoughts away and focus on the task at hand.

In the early afternoon hours, Logan and his group parted ways with Henry and his group of Rangers. They shared what information they could, along with acquired supplies and weapons from the dead Russians. Logan had even gone as far as to tell Henry where they were going. He didn't see the harm in it, since they had saved their asses the night before. Plus, there could be the added bonus of them returning. Having some Army folks around could really step up their chances of survival. Henry was even forthcoming with where they were going too. Apparently, they were heading out to San Diego again. Some base called MCAS Miramar, to regroup and disseminate the information they acquired. In the end they wished each other luck and their group watched the Chinook take off and the group of Army Rangers continue on with their mission. The kids were excited and waved goodbye to the soldiers, and Logan had to admit to himself... it was pretty damn cool.

It was nearing dinner time on a mid-September day, driving through the wilderness. It was warm, but it seemed cooler than previous days for some reason. Even with it still being summer. Maybe it was the relief that they were alright and the Russians had no way of tracking them anymore. Maybe it was the relief and joy he found on Emily's face, with her son finally being awake. Maybe it was the simple fact that they had made it this far, and with most of them still alive.

Which, if Logan had been a betting man, he would have wagered there would have been a lot more deaths along the way if chance had not been on their side... after the death clouds, that is.

Damn! We really have been lucky with not dying and all. Plus, finding food and supplies, lions killing the freaking Russians when they were about to kill us, and a group of damn Army Rangers showing up to help us out in a battle with even more crazy ass Russians. Logan thinks to himself, lost in thought.

"Hey, Logan. Are you seeing this? What do you make of it, man?" Cole asks him.

"I don't know bro. Kinda looks like a road block. And is that a little kid with a rifle?" Clint chimes in, questioning.

Logan is knocked out of his thoughts and looks ahead to the South Rim Entrance to the Grand Canyon.

"Sure as hell looks like it. On both accounts. Slow down and come to a stop, Cole." Logan replies, looking out the front windshield.

Ahead of them, probably roughly 100 feet or so, is a tanned skin girl that looks to be a teenager, sitting on the tailgate of a truck. The truck is under the Station three sign of the South Entrance Station, with the girl in the shade of the overarching roof of the station. The truck is one of many vehicles lined up in rows from tree line to tree line. It looked like their makeshift blockade in San Diego, just much bigger and better. It looked to be three cars deep at every point and there were no gaps between the four entrance standings, the side parking lot, or the two side roads on either side of the South Entrance Station.

Logan watches in amazement as the teenage girl kicks her feet on the tailgate and waves at them as Cole brings the 4Runner to a stop about 50 feet away from the girl and the blockade, blocking their entry into the Grand Canyon.

Shit. This can go one of two ways. Logan thinks to himself, as he scans the well-developed blockade of vehicles and the seemingly alone teenage girl in front of them with a lone rifle.

"What the hell, bro? What would a little girl be doing out here all by herself?" Cole asks, as he puts the vehicle in park.

"I'm more concerned with who the hell built this barricade of cars?" Logan admits.

The radio crackles to life with Emily's voice. "Is that a kid in front of that huge barricade?"

"Cole, Clint. You two stay here..." he says to them and then picks up the radio and opens up his door.

"What? Where are you going?" Clint responds.

"I'm going to go see what's going on. Because something isn't what it seems. Something doesn't add up." Logan replies.

"Okay, boss man. But shout if you need us, dude." Cole answers back.

"Will do, guys." Logan responds and exits the 4Runner.

He feels his body creak and groan with pain. *Ugh. Push through the pain, Logan. Now let's just hope this turns out with a better scenario than of us being totally screwed and just having walked into a trap.*

He keys the radio to life, standing next to their vehicle and looking back to the truck. "Alright folks. No sudden movements. I'm walking up there to find out what's going on. But no sudden movements."

"What do you mean, you're going up there and no sudden movements?!" Emily blurts out over the radio.

"Em..." Logan says back over the radio. "That little girl did not move all of those cars on her own. This is something else. Give me a minute and no sudden movements."

Logan unholsters his Glock G45, holding it up in the air with two fingers and then places it on his seat inside the 4Runner. He then slowly steps aside and closes the door and holds up his radio and turns around in a circle, looking all around him.

"I'm unarmed, now. This is just a radio to communicate with my group! I'm walking forward now to meet the girl and whoever else is out here with us!" Logan shouts out to no one in particular.

He sighs and looks back at the tanned skin teenage girl, still kicking her feet off of the tailgate of the truck. *Well, may as well figure out how screwed we are.* He thinks to himself.

He walks forward with his hands in the air, listening to the forest around him. There is a slight breeze and he can hear birds chirping but nothing else. He approaches the girl and stops within 15 feet of her. Close enough to see that she is indeed way too damn young to be standing watch out here by herself.

"Hey Mister! How's it going? Who are you yelling at out there?" The teenage girl asks.

Hmmm. Kid seems nice enough. But this feels like a game of some sort to her. He thinks to himself looking at the teenager.

"I'm not sure, young lady. But my name is Logan, and me and my friends don't mean you any harm. Who's out here with you?" Logan replies.

The kid gives him a curious look and tilts her head. Logan begins to look around him once and then she follows his gaze and looks around too.

"Who are you looking for Mr. Logan? It's just me out here. And it's nice to meet you. My name's Bonnie!" The teenage girl, apparently named Bonnie, says to him.

Hmmm. He thinks to himself. *If this was a trap, it would have been sprung already. Either that or they're waiting for something. But what?*

"Well. Hi Bonnie. And I don't mean to be rude, but, I really don't think you're the only one out here. My friends and I were just looking for a safe place to stay and thought one of the lodges in the Grand Canyon may be a smart choice. We have some kids around your age, and a few a tad bit younger. We really don't mean any trouble. We'll leave if you folks don't have the room." Logan explains.

"Hmmm..." Bonnie says, kicking her feet in the air while she sits on the tailgate of the pickup truck. "What do you think, Jeff?" She adds, as she stares directly at him.

An older man, with gray and white hair steps out from the toll booth of Station two with a rifle at the ready, and Logan can see a pistol on the man's hip.

"Well, Bonnie. I think our traveler friend is telling the truth. At least it seems that way." The older man says as he looks off to his right and swirls his index finger and middle finger together in the air.

A moment later, Logan can hear a low buzz and he looks up to see a small drone take off from atop the roof. He turns to see it hovering over the 4Runner first, then the Tundra towing the Attitude trailer, then the ambulance, and then finally the Honda van. The drone then goes further down the road they just came from and the buzzing sound of the drone dissipates.

Logan turns back around to see the older man having positioned himself at the corner of the tailgate and leaning up against it.

"Nice to meet you, Logan. At least I hope it's nice to meet you. Name's Jeff, as Bonnie let slip so quickly." The older man named Jeff says to him as he gives the teenage girl a quick look.

"What, Jeff?! He said they have kids and he didn't try to do any creepy shit. The others always did creepy shit the second they showed up." Bonnie replies.

So, it is a trap! But it doesn't sound like it's for people like us... He thinks to himself, looking at the teenager and the old man.

Jeff chuckles and shakes his head. "Language please, Bonnie."

Bonnie rolls her eyes. "We're in World War III, Jeff. I don't think me cussing is going to make it any worse. But okay... whatever."

"Nice to meet the both of you. And like I said, we mean no trouble..." Logan begins.

A radio crackles to life on Jeff's belt, with a voice coming in over it. "All clear, Mr. Cooper. Sounds like they're on the up and up. Just the four vehicles and the trailer, with their heat signatures, and some of them being a lot smaller than the others. So, yeah, they have kids with them."

"How did you?..." Logan questions.

He watches as Bonnie reaches for something next to her and it was a small camera attached to a cord, attached to what looked to be a solar charger.

"Can never be too careful, Mr. Logan." Bonnie says to him with a smile. "Most folks these days see someone like me, and they get the wrong ideas in their heads. But you didn't, Mr. Logan. That's why I asked Jeff about you."

"*Most folks* is damn right. Crying shame that when the world comes to an end, most of what's left is shitheads and douchebags." Jeff replies.

Wait a minute... Logan thinks.

"Is this a damn honeypot trap? Some sort of test? But why? Why put a teenage girl in danger?" Logan says, concerned.

Jeff nods in understanding. "Let me assure you, Logan. You all were the ones in danger, not little Bonnie here. We have a dozen people on watch every day out here, at least. You were surrounded from the moment you rolled up. Now if you were the type of folks to think they can have their way with a young lady, such as Bonnie or any other of our very nice occupants of the female variety... today would have been your last day on this earth of ours. "

"We were in danger? As in, we're not in danger anymore?" Logan questions, picking up on the past tense of the danger reference.

"Yes, Sir! You are correct!" Jeff replies. "You all passed our little human decency test, and with flying colors I might add."

He then whistles and Logan hears car engines roar to life off to his left past a small parking lot. He then clicks his radio and speaks into it. "Hey, this is Jeff Cooper up at the gate. Can someone send me and Bonnie some replacements? We're going to show our newcomers around."

A moment later, another voice comes over his radio. "Sure thing, Mr. Cooper. Be there in a few."

"Wait, so that's it?" Logan questions.

Jeff chuckles. "That's it, my good sir. If you were bad folks, you would have done what bad folks do. But you didn't. And these days, we need all the good folks that we can find. Now jump back in your cars and drive around the barricade and meet me right there." He explains to him and points directly behind Station three of the South Rim Entrance Station.

His own radio then crackles to life. "Is everything okay up there, Logan?" He hears Emily say.

"Better make sure to tell you friends that all is well and you all have a place to stay for the foreseeable future of our doomed world." Jeff says with another chuckle.

"Our world is not doomed, Jeff! Stop saying that. It really gets on my nerves! Geez!" Bonnie replies.

What is going on here? Kinda seems like they have a lot of people here and sounds like they're filtering out the bad people. He thinks to himself as he keys his radio. "Yeah, Em. All is good. They are letting us in. I guess we passed their test and they seem like nice people."

"Are you sure, Logan? What if they're lying?" Emily questions back over the radio.

Logan looks at Jeff. "She has a fair point, Mr. Cooper. How do we know if it's not all just a huge trap? You did just try some sort of twisted ass honeypot scheme on us."

Jeff scratches his chin and nods. "Fair enough... you got room enough for me in that 4Runner of yours and an extra seat for our little hellion, Bonnie, here?"

Hmmm. Interesting. He's giving himself up kinda like a hostage to be our host, to make us feel more at ease. The guy seems nice enough. Bonnie doesn't seem like she's worried about any danger and seems normal enough too. And we did want to come here for safety. But I didn't really give much thought to other people having the same idea, or already being here. I guess if there are good people here, that can do nothing but help our situation. Right? He thinks to himself.

Logan looks back at the vehicles, and then back to Jeff and Bonnie. "Okay. Yeah. I believe we do, Jeff. And for you too, Bonnie. Jeff, you can ride with me and the twins. And Bonnie, you can ride with Emily and most of the other kids."

Jeff looks at Bonnie and he shrugs. "Wanna go for a ride and show these folks around, Bonnie?"

Bonnie looks at him. "Are there boys my age? I'm 14!"

Yup, definitely a teenage girl, and she seems pretty damn normal. This feels alright, and I'm not getting any big red flags going off. He thinks and he can't help but smile.

"Yes, Bonnie. Actually, Emily has a 13-year-old son that just woke up from a coma. His name is Bryan." Logan replies.

"A coma? You don't say..." Jeff replies and whistles.

She smiles wide. "I'm in then! Everyone is either mostly old like you and Jeff here, or super little. I'm riding in the big green truck, right?" She says as she hops off the tailgate of the truck.

"Yeah, and old? Really?" Logan says, looking back at the teenager walking past him toward the Tundra.

She pauses, turns back, and leaves her rifle on the bed of the truck. "Don't want to look like I'm up to no good." She says with a smile and then heads off toward Emily and the other kids.

"Don't worry, Logan. She thinks anyone older than 20 is old. You get used to it." Jeff replies.

"Logan?" Emily says over the radio.

He clicks the radio to tell her what's happening. "Em. To show us they mean no harm, Bonnie... the teenager, is riding with you guys. And Jeff here, is riding with me and the twins."

"Alright..." Emily says back over the radio.

"It'll be fine, Em... and everyone else. Sounds like there's good people here and we may finally be able to breathe for a minute." Logan says over the radio.

"Copy that, Logan. Following your lead." Dr. Lewis says over the radio.

"Count us in." Paul says over the radio, too.

"Roger dodger, boss man." Cole says over his spare radio.

"I suppose that sounds pretty nice, Logan. As long as you think it's a good idea." Emily responds back over the radio.

Logan looks to Jeff, and then keys the mic again. "I do, and it seems like these folks have a pretty good set up and more people than we do. Strength in numbers sounds like a good idea. Especially if any more Russians show up."

"Copy that, Logan. Following your lead." Emily says back over the radio.

He wasn't sure if he liked the idea of the group all following his lead. Sure, he guessed they could argue that he had gotten them this far. But it was because of all of them for their group getting this far. Plus, they had almost died on several occasions. Then again, they didn't die. He was certain that he liked being around them and he liked being a part of their little group. Emily, Laura, Diego, now Bryan, and all of them.

"Russians, huh?! You all must have some interesting stories!" Jeff blurts out.

"Mr. Cooper, you don't know the half of it." Logan replies.

"Jeff is just fine, Logan. You can tell us all about it over dinner tonight. And welcome to The South Rim of The Grand Canyon. Our home is your home, as long you need or want it to be. Bonnie, me, and some others stay at The Southside Haven Lodge. There's plenty of room there and at the other lodges. There's only a couple hundred of us that stayed after the world went to shit. But I have to warn you, we all work around here, except for the little ones of course." Jeff says to him, patting him on his back as they walked back to the 4Runner.

Wow! A couple hundred? That's amazing! We haven't seen that many people since before this whole war started. Logan thinks to himself.

"Wait? Did you say The Southside Haven Lodge?" Logan questions.

"Yes, I did. Have you heard of it?" Jeff asks as they get closer to the 4Runner.

Logan shakes his head and chuckles, letting himself relax somewhat. "Yeah, you could say that, and it all sounds like a nice change of pace, Jeff. It really does."

Reaching the passenger side door, he opens it and Jeff opens the one behind him. Jeff nods to him and climbs in and starts introducing himself to the twins. Hearing them all chatter inside the SUV, he looks to the truck, seeing Emily in the driver's seat. She looks back at him and he gives her a smile and thumbs up. She looks to her side with Bonnie in the middle between her and her son Bryan, then looks back to him, shrugs, and gives thumbs up.

He sighs, exhaling through his nose. *Alright then. We made it to the Grand Canyon, finally. Let's hope this all works out well enough. We've all lost so much.* He thinks to himself, as he looks to the sky and will his thoughts to his dead wife. *Kelsey, I know you're up there somewhere, babe. Please watch over little Harper and me. Know that we miss you every single day, and that we love you.*

He goes to climb back into the vehicle to allow Jeff Cooper to lead them to other survivors of this brutal and tragic third world war, or the Rh Factor War. He had always known that if World War III were going to happen, it would be horrific, but he had never imagined this.

"Alright, then. Let's see what's in store for us at the Grand Canyon." He says as he fastens his seatbelt.

"Glad to have you join us Logan, and your friends seem mighty nice and very chatty to boot." Jeff replies.

Logan chuckles. “Oh, they’ll talk your ears off. And not only are they nice, they are resourceful and great to have around.”

“Ah shucks, boss man... you’re going to make me cry.” Cole replies with a grin.

“Like I was saying, Mr. Cooper. My brother takes some getting used to and he’s somewhat of a jokester.” Clint adds.

“Maybe so, bro. But I’m also the better shot! Right, Logan?! Remember how we took out those crazy Russian dudes?!” Cole responds back with his boyish charm.

These two are too much sometimes. But I’m sure as hell glad they’re here... I’m sure as hell glad that we’re all here and that we finally made it. Logan thinks to himself and can’t help but laugh and feel hopeful.

Moments later they are all talking amongst themselves and driving through the open spot of the barricade, with the others following behind them toward the South Rim of the Grand Canyon.

Chapter 26: Henry Torres

Day 15: MCAS Miramar, California

"Hey, *Bleak*? Can you turn that up, or at least put the closed caption bullshit on for us?" Torres says to Blake.

"Sure thing, First Sergeant." Staff Sergeant Blake replies.

"Thanks, *Bleak*. Much appreciated. Looks pretty damn important with all those suits and brass up there on a stage." Torres says, as he tries to decipher what was happening on the T.V. as he sips his coffee in the ready-room of a hangar belonging to a helo-squadron on the flight line at MCAS Miramar.

"What do you think's going on, First Sergeant?" Specialist Conner questions.

"Not sure, Conner. That's why I asked *Bleak* to turn on the captions and turn the damn thing up. So, we can find out." He replies to the young man.

"Oh. Yeah. Right." Conner answers back.

Torres shakes his head and smiles, taking another sip of his coffee. *Freaking kids, always with the obvious questions.*

It was still the morning hours of the day and he was already exhausted. Talking to the brass usually did that to him. He had already provided them with the intel they gathered from the civilians in Flagstaff and the prisoner of Major Michail Lenkov. But for some damn reason they needed to be briefed in person this morning again at 0700, with more brass around this time over at headquarters. So, he did what he was told and then headed back to the ready room of the helo-squadron afterward, wanting to be close to his ride and his troops.

After arriving back in MCAS Miramar late yesterday, they set up shop in this ready room. It wasn't a five-star hotel, but it served its purpose. Miramar had been hit pretty hard with the death clouds from the CWAs in the beginning, but they were still up and running. And actually, thanks to his team's intel, they were all planning an assault on Point Loma 20 miles South of them.

This morning he was given orders to fly North, around the anomaly surrounding what used to be Caltech, and pretty much 70 miles in every direction away from the damn place. His team was tasked with gathering more intel, but on the other invading forces along the West Coast. Apparently they did such a bang-up job the first time, this is what they did now. They were supposed to leave immediately, but he wanted to enjoy his damn coffee.

What were they going to do? Fire him? Besides, *Hornet* and *Wiz* were already downstairs on the flight line turning up their Chinook. He had a few minutes.

Nothing quite like a hot cup of coffee. Could be better with some whisky... maybe later, it's still morning, he thinks to himself as he takes another sip.

Torres didn't really care one way or another where the hell they sent him. Right now, he was sipping on coffee, had a decent night's sleep, none of his men had died engaging the Russians, and they even got to get some Russian kills under their belts. Nope, this was a damn fine day according to Torres, all things considered.

"Closed captioning, huh, First Sergeant? That age finally getting to ya? Should we find you a hearing aid before we get going?" Sergeant Jackson says to him with that sly smirk of his.

Torres looks over at him, giving him a stare. "Shut your damn hippie mouth, *Thriller*. Or I'll have *Bleak* do it for you."

Jackson looks at Bleak and she turns back to wink at him, and Jackson puts his hands in the air. "Nope, I'm good! Shutting my hippie mouth, First Sergeant!"

Torres chuckles as he sips his coffee and the closed captions on the T.V. start scrolling and Blake turns up the volume loud enough for it to echo in the entire ready room.

"These are uncharted, chaotic, and dangerous times. And we need to take decisive and direct action to determine the survival of our way of life." The suit on the T.V. says, with the suit standing behind a podium, with other suits and military brass on both sides of him.

"Damn, *Bleak*! Are you hard of hearing too?!" Jackson says to her.

"What about shut your trap, don't you understand, *Thriller*?! Shit sounds important and I'd like to know what's going on before we kick rocks and head out on our next adventure." Torres says to the Sergeant.

He doesn't reply back, giving a defeated and hurt look to him. Torres focuses back on the T.V. Torres knew the guy was still screwing around with his pouty face, but he really did want to know what the hell the big fuss was about.

"The former Vice President, and former Senator James Boyd has graciously taken over command of the N.A.C. during our time of need. Our humble autocratic leader now oversees the congressional senate, built up of the surviving 37 congressmen and women from what was formerly the United States of American, Canadian, and Mexican governments."

Autocratic? Humble?... Son of bitch! The alliance shifted to a full-throttle newly developed government already? And it sure as shit sounds like one very humble, and likely all-knowing, politician is in charge of the whole shebang. Shit on fucking toast and spread on thick and heavy. Dammit. This is going to complicate shit. Torres thinks to himself.

The speaker continues on. "In our current times of chaos and dismay, the Republic of North America found it necessary to bypass an election for the time being... James Boyd, having accepted the massive burden gracefully and with great humbling demeanor, is now the Autocrat of the Republic of North America. When times have calmed and reached some sort of normalcy, our courteous and civilized leader, James Boyd the Autocrat, will step aside for democracy to once again reign over North America. Only this time, through the guidance and structure provided by the Autocrat and the Republic of North America Government, all of North America will be united and striving for the common good of us all. We shall all prevail through this war we did not need, nor want, or as some are calling it, The Rh Factor War. In the end, we will, under the direction and guidance of our newly appointed Autocrat, usher in a new era of prosperity and stability."

Republic of North America?! You have got to be shitting me! Most places that have names like those are not very republic-like. Not at fucking all. And sure, he'll step aside. Our new humble Autocrat leader... fuck me. Shit just got a whole lot more complicated. He thinks to himself.

Torres and the others watch as the man previously speaking steps off to the side and a very smug looking man takes the podium, assumedly the former Senator James Boyd, and now their humble autocratic leader.

"Turn that crap off, *Bleak*. I've heard enough. Let's pack up and be on our way." Torres says to her.

Blake goes to turn off the T.V.

James Boyd begins speaking. "Hello, citizens of the Republic of North America..." And the T.V. goes black.

"Don't you want to find out what the guy has to say, First Sergeant?" Conner asks.

Torres shakes his head. "Already have a pretty damn good idea of what our non-elected, humble Autocrat is about to say. Now let's get going."

"But..." Conner replies.

"You heard the First Sergeant." Bleak adds. "Move out!"

No one else interjects as they grab their gear and head out of the ready room, down to the Chinook, where *Hornet* and *Wiz* are likely wondering where the hell they are.

Reaching the Chinook, it was turned up and ready to go. Climbing aboard, he puts on his headset and takes his seat. The other three follow his lead and they get ready for take-off.

Once they are all onboard and strapped in, Torres speaks into the Chinooks onboard comms. "Ready back here, gents. Take us away."

"Copy that, *Hawk*." Wiz replies over the comms.

The Chinook lifts off the ground.

"And awaaay we go." Captain Turner says over the comms.

"After a few minutes of silence, they are heading East to bypass the quarantine anomaly sphere-thing, Conner speaks up over the comms. "First Sergeant. Does that mean the U.S. is gone?"

"Shit, Conner! The U.S. has been gone for two damn weeks already. Where the hell have you been? Hell, most countries are gone!" Jackson replies back over the comms.

Torres watches as Blake gives Jackson a look.

"What?! Am I lying, *Bleak*? The great U.S. of A. is gone. Sounds like it's the great R. of N.A. now. As long as we get to keep killing these invading pieces of shits. Don't bother me one bit." Jackson says to her over the comms.

"You're missing the bigger picture here, *Thriller*." Bleak says back to him.

Before Torres can think of a way to explain to them how royally screwed they were, explosions begin to hit down below them and to the west. A lot of them...

"What the shit's going on now?" Jackson blurts out.

Torres looks out the Chinook's windows to see multiple explosions and more incoming missiles heading for where they just left. MCAS Miramar. No one answers Jackson, but they all watch as MCAS is decimated with multiple missiles. More than Torres wanted to count. It was surreal and they were likely all thinking the same thing. *We were just fucking there.*

Torres is the one to finally break the silence over the comms once the missiles stop bombarding the military base. "I know not with what weapons World War III will be fought with, but World War IV will be fought with sticks and stones." Torres says over the comms, thinking about a quote he heard years ago that stuck with him. It probably wasn't exact, but it was close enough.

"What's that, First Sergeant? What does that mean?" Jackson questions.

"War is fury, is what that means, *Thriller*. And before this is done, we may very fucking well be knocked back to the damn stone age." Torres replies.

"*Hawk*. If it's alright with you, I wouldn't feel right if we didn't go look for survivors down there. I mean, I doubt there are many and I know we have orders. But still." Captain Turner says over the comms.

"I'm with *Hornet*, *Hawk*." 1st Lieutenant Sanchez adds from the cockpit.

"Yeah. Fuck orders. Let's head back down there and see if we can find anyone that was lucky enough to survive. No man left behind." Torres responds.

The Chinook shifts and tilts, changing direction for what's left of MCAS Miramar. Torres looks around the Chinook at *Bleak*, *Thriller*, and Conner. All of them nod, but Conner is the only one to gulp afterward.

"Damn right! We don't leave anyone behind, First Sergeant. You know I'm in." *Bleak* says over the comms.

"I know the hazards of our profession, First Sergeant. Let's do this. Rangers lead the way." Jackson adds.

Conner just nods and gives a thumbs-up, likely with nothing fancy or heroic to say, being too scared shitless. Torres couldn't blame the kid. He did pick him up from a logistics unit, but he was a good kid.

"Good to hear it, *Bleak* and *Thriller*. Wouldn't expect anything less from you two. And Conner, you'll be fine. We'll save as many as we can... if there's anyone left down there after all of that.

He looks back out the windows of the Chinook as they make their way to the destroyed military base.

War is fury alright, and before this war is over, you're going to see my fury, Major Lenkov. I know this was you, you commie sack of shit.

Epilogue

Michail Lenkov

<u>Day 20: San Diego, California</u>

"I said fucking surface, Captain Zakharov!" Micha yells into the comms aboard one of the three Yasen-class submarines submerged in the depths of the Pacific Ocean.

"Major Lenkov. It has only been five days since we launched ICBMS and Kalibr-M missiles at your designated targets. We know the Americans still have retaliation capabilities and they may have gathered intelligence on our location. I advise that we wait longer, Sir." Captain Zakharov replied over the comms after a quick pause.

Fucking coward of a man. Should have killed you with the other two shit ass cowardly Captain fucks! He thinks to himself. *Luckily, I foresaw your inability to follow orders, Captain Zakharov.*

"Captain Grinkov." Micha says into the comms.

After a short pause, his trusted Captain answers back over on the comms. "Yes, Major. What are your orders?"

Micha smiles and speaks into the comms aboard the submarine. "Relieve Captain Zakharov of his command of my submarine, Captain Grinkov. I will deal with him later, once we are on land again. Surface and take most of your men to survey the area of San Clemente Island and report back in one hour."

"Yes, Major Lenkov. Right away." Captain Grinkov replies.

He had spent the last five days beneath the surface of the ocean and was eager to get back to the surface to commence his mission. It was his mission and command now, since it looked like no one else would be joining them from Mother Russia.

It wasn't a bad thing at all, in his mind. But being stuck in this fucking submarine for five damn days. He did have two *pindo* women to keep him busy during their time submerged. But he still missed the smell of fresh air. He had been down here for several months on the long journey over to the wasteful and lazy American *pindos*, and he sure as fuck wasn't happy about being back down in the darkness of the ocean once again.

It was the best tactical approach however, given the circumstances. He hadn't heard word back from Lieutenant Petrenko, and their transponder was in the exact same position for over a full day, along with the transmitter placed on the caravan with the American Cowboy named Logan. It had infuriated him that more of his elite Spetsnaz soldiers had likely fallen at the hands of some cowboy and his disgustingly wasteful *pindos*. So, the way he saw it, they all deserved to burn in a fiery hell of a death. And why not other targets as well? He knew damn fucking well there would be retaliation against their location, but it needed to be done... and they would not be there when it came for them.

The other two captains hadn't agreed with him and didn't want to use their arsenal on the submarines to attack the American *pindos* out of fear of retaliation. They quickly died as cowards and he took command over the remaining 169 Russian Spetsnaz soldiers combined with the submarine crews and the three Yasen-class submarines and all of the arsenals at their disposal.

After ridding himself of those that did not see their true situation and what needed to be done, he split up his truly loyal forces amongst the submarines, with the *pindo* women that they had captured on their last venture into the surrounding cities. They had captured some younger men and children as well. The children were to be molded into a new generation, and the men were to be used as workers until they were no longer needed. But he decided against evacuating them to the submarines and left them locked inside a building on Point Loma.

If the Americans were going to retaliate, they were going to kill their own. They would kill their own children. They certainly would not fucking kill him.

He would breed and train the *pindo* women and build their own new world and next generations. There was the added bonus of how much it lifted his troops spirits and morale. It may not have been for his female subordinate comrades, but he could give two shits less. He had two beautiful and willing *pindo* women in his quarters waiting for him.

On day 15 of this third world war, Micha decided what should be done and his men followed him. As he knew they would. Before leaving for the murky depths of the Pacific Ocean to evade a most certain retaliatory strike on their launching position at Point Loma, he ordered the launching of ICBMs and Kalibr-M cruise missiles. In the end, the American cowboy would be dust with an ICBM heading directly to his location in Flagstaff, Arizona.

He wasn't going nuclear, but it would be more than enough to level the area of the cowboy, Logan, and his *pindo* friends in Flagstaff, Arizona. Micha also ordered ICBMs, along with Kalibr-M cruise missiles to target San Clemente Island, MCAS Miramar, MCRD San Diego, Camp Pendleton, El Centro, MCAS Yuma, and even the San Diego International Airport.

Micha decided upon these areas to strike first, to wipe out any surviving enemy combatants, and greatly diminish their ability to travel by air and resupply. He hadn't seen any military combatants since reaching San Diego of California, which was once the United States of America. He had assumed that the surviving remaining forces either fled for their lives or were attempting some resemblance of regrouping to commit to a campaign.

It didn't matter though. He knew they would all eventually die, and *he* would be victorious. The original mission hadn't gone according to plan. But plans rarely do. So now, Micha was making it his own mission to take control and command of the region.

This is just the beginning, you wasteful and lazy fucking Americans. You should have died like you were supposed to. Now you will burn and be eradicated from our new Russia, our new homeland. These were his thoughts as the missiles were launched and his three submarines submerged to evade detection from the North American Coalition.

He commanded one of the submarines, with Captain Grinkov and Lieutenant Mashkov each commanding the other two. They still had a combined force of 169 Russian might, along with 22 American women prisoners... to be utilized, repurposed, and retrained. That was five days ago now, and he was more than ready to get back to the surface, and his new home. To continue on with his mission, his vision. He knew his troops were ready too.

"Very good, Captain Grinkov. Kill all that stand in our way, and we will be victorious in our new world!" Micha says over the comms.

"Yes, Major Lenkov. We will follow you to the world's end, for glory and Mother Russia. We'll talk again in one hour, Sir. Telling you of our success." Captain Grinkov replies.

Good! I can still trust my men to follow my orders. Looks like the ICBMs and cruise missiles reaffirmed their faith in their leader. Even after losing ten of our comrades in battle against the fucking pindos, and two more because of their cowardice. But they all got what they deserved... he thinks to himself, walking away from the comms unit, believing the Americans that were thorns in his side to be dead and gone...

He looks over his shoulder at his men, now all under his own command. "Contact me once Captain Grinkov reports back in, I'll be in my quarters. Enjoying my spoils of war."

He walks off to his quarters with a smile on his face thinking to himself, *It is the end for most of the world, but this is a new beginning for you, Micha.*

Afterword

Thank you so very much for reading *Negative: The Rh Factor War*. It is my hope that you enjoyed the first book in this series of stories of survival in a daunting and dangerous new world, as much as I enjoyed writing the story. This is not the end of the story and book two is already being written. If you would like to read more of my stories, there is also *The Radius Series*. If you enjoyed reading this book, please consider leaving a review on Amazon.com. As always, it would be greatly appreciated. You can also find me on my website www.dmmuga.com and on social media: Facebook: @DMMUGA, Instagram: @dmmuga.

At the risk of redundancy, please remember to think for yourself, enjoy the times of peace, and cherish every moment in this wonderful world of ours. When the chaos does eventually come, handle yourself accordingly and best of luck to you all. Stay safe out there, and make smart choices. Again, thank you for reading my stories, truly.

Respectfully,

David M. Muga

About the Author

D.M. Muga is a diversified writer, currently writing in the areas of Sci-Fi, Apocalyptic, Post-Apocalyptic, and Survival. He is a survival enthusiast and considers himself somewhat prepared for varying scenarios, based on the concept that no one can truly be perfectly prepared for any given scenario. *Chance* will always be an unpredictable variable in the equation of life and survival.

D.M. Muga is a United States Marine Corps Veteran. He has earned several academic degrees, including a Master's in National Security Studies and a Doctorate in Educational Leadership. He is a history teacher by day and writes during the twilight and early morning hours of the night. He resides in Southern California with his wife and their two daughters. He is adamant with his hopes of living out the rest of his life in peace, but prepares for the future, "planning for the best, but preparing for the worst."

Made in the USA
Columbia, SC
06 July 2025

60387197R00139